memories

and

matchsticks

A Sam and Bump Misadventure, Book 1

cader idris
press

Also by N. Gemini Sasson:

The Sam and Bump Misadventures:
Memories and Matchsticks
Lies and Letters

The Faderville Novels:
Say No More
Say That Again
Say Something

The Bruce Trilogy:
The Crown in the Heather (Book I)
Worth Dying For (Book II)
The Honor Due a King (Book III)

The Isabella Books:
Isabeau: A Novel of Queen Isabella
and Sir Roger Mortimer

The King Must Die:
A Novel of Edward III

Standalones:
Uneasy Lies the Crown:
A Novel of Owain Glyndwr

In the Time of Kings

memories
and
matchsticks

A Sam and Bump Misadventure,
Book 1

N. GEMINI SASSON

MEMORIES AND MATCHSTICKS
(A SAM AND BUMP MISADVENTURE, BOOK 1)

Copyright © 2014 N. Gemini Sasson

ISBN 978-1-939344-06-9 (paperback)

Library of Congress Control No. 2014921142

For more details about N. Gemini Sasson and her books, go to:
www.ngeminisasson.com

Or become a 'fan' at:
www.facebook.com/NGeminiSasson

You can also sign up to learn about new releases via e-mail at:
http://eepurl.com/vSA6z

This book is dedicated to Chloe, my first obedience dog and the only Long-Haired American Brindle Shepherd to ever exist.

MEMORIES AND MATCHSTICKS

A Sam and Bump Misadventure, Book 1

There's an arsonist on the loose in rural Wilton, Indiana — and he'll do whatever it takes to keep from being found out. Even murder.

Out of work, accident prone, and dateless, Sam McNamee packs up her belongings and her daughter to move to the Florida Keys, where she can pen love stories as S.A. Mack to ease the lingering pain of her husband's death. First, though, she has to help her dad sell his home of forty-plus years. It just might be the hardest job she's ever tackled. He's a hoarder; she's a neat freak.

The night she returns to Wilton, Sam plows into a mangy mutt on a rain-slicked country road. Bump, the dog she rescues, has a history that drags Sam and her family into a web of danger, making her father a prime suspect.

Feuds and secrets run deep in Humboldt County. Sam can't leave until the arsonist is uncovered. Not that she'd want to anymore, since veterinarian Clint Chastain has stolen her heart.

chapter 1

THIS WASN'T HOW I'D planned things. I was supposed to be ensconced somewhere in the Keys by now, sipping on a mint mojito, sea foam swirling around my Adirondack chair while I tapped furiously at the keyboard of my netbook.

Instead, I was headed deep into the cornfields of Eastern Indiana. So much space. So few people.

The next few weeks were going to be hell.

Rain slapped against the windshield in a percussive roar, drowning out the melody of the song on the radio. I fumbled blindly with the knobs, afraid to take my eyes off the road. I flipped through the stations until I found some obnoxiously upbeat techno dance music and cranked the volume. Anything to keep myself alert. With every swish of the wiper blades, I had a clear view for about half a second; then water gushed down from the sky, distorting the world beyond my hood into an out-of-focus black and white photo.

I knew these roads too well. Knew the exact spot where it had happened, just around the bend from where we were now. My heart clenched at the memory of that night: the phone call at fourteen minutes past midnight, the twirling lights, the unremitting drizzle, the mangled metal . . .

My eyes drifted shut. As my head bobbed forward, I snapped back to awareness, adrenaline crashing through my veins, my senses sharpened. My pulse drummed in my ears, the rhythm of my heart a rapid staccato.

Stay awake, Samantha Ann McNamee, I told myself. *This is no time to fall asleep at the wheel. You have precious cargo in the backseat.*

A burst of red and white flashed in my rearview mirror, spiraling me into memories of that fateful night. I focused on the vehicle approaching from behind: a police car. The piercing wail of its siren rose above the roar of rain. Behind me, my daughter Tara mumbled and pulled her hood down over her eyes.

Had I been speeding? Swerving, maybe? I started to pull off to the side, sure I was going to get a ticket. Both right wheels had barely hit the gravel shoulder when the patrol car veered into the left lane and edged up beside me. Blood pounding, I lifted my foot from the accelerator and tapped at the brake.

A wall of water hit my windshield as the police car sped past. I breathed a sigh of relief. It barreled down the rain slicked road, then turned into a lane partly shrouded by a thick stand of trees.

There, the uneven silhouette of a house set close to the road appeared in scattered bursts of lightning. Yellow caution tape was draped from tree to tree all around the house. Fire trucks surrounded the house, but there was no fire. Not anymore. An ambulance was parked in front of the house. Two EMTs were wheeling a stretcher out the front door. On it was a body bag.

Whoever it was, they'd arrived too late.

I glanced at the road for a second to make sure I wasn't drifting off onto the shoulder, then looked back at the house. Another lightning flash, prolonged, revealed part of the roof was missing. Jagged trusses, charred in places, poked above uneven exterior walls.

Looked like the place had been ravaged by fire. I stepped on the gas, eager to get away from there. Vehicles with flashing lights brought back too many terrible memories. The farther away I got, the better.

The house slipped from my peripheral vision and I returned my sights to the road ahead. It dipped into a small valley carved by a narrow, but swift-moving creek, then rose again before curving to the right.

I slapped my thighs to keep myself awake. We should have arrived hours ago. Damn those movers for taking their sweet time. Except for the few suitcases and gym bags stuffed into the rear of my Subaru Forester, all my belongings were now sitting somewhere in a moldy, cockroach-infested storage unit on Chicago's West Side. Why hadn't I stopped a couple of hours ago down the road? I could've called ahead, told my dad we'd gotten a late start and the storm was just too much.

Too late now. We were less than ten minutes away. Not that I was eager to return to my childhood home, mind you, but when you were tight on money and had just lost a steady job —

The scope of the headlights caught a reflection in a nearby field. Instinctively, I yanked the wheel to the left, my foot drawing back from the gas pedal to hit the brake. A pair of glowing orbs stared back at me, hovering at road's edge, ready to bound out into my path. This time I punched the brake, inadvertently steering right. The wheels chattered over rain-slickened asphalt as the anti-lock mecha-nism kicked in. The rear end of my Forester fishtailed toward the ditch, the muddy channel carved deep by a recent backhoe job. Rubber squealed as the tires bit into the road. My hands locked on the steering wheel. I let up on the brake, momentum still propelling the car irretrievably forward as the bright yellow dots flew toward me.

A squeal ripped from the backseat. Tara slapped her palms against my headrest as she grabbed hold.

The right rear tire plunged off the edge of the pavement, thudding loudly, and then scudded on the gravel shoulder for what seemed like an eternity, although it was no more than a few seconds.

There was a soft thump as the front bumper clipped an object. The car lurched to a halt, one tire dipping into the ditch.

For several seconds, all I could hear were the sharp, rapid breaths of my daughter behind me. Finally, I remembered to breathe, too. The steady pounding of rain on the windows came back into focus.

After throwing the shifter into park, I peered into the rearview mirror, but the glow from the dashboard wasn't enough to see anything. I groped at the ceiling, flicked the overhead light on. "Are you okay, honey?"

Silence.

Please, please, please be okay.

The car was still in one piece. At least as far as I could tell. The airbags hadn't even deployed. Why wasn't she answering me?

I glanced in the side mirror to make sure there were no oncoming cars, then unbuckled myself and twisted around to look in the backseat. Tara was curled into a ball, arms over her face. "Tara?"

"Yeah," she croaked in a whisper, "I'm here."

"You okay?"

"I think so. You just scared the crap out of me, that's all." Her hands peeled away from her face. She looked up sheepishly. "I *was* asleep. What happened?"

Groaning, I sat facing front again. Pain hammered at the top of my skull. "I think I hit something."

"Like what? A tree, a mailbox?"

I didn't want to get out of the car and look. Didn't want to know. Maybe I could just put the car in reverse, back out of the ditch, and go on?

"A deer, maybe?"

"No," I said, "not that big."

The faux leather of the seat squeaked as Tara scooted upright and pressed her nose to the window. "I hope it wasn't a skunk."

"We would have smelled it by now."

"Oh. Guess you're right."

Clutching the shifter, I slid it into reverse.

"No!" Tara's frantic scream bored into my ear canal.

"No what?" I wanted to yell at her to calm down, but she was hyperventilating already. The best course in this situation was to remain calm and act like it was no big deal. If I keyed in to her anxiety in the smallest bit, she'd erupt in full blown hysteria within a minute.

"You might back over it," she said quietly. "Hurt it worse. Whatever it is."

I flicked on the hazard lights and cut the engine. "I'm sure it's all right. Probably just a raccoon or possum. Bet it ran off into the cornfield already. I'm going to check, okay? Then we'll go on. Should be to Gramp's place in fifteen, twenty minutes, tops."

She stared out the window into the darkness. I wasn't surprised that she had no reaction to arriving at my dad's house. After all, she probably barely remembered him.

After another long silence, Tara turned her face toward me, her earthy brown eyes pressed into a squint. She pointed above her head. "Can I turn off that light? It's really bright and I can't see outside."

"Sure, honey."

Tara punched the light off and turned back to the window, her breath steaming it in drifting circles.

"Be right back." I tugged the hood of my Nike jacket over my head and pulled on the door latch. I gave it a light push, expecting it to open wide, but the tilt of the car leaning into the ditch had gravity working against me. My left foot was barely dangling out of the car when the door swung back and smashed into my ankle.

"Shit! Shit, shit, shit —"

"Mom."

I knew what was coming before she said it. At just shy of fifteen, she was just entering the height of snarkiness. She'd inherited the trait from her father. It was one of the things I had loved most about Kyle

— that edgy wit. Humor, in whatever form, was its own special kind of intelligence and Tara had it in spades. It also annoyed the hell out of me.

"Unless you just stepped in a cow patty, that is not —"

"How about 'damn it'?" I snapped. It had been a long drive already and I wasn't in the mood to debate semantics. "I just slammed the door on my leg. Is 'damn it' appropriate?" Cursing was my biggest vice — if you didn't count my lack of social interests — and Tara had picked it up early. Two years old, if I recalled. Since I couldn't tell her not to do what I so freely and often did, I'd tried hard to teach her to use language selectively. If you're going to cuss, I'd told her, do it under your breath. It hadn't always been successful. Nothing like getting a call from your daughter's second grade principal telling you she had told a classmate to "shut the hell up" for talking during an assembly. I'd had to stifle a laugh. Chronologically, she may have been eight then, but mentally she was twenty-eight.

"Sure, I suppose you could damn the door." She wiped at the breath-fog on the glass with her sleeve. "If it makes you feel better."

If I said anything else, this was going to turn into a parent-child verbal brawl. I was too tired to go there, so I let it slide. I'd talk to her tomorrow about toning down the sarcasm. Right now, I just wanted a pillow and a soft bed. Heck, even a couch would do. Knowing my dad, that was probably the best I could hope for.

I probed both sides of my ankle where the door edge had pinched it. No swelling. Yet. But I wouldn't be surprised to find a bruise there tomorrow. I may have had the physique of a natural athlete, but in grade school I'd managed to fall flat on my butt while playing tetherball, hopscotch, and musical chairs. I'd long since figured out that avoiding physical activity was the best way to avert my own early demise.

"Hand me the flashlight from the glove compartment, will you?" Tara said.

"Why?"

"Well, if you aren't going to find out what you hit, I will."

I pointed a finger at her to shush her, then realized she probably couldn't see it in the dark. "You just sit tight and keep your seatbelt on. I'll be back in a second."

Even her sigh was surly. I dug around in the overstuffed glove compartment until I found the skinny LED flashlight my boss had doled out to all the employees last Christmas. Former boss, actually. At first it had seemed like such a cheap gift, but it had come in handy more than once already. Little did I know that Top Floor Media's parent company was already starting to shave off its unprofitable subsidiaries. Had I been aware, I would've started looking for a job sooner.

In the end, though, it was a blessing in disguise. If I'd had time to think about it, I probably would've started looking for a new job. A real job. The kind where you had to clock in at 8 a.m. sharp, then would spend the next nine hours watching the second hand on the clock crawl backward. I'd just spent sixteen years doing that, jotting down grocery lists in the margins of the manuscripts I was supposed to be proofreading because the sex scenes were so boring that snagging a crate of Clementine oranges on sale provided more excitement than suggesting synonyms for private body parts.

With a grunt of exasperation, I kicked the door open wide. A wall of rain slammed into me. Muttering under my breath, I yanked my zipper up all the way, then heaved myself out into the typhoon and shut the door. I clicked the flashlight on and shone it down the length of the driver's side. Nothing. No dings, no scrapes. No dead bodies. So far so good.

A quick scan up and down the road told me all was clear. Amazing how remote this place seemed for only being a few miles off the highway. Back in Chicago, you couldn't go two minutes without a car going down the road, even after midnight — and that was in our suburban neighborhood in Naperville.

Better get used to the isolation, I told myself. At least for the next few weeks. Or however long this was going to take until I got Dad packed up and skedaddled myself out of Sticksville.

The rain was coming down heavier now. It was the kind of rain where it was good to sit inside, curled up under a blanket and sipping a cup of hot tea while watching old movies. No such luck tonight.

My shoes squished as I worked my way toward the back hatch. I hadn't even made it five steps and my pants were already soaked. I grasped the rear bumper and went down on my knees, aiming my tiny flashlight under the car. Nothing there. Thank God.

I began to straighten, but misjudged. My forehead smacked the corner of the bumper. This time the expletives were even more colorful.

When I was done cussing and finally stood up, I saw Tara gazing at me through the rear window. Had she heard the thunk? I faked a smile. The space between her eyebrows pinched with a questioning look. I held my hands wide, palms up, to indicate I hadn't found anything.

Tara cracked her window open. "Did you look in the ditch?"

I held a finger up and stepped to the far side of the car, scanning the panels on the passenger side to look for damage. The scratch was still there just in front of the right rear wheel from when I'd clipped the cement barrier post at the bank drive-thru last fall, but otherwise it all looked good. I swept my light back and forth over the ditch in a forty-foot arc. Nothing but muddy runoff, weeds, and a couple of smashed beer cans.

Spinning in my daughter's direction, I shone the light on myself briefly and shook my head.

"You didn't look very hard." She closed the window, then pulled her hood over her eyes and slumped down in the seat again. Satisfied that whatever I'd hit had crawled off into the field relatively unharmed, I returned to the driver's side.

A long, pitiful whimper rose above the incessant pounding of the rain. I froze with my hand on the door handle. Damn it. I couldn't leave now. I *had* hit something. But what on earth would make that kind of noise?

Reluctantly, I went toward the ditch, the beam of my light swinging back and forth over the rain-gorged channel. To my left, a field of low bushy soybeans spread. I looked for paw or hoof prints or breaks in the rows to reveal where an animal might have gone through, had it retreated into the field, but there was no indication of that. I almost turned back when it occurred to me the car had skidded a good hundred yards before coming to a complete stop.

So I walked on. The cool rain drenching me. The world beyond the column of my flashlight as black as coal. The dampness stabbing the misery deep into my bones.

A ragged mound of fur came into view, its inert body sprawled across the shimmering white line at the road's perimeter. Too small to be a deer. Too big for a raccoon. The fur was a non-descript grayish-brown, the tail a thick plume. Coyote, maybe? If it was, I'd leave it where it lay.

Tentative, I crept forward, ready to bolt back to the car. Closer now. Fifty feet. Thirty. Fifteen ...

Its tail flicked, the tip of it plopping into the silty rivulet of the ditch. I stopped dead in my tracks, trying hard not to pee my pants, wishing I'd brought something with me that could serve as a weapon if it suddenly attacked. What if the coyote were diseased or rabid? There was no way I could outrun it. At least with my tire iron, I could've beaned it in the head a couple of times, bought myself a few seconds to sprint to the car and dive in.

A front paw twitched. I backed up slowly, keeping the narrow beam of my LED light aimed straight at it like a light saber. If nothing else, if it sprang in my direction, fangs gnashing, I could momentarily blind it. Its tail flicked again. Straining with effort, it stretched its front legs. Gaunt ribs expanded with a single meager breath. A plaintive whine leaked from its maned throat.

I took a step back, and another. Cold water rushed into the mesh of my running shoes as my heel sank in a puddle. My ankle buckled with the sudden motion, and I stumbled sideways, biting back a yelp of pain as I turned to run.

I'd only made one limping step when my daughter's plea rose above the pounding rain.

"Mom?" Tara jogged past me in her flip flops, the foamy material slapping up water.

Grabbing her by the elbow, I reeled her in. "Tara, what are you doing? Get back in the car — now!"

"But ..." She tugged toward the sodden lump of fur, twisting her body as she struggled to free herself from my protective grip. The long strands of her wet hair slapped against her cheek. "You have to help him! You can't just drive off and leave him to die! Not after you hit him."

"It's a coyote, Tara. A wild animal." Rain filled my mouth. It was coming down in sheets so hard now I could barely see the car from where we stood.

She snatched the flashlight from my hand and wheeled around. "*That* is a coyote?"

At the sound of her shrill voice, it lifted its head to show a pair of mismatched ears, one semi-erect and one upright, framing a gentle face. A thin white blaze ran between its eyes, one dark, one a pale azure. It stretched its legs, the fur heavy with ticking, groaned, and flopped back over sideways.

A gash on its right shoulder, the width of my palm, glimmered bright with blood.

A dog. I'd hit someone's dog.

chapter 2

THE HAIR ON MY forearms prickled. Lightning speared down from a low cloud to the south. Tendrils of light snapped at the treetops next to the adjacent field. Thunder pealed across the open expanses, shaking the earth. Instinctively, I hunkered down, hauling Tara with me as I cast a glance skyward.

"Bring me the blanket from the backseat," I said. "And grab one of your knee-highs out of your suitcase, too."

"What do you need a sock for?"

"To muzzle it. In case it's not friendly."

Tara sneered. "You really don't like dogs, do you?"

What was there to like about them? They smelled, they cost too much to keep, and they were unruly and unpredictable. "Just being safe. Now do what I told you."

She returned a deadpan look. "Wow. I can't wait to see this. You knotting a sock around the mouth of a rabid dog. Care if I take video?"

"Get them or you can walk to Gramps' house in the rain right now."

Indignant, she screwed her face into a scowl that only a teenager could manage. "I don't know the address or how to get there. And my phone's in the car."

"That would make it a pretty long, miserable walk, wouldn't it?"

"You'd get arrested for child abandonment."

"You see any cops out here?"

She snapped her fingers. "Got it. Back in a jiff."

As Tara shuffled away, her flip-flops squishing, I inched back toward the shaggy heap that was my canine victim. What was I supposed to do with an injured dog at this hour?

Only fifteen feet from it now and the thing hadn't moved an inch or lifted its head again. I wasn't even sure it was still breathing. If only I could be so lucky. But while that would have solved my immediate problem, it would also create an even bigger one. If it died on me, Tara would never forgive me. Didn't matter that I hadn't even seen the animal when *it* decided to rush in front of an oncoming car. Didn't matter that some moron had allowed their dog to run loose. Or that the rain had reduced visibility to a mere ten-foot crescent in front of my headlights.

I'd been at the wheel, operating the vehicle at the time of the murder. Or vehicular manslaughter, technically, as it wasn't pre-planned. Or was that dogslaughter?

Cautiously, I bent down, muscles coiled tight, prepared to bolt. It was breathing. Barely. Its fur slicked down and darkened with rain, it was hard to tell what color it was. Brindle, maybe? No, not mottled enough. Sable, possibly. A wolfish shade. The hair was short over most of the body, with a slight ruff at the neck and a plume to its tail. Three white feet. On the fourth paw, only the toes to the first knuckle were white. Like he'd forgotten to pull that sock up. And yes, it was a 'he'. No mistaking that. With all his reproductive parts still intact.

Breed? Unknown. He looked like one of those non-descript feral Russian dogs from the Sochi Winter Olympics: long legged and lean, built to spend his days trotting from dumpster to dumpster. He certainly wasn't some pampered pet who spent his days curled up and napping next to the fireplace, waiting for a bowl of kibble to be plunked down in front of him.

The longer I stared at the dog, the more I realized the shape it was in. If this dog had belonged to someone, they hadn't been taking very good care of him. He was thin and his fur was patchy from allergies. But the dog had a collar on, so maybe he'd been lost awhile, searching for his home? Clipped by an S-ring to the metal loop of the dog's tattered and faded collar was a tag. I laid my LED beside him. Slowly, I reached for the tag, tilting it to catch the light.

A rabies tag. Expired two years ago. The owner must have forgotten to attach the new tags. There was a vet clinic's name and phone number on it. At least it would give me some way of tracing the owner.

I released the tag and it fell against the animal's chest. I expected him to react, but the dog still didn't move. His eyes were closed. No obviously broken bones, but the wound on its side was seeping a steady stream of blood. The gash wasn't wide, but it looked deep.

"Is he going to be okay?"

Startled by Tara's voice, I almost fell back into a puddle, but steadied myself with a fist against the asphalt.

"Hard to say," I said. "He could have some internal injuries. Spinal, maybe. I'm not sure we should move him, sweetheart. We might make it worse."

Tara sank to her knees on the wet road, her voice coming out in a worried squeak. "You can't *leave* him out here. Some truck will come along and ... and ..." Her face froze in a look of horror. "Splat," she whispered.

If Tara intended to manipulate me into rescuing the mongrel, she was doing a fine job of it. And if she wasn't, I was starting to feel plenty guilty anyway.

Dogs weren't my thing, but I never wanted to harm them. I hadn't owned a dog since childhood — and I barely even remembered that one. A Rat Terrier named Montecristo, after Dumas's *The Count of Montecristo*. Monty for short. The dog had died at less than three years old. A heart problem. Or maybe it was liver. I couldn't remember. My dad had told me no more dogs after that. The vet bills were too much. No loss. The dog liked to bite the ankles of visitors. Attempts to keep Monty contained while we were out of the house or expecting visitors had resulted in a four square foot section of bathroom linoleum being peeled back and a hole chewed through the door just big enough for a rodent, or a very determined terrier, to squeeze through.

As far as I was concerned, dogs were destructive, expensive, and inconvenient. They required training, which meant time. I didn't have the time, let alone the patience, to even housebreak a puppy, forget formal training.

The weight of Tara's body sagged against my shoulder. She reached out and stroked one of the dog's forelegs.

I snatched her wrist back. "Don't."

"Why not? He must be hurting. If I were hurt, and alone, and scared, I'd want someone to comfort me."

"You don't know anything about this dog. He could have rabies."

"Rabies, right." She stared back at me with misty eyes. "And he could die if we don't help him."

Guilt, delivered with such subtle expertise, like a laser aimed at my conscience. She was *just* like her father. Dang her for being so perfect.

"Okay, okay. We'll put him in the backseat. You can sit up front with me. Do you have the blanket?"

Wrinkling her nose, she extended the bundle of cloth. "It's wet."

"We're all wet. Help me carry him." I cringed at the thought of a soaked dirty blanket touching my upholstery, but better that than laying a mangy dog directly on the seat. I unrolled the blanket and together we put him on it. The mutt had to weigh a good fifty pounds. Gently, I lifted him. Tara scooted her arms underneath to support his hind end.

The walk back to the car was long and awkward. Tara was six inches shorter than me. Average height, like Kyle had been. Not freakishly tall, like me. If only I'd possessed some poise, I could've been a runway model. Like my mom. Unfortunately, I'd been cursed with the coordination of a three-legged giraffe. I had to shuffle, stooped over, so that my longer stride wouldn't cause Tara to drop her half.

Thunder cracked overhead. Tara flinched. Wide eyes cast skyward, she started gasping for breath. I could feel her trembling as her arm bumped mine. Even in the bleary darkness, I could see the goose bumps on her flesh. If we didn't get to the car soon, she'd be in a full blown panic attack. She hadn't had one of those in … a year? Two?

"It's okay, pumpkin," I reassured her. "Almost there. See the car? Right ahead of us. In less than a minute, we'll be on our way to Gramps' place. Half an hour from now, we'll be sitting at the kitchen table in dry clothes, drinking hot chocolate."

"Half an hour?" she echoed, her voice pitching high. She drew in a lungful, wheezing. Her body jerked backward half a step. I clutched tight onto the dog, barely stopping in time as the dog's rear dipped.

"Tara, Tara, honey. You're fine. Just fine. We're helping this dog, remember? Going to get him home. To Gramps', I mean. In the morning, we'll take him to the vet. He has tags. They can find his owner. You have to help me, Tara. Okay?"

Squinting now, she scanned the night sky, rain hitting her face hard. Her head bobbed in a feeble nod. "Okay. The car. Right there. I see it." She inched forward.

I paid close attention to her pace, matching it. "Hopefully, he'll be fine by morning. Maybe I just kind of knocked the wind out of him, do you think?"

Tara looked at me sideways, dubious. "Yeah, maybe."

"You know, if he was running loose, maybe he's just lost? If so, me hitting him wasn't such a bad thing after all. We'll have the vet run a check on his tags, call the owner, and he'll be home by tomorrow afternoon, right?"

"Right."

She was moving a little quicker now. But her breathing was still an erratic pant. If her anxiety ever got worse than it was now, or more frequent, I'd take her to a counselor, help her learn how to handle it. In reality, I knew full well what had caused it to begin with. Everyone dealt with trauma in their own warped way. I was no exception.

"Tara, hold up." I eased to a halt beside her. "I've got the dog. Open the back door so I can put him in the car, okay?"

"Okay." She stumbled to the car in a zombie-like state, her head tipped up to watch the sky.

"Watch it, Tar—"

"I got it." She plowed into the car, smacking her hip bone against the rear quarter panel. "Ow, sh—" She flailed a hand at the door handle. "I'm all right. I'm all right. Hurry up, okay?"

I half-sprinted forward. The bouncing stirred the dog to awareness and it twisted in my grasp. Readjusting my grip, I pulled him tighter to my chest. My fingers slid across the open gash on his side, warm and slick with blood. A tiny yelp split from his throat and he threw his head up, smacking the back of his skull against my sternum. The moment he did that, he thrashed his legs, as if he might leap to the ground and take off into the darkness.

"Now! Now!" I yelled at Tara.

She blinked at me for a second, then yanked the door open wide. The dog slid sideways in my arms as he arched his back against my chest, pushing outward. His weight shifted suddenly. If he slipped one more inch to the right, I'd lose my grasp.

So I did the first thing I could think of to save him. I plunged into the backseat with him.

"Shut the door, Tara!"

"What?" She leaned toward me, her forehead creased as if she didn't fully comprehend what I'd said.

This time I bellowed. "I said 'shut the door'!"

Bam!

The door slammed into my shoulder, jarring me hard. Which sent the dog into a fresh conniption. He struggled against my hold. I held him tightly, but calmly, my mind racing for a solution. Rescuing panicked dogs was not in my arsenal of survival skills.

Tara hopped into the driver's seat and tilted the mirror down. "Just tell me where to turn. I'll drive. Keys?"

"No, no!"

The dog was wriggling wildly. His low, broken whine rose to an ear-splitting shriek. For the moment, I was glad he hadn't clamped his jaws on my face or hands.

"Calm down, Mom. I know how to drive."

"How do you know how to drive?"

"Well ..." — she craned her neck forward, then right, scoping out the dashboard — "it can't be that different from a go-cart, can it? Or the Dixon's big lawnmower. I mowed their yard all last summer, you know, and they said I was —"

"You're not old enough to drive a car."

"Legally, but —"

The dog screamed. A very human scream. Like someone was pulling his toenails out with a set of pliers, one by one.

Tara twisted around, reaching toward the dog to lightly grab a paw. "Ohhh, baby. I know. It hurts, I know. But everything's going to be fine. Just fine. Trust me, okay?"

She squeezed its foot and the dog instantly relaxed in my arms. As her fingers moved up his foreleg in slow, soothing circles, the dog bent his neck and began licking her hand.

I had an idea. Not that that was a rare thing, mind you. I was the creative sort, after all. It was risky, this being a strange dog, but it seemed like the best option at the moment. "Tara?"

"Huh?" Her head tilted, but she kept her eyes on the dog. They were gazing at each other like star-struck lovers.

"Why don't you climb into the backseat and take my place? You could keep the dog calm until we get to Gramps'." I scooted the dog over to the side, one hand firm against the top of his ribs.

"Sure, Mom." Tara scrambled between the seats and wedged between me and the dog. Cramped was an understatement. "I got him now."

As quick as I could, I exited the car and then dove into the front seat. I was already drenched, but another soaking drove the chill air deep into my skin. I was shivering now. The temperature had dropped with the arrival of the storm.

I turned the key in the ignition, dialed up the heat, and flicked the hazard lights off. Twisting around, I looked Tara over. She was stroking the dog's neck, reassuring him. When did she get to be so maternal? I'd never allowed her to keep anything more than a pair of goldfish — and she forgot to feed those most of the time.

My eyes dipped to the floor. There were spots of blood on the carpet. I suppressed a groan. The neat freak in me was having a coronary. "Buckle up. We'll be there soon."

We started down the road, the crisis temporarily under control — although I had no idea what I was going to do with the dog at this hour. Rouse a local vet I didn't know? Take it to an emergency clinic the next town over? Either way, it was going to cost way too much. For a dog that wasn't mine. A dog that might die anyway.

"Mom?"

"Yeah, honey." The headlights of another car appeared around the bend. I blinked against the glare, keeping my eyes focused on the blurry yellow stripe running down the center of the road.

"If he could, I'm sure Bump would thank you."

"Bump?"

"Well, we have to call him something, don't we? And that *is* how we met him — you bumping into him."

I didn't have the heart to tell her the dog surely already had a name. Besides, by late morning, he'd be back with his owner, and I'd be scrubbing out my car. Until then, Tara could call the dog whatever she wanted. 'Adios' would've been my choice. But why even name something you'd have no chance to get attached to anyway?

chapter 3

KNUCKLES RESTING ON THE front door, I inhaled deeply. The damp air was thick with the scent of spruce needles and hyacinth. I blew out a breath. All I had to do was get through the next few weeks. Then Tara and I would be living the good life in Florida, surrounded by sea and sun, Midwest winters a distant memory, my mucked up childhood a faded photo in my mind.

I knocked softly, hoping he wouldn't hear and I could just tell Tara that no one was home. In less than a minute, we could be on our way, find a hotel somewhere, and deposit the dog at a vet on the outskirts of town early. I'd make up some story later, tell her my dad already sold the house, and that rusted out Chevy truck parked beside the garage was someone else's.

Through a sprinkling of rain, I gazed at the truck. The brunt of the storm had passed, but the clouds were still thick. Was that beater actually still running? It had to be twenty-five years old.

In the backseat of the car, Tara rested her head against the glass of the window. The dog had gone to sleep halfway here, its whimpers diminishing to a fluttering snore. But the fact that he wasn't alert, given that he had just been sideswiped by a car and was in the custody of strangers, concerned me. I half wondered if he had ruptured some vital internal organ and was silently bleeding to death.

Maybe I should've gone straight to the veterinarian's? Did they even have one of those all-night emergency clinics in Wilton, Indiana? Not that I could recall. More likely there was one in Fullbright, but that was twenty-five minutes away. At any rate, Tara needed some sleep. I'd get her settled in here — if anyone answered — and then take care of the dog. Having to rush out after just arriving would avoid any drawn out conversations with Dad.

Splinters dug into my knuckles. I drew my fist back to knock again.

The latch snicked and the door let out a long groan as it swung open.

My father, Walter Schimmoller, swallowed back a yawn and dragged a hand down over his stubbled face. "You were supposed to be here two hours ago."

"Sorry, I know, Dad. We had an emer—"

"Fell asleep in my recliner," he went on. "Watching the news. Big house fire not too far from here. Then there was some old science fiction flick on with God awful cinematography. Aliens looked like some kids dressed up for Halloween."

"Um, yeah, sorry we're so late, but Tara's in the car with —"

"Now the movies they make today," — Dad opened the door a little wider with his elbow, but he was still blocking the way — "they got all those special effects. Look so real you wanna jump out of your seat when something comes at you. Cost millions of dollars to make. But you know what? Back then, before all that hocus pocus, we still thought it looked real. And you know why?" He tapped a finger to his temple. "Because we had imaginations, that's why."

Oh man. This was going to be a looong few weeks.

"Can we come in?" I blurted before he could launch into another tangent.

He blinked at me several times. "Who's we?"

Patience, patience, I reminded himself. My dad was in his late seventies. His mind wasn't what it used to be. A call from Walt's next door neighbor, Ida, had alerted me to his condition. Last fall he'd tried to kill the weeds in his vegetable garden by piling dry straw over it to do a controlled burn. Unfortunately, there'd been a drought that month and the lawn caught fire. Lucky for him, Ida saw it and called their neighbor, someone named Archer, chief of the local fire department, whose quick thinking saved the garage and house.

Then there was the accident a few weeks ago. Starlings had taken up house in his soffits, two stories up. So Dad hauled out his ladder and climbed up to clear their nests out. He fell, fracturing his elbow in two places. Which would explain why there was grass growing up underneath the truck. With the stick shift, he probably hadn't been able to drive it.

Several painful phone conversations later, I had convinced my dad it was time to sell the house and move into an apartment. One where there would be nearby assistance, should he need it. One where he didn't have to mow five acres or climb onto the roof to sweep the snow off the satellite dish. Still, there was no guarantee that my dad would remember any of those conversations at this hour. Or at all.

"Me, your daughter, Sam." I motioned at the car. "And your granddaughter Tara."

After glancing into the darkened house behind him, Dad craned his neck sideways to peer past my shoulder. "Why're you making her sit out in the car? Is she in trouble?"

"She's with a dog. I accidentally —"

"When did you get a dog?"

"I didn't. He's not —"

"Then why is the dog in your car if he's not yours?"

I counted to ten in my head. I was sure if I opened my mouth and started to explain, my dad would talk right over me again. But he just stared back at me blankly, waiting.

Fists clenched, I said, "I hit the dog with the car. I need to take him to a vet."

"Now?"

"I'm not sure."

"Any broken bones?"

"Not that I can see."

"Blood coming out of his mouth? Vomit? Gums white? Lost consciousness?"

"'No' to the first two and 'I don't know' to the rest."

"So you left your ten-year old daughter in the car with a strange dog?"

"She's almost fifteen and —"

"You don't have a fifteen-year old daughter."

I wheeled around and marched back to the car. If I stood there a moment longer arguing in circles, any dust speck of violence in my being was going to explode to planetary proportions. How did this man, in his current condition, even manage daily life? It was worse than I'd imagined. Ida Oldingsells had downplayed the extent of it, probably afraid I would avoid returning to Wilton.

I tapped on the window and curled a finger at Tara. "We'll get our suitcases in the morning," I said loudly through the glass. "I'll take care of the dog."

Her eyelids heavy with sleep, Tara got out of the car. I pulled her to my side, sheltering her from the mist with my jacket. Little good that did. Our clothes were soaked.

"Gramps awake?" she mumbled.

"Yes, unfortunately."

I half-lifted Tara up the porch steps. Now under the overhang, I propped her against the wall. Why was the door shut? I reached for the knob, turned it. Locked. Damn it.

This time I pounded on the door. So hard the hinges rattled and the frame boomed.

Dad flung the door open wide. He took one look at Tara and burst into a toothy smile.

"Come on in!" He gathered her in a stiff hug; Tara's arms flapped at her sides as he squeezed the air out of her. Then he yanked her just as awkwardly inside the foyer. For a moment, I thought Dad was going to slam the door on me, but then he said, "Don't just stand there like a fence post. Get out of the rain."

Inside, I let my eyes adjust to the darkness. As Dad hobbled down the central hallway and into the kitchen, flicking on a single light, I leaned close to Tara. "Just smile and nod, all right? If you ask him questions, we'll be up until dawn. Let me handle it, okay?"

"No problem."

Shivering, we stood in the foyer a minute longer while Dad made noise in the kitchen, our clothes dripping onto the shiny linoleum. I stared down at my feet, watching the water collect in the grooves between the simulated tiles. Harvest Gold, circa 1970. This house wasn't going to be an easy sell. The word 'fixer-upper' came to mind. Although the retro look was big now, so there was hope.

"Mommy?"

"Yeah."

"What are we gonna do with Bump tonight?"

"I don't know, sweetheart. Honestly, I'm too tired to drive all the way to Fullbright right now. I'll make him a bed in the laundry room for the time being. Soon as I wake up, I'll drive him to the vet's in town. Okay?"

Her doe-brown eyes plied at the layers of my soul. "Promise?"

For the first time, I noticed a one-inch streak of red in her dark brown hair, to the right of her part. It suited her. But it also summoned forth worries that she'd show up one day with one side of her head shaved and her tongue pierced. I'd broach the subject with her tomorrow. I ruffled the top of her head. "Promise."

Maybe things between us weren't so bad after all. We may have both had our quirks, but down deep she was just a normal teenager and I was a regular single mother, dealing with life the best I could.

What was taking Dad so long? And why did it smell like burnt toast? I moved to the end of the foyer, but before going into the kitchen, I looked down the hallway toward the bedrooms. It was crowded with containers, boxes, stacks of magazines and books. When and how did it get like this? I remembered the place being nearly spotless the last I'd been here — ten years ago.

I turned just as my dad barreled through the doorway, almost knocking me over.

He waved a spatula in front of my nose. "I forget. Does she like ham on her grilled cheese?"

"Dad … not now." I dug my phone out of my pocket and checked the display: 2:07 a.m. Later than I thought. Like an hour had mysteriously disappeared. "She needs to sleep more than anything. Just tell me which bedroom to —"

"Bedroom?" He lowered the spatula. "Oh, I forgot about that. She'll have to sleep on the couch tonight. I'll work on cleaning out the bedroom in the morning."

If the hallway was any indication, I didn't want to know what the bedroom looked like. "And me?"

Dad flashed a polite grin. "Recliner's open … unless you'd prefer the floor. I think I have a sleeping bag somewhere."

"That's okay. I'll take the chair. Just bring us some blankets."

"Get the blankets yourself," he grumbled, turning on his heel as he strode back to the kitchen. "You know where everything is."

He stalked off, shoulders hunched, head down. I hadn't been here in ten years. How was *I* supposed to know where things were? He sure didn't.

I GAVE UP ON finding the extra blankets within the first five minutes. Tara had already fallen asleep on the couch, her denim jacket clutched around her. I claimed the only throw in the room — a small afghan woven in autumnal colors to cover my upper body — and a lightweight coat I found in the hall closet for my legs. The prospect of searching anywhere else was too daunting. Things were not where I remembered them. In fact, there were a lot of *extra* things in the house, compared to the day I last walked out of here.

For someone like me, a semi-neat freak, looking around at the clutter invoked feelings of anxiety. I'd seen worse on TV — fly-infested, rodent-riddled homes, the floors piled high with discarded papers and rotting refuse — and even though this wasn't yet on the verge of being condemned, surely this was how those hoarding cases started? It was only a matter of time.

I was two blinks from slipping into a vegetative state when I remembered the dog. Dead tired, I trudged out to the car and hauled his lazy carcass inside. Twice, he peeked at me, then closed his eyes, pretending to sleep. He didn't seem to be in any distress and the wound had stopped bleeding.

After settling him in the laundry room on a sheet I pulled out of the dryer, I plopped down in the recliner. The footrest kicked out with a loud *thump*. My head flew back, smacking into the wall behind me.

"Ow, ow, ow!" I clamped a hand over my mouth before the curse words could start spilling out. Geesh, I couldn't even sink into a comfy chair without having an accident. Tara was dead to the world, thankfully.

When the throbbing in my head went down, I grabbed the remote control and flicked through a few channels, stopping on a rerun of the local nightly news. There was a segment on a Labrador nursing a pair of orphaned opossums, another one on the construction of a new elementary school, and a tease of the upcoming weather forecast that hinted at heat and humidity before a string of commercials followed. I faded in and out of sleep, plans for tomorrow racing through my head. Before I dozed off, a news clip of a house fire came on. Beneath the reporter scrolled the caption:

LOCAL FIRES SPARK INVESTIGATION INTO COUNTY-WIDE THEFT RING.

SEVERAL HOURS LATER, I woke with the taste of ashes on my tongue, damp clothes plastered to my skin, and the sun stabbing through the big picture window directly into my eyes. I didn't know whether to retch, shiver, or hide beneath my blanket. In my dreams, I'd been surrounded by a wall of flames, trapped in a room without windows or doors. The strange thing was I'd been low to the ground, as if I were on my hands and knees and couldn't stand up. I'd say that like most dreams it didn't make sense, but the truth was Dad's house was one big pile of kindling. No wonder I was having nightmares about perishing in flames. All it would take would be one spark from a faulty wire.

Then I remembered the news story about the series of house fires in the area. My memory of the details was sketchy, but before I conked out I remembered the reporter suggesting that the evidence indicated the fires were a cover-up for burglaries. I pulled my phone out of my pocket and typed myself a reminder to check the smoke alarm batteries later today.

The smell of burnt toast still lingered in the air. It conjured memories of when I was six and my dad tried to make us a breakfast of toast, eggs and bacon. The toast was burnt to charcoal, the scrambled eggs were rubbery, and the bacon grease hitting the other burner — which he'd forgotten to turn off when he removed the skillet of scrambled eggs — had set the smoke alarm off. Which of course had made him remove the batteries from it. After that, Dad resorted to stocking the cupboard with a variety of sugary cereals. That would have been fine if he'd ever remembered to buy milk.

My gaze drifted to the clock on the wall above the couch where Tara was snoozing. I had to blink several times before the numbers came into focus.

9:45.

I leapt from my chair and promptly stubbed my big toe on the corner of the couch. As I hopped on one leg, my shin smacked into the coffee table. Biting my tongue, I hobbled into the bathroom, where I shut the door and muttered a string of profanities, marveling that I still hadn't woken Tara up.

When I'd run out of expletives, I splashed cool water on my face, then yanked a comb through my dreadlocks. The figure that looked back at me from the mirror resembled the walking dead. The cowlick from my widow's peak was in major rebellion mode. Hat or ponytail day? I fished a rubber band out of the drawer and pulled my hair back so tight it was hard to blink. Instant face lift.

Slapping my cheeks, I rounded the corner and opened the laundry room door. The small cubicle was littered with shredded softener sheets and bits of cardboard the size of confetti.

Bump lay on his stomach, snout pressed between his paws as he gazed up at me guiltily with those mismatched eyes.

I wasn't sure whether to be mad as hell at the mess or grateful that he wasn't dead. "Guess you're feeling better, huh?"

He thumped his tail against the flecked linoleum so hard I was afraid he was going to give himself an embolism.

Crouching down, I began to pluck up the finely tattered sheets. As I reached toward him, Bump's long tongue flicked out between yellowed teeth, swiping a sloppy kiss across the back of my hand.

Adrenaline flooded my veins. A picture flickered in my mind, a snapshot at first, but then images began to connect together like a video clip: a skulking figure silhouetted against a window, the sounds of someone rummaging through drawers, belongings strewn over a carpeted floor, and a man, maybe sixty years old, in just his boxers, flipping on an overhead light and mumbling, *"What the —?"*

Then, a thump, followed by a spark of light that grew, and grew, and grew. Until flames consumed my vision. A wall of flames.

I snatched my hand back, stroking the back of it until the fear and panic ebbed. The skin beneath my fingers was hot. I inhaled, sure I smelled smoke. Then I realized it was just the lingering odor from Dad's late-night cooking efforts.

Rising, I glanced down at Bump. For a second, I thought I saw the reflection of a fire in his eyes.

No more falling asleep with the TV on, I told myself.

And the sooner I got this place cleaned up, the better.

chapter 4

By 10:45, I WAS sitting in the waiting room at the South End Animal Hospital. The name was a major misnomer. Firstly, the 'hospital' consisted of a tiny waiting room with three plastic lawn chairs and a wooden bench, two examining rooms no more than eight by eight, a supply closet with a fridge, and possibly a surgery room in the back. Secondly, south end of what? It was more or less east of Wilton. But whatever. Let it remain a mystery. I'd be out of here in half an hour, tops — dog-less.

The waiting room was packed when we arrived. 'Packed' being a relative term. A middle-aged couple occupied two of the chairs, each with a small, fluffy white dog that yapped and growled every time anyone moved. Bump cowered with each threat, quivering at my feet. An elderly gentleman was seated on the bench with a plastic carrier beside him. Two triangular pink noses peered from the shadowy confines behind the wire grid of the door. Bump stared at them with predatory intensity, but eventually lost interest. A nap was more pressing business.

Fifty minutes crawled by. The yappy dogs were seen and left. The cats endured their examination with quiet disdain. I was nodding off, cheek propped against my fist, when the receptionist called my name.

"Samantha McNamee? You can take your dog into exam room two."

It wasn't my dog — I'd informed her of that fact when I checked in — but I was too tired to remind her. I'd wrestle that alligator when it came time to pay the bill.

A cheery twenty-something brunette who'd been ping-ponging back and forth between the two exam rooms stood holding the door open. I led Bump in — or rather Bump dragged me in — on the makeshift leash I'd fashioned out of a length of clothesline. Trailer-park chic, but it served its purpose. The dog was favoring a front leg, but it didn't seem to slow him down much. I had fed him cold grilled ham and cheese for breakfast, even scraping the burnt parts off for him. Maybe he wouldn't have cared, but I figured no one, not even a dog, deserved to eat charcoal.

The vet tech checked her clipboard. "So this is Bump, huh?"

"For now. I mean, that's what my daughter decided to call him last night. No clue what his real name is. You see, I accidentally hit him with my car — Sorry, that was dumb. I guess I wouldn't intentionally hit a dog, would I? That would be kind of sick. Anyway, we took him home — I mean to my dad's house. I'm just passing through. On my way to Florida." I had a tendency to over-explain, but I wanted this woman to understand I didn't regularly plow down defenseless animals with my car. More than that, though, I wanted her to know the dog wasn't mine. I grabbed Bump's collar and twisted it around so she could see it. "See, this is his rabies tag and number. Can you trace it?"

She bent over and peered at the information stamped on it. Bump craned his neck, despite the fact that I was trying to hold him back, and washed the vet tech's face thoroughly. She rubbed her face dry with a sleeve. "Friendly, isn't he?"

"Too friendly, if you ask me," I said. "Although I suppose that's better than the alternative." I would have preferred the dog be properly reserved, so he had some manners. The shaggy beast had nearly yanked me halfway across the parking lot with the first stranger he saw. At least I hadn't had to muzzle him. Fair trade. A pulled muscle was always preferable to a lawsuit. "So, can you locate his owner?"

"Hmm, the tag was issued here, although it's a few years old, from when Dr. Barnes was here. The records from then aren't too organized, but I'll try. First we need his vitals, all right?"

While the tech took his temperature, I distracted Bump by rubbing his ears. After asking me a few questions about the dog's symptoms and behavior, she gave the wound on the dog's side a cursory look and told me the vet would be right in.

Twenty minutes later, I was still waiting. Apparently in Wilton, 'right away', 'soon', and 'shortly' meant an unspecified time in the future.

The plastic chair was hard and cold, but I still could have fallen asleep, I was so exhausted. Every once in a while, I'd flick my leg with my fingers to keep myself alert. Somehow, I'd managed to memorize the life cycle of the flea from the wall poster in the interval. When the novelty of that wore off, I pulled a pamphlet on heartworm prevention from a display on the counter and was deeply immersed in it when a rapid knock sounded on the door. Did they think I was sitting there in a paper gown, like a visit to the OB-GYN?

"Hello." A tall, suntanned man opened the door and peered at me through the glare of a pair of black-framed reading glasses. Tipping the frames back to rest the glasses on top of his head, he flashed an obligatory smile. In one simple action, his look changed entirely. "Mrs. McNamee?"

For a moment, I forgot my own name. I gazed up at him, drowning in eyes the color of rich earth, unsure whether I should stand or stay seated. Actually, I don't think I could have stood up without falling over at that moment. I was in the company of Adonis.

Or at the least, a Calvin Klein model. He had the lean build and chiseled cheekbones of a man who exercised obsessively. I dabbed a fingertip at the corner of my mouth to check for drool. Dry, thank God.

While I fixated on his appearance, he clicked his pen a couple of times, blinking with obvious discomfort. He checked his clipboard again. "Or is it *Ms.* McNamee? Do I have the right patient here?"

I nodded, still unable to speak.

The barest hint of smile crinkled his cheeks, reaching the corners of his eyes. "This *is* Bump, correct?"

"No." I sorted through a stream of muddled thoughts. Why did he look familiar?

"Oh. Melissa must have handed me the wrong forms. What's his name, then?"

"I ... don't know."

"Don't know?"

I repeated the story to him — although in significantly fewer words this time. "— and I hope to be in Florida soon. If not next week, then the week after. So I'm hoping his owner will come and get him today. My daughter's worried about him."

"She sounds like a good kid."

"Thanks, Dr...?" I touched my temple, like I could reach into my brain and pull out a memory. "I feel like I should know you, but —"

"Oh, I'm sorry." He stuck his hand out. "I thought we'd met before. I'm Dr. Chastain. But everyone around here just calls me Clint — or Dr. Clint, if they feel the need to be formal. I'm new here. Well, new *here*. Not new to town, exactly."

His palm molded against mine. A giddy warmth flowed up my arm and spilled into my chest. Why did I feel like a teenybopper who'd just met Harry Styles from One Direction?

"You've lived here awhile?" Thankfully, I was starting to regain control of my vocabulary. The last time I'd been this tongue-tied was in 10th grade. Of course, Kyle had affected me in a lot of ways. It had taken me two weeks to say 'hi' to him, the new guy at school. I was doing considerably better this time.

"Just a year," he replied. "But I was born here. Graduated from Wilton Memorial High School."

"Home of the Fighting Maple Leafs." I imitated a pair of claws with my hands and made a scary face. He cracked a wider smile, which I took as a sign that I hadn't totally put him off. I pointed to the center of my chest. "Class of '93. You?"

"'94." He leaned back against the stainless steel examining table, his perfectly toned rump barely indenting with the pressure. His dark eyebrows jumped up. "Now I remember!"

Frick. Why was I still drawing a blank? Had I dated him before Kyle and I became serious? Doubtful, since I'd only gone out with two, maybe three guys before Kyle. Had I danced with him, maybe? Kissed him under the mistletoe? I would remember if I'd kissed a guy as gorgeous as him, wouldn't I? *Wouldn't I?*

"You remember what?" I probed.

He waggled a finger. "You were the gal with all the academic awards. The quiz team captain. National Honor Society president. The one who went off to college in Chicago. On full scholarship, right?"

He remembered all that? Most of high school was a fuzzy snapshot to me. No, to be truthful it was more like a kindergartener's tempera finger-painting, complete with stick figures. I couldn't recall a lot of details about it. Just that I wanted to get out and on to better things.

"Yes, that was me," I said.

Pride welled in my chest. I'd worked hard for that scholarship, welcomed the chance to get out of Indiana and immerse myself in the one thing, besides Kyle, that I was passionate about. Literature had been the core of my being since I was old enough to read. In fifth grade, I cried when a teacher confiscated my copy of *Romeo and Juliet*, telling me it was inappropriate material, that proper young ladies shouldn't read stories about promiscuous teenagers who committed suicide. I placated her by slipping a copy of *Tess of the D'Urbervilles* beneath a dust jacket for *Little House on the Prairie*.

"You were so stuck-up," Dr. Clint said. Very seriously.

My brows lifted. Wow, that was bold.

He set his clipboard on the table and waved his hands in front of him. "Sorry, I didn't mean it like that. Geez, I've already apologized twice and it's only been, what, three minutes? I meant a lot of kids at school looked up to you, but you kind of kept to yourself. Barely spoke to anyone. I must've said good morning to you a dozen times one semester and I was lucky if you nodded back at me."

Okay, his confession was sort of pissing me off now. Talk about judgmental. "It's unfortunate you had that impression of me. It wasn't anything personal. Introverts get a bad rap."

He clasped his hands together. "Yeah, we were all different back then, I suppose. I couldn't have been a bigger geek. Totally obnoxious, I'm sure. Science was my thing. I used to recap *Cosmos* episodes to unwitting classmates. No wonder they avoided me. And I had those *big* eyeglasses. The kind that looked like you had a pair of magnifying glass lenses stuck to your face. And not just braces, but headgear. Is there any better way to torture an insecure teenager? Frizzy hair, too. I also weighed fifty pounds more than I do now."

"Really?" No wonder I didn't recognize him. "I find that hard to believe."

And I did. Nothing about his looks now said 'pudgy, awkward teenager'.

"Yes, really. Call it baby fat if you want, but the truth is I had a thing for deep-dish pizzas." He stooped down, and Bump sidled up to him, nuzzling his palm. From the end drawer, he took out a scanning device and waved it over Bump's shoulders.

"Hmm, no microchip."

The dog leaned into him as Dr. Clint scratched his neck with one hand and probed near his wound with the other. Bump's tail thwacked against my leg so hard I expected bruises to appear later. After a bit of prodding, Dr. Clint listened to his heart, then inspected his eyes, ears, and mouth.

"We could x-ray his shoulder and leg, just to be on the safe side," he said, "but I suspect it's merely deep bruising and muscle soreness that we're dealing with here. He could stand to gain a little weight and by the looks of it he has flea allergies, plus some ear mites, but that's all easily taken care of. There's no indication of internal bleeding, however; but look out for any changes in behavior: vomiting, lethargy, lack of appetite, that sort of thing."

"Appetite doesn't seem to be a problem." I withheld mentioning the softener sheets. I didn't think Bump had actually eaten any.

"That's a good sign."

"What about the gash on his side there?"

He bent over to study it more closely. I resisted the urge to twine my fingers in that dark, tousled hair of his — Dr. Clint's, not the dog's.

"I'll clean it out and put in a few stitches as a precaution." He straightened. "You'll have to bring him back in a week to ten days to have them removed, though. Meanwhile, I'll send you home with some shampoo for his skin condition, pills that will kill the fleas, drops for his ears, and I'd also suggest some flea bombs to treat your house."

"I was hoping that his owner —"

"Right. I keep forgetting. It's not often we have the same person who hit the dog actually bring it in for care. I think Melissa is following up on the tags. I'll check on it after we get this taken care of." He opened a drawer and began to lay out items for suturing. Bump tipped his head sideways like a bobble-head doll every time one of the metal tools plinked on the steel counter. Armed with wet cotton balls, Dr. Clint sank to the dog's side. "Hold tight onto his collar, Mrs. McNamee. This is going to sting."

I barely had my fingers hooked beneath the flat of the nylon collar when he dabbed the first cotton ball over the wound. Bump screamed, bucking sideways. His mouth went wide, enormous, gleaming fangs snapping at air.

"Whoa there, buddy. Just a few more seconds." Dr. Clint continued to dab at the open wound, even as Bump thrashed in my grip.

"Aren't you going to muzzle him?" I suggested over Bump's hyena-like screams. I held the dog at arm's length, afraid the banshee would rip into my flesh at any moment.

"Muzzle? No, I don't think we need to. He's all bark and no bite." He patted Bump on the withers. "All done." The dog's shrieks diminished to a plaintive yowl, making him sound like a cat in heat. Dr. Clint gave me a squinty-eyed look. "It would help if you'd hold a little tighter, though."

"I was trying. The dog's strong enough to pull a sled of cement blocks."

"My guess is he's part Siberian Husky, so that figures." He cocked his head. "Why don't I fetch Melissa for the suturing?"

"Sounds like a good idea to me." I wondered if he was this patronizing toward all his clients. If he was, the only reason he stayed in business was because there was only one other vet in town and he was primarily a farm vet. The door closed behind him. "Smart ass," I muttered.

Bump stood there shaking like a leaf, his nails scrabbling at the slick linoleum as he strained toward the door. I wrapped the leash/rope around my hand several times and held tight, even though it was cutting off my circulation. "No dice, buddy. You're staying here until they put you back together. And then your grateful owner is going to come waltzing in that front door, overjoyed to see you. You will leap into his arms, cover him with sloppy kisses, and rainbows will spring from your paw prints."

Spinning around to face me, Bump started licking my hands.

"Stop it, stop it," I said. "Stop. It." But the more I tried to curtail his affections, the more he lathered me with saliva.

Dr. Clint came back into the room with the vet tech in tow. A hank of dark waves fell across his forehead as he set his glasses back down on his nose.

For a few seconds, I pretended to study the flea poster, but then I couldn't help myself. My eyes flicked to his face. Deep brown eyes impaled my heart. Suddenly, I imagined his lips on mine, strong hands wandering down my back, over my hips ... Blushing, I ripped my eyes away and handed Bump's leash to Melissa.

Wow, I hadn't felt longings like that since ... I couldn't remember.

Wait. Yes, I could.

Since Kyle.

THE SUTURING WENT REMARKABLY better than disinfecting the wound had — or at least it did once they'd shaved the area around the cut. After that, Bump only bitched a little. He didn't even try to take anybody's hand off during the ear cleansing, although I wouldn't have blamed him if he had.

Afterward, I sat in the lobby, now clear of other clients, while they checked their records to locate Bump's owner. Bump lay stretched out on his side, the gash neatly closed up with little white Xs. His legs twitched and a muffled 'woof, woof' sounded from his closed mouth.

"Awww." Melissa wandered in to the lobby. "He must be dreaming that he's chasing bunny rabbits."

Dreaming of bunny stew maybe, I thought. "Did you get a hold of his owner?"

Her smile faded, although she made a valiant attempt to fake one. "Dr. Clint will be back in a second."

Which wasn't really an answer. Her tone hadn't implied hope, either.

Just dandy.

I had to get back to the house. I'd left poor Tara with Dad. A bitter, confused curmudgeon and a smart-mouthed teenager under the same roof? Dad and I had butted heads far too many times during my own adolescence for me to imagine it would go well for my daughter. Besides, her sarcasm had a tendency to get her in trouble when someone got in her craw.

The receptionist had abandoned the front desk, but I could still hear her alternately chatting on the phone and munching on potato chips. The front desk was piled with papers needing filed, assorted pens, an opened can of Dr. Pepper, an unopened bottle of Kiwi water, and manila folders with names scribbled on the tabs. In the far corner of the chest-high counter, two brass plaques were shoved. The first one said: 'Payment at time of service is appreciated. Make checks payable to South End Animal Hospital.' The second plaque, nearly hidden by a calendar displaying fluffy white kittens tumbling out of a watering pail for the month of June said: 'Clint Chastain, DVM.'

Clint Chastain, Clint. Clint, Clint, Clint. Nope, the name still didn't ring a bell. There'd only been about sixty kids per graduating class at Wilton Memorial High School.

Had he been wearing a wedding ring? I thought hard. No, he hadn't. He could have been divorced. Or maybe even widowed. Like me.

Why hadn't I mentioned that when he kept calling me *Mrs.* McNamee? Then again, why *would* I mention that, unless I wanted to clue him in that I had a fan-girl crush on him already?

Still, I couldn't remember a Clint, or even a Clinton. Or anyone by the last name of Chastain.

"Mrs. McNamee?"

He was standing right in front of me. When had he come into the room? And what was he? Some kind of ninja?

I glanced up at him, flashed a grin, then looked down at the dog, still snoring away. "Good news?"

"Wish I could say so. We found the owner's name, but the phone number we had on record was disconnected."

"Oh." I couldn't look at him right then because there was no way I could have hidden the disappointment in my face. I was aware, however, that it was probably just as obvious in my voice. "So what now? I really didn't have plans to take a dog in. I'm helping my elderly father sort through his belongings and sell his house." I left out the part about finding an assisted care facility. I didn't want it to sound like I was shuttling my father off to an old people's home just to get him out of the way. It wasn't like that at all. It had been his idea — well, after I dropped a dozen hints. Still, I had a life of my own. Plans. And staying in Wilton, Indiana was not part of them. Besides, Dad needed someone who could be on call to care for him: run him to doctor's visits, cook, clean, walk him through how to use a computer, remind him to take his pills. Just the thought of it exhausted me.

"I looked the name up in the phone book, though," he said. "Oren Rickman. Retired deputy sheriff. He was a client before I came here. I called that number, which was different from the one we had on record, and … well …"

My gaze drifted upward, from his scuff-free Adidas running shoes that looked like they'd never been worn, much less run in, to his well-fitted jeans, to his crisp blue scrub top. "And what?"

"He's deceased. About a year ago. It was his daughter who answered. She said he gave the dog to a friend a few months before he passed from lung cancer. She couldn't remember the person's full name."

"Not even a first name? Where they might have lived? Anything?"

"Somebody named Bud, which I'm sure doesn't help much. She said she never met him. And I'm guessing Bud probably isn't his given name."

"So what do I do with … him? What *was* his name, anyway?"

"Funny you asked. All we have in our records is 'Unknown'. Since there are no prior records, my guess is he'd recently acquired the dog — although whether Bump here was a stray, a shelter adoptee, or he'd gotten the dog from someone else, I don't know. As for what to do with Bump, there's really no reason for him to stay here. You could take him to the shelter, but I should warn you … prospects for adoption, particularly for an adult dog are grim and … it *is* a high-kill shelter. We're a rural community. There are a lot of Amish farmers in this area of the state who raise puppies like they're a crop of wheat. They minimize costs, put out a lot of product, and don't screen buyers. That means a lot of dogs get abandoned, simply because they're not properly placed to begin with. Or sometimes those puppy mill products don't get spayed and end up having puppies of their own as soon as they're sexually mature."

That, right. The dog wasn't neutered. Had he segued into that to urge me to set up an appointment? Not my problem. Surgery could happen on someone else's dime.

Dr. Clint sat in the chair next to me. His knee bumped mine and I felt it like the strike of a branding iron, even through the layers of clothing. A warm flush spread over my skin. I leaned away, drawing my knees together.

"There just aren't enough good owners around here to keep up with the population explosion," he went on. It wasn't so much a soapbox sermon as it was a lamentation of the way things truly were. I could sense that he had seen more than his share of abandoned and neglected animals. "And there isn't enough money to feed and house all the unwanted dogs. So the shelter does what it has to."

Bump's eyelids fluttered. He stretched and let out a yawn.

"Isn't there a rescue group that will take him in?" That probably sounded like a cop-out, but the fact was that adding a destructive, untrained, overly dramatic dog to the potentially volatile situation I was already in was not going to help matters. "I mean, he's part Husky, so … maybe …?"

"I can look up some names and give them to you, but most are already full up around here. You might be able to get him in somewhere farther away, but that's bound to take a while. And to be honest, he's only part Siberian. A quarter, if I had to guess. There's also maybe some Collie, German Shepherd, terrier of some sort. Who knows? Breed rescue groups are pretty specific about what they'll accept, not because they don't love all dogs, but because they can only help so many."

Lifting his head, Bump almost winked at me with his one blue eye.

"A shame," Dr. Clint said wistfully. "He's a wonderful dog. Lots of love to give. He just needs someone with the time and patience to mold him, make him into the great dog he could be."

Then, as if reading my mind, he added, "I'd take him home myself, but I have two cats already, one a cranky senior who doesn't like rambunctious youngsters."

"Sounds like my dad." It wasn't a joke, but he laughed. I laughed, too. The little bubble of tension that had hung suspended between us burst not like a balloon stuck by a pin, but like a soap bubble landing softly on a rough surface.

"I'm sure he's not all bad," he said.

I could feel his gaze on me, warming the side of my face. "Maybe I'll introduce you someday, let you judge for yourself." I glanced at him then, but he immediately looked down at his lap. Maybe offering to introduce him to my father was getting a little too familiar? Time to change the topic. "So, if you could give me those phone numbers, I'd really appreciate it. Meanwhile, I'll put some signs up at the town grocery store, the bank, run an ad in the paper ... They do still have a newspaper in Wilton, don't they?"

"Yes, I think so."

"And where do people buy dog food around here?"

"Either Garber's Groceries or the Feed & Seed. No place else, really, unless you go all the way to the north side of Fullbright."

"Thanks. I'll ask around. See if anyone knows a guy named Bud who's lost his dog." Not that I had time for any of that, but I sure as heck wasn't going to keep the dog.

"That's noble of you, trying to find his owner. I hope it works out."

"Yeah, me, too."

Dr. Clint excused himself to look up the numbers. Meanwhile, I texted Tara to see how things were going on the battlefront.

Fine, Mom. I taught him how to make an omelet. Can you believe he didn't know how?

Yes, I could. I'd grown up on Hamburger Helper, which I learned to make myself when I turned eight. Due to my accident-prone nature, any dish that required chopping, dicing or sautéing was out of the question. Same went for anything with more than four ingredients. Or fresh vegetables, because there were never any in the house. I typed a reply and hit send.

Be home soon, sweetie. Ten minutes?

Don't rush, Mom. Everything's fine.

For now everything was fine. Give it five more minutes.

Paper crinkled. Dr. Clint stood in front of me, holding several sheets of paper.

"Rescues. I just ran them all off." He handed me the stack of paper. "I don't know how helpful they'll be, but it's a start."

I stood up and Bump immediately sprang to his feet, the thick cord of his tail thumping against my shins.

"You, uh, said you were on your way to Florida." He neatened a stack of papers on the counter. "New job?"

"Sort of. I was laid off a few months ago. Used to work for a big publisher in Chicago. My job title was editor, but mostly I was a proofreader and gofer."

"So you're looking for a new line of work, then?"

"I'm not sure. I've been writing. For years, actually. It's going pretty well." As soon as I said it, I regretted doing so. Nobody but Tara and my editor knew about my writing. It wasn't something I liked to talk about, so I'd been telling people I had squirreled away a lot of money and was going south to live and do some freelance editing for science textbooks. That usually stopped the conversation dead.

"That must be wonderful to pursue your dream like that. I hope you have a lot of success at it." And he said it like he really meant it, which took me completely off guard. But then, "What do you write about?"

Bang!

Bullet to the brain.

I stood there so long he must have thought I'd gone spontaneously mute. Or that I was having a stroke. "It's, uh … kind of hard to explain." I flipped my wrist over, then remembered I wasn't wearing a watch. So I pulled out my phone and said a little too loudly, "Wow, look at the time! I *really* have to go. What do I owe you?"

When I walked in, I had no intention of paying the bill, but it didn't seem right to stiff him at this point. He was trying to help me find the dog's owner. I started to pull my wallet out of my purse.

"Don't worry about it." Dr. Clint waved a hand dismissively. "I'll send you the bill in the mail. Say, I know I kept calling you Mrs. McNamee, but I noticed you're not wearing a wedding ring. Did I … did I get that wrong?"

I almost remarked that he wasn't wearing one, either, but that would have made the moment even more awkward than it already was. "No, not really. My husband, he, uh …" I looked down. It was still hard to talk about it, even now. "He died ten years ago."

"I'm sorry — I normally don't ask such personal questions of clients. It's just that, well, you're new in town, kind of, and I was just curious."

"No problem. Really." I grasped the doorknob. "If it helps, just call me Sam."

"See you around … Sam." He lifted his hand in a wave. "Maybe we'll run into each other?"

"Sure. Hard not to run into folk in a town as small as this."

With Bump pulling on the lead, I darted across the parking lot. I loaded the dog in the backseat, which I'd covered with an old checked blanket that I vaguely remembered from childhood.

Five miles down the road, it struck me: Lambert Clinton Chastain had sat behind me in biology class for two years. I'd been aware of his existence, but in all that time I'd barely spoken to him, except to hand him a stack of quiz papers, saying, "Please pass these back."

He was right — I had been stuck-up back then.

Another five miles down the road, another thing occurred to me. If I found Bump's owner and gave him back, I wouldn't have a reason to see Dr. Clint again.

Then again, I'd be on my way to Florida in a few weeks. I didn't have time for a relationship. Just like I didn't have time to study yoga or take a trip to Myanmar. I had a plan and nothing was going to derail me from it.

Unless he asked me out. After all, it would be impolite to turn him down outright. He should at least have a chance to seduce me. Not that I'd be that easy, mind you. Although I could be swayed.

chapter 5

SINCE THERE WAS NO fenced-in yard at my dad's house, I rigged a cable line for Bump by attaching a clip at the end of his 'leash' to the clothesline. The dog was deliriously happy running back and forth — although it took him a few times of hitting the end of the line to understand its limitations. I found a pan in the kitchen, filled it with water, and brought it out to him. Bump lapped greedily, his plush tail swinging.

"Hey, Mom."

I swung around to see Tara standing by the garage in the clothes she'd gone to bed in. Her hair stuck out in all directions and she still had pillow lines on her face. "Hey, sleepyhead. You going to change clothes today?"

She stuck a hip out and did the slightest eye roll. "I would have, but somebody had my suitcases in their car."

"Oh ... right. Sorry. I'll bring those in." I started toward the front of the house, then stopped. "Say, I'm going to need to run to the store later to —"

"Can I go with you?"

She said it with such sudden desperation that it set off alarms in my head. "Is everything all right, pumpkin? Did Gramps say something to upset you?"

"No. Nothing like that." She twisted the tail of her T-shirt between her hands, stretching the front of it down past her hips. "It's just that …" She looked behind her, then peered around the corner of the garage at the back of the house and said quietly, "He went to clean out one of the bedrooms and, well, I heard him talking to him-self and then … he started crying. I knocked on the door, but he told me to go take Monty on a walk. Who's Monty?"

"Oookay, yeah. I understand you probably need to get out of the house. Monty was a dog I had as a kid. I'm sure he meant Bump. Let me talk to him, then I'll check with Ida next door and see if she can come over and play cards with him for a while or something. We'll go to the store then, all right?"

I was halfway to the car when Tara jogged after me and tapped me on the elbow.

"Mom?"

"What is it?"

Her hands were folded before her pleadingly. "Are we keeping Bump?"

The sad look in her eyes tore a tiny hole in my heart. She may have been a sarcastic teenager, but she seldom asked for anything unless she really, truly wanted it. We weren't in the position to take on a dog, not with our living situation up in the air. Besides, I knew who'd be walking and taking care of him once Tara started back at school in the fall. I rubbed Tara's upper arm — a meek attempt to console her. "I don't think so, pumpkin. I've got some leads on his owner. Just have to make a few phone calls."

Her face fell. "Oh." Then, "Is he going to be okay?"

Bump was watching us with the intensity of an eagle, his ears perked at full attention. "Just a few stitches, but yeah, he'll be fine."

"Can I throw a tennis ball for him? I found one in the garage."

"Yeah, he'd like that. But take it easy. Just toss it a few feet, okay?" I handed her the stuff the vet had given me. "Here, first put his pills on the kitchen counter and the shampoo in the bathroom, okay?"

Nodding, she ducked into the kitchen to set the items down, then hurried off to the garage to rummage around. There were dozens of plastic bins in there. And buckets filled with yard tools and sporting equipment. And shelves lined with rose fertilizer and bug spray and gardening gloves. And boxes. Lots and lots of boxes. Stuffed full of who-knew-what. There wasn't room left to park a car in there.

In that moment, I was overcome with the enormity of the task I'd volunteered myself for. Anxiety compressed my ribs, a hint of what Tara's panic attacks must have felt like. One task at a time, one day at a time, I reminded myself.

Blowing out a breath, I forced myself to walk away. I'd be lucky to make it to Florida in time for Christmas.

Think positive, I told myself. Just to back it up, I thumbed through my contacts and dialed.

"Rosa? Hi! It's me — Sam."

"Sam. Hello. Have you decided yet?"

"Yes, I'd like you to find me something right there in Big Pine. Small is fine. It's just my daughter and me. You know my budget. I don't need to be on the water, but I do need to be able to walk to it."

She rattled some listings off the top of her head, her enthusiasm bubbling through the phone line.

"A lanai?" I interrupted. "Yes, look into that one, please. It sounds perfect."

"DAD, DO YOU WANT me to make lunch?" I stood in the doorway of my old bedroom. I'd knocked once, then hearing no answer had opened the door.

In his lap, he held a yearbook. A moment passed before he

looked up from the pages. I couldn't tell if he'd been crying, had allergies, or the redness rimming his eyes was just an effect of old age.

"When did you get here?" he asked.

"We got in late last night, remember? I took that stray dog to the vet's this morning. Just got back a few minutes ago."

"I *know* you got here last night," he groused, snapping the yearbook shut and flinging it across the bed to land in a haphazard pile of magazines. "Do you think I forgot already?"

I redirected the conversation. "I'm making some ham sandwiches for Tara and me before we go to the grocery store. Do you want one?"

"No, still full from breakfast. And no, I don't want to go to the store, either." Which was good, because I wasn't going to invite him. His gaze drifted around the room, then stopped on the far wall where a row of my old plaques and framed certificates lined a shelf. "Ever since they updated the interior of Garber's, I can't find a damn thing. I think they confuse you on purpose, just so you'll spend more time wandering around and put more in your shopping cart."

He had a point. Still, what did he do when he needed a loaf of bread or jar of jam — pay for a delivery service? No, he was too cheap for that. Besides, I doubted Garber's had a delivery service. "Say, I was just talking to Ida and she wanted to know if you wanted to go over to her place and play some pinochle? Said she made too much pumpkin bread and you're welcome to some."

"Did she now?" Dad gave me a skeptical look. "I have a lot to do here, Sam. I don't even know where to start."

"This was my room, Dad. Why don't you let me —?"

"What if there are a few things here I'd like to save? Mementos, you know. Maybe all this stuff didn't mean much to you, but I was proud of you, Sam. Proud of how you set your mind on things and what you accomplished."

If he was proud of me it was the first time he'd ever said so. My guess was that he was making up an excuse not to purge. After all, what if he made the wrong decision and next week learned he could have made a thousand bucks on eBay off that mangled plastic Smurf figurine that Monty had chewed on?

"Besides," he went on, "if you'd wanted any of this for yourself, you'd have taken it a long time ago. And since you didn't, I suppose it's up to me to decide what to pitch and what to keep. You try distilling seventy years of your life into a dozen boxes."

I could taste the bitterness in his words. I'd known it would come to this: the resentment, the procrastination, the reluctance to part with material things. And I understood, in a way. But when I walked out of this house the day after high school graduation, I vowed never to look back with regret. I'd told myself that *things* didn't matter; relationships did.

Yet ever since Kyle died, relationships were the one thing I was good at failing.

"Okay, Dad, take your time. I need to pick up some storage bins, boxes, markers and stuff, so we can organize everything. After I get back from the store, I'll start in the garage. We can discuss then whether you want to do a garage sale, some kind of auction, or just donate to Goodwill. I'd suggest a dumpster, too."

There, I said it like it was. Better to deal with it out of the gate than tiptoe around the subject for the next month.

Still, I didn't feel good about it. Whether I was honest with him or kept my opinions to myself, either way I lost.

Snorting through his nostrils, he turned away.

AFTER TARA AND I gobbled down our sandwiches, I did a few last minute things, then gathered up my purse and car keys to take my daughter into town.

Holding open the front door, I shouted into the house, "Today,

Tara! I told you half an hour ago we were leaving in ten minutes."

She appeared in the foyer, sleeves pushed up past her elbows, her tie-dyed cross-body purse slung from hip to shoulder. She wiped her hands on her jeans, leaving wet handprints on her thighs. "Sorry. Bump jumped out of the tub five times. I ended up tying him to the post of the birdfeeder out back and chasing him around with a hose until he let me finish. He's back on the line now."

My jaw agape, I held the screen door open for her. This was the kid who couldn't remember to feed her goldfish more than twice a week. Getting her to clean her room was like trying to negotiate for fewer vacation days with government employees. "You washed the dog?"

"Sure." She flicked a wad of soapsuds from the front of her shirt. "Why do you sound so amazed? He was itchy. You brought home flea shampoo. I'm pretty sure if he could thank me, he would."

"It's just that …" I stood moored in place as she walked past me to stand on the front porch.

"What? I'm almost fifteen, you know. I think I can wash a dog by myself."

"It's not that." A little fountain of pride sprang up inside my chest. This was a change. A good one. "I'm just amazed you did it without even being asked."

Her shoulders hitched in a nonchalant shrug. "I'm growing up, Mom. Deal with it."

Ah, there was my snarky little angel. I was starting to get suspicious that Mother Teresa had swapped bodies with her.

TARA LOADED THE CART with frozen pizzas, while I piled fresh vegetables in the child seat.

I selected a nice cut of steaks and showed Tara. "I was thinking of making garlic asparagus drizzled with balsamic vinegar to go along with the filets. What do you think?"

She wrinkled her nose. "Asparagus sounds good, but I'll skip the steak."

This day was getting stranger by the second. "Wow, that was backward from what I'd have guessed. Are you going vegetarian?"

Her thumb slipped beneath the strap of her purse. "Been thinking about it."

"Guess we should put the pepperoni pizzas back, then." I reached toward the top carton, but Tara flung her hand out.

"That's okay." There was an edge of panic in her voice. Thin crust pepperoni pizza was her fallback comfort food. "I'm not totally committed to it. Just thought I'd, you know, give up some meat, see how it went."

"Do you want beans with your asparagus?"

Wrapping her hands around her neck, she stuck her tongue out and made choking sounds. A nice-looking boy about her age rounded the corner and came down our aisle. Hands in pockets, the Justin Bieber lookalike slipped a glance at Tara from beneath his swoopy bangs as he inspected the frozen meat section. For a split second, Tara's face froze in embarrassment. She faked a cough, then pounded on her chest in an attempt to salvage her composure. The boy grabbed a package of ground beef and turned away without a second look.

Tara's shoulders rolled forward in disappointment. Then she tossed her head back and, pulling her spine straight, muttered, "Arrogant jerk."

"So, black beans, kidney beans, navy beans?" If I didn't redirect her attention right away, she'd sulk for hours before launching into an obsessive makeover routine, including a request for a new haircut and wardrobe.

Her lip curled. "No. Way."

"You have to get your protein from somewhere." So now she was a vegetarian? I was always suspicious when Tara got on a new kick. Last year she'd decided that her shampoo was killing off all the aquatic life in Lake Michigan. This was about the time there was a lice outbreak in her school, which I promptly brought up. The next day she switched from not washing her hair at all, to doing it two or three times a day.

"How about tofu?"

I tilted my head at her. "Have you ever actually had tofu?"

"Yeah ... I think." She sucked her chin back. "I can't remember. Maybe."

We went in search of tofu. Fifteen minutes later we were still looking. Turned out that Garber's Groceries didn't stock it. No wonder folks drove all the way to Fullbright to buy food.

Welcome to small-town life. I remembered why I left here.

Well, one of the reasons, anyway.

Since the shopping cart was practically child-sized, we stopped stockpiling when our heap threatened to overflow. After checking out and loading up the rear of the car, we drove around to the back of the store where the manager/owner was waiting with a stack of boxes for us.

He pushed up his sleeves and shoved an armload into the tiny backseat with a grunt. Big circles of sweat stained his armpits. His hairline had already receded halfway back his head, but something about him looked vaguely familiar. I squinted to read his name badge: Newton Tipton. Now I remembered. He'd been two years behind me in school. I remembered him because he rode my bus. Well, that and the name. Who names their infant Newton? The other kids teased him for his overbite — until he had corrective jaw surgery and got braces. Then they teased him about his ears sticking out, which actually weren't all that bad. I wondered if buying out the local grocery store was the Wilton version of success and the bullies were all picking up trash in their orange vests beside the highway now?

"I'll come back tomorrow for the rest," I told him.

"They'll still be here, I'm sure." A river of perspiration cascaded down his face and neck to drench the front of his shirt. He narrowed his lashless eyes, his gaze sweeping over me from head to foot before jumping to my modest bustline. Okay, I had a boy-flat chest practically. But for some reason, he found it fascinating. I glanced down at my top, wondering if the neckline had shifted and my lacy purple bra was showing. Nope. Guess he was just creepy.

"Do I know you?" he said.

"Doubt it. I just moved here from Chicago." I waved a hand off to the side. "It's temporary." Before he could ask why, I jumped to another topic. "Say, we found a dog out on Harmony Road last night. Do you know if anybody's missing a mixed-breed dog, part Husky, about so tall?" I held my palm to just above my kneecaps.

His gaze jerked from my chest to the back door, where a cashier had stepped out for a smoke break. "Can't say I do, but you could check our bulletin board at the front of the store."

"I already did. The only missing pet was a cat. This dog had expired tags. The vet thinks some guy named Bud owned him last. But we don't have a last name. Any guys named Bud who come here to buy dog food, maybe?"

"Bud, Bud ... There's Bud Wozniak. Wait ... he died a few years back. Never mind." He wiped his forehead with a monogrammed handkerchief. "I know a Buddy Baxter. His wife has rescued fifteen, maybe twenty cats, though. Pretty sure they don't have any dogs. Selma!" he shouted at the checker, although she was close enough to have heard him had he spoken at a normal volume. "Know any guys named Bud who buy dog food here?"

Flicking the ashes from her cigarette, she pushed away from the wall and came toward us. "Who wants to know? Are you the state police? FBI?"

"This is a customer, Selma. Just answer her."

"Maybe I do." Selma took a drag, then blew the smoke in my general direction as she took me in. "What's it to you?"

"She's just trying to find the owner of a lost dog," he told her.

Selma turned her heavily lined eyes on her boss. "Can't she talk?"

Newton's neck reddened. "Of course she —"

"Look," I said, stepping between them, "I just want to give the dog back to whomever he belongs to. All Dr. Clint could figure out is that he's owned by some guy named Bud. Now, do you know a Bud or not?"

Her hip jutted to one side. "Sure."

I stared at her for half a minute, waiting for more. She was too busy sucking down every puff of her cigarette and gazing down the alley. Finally, I prompted her. "Last name?"

"Crawford. But he doesn't come here much anymore." A motorcycle turned off the street and blasted our way. Selma sashayed to the middle of the alley. As the motorcycle slowed to a halt, ridden by a man with platinum-blond hair and wearing an oil-stained muscle shirt, Selma said over her shoulder, "Taking my lunch break now, Newt. Back in fifteen."

The rider smacked Selma playfully on the rump, then flashed a gap-toothed grin at Newt and me before he revved his engine and roared away with Selma clinging to his chest.

I mumbled, "Wonder how much she makes an hour?"

Newton swung his head toward me, his nostrils pinched. "What was that?"

"Uhhh, oh yeah, my daughter and I were talking about part-time jobs, you know, for when she's old enough. I was wondering how much cashiers make per hour?"

He flashed a glance at Tara — or Tara's feet, rather. She'd reclined her seat, propped her bare feet on the dashboard, and fallen asleep. Tugging at his collar, he stretched his neck. "Dollar an hour over minimum wage to start. But we only hire people with previous experience."

"I'm sure you do." To which he gave me a baffled stare. "Right, well, thanks for the boxes. I'll be back soon."

Or never, if I could help it. Maybe the hardware store next door had boxes?

chapter 6

WALKING THROUGH THE KITCHEN doorway, I pulled the tab on my pop can. Foam exploded over the rim and bubbled down my arm. I stopped dead, holding the can away from my body so that I didn't ruin the phone book tucked under my arm. There were no Crawfords listed in it. Which didn't necessarily mean there weren't any Crawfords living in Humboldt County — they could've been unlisted. Still, it was another dead end. I didn't want to hang on to Bump forever. Tara was already growing attached to him, so the sooner he found a home, the better.

I gazed down the hallway, stifling the anxiety that had begun to compress my rib cage. Meandering around this labyrinth of junk for less than a day already had pushed me toward the edge. When Tara and I packed up our belongings from our suburban Chicago home to place them in storage, we cleaned the house from top to bottom, so that its new inhabitants would have a fresh start. But I had been so diligent over the years about regularly re-purposing items we no longer used that we had very little excess to sift through. Dad's house was going to be another story altogether.

Guzzling a long swallow of root beer, I resolved not to let myself get overwhelmed with the monumental task before me. All I could do was tackle one room at a time. The question was where to start? I could see Dad looming over me every time I handled an item, saying, "Don't throw that away. I'm saving it. It has sentimental value." Or, "Keep that, Sam. It might be worth something someday. Don't you watch the *Antiques Roadshow*?"

Outside, Bump barked, yanking me from my reverie. Several times this afternoon he'd gone off and I'd rushed out to investigate. The first time was because of a squirrel, although it had taken me awhile to figure out what it was since the tree the squirrel was in was a good two hundred feet away. The next two times I had no idea what the problem was. After that I gave up. He barked again and my shoulders tensed. Looked like I'd have to go back to Garber's and pump Selma for more details. The town wasn't that big. Somebody had to know who this Bud was.

"What the blazes is he doing here?!" Dad bellowed from the bedroom. He stomped down the hallway, a rolled up magazine in his tightfisted hand.

I followed him to the foyer to peer out the sidelight of the front door. A full-sized white sedan trundled over the uneven driveway, weaving around the potholes. "Who's that?"

"Kenny Driscoll, that's who." Dad smacked the magazine against his palm like a member of the Jets getting ready for a rumble.

"And he is…?"

"The law." He peeked around the doorframe, then flattened himself against the inside wall.

"Is there a reason you're hiding?" I asked as the car pulled to a stop in front of the house. On the side, in blue, it read: Humboldt County. And right below that, in big block letters: SHERIFF. "Do you want me to handle this?"

He shushed me, then muttered something about 'paying dues'. That sealed it. There was no way I was missing this.

I opened the door and waved. "Hello there! Can I help you,

officer?"

A gentleman with dark hair that was just beginning to silver at the temples got out of the patrol car and approached the house. He wore his uniform like he was born to it: pins and badges polished to a radiant shine, his shirt collar starched, his slacks perfectly pleated.

I started to close the door behind me as I stepped out, but Dad wedged himself past me.

"Hey, Kenny! How d'you do?" Dad shouted. "How long has it been? Three, four months?"

Sheriff Driscoll tipped his hat back. "More like nine or ten. The guys miss you down at the lodge, Walt."

"Ah well, you know how it is. Old age catching up with me. Can hardly see to drive at night, anymore."

"That so?"

"Yyyep. Blind as a bat once the sun goes down." Dad shoved his hands in his back pockets, ignoring Driscoll's outstretched hand. "So what brings you out here?"

Driscoll withdrew his hand, nodding at me. I thought Dad would introduce me properly, but he seemed eager for the sheriff to get back in his car and be on his way.

"You've heard about the house fires?" Driscoll asked.

Tara peered through the living room window, then came to stand on the porch.

"You mean the ones out on Haystack Pike and Eagle Ridge Road?" Dad said. "Who hasn't? What about 'em?"

"Last night there was another on Harmony, just past Five Mile. The homeowner died in the fire. They're investigating to see if it was a burglary cover-up, like the others."

"You don't say. That's a shame. Real shame. I haven't read the paper in a few days. Anyone I'd know?"

"Probably not. His name was Jonathan Crawley. He only bought the place last year and was retired from the auto plant over in New

Herron, so not from around here."

"My condolences to his family, all the same." Dad stared at the sheriff, nodding. "Well, thank you for alerting me. I'll keep an eye on the neighborhood, let you know if I see anything suspicious."

Sheriff Driscoll shifted on his feet. "Actually, that's why I'm here. One of the victim's neighbors said they saw an old red truck in the area shortly before the crime would have been perpetrated. A similar vehicle was spotted near the other two fires. I remembered that you —"

"Oh, now, just wait a doggone minute. Just because I own a red truck you think that I ...?" Dad threw his hands in the air, then let them drop to slap against his thighs. "How long have you known me, Kenny? I used to coach your little league team, for Pete's sake."

"Just doing my job, Walt. Checking out every lead I can, no matter how unlikely."

"Well, I'll kill this lead for you right away. Last night I was watching *NCIS* on TV with Ida Oldingsells next door. Her idea, not mine. And there's nothing going on between us, in case you were wondering. Anyway, that's where I was. Check with her, if you don't believe me."

"What time was the show?"

"What?"

"When did it begin and end?"

"Nine to ten, I suppose."

"And you left right after that?"

"Pretty much."

Driscoll took a small notepad out of his pocket and flipped through it. "What about the night of April 14th?"

Dad bristled, puffing his chest out. "Doing my taxes, like most other Americans."

"At home?"

"Where else would I be doing them?"

"And the evening of May 19th?"

"Home. I broke my elbow awhile back. Hairline fracture, hurt like the blazes. The Chevy is a manual. Haven't driven it for almost two months, 'bout the week after I filed my taxes. Just got out of the sling ten days ago."

"Did you happen to loan the truck to anyone?"

"For crying out loud, no."

"Not even your daughter or granddaughter here?"

So I guess he had figured out who I was. Like I said, Wilton was a small town. Didn't take much for word to get around.

"Hell, no. Sam just got here last night from Chicago and the grandbaby doesn't know how to drive. So go chase leads somewhere else. You're way off base here."

Sheriff Driscoll removed his hat and turned it in his hands. "Sorry, Walt. Like I said, just doing my job. The Crawley family —"

"Wait," I said. Maybe Selma at the grocery store had been wrong? "This Jonathan Crawley, did he happen to go by 'Bud' sometimes?"

"Yeah, he did," he said.

The skin on the back of my neck prickled. "And he had a dog?"

The sheriff didn't answer right away. Instead, he narrowed his eyes at me until I squirmed. "How would you know that, ma'am, seeing as how you just got into town last night?"

I pointed to the backyard. "Because I think I found his dog. Hit him with my car, actually. I took him to the vet this morning — he's okay, by the way. I've been trying to find his owner. The only lead I had was that he belonged to someone named Bud. When I asked at the grocery store if there was any Bud who bought dog food regularly, one of the clerks remembered, but they called him Bud Crawford." He still looked dubious. "Crawford ... Crawley. Close enough. Anyway, I figured Bud wasn't his real first name. Right?"

Again, Bump barked. This time his woofs morphed into a plaintive howl, like he was the loneliest creature on the planet. It was impossible to ignore.

Driscoll stepped back from the porch to peer toward the backyard. "That the dog?"

"Yeah."

"Mind if I take a look?"

We tromped around back. The moment we rounded the corner, Bump started bouncing up and down at the end of his tether. Every time he jumped up, the shortness of the line yanked him back down, twisting his body in midair. He backed up a couple of steps, then started spinning in dizzyingly tight circles as he made a sound that was half chortle, half shriek.

The sheriff stopped dead and gave me a look of pity. "Is he like this all the time?"

"All the time? No. Only when he's excited. Or happy. Or feeling playful. Which is pretty much whenever he's awake." I looked behind me and noticed that Dad hadn't followed us. "So, was this Crawley's dog?"

"Could be." Sheriff Driscoll walked closer and knelt just within arm's reach of Bump. He extended his hand. Bump crawled to him, then flopped sideways, spreading his legs to expose his belly. Driscoll scratched him a few times before standing up. "There was a lot of damage to the house, but I did notice some dog bowls in the garage and a fenced-in backyard with a doghouse and a path worn around the outside, like a dog would make if it paced all day. The back gate was open. Not just open, but the chain that locked it closed had been cut."

Cut. Like someone would do if they wanted access to a back door or window through the backyard.

"Did he have a wife or any close relatives who'd take the dog? I really, *really* can't keep him."

"I'll ask. He had an ex-wife, but that ended awhile back. Couple of sisters, but they're out of state. A brother who lives between here and Fullbright. I don't get the impression that they were close, but that's your best bet. Once I confirm this was Crawley's dog — if he had one, that is — I'll pass your name along to his brother."

"Thank you, Sheriff Driscoll. Thank you." I could have kissed him on the lips right there, I was that happy. Finally, something was going right. I could only hope it would continue that way.

We were halfway around the side of the house when Sheriff Driscoll stopped and said, "Just so you know, I'd advise your dad to stick close to home for a while. The tip we got about the vehicle that may have been involved with the crimes matched your dad's truck pretty closely."

"You mean he's a suspect?" Dad may have been many things, but a burglar, an arsonist, and a murderer were about as far-fetched as claiming Hillary Clinton was born in Ethiopia.

"Person of interest would be a more apt term." Driscoll sidled in closer, lowering his voice even further. "Look, knowing Walt, I don't believe it was him. But in my thirty years in law enforcement, I've seen some unlikely things. You make sure he keeps his nose clean and maybe if we get some fresh tips, this'll all blow over. It could take a few months to get to the root of it. Heck, sometimes these things drag on for years. But you have to have faith in the justice system." He touched the brim of his hat. "Have a good day, Ms. …?"

"McNamee. Sam McNamee."

After giving him my cell-phone number, I watched him leave. It wasn't until his car had disappeared around the turn in the driveway that I saw the curtains in the front picture window flap shut. Dad had been watching. Why was he avoiding Sheriff Driscoll? Chalk it up to his anti-social tendencies, I told myself.

I sank down onto the front steps as the sheriff's words sank in. Months? *Years?* I didn't have that long.

Yet I couldn't abandon Dad and let him be thrown in prison based on circumstantial evidence. If there was any way I could prove his innocence so I could get on with my own life, I would.

chapter 7

MY PLANS FOR THE day were trashed when Bump decided to tunnel to the center of the Earth. Thinking he might need fresh water, I had gone out the back door to check. He was nowhere to be seen. Fortunately, the mystery was easily solved by his tether line leading to a narrow hole just off the steps and a tiny, pathetic whimper. I peered inside the hole. Sad blue and brown eyes stared back at me from above a dirt-smeared nose. Somehow, in the span of three hours — during which I'd sorted through the hall and linen closets and started on the kitchen cupboards — he had burrowed beneath the cinder blocks of the porch off the kitchen, backfilling as he went until he'd closed off his own escape route. It took me a shovel, a pickaxe, a hand trowel, and thirty minutes to free him. Not to mention all the self-restraint I could muster to keep from strangling him for his antics.

After I hosed him off, which was his idea of punishment judging by the look on his face, he retrieved his ball from beneath the tree and tried to tempt me into a game of fetch. I picked it up and hurled it well beyond the reach of his line. He dashed toward the ball as it bounced away, hit the end of the line, then sat there for five more minutes while I swept the dirt from the steps, alternately looking from me, to the place where the ball had rolled to a stop, and back.

This dog had enough energy to fuel a rocket to Pluto. I'd have to take him out for some exercise after my temper cooled. So after I took my second shower for the day, I left Dad to clean out the spare bedroom with Tara as his helper.

Somehow Tara and Dad had connected. A risky pairing, but it was working. For now. Earlier, when Tara had found a Beta videotape and asked him what it was, he had launched into a history of moving pictures, television, and video recording. Tara had recently developed a fascination for anything retro, and Dad's house was like a time capsule from forty years ago. She was in heaven.

Meanwhile, I put Bump on the rope leash I'd made. I thought about driving to the pet store in Fullbright for a new nylon leash and a few bones, but since Sheriff Driscoll was sure to send one of Crawley's relatives to get the dog, I didn't see the point.

After a short car ride to tiny Founder's Park on the edge of town, during which Bump drooled all over my backseat, we stepped onto the old railroad that had been converted to a bike path. The path was neatly paved and lined with old-growth trees and thick underbrush, which made it ideal for a walk on a sunny day. If we wanted to, we could hike all the way to Oil City. For now, I figured an hour would be enough to wear him out. Or, it could get him wound back up. At any rate, I needed to get out of the house. All those piles and boxes were making me feel like the walls were about to cave in on me.

My arm jerked forward, wrenching my shoulder as Bump surged down the pathway, his tail whipping side to side and a smile on his wolfish face. I'd found a pair of gardening gloves while rooting around the garage and had put them on to keep the rope from burning my hands. Bump was pulling me along like an Iditarod sled dog. I locked my elbows and leaned back, so he had to pitch against my weight — all one hundred and twenty-five pounds of me — to move forward.

For about a hundred yards, I had hope that my plan was going to work. Bump plowed forward, head down to catch the scent of those who'd gone before us. We passed an older couple wearing straw hats and what smelled like a gallon of coconut-scented sunscreen. They said hello, complimenting me on my well-behaved dog, and I thanked them. A pack of cyclists zipped past. Bump had no reaction to them, either. So far, so good.

A mile later, a runner in a neon green singlet and mirrored sunglasses strode gracefully in our direction. The wind kicked up, rustling through the leaves so that shifting patches of sunlight broke through and fell on the paved pathway. I guided Bump toward the edge, where the shade was strongest, so his feet would stay cool. Shifting my eyes from Bump to the path ahead, I noticed the runner was closing on us. He had the lean muscled legs of a marathoner — and the short shorts to prove he wasn't ashamed to show them off.

I tightened my grip on the rope, looping it around my hand an extra turn, but thankfully Bump was paying no attention to the other pedestrians. His long tongue lolled out the side of his mouth, saliva dripping in foamy globs on the asphalt. All was going well.

Until a squirrel crossed our path.

Nostrils quivering, Bump's head snapped up. His ears flipped forward. I saw it unfolding before me like a movie playing in slow motion as the squirrel darted: beady eyes shifting nervously, tiny claws scrabbling over black pavement, the plume of a bushy tail streaking from left to right.

Then, like he'd been injected with a dose of hyper speed, Bump bucked up in the air. He landed hard on his paws and sprang after it, yanking me in an oblique line across the path. Directly in front of the oncoming runner.

My feet flew out from under me. I wasn't sure which part of me hit the ground first. I had just enough time to scream, "No, Bum—!"

My jaw hit the pavement at the precise moment my lips formed the 'p' of his name. And as my jaw collided with the hard surface, it shifted forward just enough to catch my lower lip between my teeth.

Bump hit the end of the rope, yanking me forward a few more inches. Hot asphalt scraped my cheek and the underside of the arm with which I still, miraculously, held the leash. But instead of pulling toward the squirrel, which was now scurrying up the trunk of a nearby tree, Bump spun around and bounded back to me. He stood over me for a moment, snorting hot breath on the back of my head. The feet of the runner pounded to a stop next to us.

"Are you all right?"

Embarrassment washed through me. I couldn't have looked like a bigger buffoon if I'd been wearing clown feet, a red rubber nose, and a suit with giant polka dots. I hesitated to move, for fear I'd broken my arm or jaw. A few moments lapsed, during which I slowly, *slowly* bent my arm. It still worked, thank God. But I had a heck of a road burn. Then I worked my jaw back and forth. Also not broken, but I was going to have one ugly, fat lip. There would be no going into town for a few days. I didn't need anyone looking at me like I was a victim of domestic abuse.

The runner stepped closer, placed a hand on my back. "Do you want me to call an ambulance? Or drive you to the hospital?"

My head turned away from him, I mumbled, "No, dath otay." Tasting blood, I ran my tongue around my mouth to make sure I wasn't missing any teeth. Still all there, none loose. As I lifted my head, Bump dove in and began licking my face, his tongue flailing strings of hot slobber from my eyeball to my chin. I threw my other arm over my head before he could start French kissing me.

Laughter rolled through the air. "Here, let me help you," the runner said in between chuckles. I felt the rope loosen from my grip as he unwrapped it.

"Fanks." Carefully, I drew my knees underneath me and rocked back to sit on my heels. When I finally mustered the courage to raise my eyes, embarrassment gave way to complete, down to the pith of my soul, mortification.

My rescuer was none other than Dr. Clint Chastain.

Reaching out, he gently wiped the blood from my lip. "Walk much?"

I might have hated him for his misplaced humor — after all, I could have been seriously injured — if it hadn't been for the charm that oozed from every pore of his sweat-soaked sexiness.

"Jus' wanned da make tur' I had your attentun." I tried to smile, but could feel my lip splitting further. "Ow." My hand flew up to cover my mouth.

Dr. Clint pushed Bump aside and took my face in his hands. I could've died right then. He tilted my chin up, then turned my face side to side. Narrowing his eyes, he leaned in close. His mouth was inches from mine. The urge to close my eyes and wait for his kiss was strong.

Then he hooked a finger inside my lower lip and pulled it out. I winced.

He let go of my lip. "Ice."

"Huh?"

He stifled a grin. "No stitches needed. Just an ice pack. Fifteen minutes, several times a day. You're going to have a pretty bruise on your chin, too."

"Gee, fankth."

His hand slipped to mine. I had to look down at my fingers to make sure they weren't melting. Then I saw my garden gloves. He was probably wondering why I had them on. He tugged them off and laid them on the ground beside me.

"Your arm …"

I let him turn my hand gently over and run his fingers around the giant raspberry that had already spread from my elbow halfway to my wrist. As much as I wanted him to keep fussing over me, I didn't want to seem like a total wuss. "Ith otay." Dang it, why couldn't I say my s's? Or k's? My lip must have been worse than he was letting on.

Maybe he just didn't want me to go into shock?

"You can at least follow me back to my car. I have some antiseptic and bandages. I'll patch you up. No charge." He winked and I was lost in the dark pool of his pupils. "Make you better than new. Practically bionic."

While Bump pranced around us, still oblivious to the pain he'd inflicted on me, Clint helped me up. I was feeling the soreness in my jaw and arm already. We turned to head back, but I stumbled with the first step. Clint threw an arm around me to catch me.

"Whoa there," he said, his breath brushing my ear as I leaned into him.

"Thorry, my dog …"

Bump had wrapped the rope around our feet. Twice. But why had I called him 'my dog'?

"Yeah, I see. Guess he didn't want us to leave without him." He stooped over and unraveled the leash. We started forward again, this time with Bump securely on Clint's left side. Bump lurched forward half a step, but Clint quickly checked him with the leash. Bump's eyes snapped up to Clint's and he instantly settled in beside him, his shoulder even with Clint's knee with every stride.

I gawked at the sight. "How do you make him do vat?" My words were coming a little better now, but not without pain.

"Communication, I guess. If he forges, I just let him know that's not where I want him."

"But I can't get him to do vat."

"Well, no offense, but he probably knows you're not in charge, so he does what he wants."

You can do whatever you want to me, I wanted to say.

I gave myself a mental slap. Where was this coming from? He was just a nice guy, doing what nice guys do. In a few weeks, I'd be out of town and he wouldn't even remember my name.

A robin landed in our path. Bump's ears perked. His muscles

twitched. But Clint gave one tiny tug on the leash and Bump instantly calmed.

"I'd athk you to teach me, but —"

"But his owner is coming to get him soon, right?"

"About vat... I mean, dat." I forced my tongue between my teeth. "Thhhat." My speech was still thick and my mouth hurt like heck, but I wanted to sound intelligent when I talked to him. "Turns out, he belonged to da guy who died in da fire a couple nights ago."

"The one on Harmony, near Five Mile?"

"Yeah, dat one. I mean *that* one."

"What a strange coincidence that you found his dog. I heard the guy was knocked unconscious, then died of smoke inhalation. Terrible way to go. You'd think Bump would be traumatized by the ordeal — someone breaking into the house, assaulting the owner, the fire, the storm ... Oddly, he doesn't seem any the worse for it." Bump gazed up adoringly, his long bushy tail thwacking against Clint's leg. "So ... you're going to keep him, then?"

"What? No!" I half turned toward him, but upon seeing the hope in his eyes dashed, I quickly looked away. "I mean, Sheriff Driscoll is checking with the guy's relatives. Soon as I get in touch with them and arrange it, he can go with them."

"Oh. I understand." But it was clear from the tone of his voice he didn't.

We continued on for several awkward minutes until we reached the parking lot. Clint's SUV, a pearl white Lincoln Navigator, was parked in the far corner, under the dense shade of a sprawling oak. I'd left my car parked out in the sun, because I didn't want birds pooping all over it. It was still sparkly clean, but it was going to be as hot as a barbecue pit inside.

Clint soaked a cotton ball with antiseptic and swabbed my arm. Air hissed between my teeth, but I managed not to cuss him out. Then he dampened a clean gauze pad with water, braced my chin between the thumb and forefinger of his other hand and brought the gauze to my lip. If only he were leaning in to kiss me, not applying first aid.

My phone rang. I sighed. "One moment," I said apologetically. "Hello?"

"Samantha McNamee? Sheriff Driscoll here." As if I could forget the liquid tenor of his voice. "I have some information for you."

"Go ahead, sheriff."

"Crawley's younger brother confirmed he had a dog. And it matches the description of the dog you found exactly."

"That's wonderful news, sheriff! When can he come and get him? Or, I could even drop him off. I'm out at Founder's Park now. Just give me the address and I'll —"

"Uh, yeah, that's the thing. He didn't seem that interested."

"What do you mean? The least he could do would be take him in and find him a new home."

"I agree with you, Ms. McNamee. Unfortunately, he's under no obligation to take the dog. If we'd arrived after the crime and found the owner deceased, the dog would have been turned over to animal control and —"

"Animal control? You mean the shelter? The place that euthanizes dogs if no one adopts them after a few months?"

"More like weeks," Sheriff Driscoll said. "Sometimes days if they're crowded. They hang onto puppies longer, but if it's an older dog …" His words trailed off, the message clear.

I looked down at Bump. His tail tapped against the ground like he couldn't be any happier, despite the fact that we were discussing his mortality. He gazed at me with those pleading puppy-dog eyes and cocked his head, so that one ear winged out sideways.

"But I found him running loose in a storm and took him to the vet." I left out the part about hitting him with my car. "There's nothing wrong with him. He's a good dog."

"That may be, but he also mentioned that he didn't want to be responsible for the vet bill."

"Oh." It was becoming blatantly clear that Bud Crawley's brother was not an animal lover. Considering the shape I'd found Bump in, Bud probably hadn't been either. It made me wonder why he'd even had a dog.

"Is it about the dog?" Clint whispered, like he didn't want Bump to know we were talking about him.

I nodded and covered the phone with my hand. "I found out the owner's name was Bud Crawley. Turns out his brother won't take the dog back because he doesn't want to pay the vet bill."

"Tell him there's no charge."

"Huh?"

"Tell him —"

"I heard you. It's just that … why?"

"Because, that's why. Do I need to have a reason?" He pointed at the phone and mouthed, *Tell him.*

I shook my head no, then took my hand off the phone. "Thanks for the information, sheriff. I appreciate the effort."

"Sorry it didn't go better, Ms. McNamee," he said.

"That's okay. It's not your fault. I'll handle it from here."

I hit the 'End' button and slipped the phone back in my pocket.

"Why didn't you tell him there was no charge for the veterinary care?" Clint asked. He looked slightly annoyed.

"Because the guy clearly didn't want the dog. Even if he could be convinced to take him, Bump would just end up in the shelter anyway."

"You're probably right." He grabbed a towel off the front seat and mopped the sweat from his brow. "What are you going to do now?"

Touching a hand to my lip, I wiped away a bead of blood. "I'm going to find him a home."

He held up a finger. "In that case, I have something for you." He went to the front cab of the SUV and dug around under the seat. Fifteen seconds later, he laid a sky-blue nylon leash in my hands. "Take this. It's been used a few times, but it still has a lot of years left."

"I can't." I thrust it back at him, but he waved me off.

"Sure, you can. It's not like it's valuable. I mean," — his eyes went melancholy — "it didn't cost much."

"But it means something to you, doesn't it?"

He shrugged, not answering for a while as he unknotted the rope and clipped the leash onto Bump's collar. Then finally, very softly, he said, "I had a Border Collie named Jazz that I ran with until about a year ago. Twelve years old and she still ran five miles a day with me."

"What happened to her? I mean, how did she …?"

"Cancer. Lymphoma. It had metastasized into her internal organs before we caught it. It was too late to do anything about it except keep her comfortable until the end." His hand hovered above Bump's head a moment. Bump stretched his neck, until Clint's fingers brushed his upright ear. Smiling sadly, he rubbed the pink inside of Bump's ear. "She had a real zest for life. Just like Bump here." The dog lifted a paw and tapped the open palm of Clint's hand. He squeezed it once lightly before letting go.

My heart throbbed seeing the two of them connect like that. They were perfect for each other. Complementary. Yin and Yang. Peanut butter and chocolate. No, more like fine, aged wine and hard, stinky cheese.

"Too bad I'm not ready for another dog just yet," he added.

And just like that my hope for a happy ending to my little predicament was dashed against a rocky shore.

"I need to get home." I marched off toward my car.

Then I hit the end of the leash. I stumbled backward, my free hand wheeling out to catch myself.

Clint grabbed my arm. "That was close. Are you —?"

"I'm fine," I snapped. Bump was still planted at his feet, gazing at him with worship. I hadn't meant to sound peevish, but I was more upset that he didn't want Bump than I was embarrassed that I'd almost fallen in front of him a second time. My whole life had been a series of mishaps: tripping over curbs, running into doorframes, falling on icy patches on the sidewalk. One thing I'd learned from all that was that you just got right back up and forged on, like nothing had happened. Which was what I intended to do this time, except Clint was developing this annoying habit of rescuing me. I tugged firmly on Bump's leash and waited to make sure he was up on his feet before I moved this time. "Bye."

"Hey!" Clint jogged after me. "We could meet tomorrow. Take him for a walk. I can teach you how to make him heel. That is, if you're feeling up to it."

"I don't know if I can. I have a lot to do." Which was true. Although I wasn't exactly on a deadline.

"That's okay. I understand." His mouth curved into a weak smile.

I went to my car, slipped the key in the lock, then turned around just as he was stepping up into his Navigator. "What time?" I shouted.

This time he smiled for real. "Five thirty okay?"

"Sure," I said, trying to act as casual as possible. After all, I didn't want to make it appear like I was desperate for a date. Never mind the fact that I hadn't had one in two years. "Meet you back here." I opened the back door and Bump jumped in. As soon as I was buckled in, I cranked up the AC.

Clint pulled out of the parking lot, but not before waving at us. A steamy cloud of hot dog-breath smothered me. I patted Bump on the muzzle. "I'm not sure that constitutes a 'date', but I'll take it. Just try to be on your best behavior next time, okay?"

Bump licked my neck and ear, coating me in dog slobber. Visions of microscopic germs having a party in my ear canal filled my head. Shuddering, I swatted him away and searched the front of the car for something to wipe myself off with. Nothing. Even the glove compartment had been emptied of its usual supply of fast food napkins. In desperation, I aimed the air vent at my slimy parts and reminded myself to pick up an industrial-sized container of disinfectant wipes when I returned to Garber's tomorrow.

chapter 8

FROM THE EFFORT IT took to open my eyelids the next morning, I could've sworn someone had drugged my decaf coffee with Tylenol PM the night before. But the truth was I was just tired to the bone: physically and mentally.

Like it or not, there was a ton of work to do. Just the thought of it made my heart race. I lay in bed for close to an hour, sorting jobs first by priority, then by how quickly each thing could get done. Meanwhile, Dad needed small, manageable jobs, like sifting through his sock drawer, and tossing out expired canned goods. I'd tackle the garage while he and Tara were out fishing. Salvageable items could go to Goodwill. Anything flammable was kindling for the burn pile. The rest could go in a dumpster. I'd have to work quickly and without remorse. The guilt trip he'd inevitably lay on me the first time he figured out something 'valuable' was missing would be worth the accomplishment of getting him moved out of this old house and into something more suitable for this stage in his life.

First order of business, though, was breakfast. I couldn't work on an empty stomach. And at some point today I had to get more boxes from Garber's.

Then there was my date with Clint. Not date, really. More like a meet-up to exercise the dog.

The dog! I bolted upright, cold sweat dampening my chest. I'd forgotten to bring Bump inside last night. I threw my blanket off, sprinted down the hallway, and flew out the back kitchen door.

Bump's tether hook hung emptily from the clothesline. I dashed to it. There was so sign of him. Crap. I'd lost him.

Then it struck me fully. He was gone. Gone. Gone!

I was free!

It only took a few seconds of giddiness for the repercussion of that to sink in. Without a dog, what reason did I have to see Clint again? And then there was the fact that Tara would hate me for losing the dog.

I *had* to find the dog. I called out his name, scouring the yard in barefoot circles.

He hadn't backed out of his collar. Maybe someone had unclipped him?

Someone named Tara.

I marched back into the house to check the laundry room. No dog. No mess. So I knocked on Tara's bedroom door. The door, unlocked, drifted open with the first rap of my knuckles. Tara was still sound asleep. And sticking out from beneath the covers were four long, gangly legs, covered in mottled fur. Bump was snoring away, tucked under her arm.

Relieved, I walked to them and tugged at the covers. "Hey, sleepyheads. We have another long day ahead of us."

Bump's tail thumped against the mattress beneath the blanket. He let out a long yawn that turned into a yowl. Tara's lids fluttered. She peeked at me between her long eyelashes.

"C'mon. Get up." I poked at her ribs.

She flinched at my touch, grumbling. "Ten more minutes. It's summer, you know."

"Yeah, but if we ever want to get to Florida, we have to help

Gramps get the house ready to sell." Besides, I had a book to deliver to my editor by the middle of next month. Rabid fans were waiting.

I brushed stray wisps of hair from her forehead, remembering when she was small and had a fever approaching a hundred and four. I'd held her hand and dabbed a cool cloth against her face, talking to her softly as she moaned in discomfort. Finally, I'd taken her to the emergency room, alternately wondering if I'd waited too long, or if I was overreacting and they'd just send me home with some extra-strength ibuprofen. It had only been a year after Kyle died and I'd wanted him there that night. Not that he would have done anything differently than I did, but so *I* would have someone's hand to hold and tell me it was going to be okay. But it was just the two of us, and while we muddled on and survived just fine, there was always something missing.

Placing a knee on the bed, I bounced the mattress, to Tara's consternation. Bump seemed oblivious. "Besides, you need to take the dog out. If he pees on the bed, you're not only washing the sheets, but hauling the mattress outside and scrubbing it with bleach."

Her lip twitched in a sneer. One eye opened. "You're serious."

"I never joke. I was born without a funny bone." I smacked her lightly on the fanny. Bump's head shot up, his muscles coiled tight. He eyed me intently. I drew my hand back. Was he protective of her already, or had I merely startled him? Relaxing, he laid his head on her pillow and closed his eyes.

Tara's bathing had made a difference in his appearance. Instead of the dull coat and coyote-like dingy coloring, the washing had brought out the sheen to his fur and made the white whiter. He was pretty, in a Wild Animal Kingdom sort of way. His rear legs twitched as he drifted off to sleep again. I gazed at him in newfound admiration, my palm resting on the top of his paw, my fingers curled around to touch the soft leather of his pads. In his dream, he barked, but it came out as an *ooofff, ooofff,* his cheeks puffing out.

Warmth spread through my fingertips, gradually increasing until they felt ... hot. How —?

G'dammit! Over here, you stupid dog.

A burst of orange shot across my vision. A silver tool glimmered above me in the wavering amber light. A wrench. Smoke filled my lungs. I heard the bark again. Loud, sharp. The wrench sailed through the air, flew over my head, although I was low to the ground.

Thud! I leapt backward, my left foot bumping into something. I glanced beside me. There on the floor sprawled a man, blood leaking out of a gash in his skull.

G'dammit, the man said weakly. *Don't you leave me ...*

Conflicting emotions crashed through me: loyalty, fear, pain. Then, a shadowy form lunged in my direction, scooping up the wrench.

I ran. Amber light blazed everywhere. Heat seared my eyeballs, my lungs, penetrated my flesh.

Then just like that, I was back in the room, seated on Tara's bed, Bump's paw in my hand. A shudder rippled between my shoulders. I seriously needed to check out the side effects on my allergy medication.

Tara still hadn't attempted to get out of bed. I threw the curtains open. Blinding white sunlight cascaded into every corner of the room. At the foot of her bed sat a box, full to the top with old vinyl records. The greats of the 60s and 70s were imprinted on the album sleeves: Marvin Gaye, Peter Frampton, Chicago, the Doobie Brothers, Aretha Franklin, The Eagles ... I remembered them all. The house used to be filled with their songs.

The day my mother left, the music stopped. A few weeks later, Dad packed his treasured record collection away and shoved it in a closet. Why had he taken it out now?

The smell of bacon drifted from down the hallway. I inhaled deeply. "Mmm, smell that? Gramps made bacon. And it doesn't even smell like he burned it."

Tara lifted her head. "That I can get up for."

"Meet you in the kitchen in five minutes. We'll go over the plan for the day then."

She arched an eyebrow at me. "Oh, joy. I can't wait to hear it."

As I walked down the hall, I paused to study the pictures on the wall. All of them were from when I was five or less and Mom was still with us. Ann Glasser Schimmoller was her name, although she always told people her last name was Glasser. She never liked Dad's last name — and while I can't say I blame her for that and had been quick to change my name when I married, it turned out to be a sign of things to come. She had been a New York runway model and it showed in every angle and every pose. In one photo, she was reclined on a dock by a lake, her willowy legs stretched out and her pointed toes dangling over the water. She wore a polka dotted one-piece swimming suit, with the sides strategically cut out to show off her slender waist. A floppy brimmed hat shaded her delicate features from the sun's harsh rays. Dad used to tell me I looked just like her, and he was right, although I had none of her physical grace.

In another picture, she was leaning against a tree, her pouty red lips slightly puckered as if she were blowing a kiss at my father. He used to love being behind the camera, which explained why there were so few pictures of him and so many of Mom. She had been fifteen years younger than him when they married. Not a scandalous age difference, but I often wondered if she felt she'd given her up career to have a family and then regretted it.

The end picture was of Mom and me on a teeter totter, a few months before I turned six. Two weeks after the picture was taken, she left for a shopping trip to Chicago and never came back. That year, instead of my usual birthday surprise where Dad gave me hints until I found my present, he gave me ten bucks and told me we'd go to the store the next day. It ended up being a week. Photography was just another one of the hobbies he gave up when she left us. He also gave up on me.

Older and wiser now, I realized he had been suffering from depression then. But he never really returned to being the caring, happy man he used to be. Over time, his sullenness turned to resentment, almost. He became irritable and argumentative. I felt like a burden and a disappointment to him. It was never so much what he said or did, but what he didn't say or do.

I became accustomed to his indifference and expected it. So it came as a surprise when I announced my intention to become an English major and attend the University of Chicago. He yelled. He threw things. Not at me, but it scared me so much I packed my bags, phoned Kyle, and had him pick me up. I slept on Kyle's parents' couch that summer and Kyle and I began our lives together sooner than planned.

Sadness seeping into every pore, I stumbled into the kitchen and collapsed onto a chair. Dad slid a plate of bacon and a toaster pastry in front of me. I picked up each piece of bacon and turned it over, trying not to reveal my shock.

"What?" he grumbled. "Don't you like bacon? I thought everyone liked bacon."

"I love it, actually. It's just … It's not burnt."

With an indignant harrumph, he poured me a cup of coffee, then set the sugar and creamer in the middle of the table. "Tara showed me how to make it in the microwave. Did you know there's a setting specifically for bacon? All you have to do is punch the button and walk away. Perfect every time."

"And the pastry? How did you —?"

"She figured out what number to put the dial on and put a piece of tape over it. No one's allowed to touch it. Including you. If you want a bagel, you're just gonna have to put it down twice." He jabbed a finger at me accusingly, like the first thing I'd do once he was out of the room would be fiddle with the toaster knobs. "Yep, that is one smart girl you have there."

He sat down across from me and snapped his newspaper open. "Do you think anyone would come to a garage sale this far out of town? More like a yard sale, probably. Garage isn't big enough to hold everything. Course, it wouldn't be for a month or so."

I couldn't believe he was seriously considering selling some of his stuff. Then, the headline on the front page caught my eye.

"Dad." I tapped on the paper. "Can I have that for a minute?"

"I'm not done yet." He flipped a corner of the paper down to peer at me, scowling. "What the hell happened to you last night?"

I touched my lip. The swelling was down, but it was probably turning various shades of blue and purple by now. "Bump took off after a squirrel."

"Maybe you should teach him how to walk on a leash."

"Thanks for the tip."

"Anytime."

"Morning, Gramps." Tara came into the kitchen with Bump's nose practically prodding her along from behind.

The second the dog caught sight of Dad, he loped to him, plopped his rump on the floor, and put his big snout on Dad's knee. Behind the newspaper, Dad fingered a piece of bacon and slid it from his plate. Bump wolfed it down in one gulp.

"I saw that!" I said. "We bought him a bag of dog food yesterday, you know. You're going to make him sick."

Dad folded up the newspaper, but kept a hand on it. "He's a dog. Dogs are carnivores, aren't they?"

"Yes, but —"

"But nothing. It's meat. One piece of bacon. He likes it. End of story." He blew at the steam rising from his coffee cup, then slurped it. "Not like I'm feeding him candy and caramel corn."

What was happening here? I was desperately trying to find Bump a home and Dad and Tara were treating him like British royalty. Soon as I snagged that newspaper and perused the headline piece, I'd phone in a 'Free to a good home' ad to the Pet section.

"Can I just read the front page real quick, Dad? There's an article about the arsons."

Pushing the folded paper across the table, he rolled his eyes. "Humboldt County's finest at the top of their game. No leads. No suspects. Just a bunch of missing stuff."

He was right. Sheriff Driscoll gave a list of items missing from the latest crime scene: a flatscreen TV, a laptop, a change jar, a Ducati motorcycle … He also said there was no way of knowing what else might have been stolen, given the amount of fire damage and the demise of the home's owner. The highlight of the piece was an interview with Crawley's brother, who wasn't named in the article. *"Bud loved that Ducati like his firstborn."* No mention of the dog existed, however.

The article ended with a quote from Wilton Township Fire Chief, Archer Malone: *"Department cutbacks have severely hampered our response time. With the failure of the most recent operating levy, we've had to let go of three full time employees and now rely on volunteers. Rural residences are at the greatest risk, due to their remote locations. Continued lack of funding may result in the dissolution of the Wilton Township Fire Department, in which case services would be contracted out to surrounding townships, further increasing response time and consequently the danger to residents."*

Especially if they lived several miles out of town and had a penchant for setting grass fires. Like Dad.

chapter 9

"HI, UH ..." — I PAUSED, mentally sounding out the cashier's name before I attempted it — "Jor-dane." My voice rose at the end like a question. Her lip twitched as her fingers froze on the keyboard. I squinted at her name tag, trying to make sure I'd read it right.

"It's Jordan. With a 'u'."

The letters clearly read: J-O-U-R-D-A-N-E. As in, rhymes with 'pain'. "Oh, did they mess it up?"

"Mess what up?"

"Your name tag, the spelling."

"No."

"Okay, never mind," I muttered, sliding my bottle of Coke and an eight-pack of batteries for Dad's smoke alarms onto the belt. I figured as long as I had a favor to ask, I'd buy something. "Say, the manager told me yesterday I could pick up more boxes out back. Is it all right if I just drive through the alley and load them up in my car on the way out? Someone has to let me in, though. The gate appears to be locked today."

She took my twenty and gave me a couple of small coins back. Wow, the mark-up in this place was astronomical. It would have been worth the gas to go to the Super Wal-Mart in Fullbright.

"Sorry," she said in a weary monotone, "I'm not authorized to allow that."

"You can't 'authorize' letting me have boxes you're going to throw out anyway?"

"Sorry, I can't —"

"Where's Newt, then?"

"Not here."

Obviously. "When does he get in?"

She huffed a sigh. "Tomorrow." Her eyes flicked to a man emerging from the snack aisle. He cradled an armload of groceries, enough to feed a family of ten: boxes of pasta, cans of crushed tomatoes, a sack of onions, tubes of ground beef, assorted beans, and a jar of pickles. Two jugs of orange juice dangled from his thumbs.

"Hey, Archer," she cooed, all merry and bright-eyed suddenly. "Getting low already?"

"Howdy, Jourdane. You know how it is with those boys. Always hungry." He winked at her and dumped the items on the conveyor belt. "B'sides, cook-off's Saturday. I aim to beat the pants off the lot of 'em. You coming?"

Jourdane ran the tip of her tongue over glossy lips, revealing a silver stud piercing. How did she eat with that thing, let alone speak properly? "I'd love to *come*, Archer."

The innuendo was enough to make me gag. To his credit, Archer ignored it. I coughed reflexively and brought a fist to my mouth. The age span between them had to be at least twenty years, but he was a handsome enough guy — in a rugged, down-on-the-farm kind of way. I was sure he turned a lot of heads in little old Wilton, horny teenagers included. He had on a T-shirt with the sleeves rolled up, a few smudges across the chest. His biceps were impressively sized, but not overly sculpted — the mark of one who did more work in the real world than pumping iron in the gym. Not quite Chippendale's material, but hunky in a Garth Brooks country superstar kind of way.

He dumped the items on the conveyor belt and swept off his ball cap to run his fingers through close-cut dark blond hair. Gold-flecked hazel eyes pinned me with an intrusive warmth. He'd caught me staring, damn it.

His cheeks creased into an even deeper smile as he replaced his hat. "Hello there, miss. You must be new in town. Need someone to show you around?"

Tempting, but totally not my type. In real life, that is. I was Big City; he was Hicksville. Okay, maybe he could make an appearance in one of my novels. Come to think of it, I needed a down-home hero for my next series. I took a mental snapshot of him and filed it away, then turned back to Jourdane. "Tomorrow, you said?"

She batted her lashes, confused. "Huh?"

"Your boss. He doesn't come back in until tomorrow?"

"Oh ... yeah. He's off today."

This chick was getting on my nerves. She had all the customer service skills of a robocaller. Was she running the store by herself? Whatever happened to child labor laws? I would have just taken the boxes without permission, but there was a locked chain link fence across the entrance to the alley, which was the sole reason I'd come inside the store to ask.

New tactic. "When does Selma's shift start?" She gave me a suspicious look, so I tugged on my ratty ponytail. Under the harsh glare of fluorescent lights, my fried split ends screamed for a beauty parlor intervention. I had a love/hate relationship with my hair. On good days, I might be mistaken for Debra Messing, at least from behind, with my coppery nest of curls and slim boyish figure. On bad days, I looked like the love child of Bride of Frankenstein and Carrot Top. "I wanted to ask her where she gets her hair done — unless you know."

Jourdane glanced at the clock hanging over the unattended deli counter. "Fifteen minutes. 'Cept she's usually running late."

"Thanks, you've been a huge help … Jourdane with a 'u'." And a silent 'e'. Maybe for kicks her parents could have spelled her name Giourdhane? Things like that build character. And here I'd been just plain Sam. How … straightforward.

Twisting the top off my Coke and taking a chug, I headed to the front door as Archer called out "Have a good day!" I flashed a perfunctory smile. I'd try, but lately I didn't seem to be in control of how my days were going.

The moment the door closed behind me, a blanket of suffocating warmth wrapped around me. Heat rolled off asphalt, bounced off brick walls, and was intensified by glass windows. It was like walking into a kiln. Perspiration pooled in every crease of my body. By the time I crossed Main Street and circled the main city block, a tour which took all of two and a half minutes, I had sweat stains in embarrassing places.

On the second go-round, I stopped to peer into shop windows. Downtown Wilton was home to three antique shops, a pet groomer, a pizza and sandwich shop named Suds and Grub, a bank/loan office, a donut shop, a consignment store, and a law office, which I'd never seen anyone go into, although the sign always said 'Open' during normal business hours.

Ten minutes down. Crossing the street again, I staked out behind the grocery store next to the locked chain link fence. The rear of the building formed a 'U', with the recessed area gated off. I'm not sure why there was a fence in the first place. All I could see were stacks of pallets, empty boxes and an overflowing dumpster. I leaned against the cool brick on the shaded side of the alley, glancing at my phone every other minute to check the time. It was already six minutes past starting time for Selma's shift. I might have given up and gone home, but Dad and Tara had made remarkable progress yesterday. I'd had no idea he had so many albums. Those things could haul in a small fortune on eBay. I slumped against the wall. Yet another project to tackle. Maybe it was something I could assign to Tara? Allowing her to organize collections and manage small jobs seemed to work wonders for stemming her anxiety attacks.

Desperate to kill time, I pulled up a game on my phone and was just getting engrossed when the squeal of rusty hinges made me look up. A pot-bellied man in a plaid button-up shirt came out of the back door of the hardware store and tossed a trash bag over the chain link into the grocery store's dumpster. Okay, now it made sense. The fence was protecting the dumpster. Although not very well.

He was headed back toward the door when the roar of a motorcycle engine broke through at the far end of the alley. Startled, he looked around, saw me, and stiffened, like the chubby kid with his hand wedged in the cookie jar.

Just to make him more uncomfortable, I snapped a picture of him on my smart phone, then waved at him. He tipped his head in a nod.

"Trash sure piles up quick, doesn't it?" I said.

"Heh, yep." He ducked inside his rear door before Selma and her boyfriend plowed to a stop behind the gate.

Throwing a leg over the seat, then sliding into a stand, Selma glared at me. Yesterday, she'd been wearing painted on jeans, but today she was in a glittery mini skirt that showed off the mermaid tattoo on the outside of her right lower leg. Around the other ankle was a tattoo of a ring of roses. Her artwork was modest compared to the palette her boyfriend sported. It took me a few moments to realize he wasn't actually wearing sleeves and that both arms were covered in inked renderings of skulls, barbed wire, and dragons.

I couldn't help but stare. Not in an 'Ooo, that's cool' kind of way. More like 'Does this man have a job somewhere, and if so, *who* hired him?' way.

"Put your eyes back in your head, sweetie," Selma warned. She tugged her too-tight baby doll shirt down to show more cleavage. On a twenty-something it might have looked attractive, but she was probably closer to forty, a few years older than me. The shocking thing was that under all that dollar store makeup and bling, she was actually striking. It was just hard to see the real her with so much going on. Like surrounding a Monet watercolor with Las Vegas strip lights. She raked her hot pink fingernails lightly down her boyfriend's thigh, then back up before sliding a hand deep in his front pocket. "Dylan's all mine."

"Now hold on a minute, Sel." Dylan cut the engine and hooked a bulging arm around Selma to hug her to his side. She clung to him possessively, writhing against his body like they were about to get it on right there on the back of the motorcycle in the alley way. In fact, I was starting to think they'd had plans to do just that when my appearance interrupted them.

"You said you were open to trying new things," Dylan said to Selma. His eyes swept over me, grinning suggestively. "Maybe this gal's up for a little two-on-one? That'd be pretty damn hot, don't you reckon?"

I clamped my teeth together to keep from vomiting. Had I said small towns were boring? Scratch that. Can't say I'd ever been propositioned for a threesome in Chicago, especially without even opening my mouth. Not even that time I stumbled through the club district at 2 a.m. by mistake.

Selma's face twisted into a scowl. "Ain't happening, babe." Shaking her hair loose from her ponytail, she slid off Dylan to stomp toward me. She circled me. "'Sides, this one's got ties to the cops."

"Why do you keep saying that?" I said defensively.

Hands on her hips, she stopped in front of me. "It's the way you keep hanging around and asking questions."

Which made me wonder what it was I should be suspicious of. "Look, here's my question today: Can I have those boxes?" I pointed to the teetering stack between the back door and the dumpster. "I swear if you let me have them I'll leave you alone. At least until the weekend. Or until I need more."

A blank look overtook her. She batted her false eyelashes at me. "Meaning you'll be back?"

"I'm helping my dad sort through a house he's lived in for forty years, so he can move into a smaller place. He has a lot of stuff."

The tough girl façade crumbled. She tilted her head, then exchanged a glance with Dylan. "Like what?"

"Huh?" I was stunned that she actually sounded interested.

"I said like what kind of stuff? Clothes? Books? Furniture? Collectibles?"

"All of the above."

She looked over her shoulder. "You wanna handle this, babe?"

Dylan flicked the kickstand out with his heel and strode toward us. I wasn't sure whether to run for my life, or stay out of curiosity. Since I had an eight-foot-high chain link fence on one side, a brick wall behind me, and a two-hundred plus pound biker swooping in, my options were severely limited.

"See that bike?" He hooked a thumb behind him. I nodded. "Ducati Panigale, less than five thousand miles on it. Been sitting in a garage under a tarp. Found it yesterday online. Paid less than half the going rate. Guy wanted to get rid of it quick, so he could buy his old lady a ring." He snorted into his fist and Selma shot him a wounded look. He didn't seem to notice. "How much time do you have to unload this stuff?"

"A few weeks, I guess."

His eyes widened. "Good. You can price higher. Make it sound like a steal. Cut whatever isn't moving, but hold out long as you can. Amazing what some idiots will pay for junk if you word the copy right." From his wallet, he produced a business card: Hawkins' Cycle Repair, Dylan Hawkins, Owner. "Text me if you have questions. The bike business is just a side. I make my real money trading online."

"Dylan's taking me to Mexico next month." Selma kissed his

scruffy cheek.

Nodding, I stuffed the card in my back pocket. I'd met more interesting people in this Podunk village in two days than I had during any two months in Chicago. I just might have to stick around here to mine for characters. "Thanks, I'll keep that in mind." Selma was still clinging to her sugar daddy, so I cleared my throat. "So, um, boxes."

She swiveled her head toward me and shot me a killer gaze. "What about 'em?"

"Can I have some … please?"

Detaching herself from Dylan's hip, she pulled a lanyard with about fifteen keys from her studded red leather purse and swung it in lethal circles. "'Kay. Follow me."

For a moment, I wondered who she was calling 'Kay' before it dawned on me she meant 'okay'.

She flipped through the key ring and shoved one into the keyhole of the heavy metal lock on the gate. Dylan started up his bike and Selma spun around, a desperate look on her face. "Hey, I'll call when I get off, 'kay? We can go to the Cowpoke Saloon — or Bub's Place, if you want."

He readjusted his gangster bandana. "Busy tonight."

Her penciled brow folded into a 'V'. "Busy with who?" she hollered at his back. But he was already halfway down the alley. "Lousy bastard. You think I'm gonna just be waiting around next time you want a quick —" She swung her purse, hard, against the chain link, rattling it.

Instinctively, I jumped back. There was a dent in the fence where she'd hit it. Made me wonder what she kept stuffed inside her purse. Definitely bricks. Probably a gun, too.

Just get the boxes and go, I told myself. Next time I needed some, I'd drive to Fullbright. First, I needed to not piss this dame off so I could get out of the alley alive.

The gate screeched as Selma shoved it open. She jabbed an elbow in the direction of the boxes. "Take all you want. Everybody always does anyway." Her lip quivered as she sniffed in a breath. Tears welled in her eyes. Shutting her eyes tight, she stretched her neck, held her breath, and flapped a hand at the stack.

I hurried in, tucking smaller boxes inside bigger ones as quickly as I could, hoping to get out of there before the histrionics started.

But I wasn't quick enough. The dam broke. A tiny moan rose to an undulating wail. I resisted as long as I could. Then, reluctantly, I turned around. Selma was hugging herself, weeping like a little kid lost in a train station.

"Rough day, huh?" I avoided patting her on the back. A hug was out of the question. When she didn't answer, I added, "You know, that was really rude of him. I'm not sure he's worth it. You should find yourself a guy who treats you right." As if I was one to dole out relationship advice. I hadn't had a real boyfriend since ... high school. Kyle. Not that I couldn't have had one. It just didn't seem worth the hassle.

A hateful look crossed her face. "You don't know what you're talking about. He's good to me."

"You mean he takes you places. Buys you things. Yeah, I get it." I set a couple stacks of boxes outside the gate, then went to grab a few more. "If you ask me, a pretty girl like you deserves better."

Her sobs faded to sniffles. She tugged a tissue from her bottomless purse and blotted at her mascara streaks.

"Thanks for the boxes," I added.

My car loaded, I slid into the driver's seat, turned the ignition, and put it in reverse. A face that looked like an extra in a zombie flick filled the rearview mirror. I hit the brake. Selma thumped the heel of her hand on the back window.

She sashayed around to the opposite side of the car. I hit the button and the window lowered. She rested both elbows on the car door and leaned in the window, giving me a clear view of the extra two cup sizes that genetics had denied me.

"D'ya mean that?" she said. "The part about me being pretty, that I could do better?"

"Of course. Otherwise, I wouldn't have said it."

A genuine smile transformed her into something far less scary. "That's the nicest damn thing anyone's said to me in a *long* time. If you need any favors while you're in town, you just holler, 'kay?"

"'Kay." I flipped her a quick wave and backed out. I couldn't imagine what sort of favors I'd ever ask from someone like Selma — although I was sure she'd doled out quite a few in her lifetime.

Maybe, underneath all those oniony layers, there was a sweet person after all? I didn't intend to find out, but it was worth pondering.

chapter 10

PEOPLE OFTEN MOVED TO the backwater known as Humboldt County not because they loved the agrarian lifestyle, unless of course they were fifth-generation farmers, but because they wanted to get away from other people. While there was a genuine sense of community among the natives of the area, the transplants were generally the reclusive type. Bud Crawley had been one such and there were more of his ilk peppered throughout the county, with their numbers increasing annually.

When Wilton's lumber yard burned down and the plastics factory relocated to Ft. Wayne in the early nineties, real estate in Humboldt County took a hit that it had yet to recover from. Property was cheap, but employment opportunities were as rare as hair on a tortoise. Less and less people born here stayed here.

I had been one of many in my class who moved away. As the older generation retired and downsized to smaller houses in Wilton or elsewhere, their houses were bought up by people from Fullbright, Muncie, or Indianapolis, looking for a fixer-upper and a mini-farm, all rolled into one. But the basement bargain prices also attracted puppy mill breeders, meth labs, and *Duck Dynasty* wannabes whose favorite pastime was target shooting. Neighbors like that meant that the thirtysomethings who'd moved there to rear their families in bucolic bliss, packed up and went back to where they'd come from. Which meant more houses for the pot farmers to move in next to the meth dealers. Needless to say, there was no shortage of activity for the sheriff's department to investigate.

Ida Oldingsells was an exception. Now in her mid-sixties, Ida had the energy level and work output of a twenty-one year old. Ten years ago, she relocated from suburban Cleveland to live closer to her schoolteacher daughter, son-in-law, and two grandchildren. Widowed in her thirties, Ida had scaled her way up the ranks of a medical supply company until she had her thirty years in, after which she retired on a comfortable pension and a mountainous savings. Never content being idle, Ida went to work as the township secretary, but she was also a member of the Lions Club, the Optimists Club, a 4-H advisor, a reading tutor at Wilton South Elementary (there had never been a Wilton North), and the chairperson of half a dozen committees at the Central Methodist Church. There wasn't a soul within a twenty-mile radius that Ida didn't know something about — even the drug dealers. Ida didn't judge. She was just the curious type.

Since her son-in-law was first cousins with Sheriff Driscoll ... let's just say that if Ida got word of any illicit dealings, the sheriff learned about it that same day, and vice versa. Every police department had its snitches. Ours just happened to wear stretchy Capri pants, floppy sunhats, and drive a twenty-year old Toyota Camry.

She was loitering at the fence, pretending to pull weeds, when I got back from the grocery store.

"Goodness gracious!" She tipped her polka-dotted wide-brimmed hat back and peered at me over the top of her big sunglasses. "Is that you, little Samantha Schimmoller?"

Ironic, coming from a woman who, at only four feet eleven inches tall, was a foot shorter than me. She clambered over the wire farm fence. Did I forget to mention that she also climbed rock walls and hiked the Appalachian Trail on her vacations?

I had a stack of boxes cradled in my arms, so I was defenseless when she tugged off her gardening gloves and pinched my cheeks.

"Would you look at you? All grown up. Haven't seen you since you came back for Paula and Jeffrey Mann's wedding. How long ago was that? Five, six years?"

My mouth slipped into a frown. "Ten."

How could I forget?

We had come back to Wilton for Kyle's best friend Jeffrey's wedding. The night of the rehearsal dinner, Jeffrey told Kyle about a tenured position that would be opening in the Social Sciences department at Fullbright Community College in the fall. Kyle wanted to apply, but I wasn't about to move back to the sticks. For any reason.

I didn't want to live in Wilton. I didn't want to be reminded of my mother. I was happy in Chicago. Happy with just Kyle and Tara as my family. Why give that up?

We argued. Loudly. In front of Tara. When she asked why we were yelling, I snapped at her, and she exploded in tears. I stepped out of the car to let my anger subside. Although it was after midnight, Kyle drove off with Tara in the backseat, headed for his parents' house.

It was the last time I saw him alive.

Paula and Jeffrey postponed their wedding to attend Kyle's funeral instead. Guilt descended on me. Not just for destroying what should have been their joyful day, but for arguing with Kyle in the first place.

"Oh, I'm sorry." Ida rubbed my arm with an age-spotted hand. "I forgot. I'm sure it's still hard for you."

As fresh as yesterday. I forced a smile, even though it made my lip hurt. Ida winced as she looked at my mouth, but didn't say anything.

"I'm okay. Really." The lies got easier the more often I told them. People didn't want to hear about your pain. "How are things in Wilton?"

One gray eyebrow tilted upward. "Now that's a can of worms. Where do you want me to start?"

"With the juicy stuff."

"All righty, then." She gathered a deep breath. "Dawna — she's the newest township trustee, also owns the beauty shop downtown — she just got divorced. Normally I'd say good for her, because her ex-husband Dylan Hawkins is a cheat."

Dylan Hawkins a philanderer? Now there was a shocker. "I can believe that."

"You know him?"

"Sort of. But go on."

"Well, there've been rumors she's in a bit of dire straits, money-wise."

"Understandable. A lot of people get low on cash, especially after a divorce."

"Word is that the township treasury has funds missing." Her brows waggled with the implication. "And, she just got back from Rio with her boyfriend. Where do you suppose she got the money from?"

"Circumstantial, don't you think?"

"Dawna lives in a mobile home and drives a fifteen-year old Buick. The bumper is tied on with baling twine. Any idea what tickets to Rio cost?"

"Hmm, a lot. Maybe her boyfriend paid for it?" I loved Ida, but she had an active imagination. "What does he do for a living?"

She hesitated. I had her there.

"Good question." She held up a finger, the joints swollen with the signs of early arthritis. She may have looked her age, but she certainly didn't act it. "I'll find out."

I didn't doubt she would. "So, what else is new?"

"The levy failed again last fall. Special election at the end of the month."

"School levy?"

"No, emergency services. Sixth time in a row." She glanced back at her own house, an early twentieth-century cottage with clapboard siding and gingerbread trim. "Archer Malone, the Wilton fire chief, tells me if that goes down, they'll close up the township firehouse and contract out to other parts of the county, which means it'll take an age for any fire truck to arrive. Anything goes up in flames, it's as good as burnt to the ground. Pretty scary, when you consider the arsons that have been happening."

That had to be the Archer who'd spoken to me at Garber's. Learning he was a first responder raised his respectability level several notches — and gave him a pass on the grungy attire and appearance. Any man who put out fires and rescued kittens from telephone poles was allowed to go out in public way overdue for a shower and fresh laundry.

"Archer Malone, huh?" I said, curious to know more about him now. "Kinda tall, really tan, looks like he lifts weights?"

"That's the one. Township fire chief. Wilton's most eligible bachelor. Every woman under sixty at the Lions Club has her eyes set on him." She set her gloves aside and took a set of boxes from my backseat.

"And how many arsons have there been lately?"

"Three confirmed. There was another fire late last year, but they think that one might have been faulty wiring."

"How do they know they were all set by the same person?"

"M.O. That's *modus operandi*. Your dad and I get together and watch *NCIS* every week. The arsons always start in the evening. Things are stolen, valuables. Like they knew what to look for and how to get inside. And except for Bud Crawley's house, all the other houses were empty at the time — folks out of town, out to dinner. Like whoever did it was watching and waiting."

This was like getting the Cliff's Notes version of Wilton's own reality show. Not to mention better than waiting on the Humboldt County Sheriff's Department to investigate the matter thoroughly enough to clear my dad. Sometimes, if you wanted things done, you had to do them yourself.

There wasn't much room to spare in the garage, but I directed Ida to put the boxes down in there. "Any leads on the cases?"

She tilted her head toward Dad's truck. "Just that Bud Crawley's neighbor reported a red truck pulling out of his driveway a little while before the fire was called in."

"Sheriff Driscoll was here."

"I know."

Of course she did.

"Walt has become something of a recluse since you left last time, Sam, and people who don't know him well are understandably suspicious. Not to mention he has a way of raising folk's dander." She helped me to the garage with another armload of boxes. "But I agree it's ridiculous to think he could've had anything to do with it."

"Yeah. How on earth would he hoist a motorcycle into the bed of the truck by himself? Dad may be a grouch and a packrat, but he's certainly no thief, much less an arsonist or a murderer."

Her thin arm slid around me in a light hug. "Don't you worry. He's a scapegoat, that's all. It'll all fall apart for lack of evidence. Why, I could probably get Stacy down at the BMV to run a check and count up how many red trucks there are within a twenty-mile radius."

Pivoting in front of her, I grabbed her by the arms so fast her eyes bugged out. "Could you? I mean, really?"

"Sure, sweetheart, sure. Not sure it'll do much good, but it's easy enough." Her lips tightened. "Now, can you let go? You're cutting off my circulation."

I PULLED THE CORD. The trap door unfolded to reveal a set of dusty stairs. Above loomed a hot, dark cavern, devoid of air. The place where stuff went and never returned from: the black hole known as the attic.

"So let me get this straight." I placed my sandaled foot on the first rung. "You're giving me free rein up there?"

Dad scratched the back of his neck. "Sure. Why not?"

I put my foot back on the floor. "What gives? Two days ago you wouldn't let me touch anything without a stroll down memory lane. Now, you're sending me up there by myself?"

"I haven't put anything up there in over five years. Haven't taken anything down in ten." Tara appeared at the end of the hallway with a tackle box. Dad waved her back into the kitchen. "That's the one, honey. Did you get the poles loaded up?"

"Yeah, but there were like eight of them. I didn't know which ones you wanted, so I put all of them in the truck."

"Perfect. Wait for me out front. I'm just going to grab the cooler and some drinks for us."

Tara disappeared. I glared at Dad. "You're going fishing, while I suffocate in a musty attic, breathing in dust mites and bat droppings?"

"You'll be fine. And don't worry about my driving. Rainbow Lake is only three miles away." He cuffed me on the upper arm. Just once. Anything more might have been misconstrued as affection. "Oh, there's a light up there. You'll have to feel around for the string, but it's somewhere between the trap door and the window. Take as many breaks as you need. It's a big job."

The 'window' he spoke of was a one foot by two foot slab of glass, with no way to open it and let fresh air in. The 'somewhere' was a twenty-five foot long space, crisscrossed with rafters and filled with who-knew-what. I didn't argue with him about taking a break. With Tara's help, he'd almost finished sorting through my old bedroom. Granted there were several rooms, closets, a garage, and an entire attic to go, but he'd done far more in two days than I thought was possible. Especially for him. Besides, reminiscing with Tara had brought out a less cantankerous side of him. Almost pleasant.

"Have fun, then," I told him. "Just be back by five. I'm planning meatloaf for supper. Before you run off though, where do you keep the flashlight?"

"End drawer in the kitchen."

I waved bye to them through the kitchen window, then dug around in the junk drawer for a flashlight. There were four. Each one looked like a 1950s version. None worked. I rummaged through three more drawers before I found batteries that weren't corroding. The ones I'd gotten at Garber's weren't the right size for any of his flashlights. Which reminded me: I still had to replace the smoke alarm batteries.

A quick look out the window revealed Bump sleeping beneath the shade of the boxelder tree. He'd started excavating around the base of one of the clothesline poles, but had apparently given up for the time being. Good thing I was meeting Clint later to walk him.

I tromped up the ladder and shone my flashlight around before hauling myself up to sit on the ledge. At the far end of the attic was a small square of light. Just enough to see by if my batteries died. Dust motes drifted in a sparkly haze, stirred by my movements. I drew my legs up and stood, stooping to avoid the rafters.

The string for the light bulb dangled in front of me. I gave it a tug and amazingly the place lit up like Times Square. Most of the junk was piled near the trapdoor, but beyond that the space looked more organized. There was an old crystal lamp without a plug on its electrical cord, a footstool with a leg missing, a globe that still had the USSR on it, a framed print of an early American farm scene that had hung over the couch when I was in my early teens, and an assortment of Styrofoam coolers reeking of fish, with cracks or chunks missing. I saved the globe and put the rest in the pile designated for the dumpster that I'd ordered to arrive on Friday.

One box revealed an assortment of old winter coats, including the red plaid one with brass buckles that I'd adored when I was nine. The more I looked around, the more I realized he had hardly ever thrown anything away. Sometimes, the examples you grow up with teach you what not to do or become. This probably explained why everything I currently owned could fit in an eight foot by ten foot storage unit. I had very little to tie me down, which meant no clutter to trip over.

An hour later I climbed down to grab an iced tea and wash the dust out of my throat. After taking Bump some fresh water with ice cubes, I tossed together a meatloaf and shoved it in the oven. Then I returned to the attic, sneezing as I poked my head back into the great abyss.

It had to be over a hundred degrees in there. I fanned myself with an old life insurance brochure. Tomorrow, I'd snake an extension cord up there and turn a fan on, never mind the dust.

I almost quit when I came across ten boxes of paperwork. If it had been organized to some degree, my job would have been easier, but there were old appliance warranties mixed in with obsolete tax returns and other, more important items, like my parents' marriage certificate. I marked a box 'IMPORTANT PAPERS' and put it in there.

With the fourth box I opened, my heartbeat slowed. Pictures. Black and whites. Old Polaroids with a reddish cast. Dad and Mom when they were younger, before me. Their wedding, outdoors beneath a grove of oak trees at the edge of a meadow. Mom showing off her baby bump in a frilly sundress.

In a manila folder was part of Mom's modeling portfolio. In the first photo, she leaned against a red Corvette and was decked out in *haut couture*: a black A-line dress with a slit up one leg, a draping of diamonds around her swan-like neck, and four-inch spiked heels. On the back of the photo, scrawled in her handwriting, it said, "To the one man who means the world to me. I give you my heart, my soul, my life. XOXO, Ann."

They had met at a gala in Indianapolis. He was the local photographer hired to cover the fundraiser hosted by a multimillionaire in the auto industry. My mother, at the time, had been the fiancée of said mogul, who was a good thirty years older than her. How my dad wrangled her away from Mom's sugar daddy would always be a mystery, but his pictures showed he was just as handsome then as she was beautiful. Their early photos showed a couple head over heels in love, their arms wrapped tight around each other, Mom planting kisses on Dad's cheek, him with his chin tucked against the crook of her neck as she snuggled against him on a porch swing.

It was odd to see them that way, because I don't ever remember them being happy together. Just a lot of yelling and slammed doors, Dad silently brooding, Mom blubbering about things I didn't understand. About halfway through the box, Mom disappeared from the photos, just like she'd disappeared from our lives.

The aroma of meatloaf drifted up through the open hole, reminding me I'd been up there for over an hour since putting it in the oven. In another twenty minutes, I'd go down to set the table and text Tara that it was time to head home.

I wasn't sure what to do with all the photos. Put them in albums? Tara would love a project like that. Or just leave them in the box they were in? The assumption being that Dad had put them up here because he didn't wanted to be tempted to look at them. Too painful, understandably.

Plunging a hand deep into the box, I pulled out some random photos from underneath: me with my fourth place rosette from the Humboldt County Fair, holding the lop-eared rabbit I'd raised — I distinctly remembered there were only four entries; me on my purple banana-seat bicycle, the stitches in my chin clearly visible from an accident I'd had the first day I'd ridden it; me in a flouncy light blue prom dress and Kyle in a tux with a matching light blue bow tie.

My heart fluttered. I missed him. Still. I always would.

I missed the way he made me laugh. The way he could make me all tingly down there with only a glance and a suggestive grin. The way he held me close after a long, hard day. The way he snored softly whenever he fell asleep on the couch behind me.

Most of all, I just missed knowing he was there. That I had a soft place to land. An ear to pour my troubles into. A partner to share my dreams with.

I slipped my hand deeper into the box. But instead of more pictures, I pulled out a rubber-banded bundle of envelopes. Addressed to my father. The handwriting was my mother's. The postmark: 'Paris, France'. Each one had been opened, the letters inside folded and refolded countless times.

Rifling through the dates on the postmarks, I saw that they didn't start until a couple of years after she'd left us.

My stomach knotted as I gripped the bundle. As far as I knew, she had never contacted him after leaving. There had simply been a phone call from her mother several years after she left, informing us of her death. My mother had been buried somewhere on Long Island in a family plot. Dead from leukemia at the age of thirty-one. There had been no funeral to attend, at least not that I knew of. I was eleven then and just as angry that she had died as I was that she had left us.

The morning she left as she packed my lunch, she didn't give any indication that anything was about to change. There was only a cool silence that had persisted between her and Dad for months, but by then I'd grown used to it. I came home later that day to find my father sitting stoically in his favorite recliner, staring at a TV that wasn't even turned on. The note on the kitchen table had said: 'Gone to be with

Etienne. I have to do this. Please understand.' No mention of me. No explanation why. No apology.

I may have only been six, but I was a precocious reader even then. I understood enough to know that my mother was with another man. And that she was not coming back. In a way, I became parentless that day. Gone were my daddy's smiles, the knock-knock jokes, the sing-alongs to Beach Boys songs.

My sweaty palms smeared the ink on the top envelope. I stared at it for a long, long time. Dying to know what she had said to him. Yet too afraid to open it.

You don't pick at old scabs unless you enjoy pain.

I'd hand the box to Dad. Let him decide what to do with it.

Tucking the bundle back beneath the pictures, I scooted the box toward the trap door. The smell of charred hamburger wafted up from below. Darn it. Had I not heard the timer go off? I checked the time on my phone. No, it should have had another half an hour. Obviously, I must have put it on the wrong temperature.

The box tucked under my arm, I started down the ladder. I wasn't even halfway when the haze of smoke drifting from the kitchen doorway catapulted me into a panic.

Fire!

Dropping the picture box at the base of the ladder, I sprinted down the hall. Spirals of acrid smoke snaked upward from the burners. Flames burst randomly behind the grimy glass door of the oven. I scoured the kitchen for a fire extinguisher as my heart pounded in my ears. There was nothing in the pantry or under the sink. Nothing on the ledge of the cellar stairs.

Another flash of flame caught my eye. The grease from the ground beef was dripping onto the heating element. Why would it do that when I'd put a cookie sheet under the casserole dish?

In the absence of a fire extinguisher, my first instinct was to yank the oven door open and douse the fire with a pot of water. But it was a grease fire and I knew enough not to do that. Plus, if I opened the door, oxygen would only fuel the fire more.

I stood there for a few seconds, listening to the *hiss* of grease and the *poof* of flames every time a splatter hit the coil. So I did the most sensible thing I could think of.

I unplugged the oven. And I prayed it wouldn't explode.

As the drips became less frequent, I opened the fridge and found a half-empty box of baking soda. I was standing there with oven mitts on, a cookie sheet in one hand and the box of baking soda in the other, wondering if and when I should call the fire department, when Dad strolled in the back door.

"Good Lord!" He swept off his fishing hat and swatted at the wall of smoke. "Trying to burn the house down?"

Bending over, I peered into the oven. The glass casserole dish had burst into pieces. "How did that happen?"

"Oh." Dad's lip twitched. "I forgot to tell you the temperature gauge was whacky. Probably overheated. And there was a crack in that glass dish."

"And yet you left the oven plugged in and didn't tell me any of this? Why?"

"Stovetop still worked. How else was I supposed to make omelets?"

Just like him to let a little detail like that slip his mind. As much as I wanted to wring his neck, I resisted. I didn't relish the thought of Tara having to visit me in prison.

Tara stood at the back door, coughing. She covered her mouth with both hands. "We're not having *that* for dinner, are we?"

"Looks like you brought dinner home. How was fishing?" I asked Tara. "Did you enjoy your time together?"

"Oh, sure, sure. We had fun." She wrinkled her nose. "Had to throw most of the fish back, though. Too small." Then she leaned in close and mumbled, "But his driving ... oh my God, I thought he was going to plow us into an oncoming car twice."

"What was that, Tara?" Dad said as he tossed the truck keys on the counter.

"I just said I don't think we caught enough for all of us," Tara lied with a teasing smile.

"Not a problem. I'm headed out. Dad, let Tara pan-fry the fish in the skillet after the smoke clears. She knows how. You two enjoy your fish dinner." I shoved the baking soda at Tara. "Here. You guard it. And make sure Gramps doesn't open the oven door. I'll clean up the mess when I get home."

"Where are you going now?" Dad said.

"Taking Bump for a walk." I didn't mention with whom. "I'll be back by dark."

Before I left the kitchen, I grabbed the newspaper. Maybe while I waited for Clint, I could skim the arson article for more clues. I also took the truck keys. Didn't need Dad running into town just to have him crash into an innocent driver.

I remembered the box of pictures when I tripped over it. Fortunately, my scraped up knees broke my fall before my head hit the wall hard enough to give me a concussion. I sat on my rump on the hardwood floor, probing the newly forming knot at my temple. By now I probably looked like an auto accident victim myself.

Tara peeked around the doorway. "You okay, Mom?"

"I will be ... eventually."

She glanced at the box, then at me. "Need help?"

I tossed the newspaper on top of the photos. "Nope, I'm good. Thanks."

She hung in the opening, her head tilted skeptically. "You sure you don't want me to duct tape some foam rubber around you before you go?"

"Yeah, I'm sure." Stiffly, I got up from the floor and braced a hand against the wall as I waited for the blood to return to my head.

"If anyone asks, I'll tell them I race motorcycles for a living and hit a barrier at two hundred miles per hour. They'll be impressed I'm not in a body cast."

Tara cast a glance behind her, then approached me. She lowered her voice. "Mom, is he always so ... contrary?"

"What do you mean?" Snatching up the box so she wouldn't be tempted to look inside, I hugged it to my side.

She shrugged a shoulder. "We stopped at the hardware store to get some bait and he went ballistic over the price of worms."

"I don't get it. Why didn't he stop at the bait store next to the lake?"

"He says they're always ripping people off. But we ended up getting worms there anyway because he got irate at the hardware store owner for raising *his* prices."

"Yeah, that's Dad. He says what he thinks and won't admit it when he's wrong. It's like there's no filter between his brain and his mouth."

"I noticed. You know, sometimes he's all right. Other times ..."

I rubbed her arm. "Believe me, I know." Then I gave her a half-hug, careful not to jab the box corner into her ribs, and reminded her to unplug the oven after she was done using the stove top. I would've suggested they use the outdoor grill, but we were out of charcoal — or maybe it was just that I hadn't been able to find it yet. Besides, knowing my dad lately, he'd probably roll the grill too close to the house and set it on fire.

After Tara went back to the kitchen, I scrambled up the ladder, clicked the light off, and then closed the trap door on my way back down. I almost carried the box into my old bedroom, which was now decluttered enough for me to inhabit, but there was still a chance Dad or Tara might come across it.

While the two of them gutted fish on the back patio, I went out to my car and stuffed the box in the rear storage area. By the time I got around to the back of the house, Bump was making little ballet leaps into the air in anticipation of our walk, his tail propelling him in circles. We would arrive early to meet Clint, but I had something to do in the meantime.

As much as it made my gut churn to open up old wounds, I had to read those letters.

My suspension creaked as I rumbled down the bumpy driveway. At the end, I paused long enough to watch a Humboldt County cruiser crawl down our road at twenty miles per hour, the deputy's head craned toward our house.

If he was expecting to see a red truck leave the house and go tearing down the road, he had a long wait ahead.

chapter 11

LEGS STRETCHED BEFORE ME, I leaned my side against the bench slats and propped my left arm over the back. Bump sniffed my hand, then turned to watch a pair of chipmunks play tag on the lawn behind us. He strained against the leash, which I'd tied to the bench leg, but as soon as it went taut, he lay down. Dad's newspaper lay on my lap, the bottom half folded under so I could focus on the headline article. Under it was the bundle of letters from my mother.

When I was the same age Tara is now, had my mother walked into the room I probably would've punched her. No, that's not right. I was never the violent sort. Just mouthy. I would've cussed her out, maybe flipped her the finger. Most likely, my verbal attack would have been somewhere between 'Why did you leave us?' and 'Didn't you love me enough to take me with you?'. Not that I'd ever really wanted to go to France or Denmark or wherever it was she had jetted off to with Etienne. It's just that, well, if your parents split up, you want to believe they both love you enough to fight over you. Instead, she had skulked off like she had something to be guilty of. Or like she didn't want the responsibility of a kid. Like I didn't matter to her.

It wasn't until Kyle and I made our own life in Chicago that I started to let go of all that smoldering anger. Time doesn't heal old wounds. It just puts them out of sight for a while. Until something sparks the memories again. Like a batch of old letters.

If I read them, would I hate her more? Or would I understand her better? I wasn't sure I was ready for either.

I tucked the letters between my leg and the back of the bench and read the front page of the newspaper again. The article was fairly vague. It read like a junior high version of a school newsletter. The only details were about the stolen items. But it was that paragraph that I kept re-reading. Like there was something, some tiny clue, that was teasing at my gray matter. It wasn't until the sixth pass that it leapt out at me like a fireball in a lightless tunnel.

Ducati. The motorcycle taken from Bud Crawley's house the night of the fire. The same kind Dylan Hawkins was riding when he dropped Selma off at work earlier today. He said he'd bought it off of someone online and that they'd wanted to unload it quickly. Was he telling the truth? Or did he make the story up and had something to do with the robbery at Crawley's? Was it even the same motorcycle?

If I wanted to shift suspicion away from my Dad, I'd have to get more information on Hawkins. First, it might pay to become friends with Selma. She'd already warmed to me. I could get information from her without Hawkins knowing.

Sitting up beside me, Bump let out a yodeling yawn. His lids drifted shut several times, but every time his head bobbed he would snap to alertness, look about, then lean against the bench again. He had developed an annoying habit of needing to touch me. If there was an upside to his newfound clinginess, it was that he was considerably calmer as long as he was pressed against me. With the contact, his serenity flowed through me, erasing the anxiety of my situation, the worry that I might never get to Florida, and the guilt of not having written a single word since I'd arrived in Indiana. My career and future may have been on hold, but sometimes, I realized, there were more important things to take care of — like taking a nap.

The dappled shade of the locust tree and a steady breeze cooled my skin. I lay flat on the bench and covered my face with the newspaper, hoping to absorb some hidden clues by osmosis. It had never worked with my textbooks in college, but I was foolishly optimistic.

Bird chatter and children's laughter filled the air. Swing chains creaked. Insects buzzed and chirped. Far away, a jet thundered.

I imagined myself strolling along a glittery white beach, the grit of sand and broken shells rough against the soles of my bare feet. Ahead, the pale blue of sky met the deep blue of ocean in an unbroken line. And in between, white-capped waves of sea green crested and crashed, gushes of froth rushing against the beach to wash over my toes.

"Lovely day, isn't it?" spoke a deep male voice in my dream.

Perfect, I tried to say, but my mouth merely twitched in a smile.

"Are you ready for a run?"

Run? My eyes flew open. Clint Chastain floated above me, a halo of sunlight burnishing the ends of his dark hair.

"I ... I thought we were walking." I sat up, the blood draining from my head too quickly. The world went momentarily black. Woozy, I clutched the back of the bench for support. When the colors and shapes finally returned to my vision, I swiveled to face Clint, who was now sitting next to me, scratching Bump's neck with both hands. I tossed the letters and folded paper in the box sitting on the ground.

"We can if you want," he said apologetically. "You don't like to run?"

"That would be kind of hard with Mr. Iditarod here."

His long tongue lolling, Bump's cheeks curved into a toothy smile. He leaned into Clint's fingers, adding commentary whenever he hit the right spot.

"Good point," Clint said. "But I don't think it will take more than a few minutes to straighten him out."

"The truth is, I'm a klutz." I tugged at my lip. "Case in point."

There, I'd said it. If my lack of grace frightened him, best to get it out of the way. Save myself the heartbreak.

Clint laughed at me. Not in a 'You're such a dork' kind of way. More like a 'You're adorable' way. Or was I just imagining that, hoping he liked me as more than a potential client? That he wasn't just hanging out with me because he liked my dog, or felt pity for me?

A wave of embarrassment rolled through me. Oh my God. I *cared* what he thought about me. I *wanted* him to like me. Because I was one hundred per cent, completely, utterly, absolutely in lust with him. A hundred naughty thoughts raced through my head. I might have stared a little too long at his waistband, wondering whether he sported briefs or boxers, because he suddenly tugged his singlet lower over his shorts and leaned forward.

"Besides," — I rubbed at my knee, desperate to ease the awkwardness — "I'm still a bit sore. We can work up to a shuffle after a few days. Maybe a jog, eventually. A run sounds rather advanced. We'll leave it on the table for future negotiations. Sound good?"

"Sure." He offered his hand and pulled me up. "Meanwhile, want me to show you how to walk him?"

Bump sprang to his feet, dancing with excitement. I pressed the leash into Clint's hand. The slight dampness of his sweat and the warmth of his palm sent shudders of delight through me.

"Show me," I said.

A devilish grin tilted his mouth. "Why Ms. McNamee, I haven't had a girl say that to me since I was fourteen, under the gym bleachers."

I smacked his arm playfully, but hard. He didn't even flinch. "Show me how to walk the dog without him dragging me. Please."

"Have any cheese?"

"Why would I have cheese?" I asked, suspicious that this was a reference to me being whiny. 'Want some cheese to go with that wine?' was a joke that Tara and I bantered about regularly.

"For the dog. Treats help keep their attention and serve as a reward."

"You didn't tell me to bring any."

"Ah, you're right. I didn't. Hold on to him for a second. I think I have some dog treats in my car. You never know when they'll come in handy during a house call." He dropped the leash back into my reluctant hands and jogged off.

His pearl white Lincoln Navigator looked brand new. Not a speck of mud on it. Pricey vehicle for a country vet. In contrast, I drove a ten-year-old Subaru wagon. His car screamed 'money'; mine muttered 'tightwad'.

Beyond where Clint had parked his SUV was a skateboard park. Half a dozen boys in baggy shorts and graphic tees were practicing their tricks, while three others hid behind a nearby shed, puffing on the cigarettes they were obviously too young to buy. I opened the back hatch of my car and put the box back inside, relieved that Clint hadn't asked me about it.

Bump was doing backflips while Clint searched the inside of his SUV. Either the dog understood English and knew food was on its way, or he was crazy in love with Clint Chastain, even though the guy had jabbed him with needles. Heck, I'd let him poke me with rusty nails if he'd put his hands on me and run them over my body the way he did the dog's.

While I admired the nice view revealed by Clint's short shorts — firm buttocks and muscular thighs, tapering above well-defined calves — I barely noticed the rumble of an engine as a vehicle cruised down the adjacent road, slowed, and drifted into the parking lot. It was a public place, after all, and since I was new in town I wasn't likely to know who it was anyway, so I continued to study Clint's physique, ready to avert my gaze the moment he turned my way again.

A door slammed. Male voices rippled with laughter. Feet pounded in my direction.

Bump hit the end of the leash, straining toward the two men now walking across the parking lot. I grabbed the loop end of the leash, trying to hang on for dear life. With a growly bark, he lunged at them. My arms ached so bad I thought he was going to yank them off at the elbows. That or drag me across the asphalt. But I wasn't about to let go. Who knew what he might do? Tear those innocent men to shreds? Or take off for the hills, all bluster and no bravado?

The hackles on Bump's withers stood on end like a porcupine's quills. Even his floppy ear was perked up straight. His teeth snapped. Drool dripped from his fangs to fly in slimy globs onto the ground — and my legs.

"Hey, fancy meeting you here."

I looked up. The men were coming straight at me now. The one who'd spoken was none other than Archer Malone.

Burning with embarrassment, I jerked back on Bump's leash with every ounce of strength I had and roared, "No, Bump, no! Bad dog!"

As quick as if I'd just walloped him with a two-by-four, Bump leapt to my side and gazed up at me like a properly scolded child. I grabbed his jowls in both hands and gave him a firm talking-to. "You can't be mean to people like that, you hear?"

He hung his head remorsefully and flattened his ears back. As I held his face in my hands, I heard a distant voice: *"G'dammit, what are you carryin' on about now? Shut up, would you?"*

For a moment, I saw a darkened scene, like looking through a lightless tunnel. No, not a tunnel. A long hallway. And then a silhouette floated before me, barely visible. Someone wearing a ball cap. And carrying … a wrench?

Not this again.

Before I could see anything more, the world around me came back into focus.

"I'm Archer. This is Jake." Archer tipped his head toward his friend, but hung back, wary. "Does he always greet people like that?"

"I'm so sorry," I said, my grip on the leash still tight, even though Bump was now sitting on my feet, his head wrapped around my legs like he was hiding from the boogey man. "I don't know what got into him. He's normally not like that."

The two men snickered. Archer twisted his ball cap around so the bill was backward. Hazel eyes sparkled with charm, while deep dimples hinted at boyish mischief. "Sorry, miss. It was probably the hat. Right now, though, your dog doesn't look even a mite dangerous. Does he, Jake?"

Standing behind him, Jake shifted the fishing pole resting on his shoulder. In his other hand, he carried a tackle box. There was a small fishing pond down a pathway a couple of hundred yards from the parking lot. Green painted benches lined one side of the pond, while wide-bodied Pekin ducks and mottled Mallard crosses paddled at water's edge, occasionally dipping their bills below the surface. Not as big or as busy as Rainbow Lake, where Dad went, but it was a quiet spot where guys spent more time shooting bull than reeling in trout or catfish.

"Not with his tail wagging like that, he don't," Jake said with a snort, although there was a nervous tremor in his voice. He looked far from relaxed. Archer, on the other hand, couldn't have looked less fazed by Bump's sudden ferocity.

I looked down. Bump's tail was whipping in frenzied circles of unmistakable camaraderie and goodwill. Geesh, why had he suddenly turned into the canine version of Jekyll and Hyde? Ah, I saw it now. Clint had closed the door of his SUV and was carrying a bag of dog treats our way.

"That's a good-looking dog you have there." Archer patted the top of Bump's head before I could tell him that maybe that wasn't a good idea. Bump barely seemed to notice, his attention fixed on Clint. Then Archer looked at me. "Funny how we keep running into each other. I know this may seem a bit sudden, but ... would you like to sit with us for a spell? We were expecting a couple more friends, but one had to bail because his kid was sick and the other's at home waiting for a satellite dish to be installed."

Behind him, I finally took in Archer's truck: gunmetal gray, dually wheels in the rear, and a gun rack with two scoped hunting rifles. All he needed to complete the look was a camouflage Carhartt jacket and army boots.

As if trying to prompt a reply from me, Archer lifted up the small cooler he was carrying. "I have egg salad sandwiches, root beer, and some of my world famous potato salad. Way too much for just Jake and me."

It was a completely innocent offer — so why was it making me so uncomfortable? I scrambled for a way to brush him off politely. "Tempting, really, but my date," — I gestured at Clint, who by then was coming toward us — "well, we had other plans. Sorry."

He looked from Clint, to me, then back to Clint. Clint raised a hand in a hello as he joined us.

They clasped forearms.

"Hey, Archer." Clint nodded at them each in turn. "Jake. How's it going?"

Jake just bobbed his head, but Archer grinned like a Cheshire cat. "I'd say good, but looks like you're doing a whole lot better than either of us losers." Winking, Archer thumped Clint on the arm. "Al-ready snagged the new girl in town, did you?"

Dang. I hadn't counted on them knowing each other so well. Then again, this was a one-stoplight town. Two, if you counted the flashing lights at the intersection of Highway 5 and North Maple.

"What?" Clint blinked in confusion. "Oh no, she's not ... we're not —"

"Not to be rude," I said, hooking an arm through Clint's, "but I told my daughter I'd be home in time for supper and we need to put the miles in. That half marathon is only a month away." I tugged him toward the bike path. "See you guys around."

Backing away, Jake pulled a flattened ball cap from his back pocket and swatted at a fly that was dive bombing him.

"Nice meeting, you, uh …?" Archer hinted for a name.

I was hoping we were too far away by then, but Clint twisted around and called back, "Ah, sorry. I forgot to introduce you. This is Sam."

"Bye, Sam," Archer yelled. "Maybe I'll see you down at Garber's again?"

Waving faintly, I forced myself into a jog, eyes down to make sure I didn't trip over any branches or rocks. Bump trotted between us, his attention firmly fixed on the crinkly treat bag in Clint's hand. By the time we were behind the tree line and out of sight of the parking lot and pond, I was sucking air so badly I sounded like a broken down cart horse with the heaves. I slowed to a walk to catch my breath.

Clint matched my pace. He was barely breathing, forget sweating. His skin glistened. "You didn't tell me you had a daughter."

"Is that a problem?" It came out sounding defensive, but the whole encounter had me on edge. Archer hadn't said or done anything out of line, so why did I feel compelled to give him the slip? And why had Bump changed from a total wimp to a frothing maniac and back in a matter of seconds?

"Not a problem at all," Clint said. "It's just nice to know."

"Didn't think we'd reached the stage where we were sharing personal information, like how many offspring or siblings we had. Besides, you're just a friendly acquaintance who offered to teach me a few tips about training my dog."

He didn't reply to that, but a few seconds later he blurted out, "Did you tell Archer we're an item?"

"I, uh, might have mentioned we were on a date."

"Why would you do that? I mean, not that I wouldn't date you, because I would, believe me, but … I just thought I was … I mean, we were … Never mind." He was digging himself a hole wide enough to sink a Mack truck in.

"Relax. I know this isn't a date." Actually, that hadn't been at all clear to me. But I didn't want Clint to feel like I'd misunderstood his intentions. Still, it stung a little, I admit. "I was trying to ditch him because he was getting a little too friendly, that's all. He invited me to an impromptu picnic. How do you know him, anyway?"

"High school. He was a year behind me. We were on the football team together."

"*You* played football? What were you — wide receiver, quarterback?"

"No, defense. And I wasn't very good. Third string. I got flattened more times than I can remember. Told you I was a little heavier back then. Actually, it would take almost two of the current me to match the weight I was then."

"I still can't believe that. Did you have skin reduction surgery?"

A chuckle bubbled up from his throat. "Now that's getting a little personal. But to answer you, no. Nothing but intense workouts and a good diet. Although it did take me a few years to get to this point, so don't think it happened overnight."

"It's just that you look … amazing." And he really did. Like he'd just stepped off the cover of *Fitness* magazine.

Stopping, he lowered his eyes. "Thanks," he said softly, all humility and no hubris. I got the sense that he still wasn't used to getting compliments. Gradually, he raised his eyes to meet mine. "You look pretty amazing yourself."

Now it was my turn to blush. For this not being a date, the air between us was suddenly popping with electricity. I was more confused than ever. That was when I realized Bump had been staring at the two of us the whole time. I felt like we'd been caught kissing in the coat closet.

"Um, so," I began, eager to steer this conversation into safer territory, "you were going to give me some tips on training Bump so I could take him for a civilized walk."

"Right, right." Bumbling as he took the leash from me, he fished out two biscuits and stuffed the rest of the bag in a pouch around his waist. In a few short minutes, he showed me how to get Bump to sit, lie down, and walk next to me, all by keeping Bump's attention on the food and rewarding him when he was good.

"What if he sees a squirrel and I'm out of treats?" I asked. "I'm pretty sure he'd rather have squirrel than some dry, crunchy biscuit."

Clint rubbed his chin. "Sometimes when they disobey, we have to let the dog know we're not happy. Can you be assertive, Sam? You may feel like you're being mean, but really you have to let them know who's boss. Do you have that in you?"

"My daughter would say so, yes."

"Good, then just do what you did back in the parking lot. Give him a physical correction if you're holding his leash, coupled with a verbal correction. He'll get the idea eventually."

"Oh, you saw that?"

"How could I miss it?" He turned to walk along the path and Bump and I fell in step beside him. "I like a woman who can take charge."

I trotted after him like a little kid following the ice cream truck. A steady breeze stirred the tree limbs. The temperature had cooled considerably from the blistering heat of afternoon. Every once in a while, I glanced over at Clint just to admire his sculpted frame. I only stumbled once, but he caught my arm before I could trip over the dog and do a face plant.

The pressure of his touch sent a surge of warmth through my body. When he pulled his hand away, I still felt the indent of his fingertips. I considered stumbling again, just so he would catch me. Maybe I could hold my breath long enough to pass out and he'd give me mouth to mouth?

"Tell me about your daughter," he inquired politely, ripping me from my fantasy. "How old is she?"

"Fourteen, going on forty."

He asked more about Tara, and the job I had in Chicago, and what my plans were for the immediate future. It was so easy to talk to him. Too easy. I kept thinking there had to be some catch. That at some point he'd mention his favorite hobbies were collecting potato chips in the shape of celebrity silhouettes or attending fancy chicken shows. Or that I'd bore him so profoundly that the conversation would drop off into a bottomless abyss and we'd wander back to the car in nerve-gnawing silence, say our goodbyes, and never speak again. I'd hardly noticed that we'd wheeled around some time ago and were nearing the parking lot.

"You said you're a writer. What do you write about?"

I write about falling in love, I wanted to say, *and living happily ever after.* But that seemed so … personal. So out of place.

"Tough question?" He grinned at me. Then his eyebrows arched high onto his forehead. "Ohhh, you write *those* kinds of books. You know, Fifty Shades of —?"

"No!" I said it so loudly, I surprised myself. I was careful to keep my voice steady this time. "Not that kind, no. But I do write romances."

"Then there's," — his brow waggled and he lowered his voice secretively — "you know, sex in them?"

A flush of heat spread from my chest to my face. "Some." Then hurriedly added, "But mostly, they're love stories."

He pondered it in silence, his steps quickening. That was that. Not only had I killed the conversation, he couldn't wait to get back to his car and drive away. I turned my attention to the wildflowers along the path: phlox and wild geraniums, chicory and blue violets. Wouldn't it be great to have a picnic in a meadow with him, get drunk on white zinfandel, and have him eat strawberries from my navel, right before we —

"Why?" He said it so pointedly that I was afraid for a moment I'd said something totally inappropriate out loud.

"Why what?"

"I've always wondered why people write what they write. Like why do some people write horror, stuff that would scare the pants off you? Or crime stories about serial killers? Or fantasies with unicorns and dragons?"

"Why are you a veterinarian?" I parried.

"Because I like animals." He winked at me. "That was too easy. Your turn. Why do you write love stories?"

"I don't know." The subject made me uncomfortable. Especially since he was so undeniably attractive, and charming to boot. "I guess because … because I believe."

"Believe in what?"

"True love. Everlasting love." I stole a glance at him, but his face was unreadable. "Don't you?"

I don't know what made me ask that, after all, this was only the second time we'd spoken since high school. Ever, actually.

His mouth tightened. He looked off to the side. "I did. Once."

"What happened?"

He shot me a pained glare that nearly made me wilt. "I lost her."

By his reaction, I could tell he was still hurt, whatever had happened. I wondered how she'd died. If he'd been married to her or not. How long they'd been together. Who she was. How they'd met.

Yet I couldn't ask. Not now. Not yet.

"I'm sorry," I told him.

Stopping, he turned to face me. "And I'm sorry about your husband. It had to be traumatic."

I bit the inside of my cheek, trying to inflict physical pain so I wouldn't dissolve into tears. I hadn't talked with anyone about Kyle's death since the funeral. It was easier to bury my grief than lay it bare.

Which was not to say that was a healthy thing to do. I just never really felt the need to burden others with it. A co-worker once suggested a widows' support group. I imagined a roomful of old ladies, reeking of muscle rub, mopping their tears with embroidered hankies. I failed to see how that was supposed to make me feel better. So I wrote instead. Wrote about imaginary people falling in love and living happily ever after, even as I hid from the world and sabotaged every date I had. Ironic, huh?

When I didn't say anything back, Clint turned forward again. We stood near the end of the path on the edge of the parking lot. The sun had just set and with an overcast sky there was just enough light left to see by. Lightning bugs flickered in the distance, glittering like tiny stars above the rolling lawn of the little park. Crickets and bullfrogs croaked their chorus. Somewhere in the trees, a cicada hummed.

"How far did we go?" I asked.

Flipping his arm over, he glanced at the bulky watch on his wrist. "I didn't start my GPS, but we've been gone an hour and a half."

"Has it really been that long?" I scratched Bump behind his lopsided ear and he tilted his head to look up at me. "No wonder my feet ache."

Clint's eyes widened for a moment, before a grin spread across his face. "Seemed like it was only minutes to me."

Encroaching darkness only made me more aware of Clint's closeness: the heat wafting off his body, the steady sound of his breathing, the manly scent of his sweat. The parking lot was now empty except for his SUV and my car. There was no sign of Archer or Jake. The children had long since left the playground with their parents. Gone were the skateboarders and underage smokers. Even the ducks had bedded down on the banks of the pond, their bills tucked against their downy breasts.

I reached out to pet Bump's head and Clint's fingers brushed mine. A flush of heat spread outward from my heart. I jerked my hand away reflexively and bent down, pretending to tie my shoe. I wasn't sure whether his touch was accidental or intentional. This was all going too perfectly to even believe it was real — and too quickly for me to process.

I'd tried so hard so many times to move on after Kyle's death, to date other men, but every time the effort had drained me so much it left me feeling empty and unlovable. Now a connection was happening without me even trying, and it frightened me. Was there something about him I should know? Why wasn't a man with a body as hot as his and a personality that would charm the rattler off a rattlesnake already taken? The whole thing was like falling into a vat of caramel. There was such a thing as too much goodness all at once.

I started toward my car. I had to take a breather, let this all sink in before I self-destructed. "Thanks for your help tonight, Clint. I can't believe how much better Bump —"

I stopped dead in my tracks to stare at my car.

"How much better he's walking on leash?" Clint finished for me. He drifted my way, like he wasn't going to let me get away so easily. "It was nothing. You just needed someone to show you —"

He came to an abrupt stop beside me. "Wow."

"I know," I said, more calmly than I felt. My car slanted noticeably to the left and rear. The tire was as flat as a crepe. Funny, it hadn't been low when I pulled in. Maybe I'd picked up a nail on the drive here?

Clint went to the left rear tire and knelt down. He ran his hands over the sidewall, his thumb probing at a flap on the lower, deflated area. He pointed to it.

"Find a nail?" I said.

"No, no nail. Your tire's been slashed."

chapter 12

CLINT GAVE THE TIRE iron one last turn and rocked back on his heels. Although I'd long ago learned how to change my own tires, he'd insisted on doing it for me and the truth of it was that he did the job much faster than I could have. So to help him out, I'd shone my trusty little LED flashlight as he jacked the car up and unscrewed all the lug nuts one by one, before replacing the slashed tire with the little donut tire.

"Why would anyone do that?" I handed him one of Bump's slobber towels from the backseat. It may not have been clean, but at least it was dry.

He twisted his hands in the towel, rubbing hard to remove the black marks on his palms. "Probably just some juvenile delinquents with nothing better to do."

"Yeah, probably." But I wasn't so sure about that. Still, even if someone had known it was my car, the question was: why would they target me? I'd been in town less than a week. I couldn't have made any enemies already, could I?

His eyes surveying the empty lot, he stood. "Why don't I follow you home?"

"Why? Do you think someone's stalking me?"

"I'd just feel better if you'd let me make sure this junky spare didn't pop off and go rolling into the ditch."

"That doesn't exactly fill me with confidence about your tire-changing abilities," I teased, trying to lighten the mood, but I could tell we were both a little unsettled. "But sure, follow me home. My dad's house is about four miles northwest of here, up on Hilltop Road."

"Practically on my way."

After I loaded Bump in the backseat and slid into the driver's side, Clint hung beside my car, one hand braced against the door. "When we get back to your place, wait before you go inside. We can exchange cell phone numbers. That way you can call me if anything else fishy happens. I mean, if that's okay with you? I don't want to overstep my bounds."

"That'd be fine." Between the tire and Bump going berserk when he saw Jake and Archer, I was more than a little on edge.

After Clint got in his SUV and started it up, I drove out of the parking lot and onto the road, reassured to see Clint's headlights beaming in my rearview mirror. We weren't even halfway home when things got ever stranger.

Gyrating emergency lights marked the road ahead. Dread squeezed my ribs. Ever since that night ten years ago, I couldn't pass an emergency vehicle on the roadside and not wonder who had been hurt or if they were even still alive.

Bump shoved his nose into my ear, snorting. I pushed him into the back and scanned the road ahead. Standing next to a deputy sheriff's car, a uniformed officer seemed to be keeping traffic clear for a residential lane. I looked farther up the driveway and saw a house, the roof smoldering as firefighters doused the shingles with their hoses. I pulled off to the side, parking my car well onto the shoulder. No sooner had I gotten out and started toward the lane, than Clint was on my heels.

"What are you doing?" he said.

"Whoever it is is practically a neighbor. Just thought I'd see if they needed any help."

"Being nosy, I'd say. Looks like half of Humboldt County is here." He hung back half a step, as if he thought I might change my mind and get back in the car. "I think they'll be fine."

"Maybe, but I just want to find out what's going on. This is too many fires too close to home."

He couldn't argue with me on that. Soon his steps matched mine, quick and purposeful. While we were walking next to the ditch, I texted Tara to see if everything was okay at home. She answered right away that everything was fine. I was skeptical, but even so, I wasn't going home without first getting some details here.

"Hi, officer," I called to the deputy, now leaning against the hood of his car. "What's going on here?"

Arms crossed, he nodded toward all the commotion. "House fire."

"Is everyone okay?"

"Yeah, yeah, they're all fine. Got here after it started." He suppressed a yawn. I suspected he'd already fielded a pile of questions from the other neighbors clustered in the yard and was wondering how he got stuck with traffic duty. "Family came home from having dinner out and caught it early. There's some damage to the home office, but nothing a good scrub down can't fix."

"That's lucky."

"I'll say."

He seemed affable enough, so I pried for more information. "Electrical fire?"

"No way of knowing just yet." Tipping his hat back, he glanced skyward. "But it certainly wasn't a lightning strike."

By now the firefighters had stopped watering down the house. I knew they'd keep an eye on it for a while to make sure there weren't any embers still smoking away. If there were any details worth sharing, they'd be in the local paper soon enough, but a little inside information wouldn't hurt. "Do you think it was the work of an arsonist again?"

Eyeing me suspiciously, he pushed away from his cruiser to flag a car by. "Can't really say."

Couldn't or wouldn't? I thanked him and turned around to look for Clint. He'd wandered up the lane a bit to stand with a group of people who I assumed was the family that lived here. I was about to join him when he came my way. As he got to me, he put a hand on my waist to turn me around and guide me back toward my car.

"Was that the family?" I asked.

"It was. Russ Armentrout and his clan."

"Why does that name sound familiar?"

"Armentrout's Hardware, that's why."

The place next to Garber's Groceries. "They all okay?"

"Yeah. Just shaken. Especially considering what I heard." He looked behind him before telling me, to make sure no one was around us. "At the diner, Russ saw his friend Toby, who hauls gravel for the cement company. Toby asked him if he got a new truck recently. Russ said 'no' and asked why. The guy told him while he was on his way into town, he'd seen a red truck pull in to Russ's lane. So Russ paid his bill and hurried home."

"Good thing he did, huh?"

"Sure was. You can bet everybody and their brother in Humboldt County is going to be looking out for a red truck now."

If Sheriff Driscoll paid us another visit tomorrow, I sure hoped he was following up on all the other owners of red trucks in the area. I'd press Ida for that list the first chance I got.

When I returned to my car, the moment Clint headed off toward his SUV, I checked my glove compartment. Yep, there were the keys to Dad's truck. I'd hidden them so he wouldn't terrorize poor Tara with another ride into town — or worse, end up in an accident. The problem was, who would believe me if I told them my dad couldn't have been responsible for this fire because I had his keys? Nobody, that's who.

A little worm burrowed inside my gut as another thought entered my head. What if Dad had an extra set of keys? The man had multiple sets of everything, since he kept losing things in all the clutter. And Tara said he'd argued with Russ earlier at the hardware store.

No, I told myself. It couldn't be him … could it?

CLINT FOLLOWED ME THE rest of the way home and true to his word he didn't let me slip inside without us swapping phone numbers. Dad was already asleep, but Tara was in the living room watching TV.

"Hey, pumpkin." I sat down on the couch next to her, even though she took up two thirds of it and her feet were jammed against my thigh. "Did you have a good evening?"

"Meh, it was okay." She had barely looked at me when I entered the room, but that didn't mean she wasn't paying attention.

"What did you and Gramps do?"

"Stuff."

"Like … what?"

Her eyes rolled ever so slightly. "Same thing we've been doing since we got here." She pointed to the hallway. "Cleaning."

I checked the hall. It was amazingly free of boxes and piles. It even looked like Tara had vacuumed, mopped the floor, and wiped down the baseboards. "Wow." I reclaimed my spot beside her. "Bet that was a lot of work."

She shrugged, the glow of TV light reflecting off her youthful face. "What else is there to do around here?"

"So, Gramps didn't go anywhere tonight?"

Her eyes slid sideways, although her head didn't move. "No, why would he?"

"Talking about me?" Dad shuffled into the living room in his blue plaid bathrobe. Same one he used to wear when I was a kid.

I held out my hand, dangling the truck keys in front of me. "Look what I found buried on the kitchen counter under a stack of junk mail. Stuffed them in my pocket without thinking."

"Hah." He stood there with his thumbs hooked in the belt of his robe, looking very unconcerned. "Put them back on the key hook when you get up. G'night, you two."

"You didn't know they were missing?"

"Why would I? Not like I was going anywhere. Told you I don't drive at night. Can't see a damn thing."

"Yeah, I forgot about that. But you never know when there's going to be an emergency. I panicked at first, afraid you'd be stuck at home. Then I figured you probably had a spare set somewhere. You do, don't you?"

"Did. Lost 'em years ago. If you come across a set around here, let me know." He reknotted the belt on his robe and then, with a big yawn, shuffled back down the hallway.

That answered that. I might have known Dad wasn't responsible for the arsons, but me claiming I had his keys or him saying he didn't drive at night wasn't going to hold up in court. Still, if word got out that he had a kerfuffle with Russ Armentrout that day, then Sheriff Driscoll was likely to come calling. Dad was a curmudgeon with a penchant for ruffling feathers. He didn't exactly have a lot of friends in Humboldt County. It didn't matter that he was a seventy-something senior with failing eyesight and a fading memory. People would think what they wanted to think.

As far as public opinion went, it was guilty until proven innocent.

chapter 13

AFTER SCRUBBING OUT THE oven and emptying about ten buckets of charred grease water into the sink, I was so alert I couldn't get to sleep. Or maybe it was the effect of being hopped up on fumes from the oven cleaner. So at 2:30 a.m., I hauled my laptop out, thinking I'd finish the novel that was only a few chapters away from being done.

An hour later I was still staring at a blinking cursor, my thoughts continually flitting to the series of arsons and all the little disconnected pieces to the puzzle. Finally, I distracted myself by writing a love scene. It flowed like water and two hours later my hero and heroine fell asleep in each other's arms, sated. I, on the other hand, went back to bed, alone and sexually deprived. Some things never changed.

It was late when I woke up. First order of business was to put a call in to the sheriff's office, just in case there had been a rash of slashed tires in the area. The dispatcher referred me to the Wilton Police Department, since the incident had taken place in the town park. When I called them, I was told their officers were too busy to respond to a non-emergency, so I would have to come down to the station to fill out a report. Between that, needing a new tire, and all the stuff in the attic and garage that still needed to be sorted and purged, who knew when I'd be able to get back to my writing? My dream of sitting in an Adirondack chair on the lanai with my laptop while a salty breeze rustled the palm trees was slipping further and further away.

In some ways, though, I was feeling more at peace than I'd felt in a decade. Slaving away at a job I hated was a thing of the past. Tara and I had spoken more in the last week than we had in the previous six months. My father and I weren't butting heads like I'd anticipated, and he and Tara even seemed to be hitting it off.

Plus, because of some mangy mutt I'd plowed over and taken in out of guilt and pity, I finally had a guy in my life who seemed interested in my company.

Then again, maybe I was reading too much into Clint's offer to help me train Bump? After all, the guy was a sucker for anything on four legs. But he had followed me home last night after the tire incident and made a standing date for after work hours to meet with me to walk Bump. He'd done that despite the fact that I was about as graceful as an elephant walking a tightrope. This morning my lip had gone from deep purple to mottled green and yellow. To be truthful, the puffiness added just enough plumpness to my normally thin lips to be an improvement.

After wolfing down a toaster pastry of unidentifiable fruit filling and washing it down with a cup of my dad's tepid coffee textured with floating grinds, I headed out to my car. I made a pass around the rear bumper to make sure no other tires had gone flat overnight and, hopeful that the wimpy little donut tire would make it into town, I opened the driver's side door.

"No, no, no," my dad pled from behind the garage. "Drop it. I said *drop … it.*"

Sighing, I tossed my purse on the seat and tromped around the side of the house to see what Bump had gotten into this time. Had he finally taken a robin down in midflight? Or stolen laundry off the clothesline to play keep-away? I rounded the garage to find Dad pointing at Bump, a smile as big as Hoover Dam on his face.

"Oh hi, Sam." He waved to me. He still had on his bathrobe and slippers. The man never walked anywhere barefoot. He once told me it was because there were worms that could burrow through the soles of your feet, although I was pretty sure that was in the mudflats of some tropical country. Whenever I tried to convince him that he was pretty safe from that threat on the carpet and hardwood floors of his own house he brought up the threat of foot fungus and broken glass. Some arguments were not worth the effort.

Bump stood ten feet from him, the frilly flag of his tail swinging back and forth.

"What are you doing, Dad?"

"Playing fetch. What the hell does it look like we're doing?"

On cue, Bump hopped closer and spit out a yellow tennis ball coated in dirt and slobber. It rolled to Dad's feet, stopping when it hit his toes. Dad picked it up and chucked it toward the row of maple trees, but it only went about fifty feet. Bounding like a spring fawn, Bump took off after it.

When he got to it, Bump didn't just pick it up, he attacked it, tumbling through the tall grass as if he'd just brought down a wildebeest. The ball in his mouth, he sprang to his feet, looked toward Dad with obvious pride, and then whipped his head sideways so the ball hurtled through the air. He pounced on it again and repeated the game four more times before finally returning to Dad.

Patting Bump on the head, Dad giggled like a five-year-old. "That's a good boy, Bump. Gooood boy." He wiped the tennis ball on the front of his beloved bathrobe. "Isn't he something, Sam? I bet he'd do this until his heart gave out."

Seeing the two of them play ball was like watching a YouTube video of kittens doing ridiculously cute things on a repeating loop. It was the first time I could remember Dad being genuinely happy since … since I was a little girl. Since before Mom left. Why did that mutt have to make my life so complicated?

"I, uh, need to run some errands this morning." I avoided telling him someone had stuck a knife in my tire. He was generally paranoid anyway. No need to fuel that fire.

"Don't worry." He flapped a hand in the air as if to usher me along. "Tara and I are going to go through the bookshelves in the living room today. Pretty sure I haven't read some of those Zane Grey novels since the early '70s. Tara said she'd help me take them down to the library later to donate for their annual book fair. We'll probably need more boxes soon, though." He started toward the back kitchen door, the hitch in his stride betraying how arthritis had taken its toll on his aging joints. As he stopped in front of me, Bump dashed to his side and looked up at him pleadingly, the ball still in his mouth and a big string of saliva oozing from between his teeth.

Dad filled his lungs, taking a long look around the yard and at the house. His eyes filled with something between melancholy and relief. "You know, getting rid of all this stuff ... it feels like I've been buried under an avalanche all these years and someone has finally shoveled me out of it. Feels like I can breathe again. I'm almost looking forward to living in a smaller place and having fewer things." He glanced at the gutters where tiny maple seedlings had germinated — one of the many miniscule tasks surrounding him. "Something that won't be so much work. I don't think I'll miss this house as much as I thought I would, but ..." — his gaze slid to mine and I swear there was a glint of a tear in his eyes — "I'm sure gonna miss you all, Bump especially."

My mouth fell open wide. I blinked. Who was this man who looked and sounded just like my father? "Are you getting attached to the dog, Dad?" Never mind that he'd alluded to Tara and me, too.

"What? No. He just appreciates me, that's all. Kind of nice to be needed for a change. Now don't you go reading too much into that." Not being one for sentiment, Dad cleared his throat and headed for the birdfeeder hanging from a branch where he could see the goldfinches and sparrows eating from the kitchen window. A large, saucer-like squirrel-guard sat cockeyed above the feeder. "God blessed furry-tailed rats." He straightened it, grumbling, then stood back and eyed it awhile before glancing at me. "You will be able to get more boxes today, right?"

I nodded. "Sure. I may be gone for a bit, though. Is that okay?"

"Take your time." He headed toward the door.

I kept expecting him to turn around and ask why I'd be gone so long, but he didn't. He just dangled his hand over Bump's head, chuckling to himself as Bump licked his fingers, and went inside.

For a moment, I felt the urge to remind him not to leave Bump unsupervised and to clip him on the line if he needed to let him outside so he wouldn't take off after a suicidal squirrel, but I resisted. I couldn't worry about the dog every minute and besides, the two of them seemed to be doing just fine.

But now, not only was the dog making my leaving hard, Dad was doing his best to, too.

I headed back around the garage. No matter what, I had to stay focused. Finish what I came here for. I knew from the start this wasn't going to be easy.

As I opened my car door and got in, my phone rang. "Hello?"

"Sam? This is Ida. I was wondering if you could stop by for a minute? If you're busy, that's okay. I can always give this to you later."

"Give me what?"

"The list you asked for. I have it."

"I'm headed out now. Be right over, Ida."

I gave the key a twist. Just as the engine turned over, Dad tapped on the window, startling me. I rolled it down.

"Say, Tara's going to a movie this afternoon with a girl her age that we met at the fishing lake. Daughter of an old co-worker of mine at the post office. Good kid. Shannon's mom is picking her up at two. Hope that's okay? Tara's pretty excited about it."

Tara excited about a social outing? Was that his interpretation of her politely accepting an invitation because she couldn't think of an excuse to bail quickly enough, or was she really looking forward to it? After reviewing her rules for being out with him, I backed out and bumped my way down the off-road adventure that was the driveway.

If there was one consistency in everything that had happened over the last few days, it was that my life was becoming more like *The Twilight Zone* every minute.

IDA'S LIVING ROOM WAS decorated in antique chic, like something out of *Better Homes and Gardens*: a tasteful floral print armchair and a pale green sofa littered with coordinating throw pillows, hand-sewn quilts, colored crystal glassware, old tin advertisement signs on the walls, and cast iron collectible toys on the built-in shelves. Every time I walked in there I saw something new, not because she swapped items out regularly, but because there was so much going on. Even so, there was never a speck of dust in the place and despite the many items, it never seemed cluttered. Each piece had been carefully selected, its place well defined, its purpose to conjure memories of a bygone era.

Ida shuffled into the kitchen to grab a glass of lemonade for me. Not that I'd asked for it, but you didn't escape a visit to Ida's house without a beverage. She always had a fresh pitcher of herbal peach iced tea or fresh squeezed juice in the fridge.

A row of hand-painted china plates caught my eye. I wandered over to the mantel to study them. The fireplace hadn't seen a fire for decades. On the wall above it hung a watercolor of a heather-covered landscape strewn with stone walls, thatched cottages, and scattered sheep. An idyllic setting that made me want to leap right into the middle of it to escape all the craziness that was going on. Maybe instead of a house on the beach, I could hide out somewhere in the remote Yorkshire countryside, my nearest neighbors barely visible across the undulating moors?

The rustling of papers snapped me out of my daydreams.

"I got this from the county Bureau of Motor Vehicles." Ida flipped through a stack of stapled papers. "But please don't let anyone know I gave it to you or where I got it from. Stacy will lose her job and I'll get booted out of office in the biggest scandal Wilton's seen since Etta Mae Denlinger embezzled six hundred dollars from the candy sales of the pee wee football cheerleaders." She pointed to one of the names on the first page. "These here are the people who own red trucks in Humboldt County. Here you have the owner. That's their address. And there you see make, model, year, and the VIN."

"What does VIN stand for?"

"Vehicle Identification Number. Actually, that's based on things like what country it's manufactured in, who the manufacturer is, the model, all that good stuff. I should tell you, though, this is from whenever they last renewed their plates. It's not completely up to date. And if someone has recently moved here, then their vehicle would still be registered in another county."

I rifled through the pages, not recognizing any of the names. "There must be a couple hundred names here."

"And that's after I had her whittle it down to just pick-ups. At first she had commercial semis, flatbeds, and box trucks on there, too. But I figured that wasn't what you meant — was it?"

"No, this is great. Really great." Or would have been, if I'd had a few more clues to go on.

"I don't know that it'll help much, but at least the next time Sheriff Driscoll accuses Walt of something ludicrous like stealing and setting fires, you can tell him to go pull up these records and see how many red trucks there are in these parts. Shoot, until someone gets a plate number on a suspicious vehicle, they might as well say it was a man with two legs responsible for the arsons. Then half the county would be suspects."

"I can't tell you how much I appreciate your help." Excusing myself, I put my hand on the knob, turned it partway, then let go. "Ida, tell me — if someone had a VIN number for a vehicle, could you tell what make it was and who owned it the last time the plates were registered?"

"Oh yeah, easy. Why?"

"Just curious if it worked in reverse, that's all." I knew what I was about to ask, and had already asked of her, might put Ida and her friend at the BMV in a delicate situation, but if I was going to get to the bottom of this soon, I needed answers. "Can you have Stacy bring up the VIN number for the Ducati motorcycle owned by Jonathan Crawley?"

"The man who died in the fire?"

"Yes."

She hesitated. "Didn't that motorcycle get stolen?"

"Yes." I knew she was fishing for an answer as to why I wanted the information, so I told her, "Look, I don't want to implicate anyone right now, but I have my suspicions. If I'm wrong, I'll drop it and move on."

Ida placed a hand lightly on my shoulder. "Be careful, Sam."

A yellow tabby cat with white markings twined between my ankles. She looked up at me and trilled. I gave her a quick scratch behind the ears. "I'll do my best, Ida. But I don't think I'm in any danger. Just need enough answers to point the sheriff in the right direction, that's all."

"Good luck with that. Sometimes it seems like all their efforts are going into busting that alleged drug ring hereabouts. I don't see them getting much else accomplished."

Tucking the paper in my pocket, I thanked her and left. So, Humboldt County had its own drug lords, huh? Maybe the Mennonites had their own mafia to combat the downtown gangs of Wilton, too?

AN HOUR LATER, I had a new tire and a decent spare, thanks to Dan of Dan's Tire Service. He lifted a wrench he was using as a paperweight and slid the bill across the counter to me. I leaned in closer, blinking several times to make sure I was reading it right. The smell of engine oil invaded my nose. I could practically feel a layer of grime caked on my skin.

Dan tilted the brim of his cap up. Did everyone in this town wear a baseball hat? The fashion police would have a heyday here. In downtown Chicago, you didn't wear a ball cap unless you were headed to Wrigley Field.

He gave me an apologetic smile. "Bit more than you were expecting, huh? Sorry 'bout that. We had to raise our labor rates for the first time in five years. Cost of living and all."

"Uh, no, not really." Actually it was less than half what I paid last time in Chicago and that was three years ago. But who was 'we'? Was he using it like the royal 'we'? I hadn't seen anyone but Dan working here.

"You sure 'bout that? 'Cause you don't look too sure."

I handed him my credit card. "No problem, really."

His face brightened with relief. "Now, if you decide to upgrade to our all-weather mega-tread, just come back in November or so, and I can pull these babies off for you and store them until spring. They've still got a good ten or twenty thousand left on 'em. But you'll need something with a little better grip for the winters around here."

"That's all right. I don't plan on staying."

"You don't, huh? Where you headed to?"

"Florida. The Keys." If I kept repeating that, I'd manifest it. Oprah was my guru.

"Never been, but sounds wonderful." He ran my card through,

then gave me the paperwork to sign. From his pocket, he produced my keys and dropped them on the counter. "You're all set to go. And remember, if you want an oil change before you head south, stop back in."

"I will." I scooped up my keys. "Say, have you had to repair any slashed tires like mine, lately?"

His forehead scrunched in thought. "Now that you asked, yeah. A day, no, two days ago."

"Whose?"

"Jake Taylor. Volunteers for the fire department. Used to help out here on weekends when he was in high school and for a little while afterward."

Archer's friend, I guessed. I'd be sure to let the sheriff's department know there was another incident.

"Good thing he got it fixed," I said. "Never know when he'd need to report for a fire, the way things have been lately."

"Oh, I don't think he was too worried about it, seeing as how it's his brother's car. I mean *was* his brother's car. Half-brother, to be exact. Or ... maybe they were stepbrothers? Ah, who knows? Cynthia Crawley Fordham Taylor had about ten kids in all. Hard to keep straight who their fathers were. And they didn't always belong to her current husband, if you follow me."

"What do you mean?"

Both shaggy eyebrows lifted up into a pudgy forehead. "I forget that you're not from around here."

I was, but I didn't correct him. Amazing how quickly I'd been forgotten after I moved away.

"Not sure if I recall the family dynamics," he began, his voice low just in case someone had snuck around the corner to eavesdrop on us, "but their mama was married to —"

"Not that. You used past tense. You said '*was* his brother's car'."

"Ohhh, that. You didn't hear about the house fire over on

Harmony the other day? Jake's brother died in it. Terrible thing to happen. Can't imagine dying that way."

A tingle crawled up my spine. If the arsonist had slashed Bud Crawley's tire so he couldn't get away, then maybe it wasn't a mischievous teenager, but the same person who was running around Humboldt County setting fires to people's houses, stealing their stuff, and resorting to murder when it was convenient? Someone had to have come to the park after Archer and Jake left, but before Clint and I got back.

"They were a good twenty years different in age, almost," Dan said. "Ol' Bud pretty much kept to himself and he and Jake didn't talk much. Word has it there was a falling out awhile back when their mama died and left everything to Bud, who squirreled the whole inheritance away somewhere. That ol' geezer sure was miserly. Always bought used tires, changed his own oil. Who does that anymore? Only thing he ever spent money on was that, uh … Oh shoot, some kind of Italian motorbike."

"Ducati," I said in a small voice.

He snapped his fingers. "That's right!"

So Jake Taylor the firefighter and Bud Crawley were brothers? With Bud's death, his possessions should have been off limits until his will went through probate, but I wouldn't put it past a conniving relative to dive in and borrow a few valuable in the interim. The real question was why was Dylan Hawkins now riding around on a Ducati just a day after one had gone missing from Bud Crawley's garage? Either it was a total coincidence or Dylan was a brazen criminal.

Time to have a talk with Selma and learn a little more about this Dylan Hawkins.

First though, I had to stop at the police department to fill out my report. It hardly seemed worth the time, but I wasn't about to let some adolescent vandal — or deranged arsonist, whatever the case — get away with the destruction of personal property. Sooner or later, they'd get caught and pay the price.

chapter 14

WILTON HAD A FULL-TIME police chief and two part-time officers. Most days, whoever was on duty could be found hiding behind a hedge row in their parked cruiser at the edge of the Meadowlark subdivision along Route 379, waiting for drivers to exceed the 25 mph speed limit as they either rolled into or sped out of town. Half of Wilton had probably been ticketed there at some point. Although the townspeople eventually all learned to punch the brakes and abide by the signs, unsuspecting passers-by kept the coffers of Wilton's police department full. Unlike the fire department, they were in no danger of having to lay off employees any time soon.

The reception area was an eight by ten room, half of it taken up by a monstrous desk filled with a bulky monitor that looked as if it were from the 1980s. The equally ancient hard drive whirred and hummed, like it was ready to give up the ghost at any moment. I shut the door behind me, but a window AC unit gurgled so loudly that whoever was in the back room couldn't possibly have heard me enter. Although the desk was free of paperwork, a full glass of lemonade sat next to the keyboard. Perched on the edge of the desk was a plate of brownies: double dark chocolate chunk, by the looks of them.

"Hello," I called, peeking through the doorway behind the desk.

"Is anyone here? I called a little while ago. I need to fill out a report."

I wasn't sure whom, if anyone, I was speaking to. Maybe they had stepped out for a minute? All I could see in the back room was a row of filing cabinets, a stack of law books and an open door to an empty bathroom. I waited, called again, louder. Nothing.

The AC unit clunked behind me and I jumped. After my heartbeat returned to normal, I inched closer to the brownies, inhaling. My stomach rumbled. It was past my lunchtime. Next to sniffing coffee beans, dark chocolate was my greatest weakness. Mouth watering, I reached for the plate. No sooner had I wolfed down my second brownie and started nibbling on a third, than a Barney Fife lookalike in a short-sleeve uniform shirt and black pants appeared in the doorway to the back room.

"Don't be shy. Have all you want."

I stuffed the last chunk of brownie in my mouth. "Fanks," I mumbled, stifling a cough as I sucked some crumbs down my windpipe.

"Dalton's mom keeps sending them in. I've already put on five pounds this month. Personally, I think she's just trying to butter me up so I won't ticket her next time she parks in the handicapped space in front of the county building." He poured a Dixie cup of water and handed it to me. "Want another brownie?"

I chugged the water. "I'm good, thanks. Probably shouldn't have had those before eating my lunch."

"I know how it is. You tell yourself you're just going to have one, and then ...three or four later, you're sick to your stomach and feeling like the Pillsbury Doughboy."

More like the Michelin Man, actually.

He shook my hand vigorously. "Police Chief Foster John."

I wondered if he meant John Foster, or if he actually had a first name for a last name and a last name for a first name. But then he would have paused between the Foster and the John, as in 'Police

Chief Foster … John.' He wasn't wearing a name tag, just a badge. It was one of those cases where you were afraid to use the person's name because you weren't sure if you had it right. He spun the chair around and sat, tossing both feet up on the desk. I had the feeling he spent a lot of time relaxing in that chair, playing solitaire on the computer. "Can I help you with something?"

"McNamee … Sam. I called about the slashed tire. Last night at Founder's Park, just after sunset. I discovered it when I returned from a walk."

He pulled his feet down and planted his pointy elbows on the desk. "You were out there by yourself at night? Pretty thing like you? Ma'am, this may be a small town, but you gotta be careful."

His tone was a tad patronizing, but then I'm sure he was used to lecturing people about safety and common sense. "I wasn't by myself. I had my dog with me." Which wasn't exactly the whole truth. First, I hadn't committed to keeping Bump. As far as I was concerned, if someone came along who wanted to give him a home, he was out the door. Just this morning he'd puked up a wad of nuclear yellow-green grass on the welcome mat in the kitchen. And I omitted telling Foster/John that I'd been with Clint. In a town this size, the rumor mill would have us procreating our first offspring before we ever actually got to the handholding stage. All right, I was getting ahead of myself on that account. But maybe I *had* begun to fantasize about Clint a little. Or a lot. I'd eventually pounded out six very steamy pages of a love scene long after midnight last night. It always helped to have some real life inspiration to make the mental wheels churn.

Foster/John's scraggly eyebrow tipped sideways, like he knew I wasn't telling him everything. He laced his fingers together. "All the same, ma'am, we have our share of miscreants in these parts. Best keep an eye out."

"That's so nice of you to be concerned about me." I refrained from jabbing him in the eyeball with my car keys and forced my most convincing smile. "Now, how do I fill out a report?"

He took a photocopied paper from the desk drawer, then started clicking away with his mouse.

I filled it out with as many details as I could recall, then pushed the paper across the desk at him. "I didn't write it in there, but you should probably know I was just talking to Dan at Dan's —"

Foster/John slapped the desk. "How's that old rat bastard doing, anyway? I haven't talked to him for a month." Leaning forward, he cupped a hand to his mouth. "My guess is he's hacked off because my wife got a new set of tires at the Wal-Mart in Fullbright."

"Right, um ... Anyway, Dan said he repaired another slashed tire a couple of days ago. From the car belonging to Bud Crawley. His brother, Jake Taylor, brought it in after the fire."

Foster/John nodded blankly. "That so? Excuse me for asking, but why are you telling me this?"

I reminded myself this was not the Chicago Police Department I was dealing with. Evidently, I'd have to spell it out for him. "Don't you think that's a little odd, that he'd repair the tire on his brother's car? A car that's probably going to be tied up in probate for months?"

He shrugged. "Maybe he needed to borrow it?"

"Sure, maybe."

"Do you know when the tire was slashed?"

"No, I —"

"Could've happened anytime, then, couldn't it?"

"Well, I suppose so, but —"

"Did Bud maybe ask him to get it fixed for him?"

"How would I know?"

"So nobody's talked to Jake about this?"

My head was spinning. If I had any confidence when I walked in the door five minutes ago, he'd managed to trample it beyond recovery. This guy could give the CIA interrogation team a run for their money. My voice, when I finally spoke, was surprisingly meek. "I was kind of hoping you would."

He gave my report a cursory glance before dropping it back in the same drawer he'd taken the blank form out of. "Thank you, Ms. McNamee. We'll call you if we find anything out."

Which, if I were to guess, would likely be never.

AFTER I HIKED THE three blocks back to the center of town where I'd parked my car, I gimped to a halt in front of the hardware store. Wearing strappy sandals had been a bad call and I now had the blisters to prove it. I considered taking my shoes off and going barefoot, but the sidewalk was probably as hot as the surface of Venus. The entire lower half of my T-shirt was soaked in perspiration, a sweat-free zone clearly delineated by the line of my double padded bra. Lovely. The flashing temperature on the digital sign by the bank read 99 degrees. Dad didn't have an air conditioner in his house, either. I texted Tara to tell her to make sure Bump was either in the shade or in the house.

"They say it's going to be like this all week."

I looked up from my phone to see Russ Armentrout leaning on a broom at the corner of his store next to the alley.

"Oh, hi." I walked closer. I had obviously been headed that way, so it wasn't like I could turn around all of a sudden. At any rate, this was my chance to learn more. "I'm surprised to see you at work today, considering ... you know, the fire and all."

A little snort leaked out from beneath his hand as he wiped at his mouth. "They're supposed to send a fire marshal out to investigate later today, so we're not allowed to touch anything until afterward. My brother-in-law had to loan me a set of clothes," — he spread his arms wide to display his tent-like attire — "and he's a good two sizes bigger than me."

"Do you think it was arson?"

His lip twitched in a sneer. "I know it was."

"How?"

Russ leaned out into the street, glancing at the doorway to Garber's as an elderly couple went into the grocery. He stepped further into the alley, motioning me to him. "Newt Tipton wants me to sell my store to him so he can level it and put in a gas station, but I'm not going to do it. No way. I started this store on my own dime thirty years ago and it'll close the day I die — which if he had his way would've been last night."

"Has he threatened you? Tried to force you to sell somehow? I mean, what makes you think he had anything to do with the fire at your house?"

He jutted his chin forward. "Some things you just know. He's a cutthroat and a penny pincher. 'Sides, he may not have threatened me outright, but he doesn't give up. Like a skeeter in my blinkin' ear. He prob'ly asks me if I'm ready to sell at least once a month."

Newt's persistence was far from being grounds for harassment, but clearly the two men didn't like each other. "So did you tell the sheriff any of that?"

He rolled his shoulders in a shrug. "What would I tell them? That the guy pesters me and gives me the creeps? Yeah, they'd jump right on that."

At least he realized he didn't have any evidence to prove Newt was involved.

"Was anything stolen?"

"From my house? A few things, but it's hard to say exactly what or how much, given the damage. Why?"

"Sounds like the other arsons, that's why." I didn't push for details. What he'd said so far was enough to let me know that this was the same person who'd started the other fires. The questions was, was Bud Crawley's death an accident, or intentional? The newspaper article hadn't said anything about how he died. At any rate, Russ

Armentrout seemed to think Newt was the culprit and I wasn't about to try to convince him otherwise. I figured it might be a good idea to smooth matters over regarding my dad in the meantime, though.

"Say, I heard my dad, Walt Schimmoller, gave you a hard time yesterday about the price of fishing worms."

"You're *his* daughter?"

I wasn't sure how to take that. "Um, yeah?"

He snorted again, then corralled a pile of pebbles at his feet with his broom. "Sorry to hear that. You seem like a nice young lady. Hard to believe you're related."

"Thanks ... I think. Anyway, I just wanted you to know that he's been under a lot of stress lately, getting ready to move and all. Medical problems, too. An intermittent cranial-rectal obstruction, or something like that." Another way of saying he had his head up his ass half the time. "I'm sure he didn't mean to be so ... so adamant about it. He's kind of stuck in a 1970s mindset. It still shocks him that a gallon of gas costs more than a dollar. He likes that your store is still family owned and operated and that he doesn't have to venture through a warehouse stacked twenty feet high with orange shelving just to find a box of nails."

"Humph, well, the customer's not always right, is all I can say."

I had to agree with him on that. During college, I'd worked part time at a fast food joint. What it had taught me was that some people just liked to complain. Unfortunately, my dad was one of 'those people'.

"Anyway," Russ went on, resting his broom against the wall, "that old geezer argues with me every other time he comes in here. The times he doesn't, it's 'cause he doesn't say anything at all. Just walks in, grabs what he needs, gives me the cash, and walks out. I consider that a good day."

Just then, Newt emerged from his store, carrying a stack of plastic Adirondack chairs in aqua, red, and lime green. He arranged them by color, then taped a sign to the seat of one that said 'Special, Today Only — $14.99'. When he was done, he waved smugly to Russ and me before going back inside.

"See what I mean?" Russ gripped the handle of his broom with both hands so hard I thought he was going to snap it.

I squinted at the chairs. "See what?"

"Mine are $17.99. That jerk has gone and undercut me." He kicked a little mound of dust and pebbles back onto the sidewalk he'd just cleaned. "I tell you, he'll do whatever he can to drive me out of business and out of this town for good. Even burn down my house."

Dad had nothing on this guy in the paranoia department. I was good at reading people and if there was one thing Newt Tipton was not, it was a criminal of any sort. I doubted he even had any unpaid parking tickets.

"Again, I'm sorry about your house," I said. "I hope they find whoever did it."

"They don't have to look far."

That went without saying. Wilton barely covered a square mile.

I hoofed it across the street and didn't look back until I was forced to wait at the next street crossing for a semi hauling market hogs. Russ had already set out a stack of plastic Adirondack chairs. He whipped out a felt marker and scribbled something on a cardboard sign, which he then set on the top chair: 'Only $13.99. Lowest prices every day.'

chapter 15

AFTER THE TRUCKLOAD OF squealing pigs rumbled past, leaving a noxious odor of manure and diesel fuel in its wake, I looked both ways and dashed across the street, heading toward Dawna's Beauty Studio a block down. It had to belong to Dylan Hawkins' ex-wife. After all, how many Dawna's could there be in this town?

Frilly yellow café curtains hung across the lower half of the front window, where a shelf displayed photos with celebrity-style haircuts. Most of the people who emerged from there, however, were women over sixty with blue-tinted bouffant hair. A small sign on the door listed their other services: tanning and nails. Time to dig around a little about Dylan Hawkins' side business and new acquisition. I grabbed the door handle.

A hand tapped me on the shoulder. Reflexively, I spun around, jerking a step to the side.

"Sorry. I called your name a block back." Selma offered a sheepish grin, her plum-colored lipstick highlighting the distortion of her mouth even more. "Guess you didn't hear me."

"Oh, yeah, I can be that way." I lifted both hands skyward. "You know, my body's here, but my mind's a million miles away."

"Me, too." She stood there blinking at me, like her tongue was stuck to the roof of her mouth and she couldn't get any more words out. I noticed her hair was a different shade today. Less red, more ... purple. It complemented her lipstick. You couldn't *not* notice it. Her style may have been questionable, but she had guts.

A few more seconds passed. Finally, I said, "So, my guess is you weren't trying to flag me down just to say 'hi', huh?"

She shifted her sparkly purple leather handbag from one shoulder to the other. It was big enough to fit an infant inside. Or a Cuisinart toaster. Perfect if you were into shoplifting. Or vying to be picked for *Let's Make a Deal*. I imagined Wayne Brady fanning a stack of hundred dollar bills, teasing, 'You can have door number two *or* ... I'll give you five hundred bucks for a Swiss army knife.'

"I was just, you know," Selma hedged, "on my way to work and realized I was a little early for my shift. Like about an hour. I start at different times on different days. Confuses the hell out of me. Anyway, I was wondering ... well, if you might like to go to lunch with me?" Her brow creased with worry, as if she were afraid I might say 'no'. Then she pointed down the street and started talking so fast I had a hard time processing it. "Ginny's Whistle Stop has real good smoked turkey sandwiches and raspberry iced tea. But there's all kinds of stuff, if'n you want something different. I kinda like the pulled pork myself, with a side of garlic mashed potatoes, but Dylan likes —"

She stopped abruptly, her brow clouding with anger. "Forget I mentioned him. Anyway, you wanna join me? If you're too busy, no problem. Maybe we can catch up some other time. I just figured with you being new in town and all that, it'd be nice to get to know people. But like I said, if —"

"Sounds good." I was afraid if I didn't interrupt her, she'd talk herself out of it, never mind me. From the sounds of it, she and Dylan had had a falling out, which made me wonder why. "Is that the place down by the train tracks? The one with the striped awning on the old railroad car gift shop out front?"

She flapped her lavender eyelids at me. "Yeah."

"C'mon then." I tilted my head in that direction.

Genuine surprise lit her face. She pinched the strap of her handbag between her thumb and forefinger. "You mean you will?"

"Sure, why wouldn't I?" The better question was why she had invited me.

"'Kay."

We started down the sidewalk, the air between us heavily silent. I could tell she wanted to tell me something, but maybe she'd relax a bit once we ordered some food.

Suddenly, Selma stopped dead in her tracks. Her eyes focused on something in the distance, then widened. Before I could ask her what was up, she hooked a hand around my elbow and flung me around so fast I felt like a kid on a merry-go-round. Inch long press-on nails dug into my flesh.

"I forgot," she said, pinching my spindly little bird-arms so hard with her talons I thought she might draw blood. "Too risky. I got food poisoning there once. Let's hit Suds and Grub, 'kay?"

"No, wait." Stopping, I peeled her hand away. "You saw something ... or someone, didn't you? That's why you don't want to go to Ginny's, isn't it?"

Without answering, she ducked into the recessed doorway of an antique shop. The metallic roar of engines rose and she cringed, pressing her face against the glass like she was trying to hide. Pretty futile, when you considered her hair color alone was like a beacon signal from the age of punk.

I looked down the street toward Ginny's Whistle Stop. Three motorcycles veered into the parking lot. I couldn't make out their faces from here, but based on the style of clothing and build I could tell who one of them was.

"Are you hiding from Dylan?" I said.

She pretended to study an assortment of doilies draped over an old roll-top desk. "Why on earth would you say that?"

"Oh, I don't know. Maybe because you jumped out of sight when he rode down the street? Besides, I'd never peg you for an antiquer."

"Just because I wouldn't buy it doesn't mean I don't appreciate a little finery." She braved a look around the window, her chest heaving with a visible breath of relief.

"Do they have salads?" I asked.

"Who?"

"The sub shop."

"I don't know. Why?"

"I need to cancel out the brownies I had for brunch. Come on. Let's go." I hooked my arm in hers and dragged her along until she was fully committed. Her platform heels clomped beside me for four blocks.

I opened the door to Suds and Grub for her. Little bells tied to the door with yarn tinkled, announcing our arrival. The sub shop's three customers turned to look at us. Or at me, rather, seeing as how I was the out-of-towner. They paid no attention to Selma, despite the fact that I was dressed in ordinary clothes and she was lit up like a Christmas tree. Maybe they were all jealous of my flaming red, frizzy hair? Okay, maybe not.

Instead of ignoring them all, I stared back. One was a Goth teenager: black clothes with more holes than a spider web, spiky black hair, and multiple piercings in his ... her ... his head. I wasn't sure if it was a guy or a girl.

The other two were a couple of farmers, decked out in denim jeans, *Duck Dynasty* T-shirts, and camouflage ball caps. Again with the ball caps. The hat industry must love this neck of the woods. While we ordered our food at the counter, I started to worry that one or both of them could be carrying a concealed weapon, so as soon as I had my salad and iced tea I picked the booth in the farthest corner and took the seat facing the rear wall. That way I wouldn't be tempted to stare back at them, because they would probably take it as a threat.

I stirred my salad with my fork. On the surface it had looked good: a layer of baby spinach, thinly sliced onions, three ripe cherry tomatoes, and a sprinkling of sunflower seeds. But underneath the appealing façade was a sea of pale, brown-at-the-edges iceberg lettuce. It was roughage, anyway. After a week of frozen pizzas, I needed a colon cleanse.

Selma peeled the top slice of bread off her sub and picked the onions out with her long, decorative nails. She sure got a lot of use out of those things. They could probably serve as weapons if she took a well-aimed swipe at an assailant's jugular. As she raised her sandwich to take a bite, the pile of bracelets on her wrist clacked. She noticed me eyeing them.

"Pretty, huh?"

I nodded. Not that I'd wear anything that gaudy, but they were sparkly. Just like Selma.

She smiled, twisting her wrist so the gems winked under the bright fluorescent lights. "They're real gemstones. 24 karat gold, too." Then her mouth plunged and she plopped her sandwich down before taking another bite. "I think he's been cheating on me."

'He' meaning Dylan Hawkins. Which came as no surprise, given what Ida had told me.

"Why do you think that?" I didn't want to go there, but I was stuck here for as long as it would take me to finish this rabbit food.

Her lips tightened. "I saw him talking to that tramp Jourdane last night at Bub's Place. And he wasn't just asking her the price per pound of ground beef, if you get my drift."

I wasn't thrilled she'd picked me for a confidante, so I tried to skirt the issue by changing topics. "Who's Bub?"

"How the Sam Hill should I know?" She stabbed her sandwich with a plastic knife and sawed at it with an abandon that would have impressed Sweeney Todd. "Sorry, I forget you're not from around here. I have no idea who the place is named after. Bill's the perpetrator."

"Perpetrator?" What the heck had this Bill done?

She took a bite and chewed while she waved her knife in the air. "You know, the guy who owns the place. Maybe someone named Bub had it before him?"

"Ohhh, you mean the proprietor."

Her lip twitched in a smirk. "Whatever. Anyway, you know how Dylan told me he was too busy to take me home from work? My car's been in the shop awhile. Dan's holding it for ransom. Says I owe him for past repairs and now the transmutation's shot —"

"I think you mean transmission."

Selma plunked her knife down. "Do you always interrupt when a person's speaking?"

Only when they commit two or more malapropisms in the span of thirty seconds. After fifteen years correcting minutia in thousands of manuscripts, it was impossible to turn off my internal editor. Hunting down homophones had been my personal mission. Heck, even now I couldn't write a text without checking my punctuation and capitalization before hitting send. I attacked my salad, wondering if I could finish it before she got to the point of exactly why she'd chosen me to confess to about her cheating boyfriend.

"Well, I decided it was a nice night for a walk," Selma continued, "so I called my girlfriend Amy Sue and asked her to meet me at Bub's for some drinks and a round of darts. You don't know this, but I was last month's dart tournament champion at Bub's. I beat out twenty-six contenders."

"Impressive." They were probably all drunk.

"You bet it was." Selma took a few more bites and stared doe-eyed out the big glass front window with a mixture of dread and excitement, like she was expecting Dylan to come walking down the street at any moment.

"So you suspect he and Jourdane are …?" I twirled my fork between my thumb and forefinger.

"I was getting to that," she said through a mouthful of Italian bread and salami. After she swallowed and took a swig of her soft drink, she went on. "That girl will steal anyone's man. Everyone in Wilton knows that. She ain't even old enough to be drinking, but Bill serves food there, so anyone can walk in the place, even though people really just go there to get smashed and lay bets on darts." She clamped a hand over her plum-colored mouth, then said between her fingers, "You did *not* just hear that from me."

"Hear what?" I winked, just so she'd get that I was joking.

To my relief she smiled. "Anyway, I got there early … Well, actually, *I* was on time. Amy Sue is *always* late, which you'd think I should know by now. Like I was saying, I walked in the back room where the bar is, thinking I'd just pull up a stool and nurse a beer while I waited for her to finish primping and show up, when I saw him." She sneered. "He was sitting at a stool on the end and that little floozy had her hand on his … let's just say *I* don't touch him there except in private. And he wasn't exactly pushing her away. In fact, he couldn't take his eyes off her butterfly tattoo. You know," — she dipped her chin — "the one on her left marimba."

Maraca! I screamed inside my head. Unless Jourdane carried around a pair of xylophones, that is. Or was flat-chested, like me, which she wasn't.

I sucked down some of my iced tea, regretful of the fact that I'd ordered a large because I was so thirsty. If I tried to finish it, my bladder would explode before she got to the end of her story.

"I figured I'd wait until things got really steamy between them and confront him about it. So I asked for the little table just on the other side of the doorway. That was when I saw Dylan's buddy Demetri come out of the little boys' room. I was behind him, so he didn't see me, but he went straight up to Dylan and sat next to him. Dylan whispered something in Jourdane's ear. She left, but I swear as she walked past me she was gloating. She made a point of tugging her shirt down, so her nineteen-year-old cleavage rode up a little higher out of her extra-extra small tank top."

"Hmmm, I can see why you suspect something's up between them." I chomped a few more forkfuls before asking her, "So if both you and Jourdane were at Bub's, who was minding the store?"

"Newt. He always works Friday nights. Saturdays, too."

"How late does he keep the place open?"

"Ten, but he's usually there for a bit longer, counting the money in the till. He hasn't had a Saturday night free since he bought the place."

So much for Russ's theory about Newton Tipton being an arsonist.

Holding a laminated weekly specials menu up to partially cover her face, Selma surveyed the sub shop, then leaned in so close I could've told from her breath what kind of toothpaste she used. "That's not all, though. See these bangles here?" She clicked a fingernail on one of her bracelets. "I think they're stolen."

My phone rang, I glanced at the number. It was Dad's landline. He didn't have a cell phone, so it would have been him, rather than Tara. He was probably calling to remind me about the boxes. I let it go to voicemail.

Maybe her story had been worth waiting for after all? The *Duck Dynasty* guys left. Goth teen had his ear plugs in and the music so loud I could hear his skull vibrating. The sandwich-maker had ducked into the restroom to replace the toilet paper.

"Why would you think the jewelry was stolen?" I asked.

"Because Demetri told him he had more 'merchandise' for him to sell. When Dylan asked where he got it from this time, Demetri told him not to ask."

"So you believe this Demetri receives stolen goods, and then

Dylan sells them online and they split the profits somehow?"

"I do. You wanna know why? I'll tell you why. I took these bracelets to a jeweler after Dylan gave them to me a month ago. I figured the guy could tell me if the stones were real and what they were worth. He told me they retailed for fifteen grand. Now, I figure even if someone was hard up for money and put them up for sale online, they still would've cost a pretty penny. And I find it kind of hard to believe Dylan would plop down that much cash for me, seeing as how everything else he'd given me up until then was a bunch of cheap shit. Not that I didn't like it, mind you. Pretty things don't have to cost much. I've gotten some really nice stuff at the dollar store. But it made me wonder where he got the money to buy them from." She took a sip of her drink. "Next time I saw Dylan, I asked him where he got the bracelets. He told *me* not to ask. At the time, I thought he just meant I shouldn't look a gift horse in the mouth. But now …"

"What are you going to do about it? I mean, you don't really have any proof, do you?"

"Naw. And even if I did, I'm not sure I could turn him in. I'm still kind of hoping things will work out for us. I like the big dope. He makes me feel kinda special." Sighing, she stirred her tea with her straw, creating a little whirlpool of ice cubes. "But there's more to what happened at Bub's that night. Demetri asked him when he was going to Cancun, so he could be sure to deliver 'the stuff'" — she made little air quotes with her fingers — "in time. Dylan told him the trip was off. That he'd decided to keep the Ducati because he'd rather be married to his hog than …" — she gulped in a breath before blurting the rest out — "than humping a dog." Her lip jutted out as tears burst forth.

"I don't quite follow you."

She yanked a tissue from her giant bag, blew her nose, and dabbed the streaks of mascara from her face. "Honey, you need to be a bit quicker on the upturn."

Uptake!

She patted my hand. "He meant he didn't want to sell his precious motorcycle to pay for the trip he'd promised me *and* that he was dumping me."

"Oh." I gave her hand a quick squeeze before pulling mine back into my lap. Our relationship was progressing a little faster than I preferred, but that didn't mean I didn't feel genuine sympathy for her. "I'm sorry." And I was. Sorry that she'd been hurt. But not sorry that he was dumping her. She was better off without him, although I couldn't tell her that right now. She'd have to figure that out for herself in time.

At work, I'd been cornered into lunch with workmates more times than I liked. I was deemed a good listener, simply because I didn't have many stories of my own to tell about relationships gone awry. To be honest, having people pour their hearts out to me made me uncomfortable. Yet they felt compelled to do it over and over again.

So, I did what I do best: I asked her to tell me more.

"Are you still going to see him?" I said.

After dumping two more packets of sugar in her tea, she shrugged. "I don't know. I thought we were a couple. But after he left Bub's, I followed him out into the parking lot. I was going to go papal on him, and then ..."

Postal, although *papal* did have some interesting connotations.

"Then I saw Jourdane get on the back of that Ducati with him and ... God, I miss that bike. I felt like a queen riding around on it. Maybe he was just giving her a ride home, huh?"

Sure, honey. Whatever you want to think.

A family of six walked in just then. Mennonites. Did I not mention them before? If there's a traffic jam in Wilton, you can bet there's a horse and buggy involved. The four children, arranged like stair steps behind their mother, peered at the menu silently: two little girls in dark smocks that came to below their knees and two boys in blue button-up shirts and black suspenders. Their father wore a black brimmed hat and their mother a starched white headpiece.

"Hey, thanks for listening," Selma said. "I'll make it up to you somehow. If I can do you any favors, you just ask, 'kay?"

I peeled my eyes away from the family to see that Selma had somehow managed to finish not only her sandwich, but her chips and drink while telling me her story. Apparently, she could talk, breathe, chew, and swallow all at the same time.

"Don't worry about it," I said. "You don't need to do any—"

My iced tea toppled as Selma ducked her head below the table. Liquid splashed across the tabletop and ice cubes skittered over the floor. I was about to ask if she'd dropped something when I saw Dylan and his two friends tear down Main Street on their bikes. When it was clear they had moved on, Selma emerged from her hiding place and nonchalantly teased her hair back into place.

"Actually, are you going to see Dylan any time soon?" I asked, grabbing a handful of paper napkins from the dispenser to mop up the mess.

"We have a date tonight." Biting her lip, she wound a lock of hair around her finger. "I was gonna cancel it, but I think we need to settle a few things. I haven't given up on Cancun. I bought the cutest little bikini to wear there — I'll have to show it to you." Her eyes lit up, then quickly clouded with worry. "I don't want to return it, but it wasn't cheap. I've never been out of the state, let alone the country. I even applied for my passport when he asked me to go. It got here yesterday."

"You'll work it out, I'm sure." I afforded her a sympathetic smile, then added with a tilt of my head, "You know, I may need that favor after all, Selma. I think there is something you can do for me. But you can't let anybody know about it, all right?"

Eyes wide, Selma grabbed both my hands. "Is it … *illegal?*" she whispered.

"Uh, no. Why?"

"It's just that, well, I've never been to jail. Can't say I ever wanna go, knowing what they do there to attractive, innocent people like me." She fanned her fingers over her chest, as if to proclaim her angelic status. "But ..." — she turned her head sideways and winked — "if you need some clandestine work, I'm your girl."

I blinked at her. She'd used 'clandestine' correctly.

She cocked her head proudly. "That means secret. You see, I read a lot. Romances, mostly, but it kinda gives me a big vocabulary."

I decided against suggesting she keep a dictionary at hand for big words. That was just too easy. But we finally had some common ground. "I like romances, too. Who's your favorite author?"

"Girl, I read anything and everything. But lately — and I have Amy Sue to thank for this — I've been reading books by S.A. Mack. They are, oh my God, *amazing*! I cried so hard when Felicity was in that accident. I thought she was gonna die, but then Alexander showed up at her hospital bed and I just *knew* everything was gonna be fine. I wish she'd hurry up and publish her next book."

"Yeah, me too." And she would if she hadn't had to make a pit stop in Wilton, Indiana to sift through forty-plus years of her father's life. I speared the last of my lettuce. "What if I told you I could get you some signed copies of her books?"

Her hand flew up to cover her gaping mouth. "Can you? I mean, how?"

"I was in publishing before I came here. I have connections."

"You'd do that for me?"

Pushing my salad bowl aside, I leaned across the table and said lowly, "If you get me what I need, I'll make sure you get advance reader copies of everything she ever publishes again. Deal?"

"Girl, I'd carry your child in my urethra for nine months free of charge for that."

Uterus, uterus. To her credit, at least she named a body part. She slid her hand forward. "It's a deal."

chapter 16

AFTER WALKING SELMA TO work and grabbing a few jumbo-sized boxes, I headed home. I was half a mile away when I spotted Dad standing in an overgrown pasture, up to his waist in thistle and burdock, his hands cupped to his mouth.

"What the —?" Swerving hard to the right, I pulled over. The ditch was deep and hadn't been mown in months, so I parked the car halfway out into the lane to avoid sinking a tire into an unseen muddy channel. I slammed the door, scrambled over a rusty woven farm fence, and waded into the forest of prickly things.

Locusts exploded beneath my feet, springing from their resting places to thwack me dead center in the chest before bouncing off. Razor edged blades of grass sliced at my shins as I pushed onward, calling to Dad. I picked my feet up high, but after about fifty yards that only tired me more, so I gave up, wishing I had a machete to blaze a trail before me. Or at least that I'd put on long pants and sneakers that morning, instead of shorts and sandals, despite the ninety-plus degree heat.

"Where are you?!" Dad's voice cracked with strain. "Come here! Come *here*!"

Who was he talking to? Had he gone suddenly and completely

senile? Then it dawned on me — he'd lost the dog.

I reached into my pocket, thinking I'd call Tara and find out what was going on. But the only thing I pulled out was a wad of lint and an empty gum wrapper. I'd left my phone in the car.

Ignoring the fact that my legs were now crisscrossed with cuts and welts were forming behind my knees and around my ankles, I started to run toward him. Without bug spray, I'd feel the insatiable itch of chigger bites soon. It was going to be oatmeal baths and double doses of Benadryl for me for the next few days.

Short mulberry bushes dotted the field, making it hard to see him as he meandered around. I was lucky I'd seen him from the road at all. Thankfully he was a lot slower than me. My foot sank in a cow patty just as I shifted my weight to my left leg. I slid forward, my legs separating. Painfully. I toppled sideways to avoid doing the splits, and crashed face first into a patch of blackberry brambles, barely closing my eyes in time.

I lay there, hidden by the tall brush, my hair tangled in thorny switches. Damn, I think I'd torn a groin muscle. Dad yelled again, but by now his words were garbled by sobs. I yanked my hair free of the thorns, leaving patches of it behind. Carefully, I rolled over onto my knees. I stood without too much trouble, but when I took my first step, I nearly screamed in pain.

Holy shhh—

"Sam?" Dad stood not a hundred feet from me, his face long with worry, panic in his eyes. "Did Tara send you? She was supposed to call you."

"No, I saw you as I was driving by." I limped a few steps toward him, but paused when the muscle inside my left thigh flared with pain. I sucked it up and took smaller steps, which helped. "Where's Bump? What happened?"

He spun partway around. There were rips in the sides of his button-up shirt and his jeans had grass stains on the knees. Sweat poured from his jawline, soaking the front of his shirt. His hair, thin though it was, hung in damp clumps. He kept rubbing his thighs and making little puling sounds, like he was going to break down at any moment. Back and forth he swung his head, scanning the field.

"It's okay, Dad. It's okay." I touched his arm and stepped closer so I could meet his gaze. I had to move to the right to get him to look at me. Tears were flooding his eyes. In the bold afternoon light, I could see every blue vein, wrinkle, and age spot on his weathered face. He gazed at me for a moment, almost looking disoriented, like he didn't know who I was or how he'd gotten there.

I kept my voice low and soothing. "Tell me what happened."

"Didn't you check your damn messages?"

"Sorry, I was kind of busy. Did Bump run out the door? Break his tie-out? Slip out of his collar?"

His lip trembled. "No."

"But he's gone. How?"

He rubbed at the corner of his eye, dashing away the tears that threatened to spill over. "He had to pee, Sam. I figured it wouldn't take more than a minute. So I just let him out the back door. He ... he did his business right away. But then ..." He clenched a fist and shook it. Anger replaced worry. "God damn that squirrel, anyway. Son of a bitch rodent! Taunting him like that. I hope he catches the idiot one day."

As much as I wanted to lecture him on keeping Bump on a leash since we didn't have a fence, I didn't. That wasn't what he needed right now. What he needed was for me and Tara to help him look for Bump.

Before I said anything, I thought for a moment. About what his reaction to Bump running off meant, about how he'd been playing with him that morning. He'd bonded with that dog, even though he wasn't likely to admit it. And I knew if I found Bump a home or moved away with him, Dad was going to be more than lost. It would be as good as ripping his heart out with my bare hands.

I couldn't do it.

The real catch was that with his unreliable memory, Dad wasn't capable of taking care of Bump himself. A heavy feeling settled in the pit of my stomach. I had a lot to mull over, but again, now wasn't the time.

"Did Tara go looking for him, too?" I asked.

Looking away, Dad cleared his throat. "Yeah, I think she said something about taking the bike down the lane."

"Which way did he go? Straight back toward the maples? East toward the fields? Toward Ida's house, maybe? If Tara went down the lane, that means he probably went in the direction of Ida's, right?"

"I don't know!" he snapped. And I was sure he didn't. Pressing the point was only going to agitate him more. He needed time to calm down, so he could be of some help. Zigzagging around in a burr- and thorn-infested overgrown meadow was not the most productive means of locating Bump. Tara would probably have more to tell me about which way he might have gone. First, I had to get Dad back to the car. Hopefully, Tara had her cell phone with her. But then why hadn't she called me?

I slipped an arm around his back to gently guide him toward the road. "This way, Dad. My car's just over there. We can drive up and down the road a bit to look for him. I'll go real slow, and we'll stop every once in a while and call for him. Okay?"

He dipped his head once in a faint nod. I jerked him along as I retraced my path, following the bent stems. After a hundred yards I gave up, having realized that I'd taken anything but a straight path from my car. I hadn't even noticed the little slope I'd gone down before, but on the way back up my strained muscle screamed at me to sit down. We could have made it back in half the time, but Dad was even slower. He had to stop partway up the short incline to catch his breath.

Once Dad retired from his postal route, he gave up all forms of voluntary physical activity, due to heel spurs. Now, most of his days were spent parked in front of the TV. If he was outside at all, he was tooling around on the riding mower. If it snowed, he stayed snowbound until it melted enough to drive down the lane. And yet he hadn't gained a pound in the ten years since. Making dinner would have required planning and effort, so he made do with cans of soup, jars of applesauce, and peanut butter sandwiches with a thin layer of butter to make them slide down easier.

Somehow we made it to my car — sweaty, bug-bitten, scratched, and breathless. I grabbed my phone and called Tara. It went to voicemail after five rings. Either she didn't have it with her, or she'd been unable to answer right away. I waited for the beep and left her a message to call me back as soon as she got it. Then I buckled up, checked both ways, and pulled onto the road.

We drove a mile down Hilltop Road, turned left at the next intersection, then made two more lefts, until we'd been around the country block, all the while both of us calling out the window for Bump. Anytime I went over twenty-five miles an hour, Dad would slap my thigh and holler at me to slow down, even as we went by open, freshly cut hayfields that spread hundreds of acres across the horizon. When we drove by woody patches, I slowed down even more. The trees in those places were so dense Bump could have been a hundred yards away and never heard us.

"There! Over there!" Dad yelled two feet from me. "That's him."

After I recovered from my coronary, I looked in the direction he was pointing. He was so adamant, that for a few brief moments I was hopeful. But when my eyes finally focused disappointment returned. I had to remind myself that Dad's vision was not what it used to be.

"Dad, that's a cow pasture, and that thing you think is Bump ... that's a calf." In his defense, it *was* a similar color and was lying down in the tall grass, but you'd think all the heifers standing around would've tipped him off. I stopped on the shoulder so he could get a better look.

"Huh," he said. "Well, keep driving. We're not going to find him parked here all day."

Another half an hour of cruising around at twenty miles per hour and two more false sightings was about all I could take for now. My voice raw, I turned into Ida's driveway to check my cell phone. I called Tara one more time. It went to voice mail again, which kind of worried me. I began driving up Ida's lane.

"What are you doing?" Dad blurted out. "He didn't go this way!"

"You don't know that!" I shot back. I shouldn't have snapped at him, but Dad had done exactly what I'd warned him not to by letting Bump off-leash.

Dad clamped his mouth shut and turned his head away, arms crossed. A few tense moments passed before he spoke again. "If the darn dog would just come when he's called, then —"

"Just stop it, okay? He did what dogs do. He chased a squirrel. In Bump's mind, that was dinner. And I'm sure to him some tasty squirrel meat would be worth ignoring you. By the time he realized he'd lost the squirrel, he probably had no idea where he was, seeing as how he's been with us for less than a week."

Dad didn't like being told he was wrong, but that was too bad. He needed to be put in his place and see things from the dog's perspective. Bump was a dog, warts and all. Dad shouldn't expect him to act like an adult human being.

"You know," I said, "this is just like that time when I was a little kid and we went to the mall. You were looking at snow blowers at Sears and I got bored and told you I wanted to look at toys. You didn't answer me, so I figured it was okay. I headed in the direction I thought the toy department was, but got disoriented and ended up three stores down in a ladies' lingerie section, crying my eyes out. When the security guard brought me to you, I was so relieved and happy to see you, because I was afraid by then you'd gone home and left me. But you berated me in front of him."

He scoffed. "You never ran off again."

"No, I didn't. And I'd never done it before that. But you know what I thought when that happened? I thought you were mad because I'd been found. Mad because I'd made you late. Mad that I embarrassed *you* in front of the security guard. I was seven. I didn't run off on purpose to complicate your life. I just wanted to look for a Furby, for crying out loud, because Christmas was coming up and I wanted one more than anything." I parked in front of Ida's garage and turned the car off. Swiveling to face him, I looked at him sternly, years of resentment spewing forth. "It was always about you. It still is. You blame the other person, or dog, for making your day difficult, without ever considering how things are for them. It's like you can't see outside your own little bubble."

I expected him to argue with me, to give his side of things, but he just sat there looking beaten and lost. Which almost made me feel guilty for piling on him. Almost. Mostly, it felt good to put it all out there. To give him a dose of his own medicine.

He took it remarkably well. After a while, he rubbed at his whiskers and nodded. "You're right. I can't sometimes. To tell you the truth, I don't know why I'm like that." A smirk tilted his thin lips. "Don't blame you for moving away. Who'd want to hang around a cranky ol' coot like me?"

"Darn straight." Good. We finally agreed on something. The air inside the car was stifling without the AC running, so I put the windows down. Ida peeked out her picture window and waved at us, her cordless phone pressed to her ear. She held up a finger to indicate she'd be out in a minute.

"Do you suppose he's scared," Dad said, "or running like crazy, happy to be free?"

"Both, probably. But more the latter."

"I bet he's chasing birds right now, stretching his legs. Nose to the air, smelling all the smells. Drinking out of puddles and ditches. Eating worms. A few mice. Maybe a baby bunny or two —"

"Okay, okay. I get the picture." I pushed my door open and swung my legs out. "Dumb dog probably doesn't miss us at all."

Dad lingered in his seat. His mouth drooped in a frown. "Yeah … but I miss him."

At that moment, he looked like I felt when I didn't find that blasted Furby under the Christmas tree. Never mind the fact that I had put it at the top of my Christmas list — bolded, starred, and underlined — then taped it to the refrigerator door two months ahead of time.

"Come inside, you two!" Ida hollered from her front door. In the middle of the porch, two old-fashioned green metal chairs flanked a small round table covered in a cloth printed with giant pink and red peonies. At the far end was a canary-yellow porch swing. Ida was carrying a tray with three glasses and a pitcher of lemonade. It made me wish she'd lived next to us when I was little. Not that she would have replaced my mother, but I would have had somewhere to go when I'd needed to get away from my dad. Oddly, Ida never seemed bothered by Dad's grouchiness. She treated him kindly no matter what. In my eyes, that woman was as much a saint as Mother Teresa.

I stopped before the porch steps. "I'm sorry, Ida. We can't stay. We're —"

"Bump ran away on me," Dad growled. Then, he quickly added in a mocking sing-song voice, "Guess I should've put his leash on. But anyway, he could be in Brown County by now."

"I know. Tara just called from your house. She had her cell phone on mute and misplaced it. Turns out it was in the bottom of her book bag." Ida pushed the door open wider with her hip and lifted the tray in offering. "Why don't you come inside? Might be worth your while. Besides, you both look like you could use a little refreshment about now. Bet your throats are parched. I heard you hollering a mile away, Walter Schimmoller."

Beside me, Dad scuffed a foot over the crumbly cement and muttered to me, "Do we *have* to? We need to keep searching."

"Walk home, if you want to. I need a drink." I marched up the steps and through the door. As I passed her, Ida smiled and tilted her head toward the kitchen. Inside, I heard something solid thunk against the wooden floor, followed by slurping and teeth grating on bone. I rushed to the kitchen.

Mismatched eyes gazed at me with contentment. There under the table was Bump, a soup bone braced between his paws. He thumped his bushy tail twice and went back to work gnawing on the bone.

I turned to Ida. "How long has he been here?"

"Ten minutes, maybe?" She reached under the table and scratched Bump's side. "He came romping through the front yard, carrying a dead squirrel. I had to lay a trail of raw hamburger up the front steps and into the house to lure him away. So much for the meatballs I was going to make for dinner. Then, soon as he was inside, I gave him that soup bone and went outside, shoveled up the squirrel, and dumped it in the trashcan. He's been so involved in that bone that he hasn't even paid attention to my two cats. Could be because Mr. Jeeves ran and hid under the bed when he saw the dog. And Tiger Lily, the toothless declawed one, she's perched on top of the cabinets, waiting for her nightmare to be over with."

"Thank you, Ida." I hugged her, I was so thankful, even though it wasn't something I normally did. Ida's quick thinking had averted one crisis, but I wondered how many more there'd be before —

Who was I kidding? This was going to happen *a lot*.

Ida wrapped Bump's soup bone in newspaper so I could take it home, then loaned me an old drapery sash cord to use as a leash for him.

I waved bye. "Thanks again. If there's anything I can do for you —"

"Forget about it. I'm certainly not keeping count."

Yeah, but I was. At this rate I'd soon owe her not only a few ginormous favors, but my firstborn *and* my eternal soul.

I loaded Bump into the backseat. Dad took one glance at him, smiled. "He got the squirrel, didn't he?"

"Yep, he did."

Nodding, he rumpled the fur on the top of Bump's skull. "Well, then … mission accomplished. I'm tired of those God damn thieves raiding my bird feeder."

chapter 17

I BEGGED OUT OF my walk with Clint that afternoon, explaining the day's events. He told me to bring Bump into the clinic in two days and he'd take the stitches out. After that I could follow him to the park and we'd take a walk. If everything looked good with Bump, we could schedule the neutering for next week.

Dad opened the bottle of steak sauce and dumped a lake of it onto his plate. "You're going to do what to him?"

"Neuter him," Tara said. She held a flattened hand to the side of her mouth and whispered to me, "Do I need to explain it to him?"

"I know what it means, pumpkin. I was raised on a farm." Dad jabbed a piece of steak and stuffed it in his mouth. "We castrated our own lambs. We'd flip 'em over and —"

Tara clamped her hands over her ears. "I didn't need to know that, Gramps."

"So you're okay with it?" I said. I'd considered just doing it and not telling him, but he would have figured it out eventually. The dog liked to lie on his back spread eagle. There was not enough fur down there to hide his private parts. Then again, Bump wasn't Dad's dog. I didn't have to ask him.

"Are you asking my permission?" he replied between bites.

Dang it. Here we go. "Not really. I was just hoping you wouldn't give me grief about it, because, well, guys can be kind of touchy about the subject sometimes."

"Wouldn't he be less likely to run away if you …?" He finished his mouthful and made a scissoring motion with two fingers

"Possibly. But it won't stop him from chasing squirrels."

Plunking his fork down, he glared at me. "What's that supposed to —?"

My phone rang. Normally I wouldn't answer it in the middle of a meal, but the interruption came at a convenient time. I slapped it to my ear and said in as perky a voice as I could, "Hello?"

"Hello, is this Samantha McNamee?" the voice on the other end said.

"It is. And Sam's fine."

"Hi, Sam. This is Janice Yoder, with Yoder & Yoder Realty. How are you today?"

Murderous, frazzled, and majorly stressed out. "Fine," I lied. Nobody *really* wants to know how you're doing. One of these days, though, some cashier was going to ask how I was and I was going to let loose like a cannon, dumping all my personal problems on them.

"Good," Janice said. "I just wanted to let you know that I have exactly what your father is looking for. There's a condo on the east side that unexpectedly opened up. The owner died from a brain aneurism while on a cruise for widowed seniors. The complex is for those fifty and over, no residents under eighteen, although visitors are allowed for defined periods. Very affordable. Frankly, his heirs have underpriced it, but maybe they're hoping for a quick sale. Fees are more than reasonable, too, well within your budget. I just had a look myself and the place is spacious *and* immaculate. Plus, there's a community center with a gym and a pool and they have an activities director who coordinates everything from European getaways to day trips to the Indianapolis Zoo. There's also a resident nurse and it's on the trolley route, which can take him to any appointments or shopping centers in Wilton or Fullbright. He wouldn't even need a car." Amazingly, she'd rattled this all off in one breath. She allowed a dramatic pause. "I was wondering if you and your father would like to have a look tomorrow morning?"

If Dad hadn't been sitting right there, I would have jumped up and run around the room, shouting for joy.

"Who is it?" Dad said.

I put my hand over the phone. "It's the realtor, Dad. She wants to show you a condo first thing tomorrow."

"Okay." He wiped the corners of his mouth with a paper towel. "What time and where?"

I narrowed my eyes at him. "You mean you *want* to see it?"

"Why not? Might be nice. B'sides, lawn's been growing like mad, what with all the rain. I'll be out on the tractor half the day. Sure would be nice not to have to do yard work ever again." He scraped his fork across his plate to corral the last of his mashed potatoes. "Oh, does it have a pool?"

"Uh, yeah. But you hate to swim."

"I know. Just thought it might be nice to read my newspaper next to the pool in the morning. I could work on my tan."

"Hello, Sam?" Janice said, her tone hopeful. "Would ten o'clock be good for you both?"

"Where is it?" I wrote down the address on the back of a grocery receipt. "Okay, meet you there at ten."

Dad grinned mischievously.

That was too easy.

I had the feeling there was a catch to this. I just couldn't figure out what.

AFTER DINNER, I WATCHED some *Dr. Who* with Tara and then stumbled off to bed. With dread, I opened my laptop and checked my inbox: one hundred and twenty e-mails. I skimmed through the senders' names and replied to the few I recognized. I'd had to contact my editor to tell her I had to push the deadline for my novel back another month due to an extended family emergency. She wasn't happy, but I was sure she had plenty of work to move up to my slot anyway, so it was more of a blow to me than her. It was, however, getting hard to dodge all the e-mails from my readers, asking when the next Felicity Lassiter novel was due out. I gave them the same reply, guilt gnawing at my conscience. I made a quick online check of my bank balance. If I wanted to keep enough in savings for a sizable deposit on a place in Florida, I needed to get that next book out or S. A. Mack was going to slip into obscurity and I'd have to get a job teaching English to immigrants at night school or correcting ad copy at a hole-in-the-wall weekly local newspaper.

A month ago, having so many loose ends hanging would have been enough to launch me into hyperdrive. I would have gone without sleep until they were all taken care of. Nowadays, all I wanted to do was crawl under a rock and hope everyone would forget who I was and leave me alone. Suddenly, running a cash register at the local burger joint was very appealing. All I'd have to do was be present and I could pull a paycheck. Writing books didn't quite work like that. Publish or perish.

For the first few nights after arriving in Wilton, I'd tried to stay up late, parked at my keyboard in the quiet hours after bedtime, but there wasn't enough coffee in the world to keep me awake. Sorting and packing was physically and mentally draining. Even when I could stay awake, my mind kept darting around like a honeybee in a field full of wildflowers. I tried getting up early, but that was even more hopeless. Before 10 a.m. my thoughts moved at the speed of a glacial retreat.

There was so much on my plate that I didn't know where to start. The usual panicky feeling had given way to inert helplessness. All I could do was take one day at a time. Except for me almost burning the house down and the dog wandering off, the three of us had survived without killing each other so far. We were making great progress going through Dad's things, but there was still a lot that needed to be sold, thrown out, or given away. I hadn't been up in the attic since the day I found the box with the letters in it. For now, the box was stowed safely in my wagon under a blanket. If I ever got up the courage, I'd read those letters, but right now dredging up old memories of a painful childhood wasn't on the agenda.

I just had to get through the next few weeks, get Dad settled, and get back to my plan. Easy as pie. Right? I mean, what could possibly go wrong?

Sitting on the edge of my bed, I pulled Dylan Hawkins' business card out of my purse. If he was dealing in stolen goods and setting fire to houses to cover his tracks, I wasn't so sure asking him for advice was a smart move. But, it *could* provide clues.

Maybe there was some other way to get information on Dylan Hawkins? I could only hope Selma would pull through for me. With luck, she could give me exactly what I needed. Until then, I didn't have anything to tell Sheriff Driscoll about. I certainly wasn't going to goad Police Chief Foster John into looking into anything. Talking to him was too much like being waterboarded.

First, though, I had to take Dad to see the condo. If he liked the place, there was a chance I could get my original plan back on track. Within the month, he'd have a new place to live with someone to look in on him regularly, public transportation, and a carefree life with copious social opportunities. Okay, nix on that last one. He'd discourage any friendly overtures from neighbors and build a no-talk force field around himself within two encounters. At any rate, Tara and I would be free to zoom off to Florida. Provided the cops didn't haul Dad off to jail first.

I just had to figure out what to do with the dog.

And then there was Clint.

But what was I to him? What was he to me, for that matter?

I should get realistic. We'd barely seen each other. Even then, we'd never had a formal date. If things between us didn't progress to something beyond dog-walking the next time we met, it was time I moved on.

I could still dream about him, though. He'd make a hell of a leading man. That was the great part about writing. I could do all sorts of naughty things in my head and no one would ever know. As long as no one figured out my secret identity.

"ARE YOU SURE YOU don't want to go with us?" I put the car in park and stared at the hundred-year-old Victorian farmhouse.

The place probably looked the same as it did when it was built. White paint had been scraped and reapplied numerous times. The front porch sprawled from left to right, partially concealed by overgrown yews. Heirloom rose bushes lined the front walkway. An old, freestanding, single car garage marked the end of the driveway and behind it were several barns, complete with all the usual farm smells and sounds. Humboldt County was so alien to where Tara grew up that I couldn't imagine her feeling at home here.

In the backseat, Tara flipped through some icons on her iPod and tapped the screen. She pulled her earbuds out. "Mom, you were always bugging me when we lived in Chicago to go out with friends, but everyone there was so" — she wrinkled her nose — "snooty. All they did was talk about their summer vacations in Fiji or Greece. What kind of car they were getting for their sixteenth birthday. Who slept with whom —"

"Kids or parents?" Dad asked, leaning sideways to look in the rearview mirror at her.

Looking up, she rolled her eyes. "TV shows, Gramps."

"You should monitor what she watches," he said sternly to me. "Kids see that kind of stuff, they think it's normal. Next thing you know they've got five babies from five different fathers, no job, no home, and a drug habit to boot."

"You need to stop watching so much Maury Povich, Dad."

"Who?"

"It's a talk show. Kind of like Jerry Springer."

"I don't know who that is, either." He nodded toward the middle-aged woman in khaki shorts descending the front steps. "Tom and Judy Mullins are good people. Tara will be fine here."

"I don't know." I unbuckled my seatbelt and put my hand on the door latch. "Maybe I should talk to them, you know, step inside the house to look around? They should probably know about Tara's panic attacks and how to handle them."

Tara groaned. "Mom, *please* don't. I'll be fine. Geesh!"

Dad put a hand on my arm. "Since when don't you trust my judgment of people? I delivered their mail for thirty-three years. You can tell a lot about people just by their mail: where they shop, what hobbies they have, if they pay their bills on time, if they have any legal issues... Besides, Tara's old enough to handle herself. She can always call you if she needs to go home."

This man sitting beside me was most certainly not my father. He was a clone. Possibly an android. Since when did he start making sense?

A girl about Tara's age tore out the front door and past her mom. She stopped ten feet from the car, bouncing up and down on the balls of her feet. She had on worn Chucks, Wrangler jeans a size too big for her, and a paisley peasant top that looked like it came from Goodwill.

"Hey, Shannon!" Tara shouted out her window. "Just a sec."

"Should I swing by on the way back from the condo?" I asked.

"How long will that take you?"

"Two hours at most, if you take into account the drive into town."

"Mom," she said in her usual churlish teenager voice, "stop worrying. I'll be all right."

I gripped the steering wheel. "Remember that birthday party you went to two years ago?"

"I was twelve, Mom."

"By the time I got there you had shut yourself in the hall closet and were hyperventilating so bad you almost passed out."

"Yeah, well, those clowns were just plain freaky. And Mikey Wishart was high on helium and trying to kiss me. Anyway, I'm older now. I need to do this."

Dad gave me a sideways glance. "In your day we used to kick the kids out the door and just tell 'em to be home by supper. Never knew where they were at." He nodded once. "They always came home."

In my day you didn't care where I was or *if* I came home, I wanted to say. But that was water under the bridge. I had to learn to let it go.

"Mom, please." Tara propped her chin on the top of my seat. "I'll call you if anything doesn't seem right, okay? Promise. Shannon and I are just going to listen to CDs and look at fashion blogs."

The thought of leaving her in a house with people I knew next to nothing about frightened the bejeebers out of me. What if they started playing Grand Theft Auto and the next thing you knew, I'd be bailing her out of juvie detention? What if her new friend introduced her to an online chat room and a stalker latched onto her? What if she had a panic attack and the Mullinses all freaked out? What if, what if, what if?

What if, in my hyper-protective mode, I smothered her to the point that it destroyed her confidence, and our relationship? In the fall, she'd be starting high school. I had to let her make her own way in the world.

Sighing, I conceded. "Pick you up at five."

She planted a kiss on my cheek and exploded out the door. She and Shannon raced up the porch steps, their dark ponytails swishing like banners behind them. With a friendly smile, Judy Mullins waved goodbye and followed them inside.

I sat there in the drive for a minute, just in case Tara rushed back out to tell me something.

"She'll be fine, Sam," Dad said. "She has her own cell phone, remember? Darn gadgets can do anything. They can even use 'em nowadays to locate missing persons, you know."

How reassuring.

"You know what cell phones remind me of?" he mused, tipping his head back. "Those communicators they used on *Star Trek*. The original series. Next thing you know we'll be beaming from place to place. Won't that be something? I think I'll pass, though. Nobody's going to scatter my molecules across space, no sir. Count me out. I mean, what if an electrical storm happened right in the middle of them sending you somewhere? Zap! Just like that."

Ah, back on familiar turf. Suddenly, I was very eager for him to see that condo.

THE CONDO WAS SO nice I almost wanted to buy it. Except that it wasn't in Florida. And I hadn't seen a resident under seventy since we drove past the gatehouse.

The units were arranged in neat rows, four to a building, two buildings per street. The streets were lined with tall lampposts and sidewalks shaded by rows of honey locusts.

Janice Yoder waited outside talking to the gardener who was

trimming the boxwoods, while Dad and I took one more walk-through of the place. It was furnished with all the essentials, including a sleep sofa to accommodate extra guests, since it was only two bedrooms. Not that Dad would ever have many guests besides Tara and me, but Janice had made it sound like a great selling point. The décor was tastefully conservative. And there was still room in the great room for Dad's recliner.

We stopped in the kitchen and turned around. Dad inspected inside a few cabinets and under the sink, then pressed his fingers on the stainless steel exterior of the refrigerator, leaving fingerprints. He pushed the lever on the icemaker. It made a clunking sound and ejected several cubes onto the floor before he removed his finger.

"Can't say I ever wished I had an icemaker. Do these things break easily? Suppose you'd have to get someone in to fix it."

It was the most negative thing he'd said about the place. Which meant the showing had gone remarkably well so far. "That's the nice thing about a condo, Dad. It's like renting an apartment, except you own it. Something breaks, they'll fix it."

"If you own it, why do you pay extra every month?"

We'd been over this before, but I explained it again. The man hadn't had a house payment in over a decade, relied on well water and over-the-air TV, and didn't own a cell phone. Yet he still complained about his monthly bills. Don't even talk to him about taxes.

"Do you still need time to look around," Janice said, popping her head in the door, "or are you ready to make a decision, Mr. Schimmoller?"

"Oh, I think I've made up my mind," he said.

Her heels clicking on the polished wood floor as she approached us, Janice looked at me in question. I shrugged. If I had to guess, I would have said he was going to pass based on the monthly fee. That and the neighbors being too close. And all the rules about keeping your garage door closed and what kinds of curtains or blinds you could or couldn't cover your windows with.

She laced her fingers together and smiled warmly. "What's the verdict, then? Is it a fit — or would you like me to show you some other places?"

"No," he said.

"No ... what?"

"I don't need to look anymore. This'll do."

Air whooshed from my lungs. The room whirled around me. I had to grab onto the kitchen counter to keep from keeling over in shock. "Dad, are you sure? What about the fees, all the restrictions? Or the fact that every unit looks exactly the same from the outside? What if you get confused and try to enter the wrong house?"

"Sam, I reckon the key won't fit. I'll figure it out."

"But ... are you sure this is what you want? You've had your own place for so long. This will be a big change."

"I know. And I didn't say it was ideal. But damn it, I'm tired of mowing and shoveling snow. This is northern Indiana, by God. It's non-stop. Long as the neighbors don't poke their noses in my business, I'll get by. B'sides, once you and Tara leave," — he lowered his eyes, his voice tinged with sadness — "it's gonna be just me. It's hard to admit, but I just can't do the things I used to do."

I felt sorry for him, then. Sorry because I understood. It had to be humbling to be so fiercely independent, only to realize one day that you needed help from others.

"You don't have to be alone, Dad," I told him.

Something in his face brightened. He looked up, nodded. "I suppose not."

Janice walked over to the dining table and opened her briefcase. "Good, we can go over the homeowner's agreement now, along with some other paperwork. I'll leave you copies of each. Then, you can take them home and talk about it before we do anything official." She shuffled the papers into order and placed the stack in the middle of the table, indicating for us to take a seat.

"I just have one question, actually," Dad said, as he pulled a chair out.

Janice sat down and crossed her legs, smiling confidently. "Certainly. Go ahead."

"Seeing as how there's no backyard here, if I tethered my dog out front, would that be a problem?"

Her smile fell. "Oh, you didn't say anything about a pet when you came to my office. You have a dog?"

"No," I said, "he doesn't."

Glaring at me, Dad thumped his fist on the table. "Look here. You keep saying how you're going to find that dog a home because you never wanted one and you're moving to Florida. Well, I'm taking him, then, because *he* needs someone to take care of *him*."

"Is the dog under twenty pounds?" Janice interjected, hoping to circumvent a family blow-out. "Because you are allowed one pet under twenty pounds, provided it has passed a Canine Good Citizen test, and all your shot records and license are on file. There is an additional fee, however, but if you can get a professional to verify it's a service dog —"

"Twenty pounds?!" Dad roared.

Here we go. I slid into a chair and put my head in my hands. No point in trying to stop the tsunami.

"I've killed rats in my garage bigger than that!" he raged. "And what's all this Canine Service mumbo jumbo, huh? Good Lord, does the dog have to have a college degree to pass muster around here? Whatever happened to just having a companion, a dog that will bark if someone comes to the door? How is a dust mop the size of a guinea pig going to deter a thief from breaking into my house? And you know something else? If I own the damn place, I should be able to have ten dogs if I want to."

I stood up and snatched the papers off the table, then grabbed

Dad's wrist to pull him toward the door. "Thanks for your time, Janice. I'll call if we have any other questions."

On the ride home, he didn't say a single word. Just stared at the road ahead, his jaw tight, his fingers splayed across his thinly muscled thighs. Every once in a while, he swallowed or cleared his throat, but even those meager sounds spoke volumes.

Questions leapt to my mind, but I swept them all aside. If I asked him how he was going to exercise Bump every day when his hips or knees ached, it would have earned me a death glare. He'd drawn a line in the sand. He wanted to keep the dog. And clearly, I didn't think he could handle owning a dog like Bump and living on his own. We were in the midst of a silent war.

If only I'd rescued a Shih Tzu or a Toy Poodle. Something he could carry under his arm, walk on a shoestring leash, or usher out the door to do its business without fear that it would see a twitchy, furry creature and flip the prey drive switch.

When we arrived home, he sat in the car for ten more minutes by himself before finally coming in the house. By then, I'd pottied Bump and let him in the kitchen. As soon as Dad sat down at the table and opened up his newspaper, Bump came and laid his head on Dad's lap. Without looking away from his newspaper, Dad reached down and scratched Bump between the ears.

It tore my heart out.

chapter 18

THE AIR IN THE attic was stifling, despite the small fan I'd brought up with me. All it did was push hot air around and propel dust up my nose. Sweat-drenched clothes clung to my skin. Who needed a sauna when you had an attic without ventilation?

I lifted an old quilt and the pile of magazines beneath it toppled to the floor, sending a mushroom cloud of dust into the cramped confines. A fit of sneezing gripped me. I blew my nose and stuffed the tissue in my pocket, just about jumping out of my gourd when my fingers brushed my phone and the ringer went off.

"Hey," Clint said, his voice cheerful. "I've got the afternoon free and I was wondering if you'd like to meet for our walk a little early today? Kind of hot out right now, but my weather radar app says there's a storm due to move in later, so I didn't want to miss the opportunity to see you."

See me, huh? My cynicism gene kicked in. "What if you have an emergency?"

"There's always that chance, but Melissa will be here until closing. She can call me in if I'm needed."

I stood up to head for the trap door, but just as I turned around, a rafter leapt out and smacked me in the forehead. All right, so it didn't move, but damn, that smarted. I dug my fingernails into my palm to keep from cussing as I rubbed at the lump forming beside my temple. The dull thudding pain passed after a few seconds, but my piss-factor ramped up tenfold. "So is it *me* you want to see ... or the dog?"

Long pause. "Um, about that. I was thinking —"

"Because I can just rent him out to you if that's what you want. Heck, I won't even charge you. Just come get him. Better yet, I can deliver him."

Longer pause. "Sam, is there something wrong? Are you ... are you mad at me? I mean, you canceled yesterday. I thought you were just having a bad day and needed to decompress. But if I've done —"

"No, no, you haven't done anything wrong." I plopped down on the little foot stool I'd been using as I sorted through boxes and manila folders. Here Clint was trying to get together with me and instead of jumping at the chance, I was PMSing on him. "I'm sorry. It's been more than a bad day. More like a bad week. I shouldn't take it out on you." I sniffed, trying to stave off another sneeze attack, but it hit me full force. I held the phone at arm's length until it passed.

"What are you doing?" he asked.

I blew my nose again. "Would you believe I'm sitting alone in an attic? The meat thermometer I found in a box of camping gear tells me it's a hundred and twenty degrees up here. And I think I'm allergic to dust mites."

"Sounds like you need a break. Meet me in thirty minutes at the park?"

"How about fifteen?" A little over-eager, maybe, but I needed some incentive to get out of the house.

"Twenty."

"Deal. See you then."

Hanging up the phone, I started toward the attic door, catching a glimpse of myself in an old dressing mirror as I stoop-walked by.

Lovely. My hair looked as though someone had beaten it with a wire whisk. Not to mention that my eyes were bloodshot and puffy and there were still welts all over my arms and legs. The fat lip didn't help. Why had I agreed to meet him so soon?

Ten minutes later, I had smoothed my hair into a ponytail, doffed a spiffy little running hat with a bill, shaved my legs (that was painful!), scrubbed the grime from my face (even more painful), changed into clean clothes, dabbed on some blush and eyeshadow, and gulped down two Claritin.

I did a quick inspection in the hall mirror before I went out to my car.

I still looked like hell. Perfect match for my mood.

"SAM!" CLINT JOGGED UP to me and gave me a good long look. "You look great."

Was this guy on drugs? I'd been trapped in a sweat box for the past three hours. Not to mention done a pretty good job of beating myself up lately.

"You, too." I wasn't lying. Actually, 'great' was an understatement. He had his shirt off and there was no sign of a farmer's tan. The man was ripped, from the firm slope of his shoulders, to his perfect pecs, all the way down to abs so defined I could count every single muscle. Clint Chastain could have beaten all the chicks out for *America's Next Top Model*. He would have looked awesome on the side of a bus. Or better yet, a forty-foot-high billboard. The imagined proportions of certain anatomy parts made my knees go weak.

A man as physically perfect as him had to know how good-looking he was. Which begged the question: why was he hanging out with me?

He looked past me, to my car. His smile dipped.

Right. He liked my dog. The dog I hadn't brought.

"Where's Bump?"

"Um, well, I checked the temperature before I left. It was ninety-two and climbing. Figured he was better off at home in the house, camped out in front of the fan with a bowl of ice cubes."

"Oh, sure. You're probably right about that. I was looking forward to seeing him, though." He flexed his open fingers, like he didn't know what to do without a leash in his hands. Then, as if he didn't want me to see the disappointment in his face, he trotted over to his SUV, wiped the sweat from his face and chest, and draped a dry shirt over his shoulders before rejoining me.

"You miss your old dog, don't you?" I said.

He rubbed at his neck, thinking. "Yeah, I guess."

"So why don't you get another dog?" *Please, please, please say you will! Because I happen to know a dog that needs a home.*

"It's too soon." He flicked at a deerfly that was buzzing his head. "And anyway, my schedule's so unpredictable. I'm not sure a puppy would fit in with my lifestyle at the moment."

Puppy? My hope sank. We were on a different track altogether. If I suggested an adult dog, a rescue, would he catch on that I was still hoping to find Bump a home? Should I just be blunt and ask? Would he think I was horrible for not wanting to keep the dog?

To heck with this. Time to get off the merry-go-round. Apparently, there was no blossoming relationship between us anyway, so I might as well put it out there. Not like he'd shown any interest in me. Besides, there was no sense keeping my whole life in limbo for a bunch of 'what ifs'. If he was meeting with me just because of the dog, then I might as well offer the dog to him. "I was wondering if ... maybe, you might consider —"

"Do you want to go out this Friday?" he blurted out.

I blinked at him. "What?"

"Out. You and me. A nice dinner, someplace special." He scuffed the toe of his running shoe over the asphalt. "Drinks later at my place, maybe?"

I had no words. As in, I couldn't have spoken then even if I'd remembered English. My mouth felt like someone had stuffed an entire jar of cotton balls in it.

Moving closer, his fingertips grazed the hairs on the top of my forearm, tracing their way upward until his hand curved over my shoulder to send a shiver down my spine. He lifted my chin, brushed the pad of his thumb across my lower lip, dragging it down to let my mouth open as he tilted his head and leaned in.

"Say yes," he breathed against my lips.

Yes, yes, a thousand times YES!

"Ummm." A buzz began at the base of my skull and wrapped around my head. My chest felt all tingly. My arms and hands started to go numb. Reminding myself to breathe, I gulped in a lungful of air so huge I coughed before I could get the words out. "Can I think about it?"

His hand fell away. I wanted to grab it and press it to my ... any part of me, really.

"I like you a lot, Clint," I said, searching his face, not sure how to put it, "but, I —"

"That's okay." He took a step back, dejection marring his perfect features. "You don't have to say anything else. I get it." He fished in his shorts pocket for his key. "If you change your mind — and I hope you will — you have my number. I'll, uh, see you around."

I grabbed his hand as he turned to go. "Wait! I was going to say 'yes'."

He gave me a quizzical look.

"It's just that ..." Releasing his hand, I let my gaze drop. This was hard, but it had to be said. "I had these plans all laid out. And they've all gone down the toilet. Right now, I'm not sure where I'll be or what

I'll be doing a month from now. I just want you to know that up front. Because I really do like you. In fact, I *more* than like you."

There, I'd said it. He could take it or leave it.

Silence stretched between us. I finally gathered the courage to look up. His eyes had brightened. I smiled to see it. He drifted closer again.

"I like you, too, Sam." Clint bent his head, his lips parting, sucking me in with his latent sexual charisma. He ran his tongue over his lips. Not like he was thirsty, or like his lips were dry. More like a teaser of the many, *many* things he could do with that tongue. He lowered his voice to a breathy whisper. "And I'd like to spend some time with you. Alone."

Alone. That could mean a lot of different things. Alone to talk. To get to know each other. Hold hands. Smooch. Get naked and —

He kissed me. As in hot, steamy, his chest pressed to mine, tongue swirling in my mouth, hands sliding down over my ass, get-to-know-me in a biblical kind of way. Right there. In public. Shirtless. Which meant technically he was more than half naked. Actually, I don't think anyone was watching, but still. What would he do when we were *really* alone?

I couldn't wait to find out.

"Friday?" I said, pulling back for a much needed breath.

A grin tilted his mouth. "You sure you want to wait that long?"

I know. I must have been crazy. But I had ...

He trailed fluttering kisses over my chin and neck.

... things to do and ...

His fingers slipped up under my tank top, finding the sensitive spot in the small of my back. The spot that was like an 'on' button.

... they weren't going to get done if ...

I turned to jelly as he pulled me against him. Which was a good thing, because my knees were about to give out. The ridge of his hip bone pressed into my belly. No, wait, that wasn't his hip. Oh, Lord ...

Suddenly, I wanted to throw him to the ground, rip his clothes off, and mount him right there. Like an animal. It had been so long since I —

Wait a minute. This was going a *little* too fast. What was I, sixteen?

Thank goodness a car pulled into the parking lot right then. Because I wasn't sure otherwise if my brain could have overridden my libido. Why did he have this effect on me? I tore myself away, wiping at my mouth like I could erase the last few minutes and regain self-control.

I fanned my fingertips over his chest, feeling the rampant thump-thump of his heart. "I'd love to go out sooner, but it's been crazy and I'm sooo far behind. So, Friday?" That would give me time to cool off, too. And buy some birth control. Just in case. Because I hadn't used any since before … since the night before Kyle died.

"Where would you like to go?" he asked.

"The movies?" An action picture, preferably. Lots of shooting, blowing things up. No chick flicks. Nothing with people writhing around under the sheets. Violence was fine. But onscreen sex? That would be like kerosene to our kindling. We needed to slow things down, get to know each other as friends before we —

"Stardust Drive-In?" he proposed. "There's a Sci Fi movie playing there this Friday that I'd like to see — if that's okay with you?"

The two of us in an enclosed vehicle, parked in the back row, in the dark? For all it mattered, the movie could have been a documentary on pottery. "Sounds great."

He smiled. "Good, I'll pick you up about eight?"

"Perfect." Even as he eased back from me, I could still feel the heat of his touch. "So, how about a walk now? Since I don't have to worry about tripping over the dog, I might even be able to manage a short jog. It might feel slow to you, but —"

His pocket buzzed. "Excuse me." He glanced at the display on his phone, then pushed a few buttons to check his texts. He rolled his eyes, releasing a forceful sigh. Any hint of a smile had vanished from his face. The muscles in his jaw tensed. "Looks like I'll have to take a raincheck on that."

"Tomorrow, maybe?" I figured he ran every day. I needed at least an hour a day to decompress after being cooped up in the house with my dad. "I'll bring Bump. If it's hot again, we can go later, or shorten the walk, maybe let him take a dip in the duck pond between laps?"

"I'm sorry. I can't. Full day." There was honest regret in his eyes, but also something else I couldn't quite peg. Discomfort? Annoyance? I didn't know him well enough yet to be able to tell, but there were times when he seemed a little, I don't know ... closed off?

"Emergency?" I said.

"Kind of."

What did that mean? A crazy cat lady with Munchhausen Syndrome?

He gave me a quick kiss on the forehead. "See you Friday."

"Can't wait," I said, trying hard not to sound as underwhelmed as I felt. Why hadn't he asked me to walk during the week? Two minutes ago he was all over me. Now, it was like he had some place better to be.

Or someone else to see.

His footsteps receded across the parking lot. I turned to wave goodbye, but stopped with my arm half raised. That wasn't just any car that had pulled into the parking lot. It was a patrol car.

And Sheriff Driscoll was walking straight for me.

"Ms. McNamee." Driscoll nodded as he approached, pinching the brim of his hat in a 'hello'. "I was wondering if I could get your father to come down to the station tomorrow morning for some questioning?"

Dang it. I'd been dreading this.

chapter 19

"DAD, I STILL THINK it would be a good idea if we consulted an attorney about this. I'm sure Ida would know someone locally who could handle this for you." I hit my blinker as we waited at the stoplight. A couple more miles and we'd be at the sheriff's station. There was still time to change his mind.

"What for?" he grumbled. "I don't have anything to hide. 'Sides, lawyers are nothing but paper shufflers. All one of them would do is buy time. And for what? I'd still end up giving a statement and be several thousand dollars poorer." He fiddled with the buttons on the radio until he found a station playing Frank Sinatra. Then he cranked the volume up so loud the bass speakers were booming.

I hit the magic mute button on the steering wheel. "Dad, we need to talk about this before you get there. I think you should consider it. It's not too late."

He snorted. "You make it sound like they're going to throw me straight into the clinker and I'll end up on death row. Sure would solve where I'm going to live, wouldn't it?"

"I don't think this is something you should joke about."

"Who's joking?"

"Newt saw you arguing with Russ before his house burned

down."

"Newton Tipton should mind his own business. And Russ Armentrout engages in price gouging. He thinks just because he has the only hardware store in town that he can charge whatever he wants."

"He can. And plenty of people shop there out of convenience, just like they shop at Garber's Groceries instead of going all the way to Fullbright. Why did you stop at the hardware store Saturday?"

"For bait. It was on the way. You know that."

"Why not buy it at the bait store by the lake?"

"I told you — because they charge too much. And if you want to know why I was arguing with Russ, it was because he raised his prices by thirty per cent — way more than inflation. He was so damn stubborn about it I bought our worms at the bait store, just out of principle."

The light turned and I pulled out onto the state highway. So far I wasn't winning this argument, but I wasn't about to let Dad implicate himself. "Did you pay more or less there than what Russ was charging?"

He turned his face away to stare at the soybean fields. "I don't remember."

Liar. "Will you at least consider —?"

"Nope. No point."

Once again, I was reminded of what frustrated me the most about him: his obstinacy. There were definitely times in life when you had to stick to your guns, but sometimes he was contrary on purpose. Normally, I'd drop it and just go do my own thing, but this wasn't about whether John Deere tractors were better than Allis Chalmers, or speculation about what baseball team was going to win the pennant. This was about getting convicted for something he didn't do all because he was too bullheaded to keep his cool.

I took my foot off the accelerator to let the car slow another five miles per hour before setting the cruise control. Anything to buy a little more time. "Look, Dad, I know you and I know there's no changing your mind once it's set, but this is important. You don't want to pay a lawyer now, but if you say something ..." I struggled for a diplomatic term.

He lifted a brow. "Stupid?"

"Well, yes. If you say something, anything, that they could misconstrue as motive, then they could have all the reason they need to lock you up and charge you, and then you'd *really* need a lawyer."

He slammed the heel of his fist against his thigh. "For crying out loud, Sam! Do you think I set any of those fires?"

"Of course not."

"And has anybody come forward saying they saw me at Bud Crawley's or Russ Armentrout's houses, or any of the other places on those nights?"

"No, but —"

"Then I don't have anything to worry about. And neither do you. So stop trying to control everyone, would you? For crying out loud, that must get exhausting, having to orchestrate everything around you."

Dad had a way of getting people's dander up. Especially mine. He was particularly contentious with authority figures, so dropping him off at a law enforcement building was like delivering a bear to a bee hive.

I took several deep breaths, reminding myself of the list Ida had given me of owners of red pickups, and that I now had reason to believe that Dylan Hawkins was somehow involved. But if I told Sheriff Driscoll anything that Ida had shared with me, it would get both her and Stacy at the BMV in trouble. And if I told him what Selma suspected, I'd be betraying her trust. I just couldn't do that. Not without proof. And anyway, if I did there was the chance that Selma could be charged with receiving stolen goods. For reasons I couldn't explain, I liked Selma. Beneath the rhinestone glam and the funky-colored hair was a good and honest soul. Maybe that was all that mattered.

I pulled into the sheriff's station parking lot. A headache threatened to crack my skull open. I pressed two fingers to my temple and rubbed.

"You didn't have to come, you know," Dad said, the implication being that he didn't want my help in this.

"I just don't want you to go to jail for something you didn't do, Dad."

He grasped the door handle, but didn't open it. "Me, either. But worrying never solved anything, did it?"

"I suppose not."

Dad patted the back of my hand. The veins on his hand, blue and bulging, pulsed beneath age-spotted skin. "C'mon. Let's get this over with. When we're done, I'll treat you to a burger and shake at Dino's Drive-In."

"You mean the root beer stand is still open?"

"Things don't ever change much in this town. That's what I like about it." With a quick tug, he straightened his blue and green checked button-up shirt. It looked like something Sam the Butcher from *The Brady Bunch* would wear. I remembered that shirt from twenty years ago. It still fit him the same.

Just as he nudged the door open, I grabbed his sleeve. "Promise me something?"

Mischief sparkled in the depths of his pupils. "Depends on what that something is."

"Promise me you'll be on your best behavior. That you won't yell at anyone or argue with them. And keep your opinion about Russ and Newt to yourself. If you sound —"

"Got it, got it." His eyes slid to my hand. "Now let go of me. You're putting a crease in my favorite shirt. I need to make a good impression."

We got out of the car and walked into the sprawling, red brick building that was noticeably devoid of windows. A deputy with flinty eyes who was about as wide around as he was tall manned the metal detection device at the entrance. Not that Dad or I were packing any heat or had any switchblades stashed in our socks, but the man stared at us in a way that made me think he was going to grab one of us by the collar, slam us against the wall, and start doing a strip search. I dumped my purse on the counter and watched him dig through all the pockets. Thankfully I hadn't loaded up yet on last-minute birth control. I'm sure he'd seen enough tampons in his day not to bat an eye. He stuck my purse on the other side, then gave Dad's wallet the same thorough inspection.

Dad approached the metal detector first. After he walked through, his arms stuck out to his sides, he pulled his front pockets inside out and patted his back ones. "Empty," he declared. Then he raised his chin, his mouth pressed into a goofy smile that was almost a challenge. "Do I need to go into a private room for a body cavity search?"

The deputy glowered at him. "Not today, sir. Please step aside." Turning to me, he motioned me through. "You next, ma'am."

I always hated being called that. 'Ma'am' sounded so *old*. Breath held, I rushed beneath the archway, eager to get through. Before I had a foot on the other side, a beeping alarm went off, nearly splitting my ear drums. I froze where I was, suddenly aware of the fact that I had to pee really, really bad.

"Any keys or change in your pockets, ma'am?" he droned.

Obviously, this happened on a regular basis. I pulled out my car keys and dumped them on the counter. Then I stepped through. This time with my eyes closed. Because, of course, keeping your eyes closed protects your ears. The alarm went off again.

Muttering, the deputy pointed to my other pocket.

I dug inside and fished out six quarters, two dimes, three pennies, and a paperclip. After that I went through without incident. However, it took five minutes for my heart rate to return to normal. And I had a bad case of cotton mouth. As soon as someone directed me to the ladies' room and I was able to empty my bladder, I felt better, but my armpits were soaked with nervous sweat. I avoided all eye contact, sure that I looked guilty of something, even though I wasn't the one being questioned. Dad, on the other hand, looked like he was just strolling into the BMV to renew his license.

During my junior year in high school, I got called to the principal's office. I was so nervous I had to stop in the restroom on the way and throw up, sure I'd done something wrong, even though I couldn't imagine what. Mr. Zook told me I was the regional champion for my essay on women inventors, sponsored by the Daughters of the American Revolution. I then passed out. I never could take much excitement.

We had to wait fifteen minutes in a narrow lobby lined with 'Most Wanted' posters. There was no TV, so the lack of noise only amplified every heel click and spoken word. I flicked through six magazines, glancing at photos of impossibly perfect patio gardens and smashing summer outfits for under a hundred dollars, unable to focus on any of the words in the captions.

"Mr. Schimmoller?"

A young female officer approached from the end of the hallway, clothed from head to ankle in her crisp khaki uniform. She looked like she'd just graduated from high school.

Dad laid aside the newspaper he'd been leafing through and stood, his knees cracking. I started to get up to go with him, but the deputy cut between us and placed a hand on Dad's lower back to guide him.

"Just Mr. Schimmoller, ma'am. You can wait here."

Reluctantly, I slumped back down in my seat and watched them go down the hall and turn the corner. The whole time I wanted to rush after them, ask how long it would be, whether they wanted a statement from me, if I should contact an attorney ... But I didn't do any of those things.

It took all the restraint I had to do nothing. So I studied the FBI posters of drug lords, bank robbers, and serial killers. Some of them looked like obvious criminals. You could see it in the squint of their eyes and harshly furrowed lines in their foreheads. Maybe it was all the tattoos, or the body piercings, bruises and scars, or that hazy, doped-up look. But one glance told that these were people who had lived life on the edge for many, many years.

Then there were others who looked just like regular people. Like my dad.

I watched the place where the hallway divided. Every time a shadow passed there, I leaned forward, my body coiled with tension. But time after time it was someone else. Amazing how slowly the hands on a clock move when you're watching them.

Forty-five torturous minutes later, Dad walked back down the hall, laughing and joking with the lady deputy. Sheriff Driscoll was a step behind them. He shook hands with Dad, nodded to me, then went on his way.

So they hadn't incarcerated Dad. That was a positive sign.

Dad walked by without a word. I jumped up and followed, my shoes squeaking on the freshly waxed floor. Together, we passed the deputy at the security checkpoint, his fingers dipping into a bag of Dorito's, a can of Diet Coke the only item on the counter beside him.

"Hang in there, kiddo." Dad punched him lightly on the arm. "Bound to be some excitement around here eventually."

I dashed out into the welcome light of day, not bothering to look back. If they were going to cuff him, I didn't want to be around. A few moments later, Dad clomped out through the doorway, whistling.

"Ready for Dino's?" he said.

I spun around. "Well? What did they ask you? What did you say?"

"Not much." He breezed past me and I hurried to catch up. For a man in his seventies, he was remarkably quick when he wanted to be. As I hit the unlock button on the car doors, he paused and looked over the top of the car at me. "Although I may have stirred the pot just a *tiny* bit." With a smirk, he ducked inside the car.

I got in. "What exactly does that mean?"

He inspected the bills in his wallet before stuffing it in his back pocket. "Did you ever wonder why I quit the lodge?"

"What does that have to do with any of this?"

"Bear with me." He snapped the visor down and inspected his dentures in the mirror. Satisfied there was nothing stuck in them, he turned to me. "You know how they have bingo night every week and how I went religiously?"

I started the car, backed out, and made my way to the exit. "Yes, I was starting to think you had a gambling problem."

"I was supporting a cause, Sam. They donate part of the proceeds to the county children's home. Anyway, it was rigged. I tried to call them on it, but they denied it. After that, I was ostracized. An outcast. Didn't matter that I'd been a member for thirty-five years. Chaired a dozen committees in my time. Organized raffles, collected donations, you name it."

I was pretty sure he hadn't done any of those things, but I kept my mouth shut, hoping he'd get to the point.

"Meanwhile," he went on, "there was some infighting going on between Armentrout and Tipton. I may have mentioned that to Driscoll. Hawkins and his gang wanted me to take sides, but I wouldn't. So I quit. Walked away, more or less. Figured I didn't owe anyone an explanation. It was worse than a bunch of teenage girls sitting around, flapping their jaws."

"So you think Newt wanted to deflect any suspicion from …?" My thoughts were racing faster than I could put them into words.

"Wait — Dylan Hawkins is a lodge member?"

"Yeah, he's the one who instituted Ladies' Night on Wednesdays. If that didn't cause a flap, I don't know what did."

"What goes on at Ladies' Night?"

"Drinking and carousing, that's what." He gave me the pirate evil-eye. "Why do you think Dylan and Dawna Hawkins got divorced, huh? Wasn't because he was spending too much time at the soup kitchen. Then again, maybe he was, you know, dipping his ladle into the pot a little too much."

"Is that a euphemism?"

"A what?"

The root beer stand came into view ahead. I turned on my blinker and slowed to make the turn. "Do you mean he was cheating on his wife?"

"Let's just say he deserved to lose his shirt in the divorce settlement."

So, Hawkins had recently lost a lot of money? All I needed was proof that he was involved in a theft ring. I still had the hand-held digital recorder that I used for dictating stories into. One little slip of admission and Dylan Hawkins would be on his way to the county jail. "What time does Ladies' Night start?"

"Seven o'clock. But stay away. Not the kind of crowd you need to get messed up with. They smoke like chimney stacks and drink like fish. 'Sides, the traffic's murder."

He reached for the pack of gum I kept in the change tray. The pads of his fingers were black.

"Did they fingerprint you, Dad?"

Turning his hands over, he glanced at the smudges. "Yup. Sure did. Asked a lot of questions about wrenches, too."

A cold shiver ran down my spine as I recalled the images I'd seen when Bump was asleep on Tara's bed: the fire, the wrench hurtling through the air, the man calling to me …

"Do you suppose Bud Crawley was killed with a wrench before the fire was set?" I asked.

"If he was, maybe Crawley knew something the killer didn't want anyone else to know?" He stuffed the stick of gum in his mouth, chewed it a few times, then slapped his thigh, snorting a laugh. "Geezy Pete, I gotta stop watching so much *NCIS*. That kind of stuff doesn't happen in places like Wilton."

There was one way to find out.

chapter 20

I PULLED INTO THE Grand Beaver Lodge parking lot at half past seven. There were a grand total of six cars and four motorcycles there, one of them Dylan Hawkins' precious Ducati. The only traffic I'd encountered was just as I passed the Humboldt Brethren Evangelical Sanctuary of Worship. It was prayer-meeting night there, which was obviously more popular than Ladies' Night at the lodge. Apparently, if you wanted to catch a man in this county, your odds were better mingling at church than hanging out at the cash bar of the local men's club.

A blast of disco music slammed into me as I opened the glass door. A dozen men swung their heads in my direction. I stiffened, wishing I'd worn my tatty old Levi's, rather than my junior-sized skinny jeans. After a quick visual survey, I made my way to the empty end of the bar. A lone older man nursing a mug of beer sat at the opposite end, his arms curved protectively around his drink as if he were afraid someone might steal it out from under his bulbous red nose.

I could count on one hand the number of times I'd been in a bar in my life. Two of those were to see bands that Kyle's friend Jeff was in. The third was so Tara could use the restroom when we were passing through a small town in northern Illinois after hours and the gas station was closed. The fourth ... Right, there wasn't a fourth.

None of those times did I ever buy alcohol. Public drinking was taboo. Private drinking showed self-restraint — at least that's how I reasoned my problem away.

Shoulders back, looking straight ahead, I sauntered across the dimly lit dance floor, where no one was dancing, and sat down at the bar. I ordered my old favorite: a mint mojito. A dozen round banquet tables were clustered against the walls. A mirrored disco globe spun in the middle of the ceiling to scatter flashes of light everywhere.

Shoot. Had I come here on the right night? I checked my phone. Yes, it was Wednesday. And the sign outside did say it was Ladies' Night. So, where were all the ladies? I rotated my upper body on my stool to gaze casually around the room.

Dylan Hawkins was beelining right for me.

Goose bumps broke out on my arms. My heart thumped so loudly in my chest I was sure someone standing next to me could have heard it over the music.

This whole thing was a bad idea. Downright stupid, in fact. I had to leave.

I thumbed through my texts. There weren't any new ones, but I made a surprised face and sighed in resignation, like I'd just gotten an important message begging me to rush home. I popped off my stool and started toward the exit.

A dart whizzed past my head, smacked against the wall not five feet from me, and clattered to the floor.

I stumbled backward, flailing a hand out to grasp the counter, but instead I whacked it against the seat of my stool and sent it toppling to the ground. My elbow hit the bar, breaking my fall. Daggers of pain shot down my arm.

"Sorry." Jake righted the stool, then snatched his dart up and handed it to Archer. He took one look at me and said to Archer, "I gotta go."

Archer shrugged as Jake scurried off. He held out the non-business end of the dart to me. "Want to play?"

I was about to say 'yes' when Dylan Hawkins slid into the space between us and shoved a stool up to the bar, blocking my retreat. "Imagine seeing you here, gorgeous."

The scent of cheap aftershave assaulted my nose so abruptly my eyes stung. Blinking, I leaned to the right, hoping that Archer hadn't given up his ground. But he'd already turned away. Apparently, once Dylan Hawkins staked a claim in this place, it was his. Dylan patted the barstool beside me.

Heck, I'd come this far. Might as well get what I came for. I sat down, my legs crossed away from him.

"I like you, Red. Liked you since I first saw you that day in the alley. Why don't you settle your cute little hind end right here and we can get to know each other?" He held up two fingers to the bartender and two shot glasses of bourbon instantly appeared. His hand slid over my thigh. I fought the urge to whack him with my purse. Besides, the digital recorder was in there. I didn't want to break it. Anyway, what was he going to do here right in front of everyone? Archer was barely fifteen feet away, flinging darts at the wall. "Forget my previous proposition — the one that involves Selma. What d'you say you and I blow this joint? Go somewhere more" — he leaned in uncomfortably close, his breath scalding in my ear — "private? Just the two of us."

"Don't you think you're getting ahead of yourself, Hawkins?" I pushed his hand from my thigh, then reached inside my purse. I dug around, pressing the button on the recorder before I pulled out a tube of chapstick. Strawberry Bliss. Must be Tara's. Tossing it back into the jumbled depths, I set my purse between us. "Maybe I didn't come here looking for a date."

"Date? Who said anything about a date? Don't you think if two people are attracted to each other, they oughtta just skip all that bullshit and get down to business? I can make a woman scream her head off and beg for more. Just ask Selma."

"I don't have to ask Selma to know that you have an inflated opinion of your bedroom prowess. I doubt that anything you do could impress me."

A growl rumbled low in his throat. Squinting at me, he downed his drink and gestured for another. Then a wicked smile lit his face. "Hallelujah, you're one of them!"

I ran my fingertip around the rim of the glass. "One of what?"

"Oh, what do they call them?" Pressing his hands together like he'd just had a prayer answered, he raised his eyes to the ceiling. "A dominatrix? You probably read that book, Fifty Sha—"

"No!" I shouted, so loudly that Archer paused with his arm drawn back, a dart pinched between his fingers. Embarrassed by my outburst, I looked down at my lap. My voice lowered, I said, "No, I am most certainly *not* a dominatrix. How did we get on this topic, anyway? I came here to ask you about your business — and I don't mean the bike repair shop, either."

He planted an elbow on the bar. "Got something you wanna sell?"

"Maybe." I swirled the contents of my shot glass. I was tempted to down it, but then I'd be too numb to control this conversation. "Let me ask you — does it matter where it came from?"

"It might." He scooped up a handful of peanuts and munched them down in between swigs of bourbon. One spark and the vapor from his breath could have burned a lumber warehouse to the ground. "Depends on what 'it' is and exactly where 'it' came from."

I swatted away the stench. "Maybe I don't want to say."

"Maybe I don't want to tell you … here. Too many people that could hear what they're not supposed to. Don't want anyone stealing my secrets, you know. What say we sneak away to the back room? There's a nice big, comfy couch there." Moving behind me, he nuzzled his chin on my shoulder. I flinched. Laughter rumbled in his throat. He slid a hairy arm around me, pressing his lips to my ear. "I'll tell you whatever you want then. For a price."

I didn't have to think hard to imagine what that price was. How far was I willing to go to learn if he was involved in the arsons? Clearly, he wasn't about to spill that easily.

The tip of his tongue flicked over my earlobe. I fought a shudder.

"Fine," I said, "but we leave the door open. And I don't pay anything without knowing the cost up front."

"I don't give information away for free, sweetheart." He smacked me on the rump so hard I let out a little yelp. "Call me when you wanna talk business. You got my number."

With that, he slid from his barstool, his biker boots hitting the floor with a *thump*, and swaggered away. I grabbed my purse and slung the strap over my shoulder. Scrambling after him, I tapped him on the arm as he shoved his way between two men clutching their red Solo cups. But he kept going. So I leapt forward, swung around in front of him, and shoved him back with the flat of my palm.

"Don't you walk away from me!" My voice boomed above the frenetic pulse of disco. Faces turned toward us with curious amusement. Jutting one hip out to the side, I placed a single finger in the middle of his beer gut and drew it teasingly downward. I hooked my finger over the top of his belt buckle and tugged once, twice, as I tipped my chin down and looked up at him pleadingly. "You promised you'd tell me *how* to do *it*, remember?"

Then I sidled in close. Turned my head to the side. "I need money, Dylan. I need it fast. Lots of it. I was hoping you could help."

Before I could spit out a protest, he hooked me by the elbow and hauled me down a dark paneled hallway, past the restrooms, and to an unmarked door.

chapter 21

NO ONE HAD FOLLOWED us. I was caught somewhere between the urge to scream for help and the desire to get what I came for.

It wasn't until Dylan slammed the door behind me and pinned me against it, that I decided screaming for help would be a better course of action. The only light in the small, musty room was the thin square of peachy-orange sunset peeking around a pull-down blind from a single high window. It was still daylight out, barely, and all I could make out from that scant illumination were the edges of a few unidentifiable objects.

I sucked in a breath, my stomach twisting like a snake as I readied myself to belt out a bloodcurdling scream. But Dylan clamped a rough hand over my mouth. Laughter rumbled from his belly as he pushed himself up against me, his mouth close to my ear. "You got fire in you, Red. Hot, hot fire. I like that. Kinda turns me on. But I swear, if you make any noise, I'm gonna shut you up *real* fast."

Even this far from the sound system, the music still made the door rattle in its frame. He gripped both sides of my face between his thumb and forefingers, so hard it felt like he could have snapped my jaw off at the hinges. Then he lightened his hold ever so slightly. "Got it?"

I nodded. His hand fell from my mouth, down over my throat, lingering there as he raised his other hand to just below it. In that moment, I decided that coming to this room was the dumbest thing I'd *ever* done.

Forget getting information from him. The new plan was to get out alive and stay the hell away from this lunatic. If I managed that, I'd do everything in my power to make sure I broke whatever hold he had on Selma. What on earth made women come back to a man like this once they realized what he was capable of?

Slowly, he drew his hands away, covered his face, and ... No. Was he *crying*?

He stumbled through the darkness and collapsed with a whoosh. By now, my eyes had adjusted. He was slumped over on a brown faux-suede couch with his head in his hands. I could barely hear his broken gasps above the music from ten feet away, but yes, he was definitely crying.

I groped behind me for the doorknob. Just as my fingers curled around the cool metal knob, his body shook with a sob. "I'm so sorry, Red," he blubbered. "You gotta believe me — I didn't mean to do that. You just ..." He looked up, his eyes rubbed red. "You make me crazy. I got it *bad* for you. Real bad. I ... I think I love you."

I kept my hand firm on the knob, ready to turn and flee. Yet, I wanted to see where this was going. Try to figure him out.

"Come on, Dylan. You don't even know me."

"I know enough." He sniffed. Swiped a big ape arm across his bearded orangutan face. "Don't you believe in love at first sight?"

Infatuation at first sight, maybe. But love at first sight? No.

Actually, that wasn't true. The first time I laid eyes on Kyle, I was smitten. The sight of him was a drug to me. The more I saw of him, the more I spoke to him, the more I was with him, the more of him I had to have. There was no cure. To me, the day he died was like a heroin addict's worst nightmare.

It had taken me this long to crawl out of that darkness, to find myself. But if I was going to fall in love again, it would be with someone like Clint Chastain. Certainly not Dylan Hawkins. The thought of even touching him made me ill.

"Won't you give me a chance, Red?" Tilting his head, he put on a pout that would have bested any five-year-old.

"My name's not Red. It's Sam. And if you aren't Wilton's best actor, I don't know who is."

He pointed at me, his pout morphing into a smirk. "See, you're a smart one. That's what I like about you." Leaning back, he tossed one arm on top of the couch, then smoothed his other hand over the fabric on the cushion beside him in invitation. "Why don't you come on over here so we can get to know each other a little better? Clear things up and all."

I stayed where I was. I turned my head to gaze at him at an angle. As long as I had an escape route, I felt emboldened. "I want to know how you sell merchandise online." I flipped the light switch on and pushed myself away from the door to stand above him. "And I need to know how to do it without the merchandise being traceable."

He blinked at the brightness. "Let's cut the bullcrap, okay? Are you asking me how to profit from stolen goods?"

"Only if you can tell me."

"If that isn't a setup, sweetheart, I don't know what is. You got a wire on you?"

I tugged my purse strap higher onto my shoulder. "No, I don't."

"Prove it. Take your clothes off, toss 'em out the window."

"Good try, Hawkins."

"All right, keep 'em on, then. For now." He glanced at the empty spot beside him. "But if you join me over here and let me … check you out, I'll know for sure."

This was going nowhere. Either he sold stolen goods, or he was just working the situation to get in my pants. Finding out wasn't worth the price.

"Forget I asked." I turned around, yanked the door open. And stopped dead.

A hulking giant with a shaved head stood before me with his arms crossed, blocking the door. He leaned his head in to look past me and lifted his broad chin in a nod.

"That's Virgil," Hawkins said behind me. "He's standing guard. Making sure no one interrupts us. Thanks, Virg."

Virgil uncrossed his arms and reached for the door. I lurched toward the opening, but too late. It banged shut in my face.

I spun around. "Look, forget about this. I obviously misunder—"

"Don't make me call Virgil back in here, Red. He gets a little worked up when gals make a fuss. Tends to knock 'em around a little until they learn to cooperate."

Holy crap! This was spiraling out of control way too fast. Panic twisted my innards. I scanned the room. No other door. One small casement window. There was no way I could squeeze out of that unless I suddenly became Flat Stanley. *Crap, crap, crap.*

Next to the couch was a floor lamp. On the other side, between the couch and the wall, a bookcase was crammed with old magazines: *Penthouse, Hustler, Playboy.* Did my dad know what went on back here when he belonged to the lodge? From the looks of the place, it didn't appear to get much legitimate use.

Think, Sam. Think.

Or if that fails — scream.

I let out the most primal scream I could conjure, squeezing the air out of my lungs until I emptied them. Then I flung myself around and started banging on the door. "Help!!! Somebody help me!"

I pounded until my fists hurt. Yelled until my voice cracked and my head tingled from lack of oxygen. I was the one crying now. Maybe he'd take pity on me and let me go?

A groping hand landed on my shoulder. Whirling around, I jerked my elbow back high, aiming for his face. But he deflected it with an upward thrust of his forearm, catching my wrist in his sweaty paw. My purse slipped from my shoulder and landed on the floor. Items spilled out, the tube of chapstick rolling past his feet. The voice recorder lay halfway out. I kicked it back in before he could see it.

Laughing, he wrung my arm as he yanked me across the room. He tossed me onto the couch, where I crumpled like a used rag, my face buried against the cushions.

"Make all the noise you want to, sweetheart. They used to use this room for band practice. The walls are soundproof." His steps thudded closer, paused. "Now why don't you tell me why you're asking about selling stuff? What could *you* possibly have that's stolen, huh?"

Slowly, I turned my head to look at him. "Not stolen, really. Just things of my dad's. He doesn't know I found them. For all I know, he doesn't even remember he has them. I need money for a down payment on a house and I don't want him to get suspicious about these ... items, if he ever figures out they're missing. Simple enough for you?"

It was the best I could come up with on the fly. Just when I thought he wasn't going to buy my story, he nodded.

"I might know someone who can help you," he said, "but I can't give you a name. And I sure as hell ain't gonna tell you how it's done. Got it?"

From the corner of my eye, I caught a glint of metal. I glanced at the bookcase, where I saw a small screwdriver peeking out from beneath an open magazine. I pushed myself up on my elbow, the ache in the twisted joint flaring. "No, it has to be you. I'm not trusting this to someone I don't know."

Pulling a hand down over the scruff on his neck, he came toward me. "All right, Red. But you pay up front."

"My money's out in the car. Let me get it." I swung my feet over the edge of the couch.

Planting his feet wide, his toes touching mine, he blocked me. "No. That's not the kind of payment I want." He reached out, took a strand of my hair in his hand and ran it between his thumb and forefinger all the way to the ends. "Don't act dumb, Red. If I want stupid, I'll call Selma. We can get this over with here, now. Or, we can do it some other time. But to be honest, I don't like waiting. It makes me crazy."

I scooted toward the bookcase, opening up space for him on the opposite side.

A lewd smile splayed his cheeks. His gaze drifted to the open magazine. My heartbeat stalled. The longer he stared at it, the more my panic resurfaced.

"I haven't had this much fun in a loooong time." His eyes glazed over. "Selma always does what I tell her to. That's gotten so damn boring." Finally, he tore his gaze away from the porn magazine and leaned over me, his hands braced to either side of my arms.

I had to time this right. Be patient. If I lashed out too soon, he'd just rip the screwdriver from my hand and use it against me.

I lowered my eyes. I couldn't look at him. "Go ahead and kiss me," I said, my voice a forced sultry. "Anywhere. But not on the lips."

Swooping in with all the grace of a mating ox, he planted his mouth on mine. Which I knew he would. Turning sideways, I lay down, my head toward the bookcase. He moved with me, planting his right knee on the edge of the couch as he brought his other leg up to straddle me. I reached back, feeling for the magazine. My finger tapped against the handle of the screwdriver and it slid further underneath. He didn't seem to notice, but I swirled my tongue around in his mouth, tasting beer, hoping to distract him. A moan rose up from his belly in response. Maybe it was because neither of us was talking now, but I could suddenly hear the disco music more clearly.

A metallic clink sounded and I realized he was fumbling with his belt. I wrapped my free hand around his neck, pulling him to me.

Stubbly hairs pricked my fingertips. He wedged his other knee between me and the back of the couch. He was over me now. I had one chance to get this right.

There it was. I closed my grasp around the screwdriver. Slowly, I drew my arm down, careful to keep my weapon out to the side. I opened my eyes, sized up his crotch, and —

"'Scuse me." Archer Malone clamped a hand on Dylan's shoulder and yanked him back. He swayed where he stood, looking like he was going to fall over at any second. "Where's the john? I'm going to be sick."

Dylan glared at him. The door stood wide open. Virgil wasn't there.

Eyes rolling up in his head, Archer covered his mouth with both hands. He turned to the side, bent down, and then ... puked beer and pretzels all over the couch, some of it landing on Dylan in mushy, undigested chunks.

"What the —?" Fire blazing in his eyes, Dylan shoved him back and shot to his feet. After he buckled his belt, he jabbed an angry finger at Archer. "Clean this up, you son of a bitch! And don't you ever come back in this room again, you hear me?"

Cussing up a storm, Dylan stomped out of the room.

Careful to watch where I stepped, I grabbed an old towel off the middle shelf of the bookcase and handed it to Archer.

An ear-to-ear grin plastered across his face, he wiped his mouth.

"For someone who's sick," I said, "you don't look all that bad."

He winked, then went to work scooping up his mess with the towel and dumping it into the trashcan by the door. "Finger down the throat. I used to use it when I had a big test and didn't want to go to school. Works like a charm."

"Who knew it would come in handy for saving a damsel in distress, too? Do you do that often?"

Archer grabbed a bottle of water from a small fridge on the floor, opened it, and took a few swigs. He looked as fresh and sober as he did the last two times I saw him. Come to think of it, he'd been drinking a ginger ale when he was throwing darts.

"Puking on demand?" Archer said. "Or saving chicks who walk into stupid situations?"

How was I supposed to respond to that? It *was* stupid of me. But I wasn't about to admit it. He didn't need to know why I was here.

"Thanks. I owe you one." I bumped his arm, grabbing my purse on my way out into the hallway. To the left was the reception hall. Disco had been replaced by foot-stomping country music. No way was I going back there. I plowed to the right, where a dim exit sign glowed above a metal door.

I shoved the release bar and pushed out into the half-light. Just past sunset, it took me a few moments to get my bearings. I'd come out on the backside of the building. I took a quick look around to make sure that Virgil or Dylan wasn't out there, hunting me down. All I saw were two middle-aged women in miniskirts and halter tops that belonged on teenagers, having a smoke beside a rusty, old, yellow Mustang with racing stripes.

The shortest route to my car was to the right. I took off that way and made it four strides before the heel on my left shoe broke. My knee buckled. My arms windmilled, catching nothing but air. I tumbled sideways as I tried to right myself, but my balance had been thrown. Luckily, a privet hedge broke my fall before the concrete block wall did.

Propped up by prickly branches, I rested there a moment, thankful I'd had the presence of mind to close my eyes before a twig could puncture my cornea. When I finally looked, I could see I was halfway into the bush, pretty much sitting in it. My first instinct was to shove a hand back toward the wall and push myself up, but I could already feel the sting of numerous scrapes.

So I just sat there, my weight resting against a network of

branches that might snap at any moment. And I cried.

Not just sniffles, or silent tears, but falling-to-pieces, losing-my-mind hysterical sobs. Because I was that darn mad at myself. And frustrated. Fed up. At my wit's end. Losing it.

"How stupid could you be?" I blubbered to myself.

A hand appeared out of nowhere to pull me free.

Archer's teeth gleamed in the moonlight. He plucked several leaves from the front of my shirt. "You are talking to yourself, right?"

Stepping back, I straightened my shirt and tucked it back in. "I should probably go home now." I kicked my shoes off and started across the parking lot. Gravel dug into the soles of my feet, slowing me.

He caught my elbow before I could get away from him. "I know it's none of my business, but why did you go back there with Dylan Hawkins? He doesn't exactly seem like your type."

He had me there. I couldn't think of a good lie. So I told him the truth. "Because I think he's dealing in stolen goods — and that he could have something to do with the arsons going on lately."

He narrowed his eyes. "What makes you think that?"

"I can't say. Just something a friend told me."

"So why go after Dylan Hawkins yourself?"

"Because they've already had my dad in for questioning, that's why!"

"Okay, I get it." His hold on my arm fell away. He slipped his hands in his pockets. "All the same, that wasn't a very bright move of you."

I bristled. "I can handle myself, thank you."

"I'm sure you thought you could, but it wasn't exactly going like you planned now, was it?"

Turning, I started to stomp away, despite the sharp rocks slicing at my feet.

Archer clamped a hand on my shoulder and spun me around.

"Please … stay away from him, okay?"

"Let me go!" I shrugged his hand off, but he came up beside me as I made my way to my car. "How do I know you're not involved in the fires somehow, huh? After all, it sure makes your department look good to be rushing around putting out fires on a regular basis now, doesn't it?"

"Really, Sam? You think I'm in cahoots with that piece of trash? You're grabbing at straws. Besides, I don't get why this matters so much to you. I just don't think you —"

"I said leave me alone." It was all too complicated to explain to someone who was practically a stranger. I brought my key out of my pocket and let my thumb hover over the panic button.

He held his hands up. "At least let me —"

I hit the button. The horn blared. *Beep, beep, beep! Beep, beep, beep!* Archer cringed. The two women leaning against the Mustang paused long enough to gawk at us, then abruptly went back to talking and puffing. The lot was still empty of people, otherwise. The only thing I had accomplished was to give myself a headache.

Backing away, Archer took one last look around. "Okay, okay. Have a safe drive home. But please, just heed my advice. He's bad news."

With that, he walked away. When he was far enough from me, I turned the panic alarm off.

The moment he disappeared into the building, I could've kicked myself. I was angry at myself, not at him. Pride made me do stupid things sometimes. Maybe I was more like Dad than I cared to admit?

No wonder we couldn't get along.

Just as I reached my car, my phone went off. I nearly jumped out of my skin. It was a text from Selma: *I got the info you need.*

There was hope yet.

I also had evidence. I pulled the recorder out of my purse and punched the 'play' button. Nothing happened. So I punched it again.

Nothing.
The batteries were dead.

chapter 22

ALL THAT FOR NOTHING. I may have prided myself on being book smart, but streetwise? Not by a long shot.

I jabbed my straw into my iced tea, sinking ice cubes with misplaced frustration. Midday traffic buzzed past Suds and Grub, where I sat waiting. If I saw Dylan Hawkins on the street now, I'd run for the hills. He'd have it out for me, that was for sure. Instead of digging up information that could have implicated him and exonerated my father, I'd painted a target on my forehead. And I couldn't turn him in to the police for assault or attempted rape when I'd willingly gone in the back room with him. It would be my word against his — and I'd lay bets that Hawkins had more friends in this town than the daughter of retired postman Walter Schimmoller did. No, chances were that would only make my situation worse once they let him go on lack of evidence.

"Ohhh, honey. You look like hell. What happened?"

Selma thrust her lower lip out in a pout of sympathy. Today's colors were shades of blue. Not many people could pull off periwinkle streaked hair, but somehow she did. The silvery blue lipstick, however, made her look like a body that had been pulled out of a frozen lake.

"Thanks," I said. "You look great, too."

Flouncing her three tiered mini-skirt, she slid into the booth on the opposite side of me. She unwrapped her meatball sub and took a couple bites before speaking with her mouth stuffed full. "I didn't mean it that way. It's just, well, you kinda look like you've had a rough day."

"Insomnia does that to a person." I'd lain in bed for hours, starting at every sound, paranoid that Hawkins was going to hunt me down. "What do you have for me?"

For a second, Selma batted her electric-blue eyelashes at me. "Oh. The information. Right." She took a slip of crumpled paper out of her purse and passed it to me. "Is this what you wanted? The vine number?"

"The, uh, V-I-N number, yes."

"What's it for again?"

Munching on the tasteless iceberg lettuce of my salad, I smoothed the paper out. Judging by the combination of letters and numbers, she'd done exactly what I asked of her. "It's the Vehicle Identification Number. Every vehicle has a unique one."

"I get it. Like a ..." She took a bite of her sandwich, chewed twice, and swallowed. "Shoot, what do they call them? Some kind of number."

"Serial number."

Selma flapped both hands at me. "No, not that." She clicked her fingernails on the table. I stared at her hands, stifling the urge to swat them and make her stop. Pausing, she cocked her head at me. "Go on. I'll think of it."

"Aaanyway. You got this from —?"

"Bin number!" She smacked her hands down on the table so loudly I almost swallowed my heart. "You know how you go to those big box stores for the furniture you put together yourself, and they say that this item is in bin number forty-five or whatever? Like that."

"Sure, sort of." I couldn't contradict her. She seemed so proud of herself. "Like I was saying, you got this off Dylan's new motorcycle, right? The Ducati?"

"The royal carriage, as I like to call it. That's the one."

"And he didn't see you write it down, did he?"

"Please, honey." She tore the tip off the paper cover of her straw, then puckered her lips and blew the paper at me. "Dylan's always out cold after a good, hard —"

"I don't need details."

"I was gonna say ride."

I plugged my ears with my fingers and started chanting '*la la la la*', but she reached across the table and pulled my hands away.

"On the bike, ding dong. We cruised down Eagle Ridge Road, went out by Hadleyville, around Fullbright, and got back just as the sun was setting. It was sooo romantic." Then she leaned in close and whispered, "But I did lubricate his shaft earlier, if you catch my —"

"Selma!"

"Sorry. You asked."

I hadn't, but I wasn't about to make a point of it. That might have encouraged her to tell me more.

Dipping her straw in her drink, she sucked the container halfway dry. "Dylan doesn't like to wait for sex. So we do it first. Says he can't concentrate on anything until he gets some."

Great. She told me more anyway. By now I was beyond shocked. Dylan Hawkins was a manipulator. Just thinking of last night made me angry. Not just at him, or at myself, but at Selma for falling for his flimsy lines. I impaled a cherry tomato with my fork. "Bet it makes him crazy."

"What does?"

"You know — waiting."

"Yeah, that's what he says." Then, tilting her head back, she narrowed her eyes as a thought struck her. "But how would you know?"

I shrugged. "All guys are the same, aren't they?"

That seemed to satisfy her. I wasn't about to tell her I'd flirted with Dylan in the desperate hope that he'd tell me something, anything. But as much as last night's events bothered me, it also disturbed me that Selma had an ongoing relationship with him. If I told her he'd come on to me, would she walk away from him for being a cheat — or would she accuse me of going after him? I didn't know her well enough yet to guess. More than what she'd think of me if she knew, my concern was for Selma. Knowing what Dylan was capable of, she could get hurt — emotionally and physically. Right now didn't seem like the best time to broach that subject, though.

Taking another slip of paper from my purse — the VIN number that Ida had given me that morning — I put it next to Selma's. I looked from one to the other, then looked again. "This can't be right. Are you sure you wrote it down correctly?"

"Dead sure, hon. I not only double checked it, I quadrant checked it."

"Quadrant?"

She held up her hand with her thumb closed across her palm. "That means four times."

Close enough. "Oh, right."

"Don't worry." She patted the back of my hand. "Stick around me long enough and you'll learn a lot of new words. Just last week I read six books. Two in one day. I've read some of that S. A. Mack's books three or four times. If she doesn't put something new out soon, I'm about to start writing my own fanfiction."

I cringed at the thought of the words she'd put into my characters' mouths.

After a few more bites of her meatball sandwich, she rattled the ice cubes in her cup to get my attention. "Anyway, you said you'd tell me why you wanted the number. So, what's it for?"

It was time to let Selma in on my little investigation. After all, I had promised her the truth. "There was a Ducati stolen from Bud Crawley's house the night of the fire. It seemed like too big of a coincidence that Dylan was riding one the next day. You don't see very many fancy Italian motorcycles in Humboldt County, after all." I laid Selma's paper on top of the other one and folded them up together. "I figured maybe Dylan had something to do with it — if not the fire itself, then maybe receiving or selling goods stolen from the crime scene. Unfortunately, the number you gave me doesn't match the one I have for Crawley's bike. In this case, Dylan Hawkins appears to be innocent."

Tipping her cup up, Selma emptied the last of her ice cubes into her mouth and crunched on them. She gazed out the front window for a while as she mulled my revelation over. Finally, she gathered her trash, dumped it in the receptacle, and plopped back down across from me, looking as serious as any chick with wild blue hair and nails could look. "You ever love someone, but not really *like* them?"

I knew exactly what she meant. "Sure. Why?"

"In some ways, being with Dylan makes me feel, I don't know, special. Like I'm the only girl in the world he wants to be with. But sometimes ..." Her nose and upper lip scrunched together. "Sometimes I think he's just saying what I want to hear. Or that he has ways of avoiding the truth. I know in here" — she thumped the flat of her palm above her left breast — "that he's not buying all these things he gives me in an honest way, but I can't really prove it, you know? So I tell myself I'm being ... Oh, what's the word? Para-something."

I hesitated. "Paranoid?"

"Yeah, paranoid. Like that night I saw Jourdane practically rubbing up against him. I mean, was it just her being the slut she is, or is he really a cheatin' scumbag? Lord knows that girl would screw old man Heffernan down at the home if she thought there was a free dinner in it for her. Until I catch Dylan lying, how do I know he is? Like, I know he is, but I don't *know*, you know?" She pointed one long, sharp claw at me. "Tell you what, though. If I catch that girl coming on to him again, I'm gonna cut her a new pie hole." Her fingernail slashed through the air.

Okay, so I wouldn't tell her what happened between Dylan and me. Maybe Jourdane or some other floozy would prove my point about him being a womanizer. Hopefully that would be sooner, rather than later. As 'peculiar' as Selma was, I didn't want anything bad to happen to her. She was the first girlfriend I'd had since … Well, ever, actually. There were some girls in high school who pretended to be my friends, but when I stopped sharing my algebra homework with them and told them to figure it out themselves, I suddenly found myself sitting alone at lunch.

"So, you gonna fess up?" A teasing grin spread across Selma's metallic lips. "I hear you got a date this weekend with the hottest piece of meat in town. Am I right, hmmm?"

How did she know? I hadn't said anything to anyone. Who was Clint blabbing to?

"Maybe." I didn't want to make a big deal out of it. The truth was, I wasn't even allowing myself to get my hopes up as to how it would go. If it didn't work out, that just opened the door for me to blow this one-stoplight crossroads the first chance I got.

Planting her elbows on the table and folding her arms, she leaned closer. "Honey, you are one lucky, lucky girl. If Dr. Clint asked me out, I'd drop Dylan like a hot potato. You should treat yourself to a new hairdo and manicure at Dawna's. Ask for my cousin Keisha and mention my name. She'll give you the family discount."

"Does she do your hair?" I needed to know if I should avoid her.

"No, I do my own. The coloring and styling, that is. I used to go to Dawna's for my nails just to catch up on the local gossip, but ever since Dylan and I started dating, I avoid it like the plague. Hey, if you want, you could come over to my place this week and I could, maybe" — she wiggled her fingers at my head, as if conjuring a rabbit from a magic hat — "do something with that … 'nest' of yours."

I covered my head with my hands defensively. "I like my hair."

"Sure, sweetie. I understand. Change is scary. If you ever do decide to try something new, at least you have a lot to work with. Will you let me take you shopping, though? I could use a girls' day out. Amy Sue has been blowing me off ever since she adopted some cocka-shih-poo puppy from the pound. I think she's just feeling sorry for herself since Foster John dumped her."

So Foster was the police chief's first name? One mystery solved. I still had a lot to figure out, though, and I wasn't about to give up on getting my dad off the hook. Maybe there *was* a way I could gather some information around this town after all? "You know, a haircut sounds like a good idea. I might get a few highlights, too."

Selma let out a squeal like a stuck pig. The teenage couple across from us turned and stared, but Selma didn't seem to notice. She clapped her hands together. "I can't wait to see what she does with your hair! Pick me up tomorrow at three from Garber's. That rat Dan still has my car. Dylan says he might be able to get me the money for it by the end of the week, which is a darn good thing. I'm getting man-calves from all the miles back and forth to work."

Selma lived three blocks from where she worked. Her commute was a little over a quarter mile. Somehow, though, I'd become her chauffeur. "Right. Three."

"'Kay, then. Three it is." She grabbed her oversized purse and swung around the table to plant a kiss on my cheek. "You're my new bestie."

Oh, goody. At least I had one ally in this town. If anyone bullied me, she could dazzle them into paralysis with her punk rocker hairdo, then chase them away with her nail file.

KEISHA TURNED OUT TO be a cousin of Selma's by marriage. Seeing as how she had an afro that would have put the Jackson 5 in their heyday to shame, I was a little leery of what she might do to my curly ginger locks. So I told her to just trim an inch off my hair, condition it, and give me French nails.

My hair was still wrapped in a towel, Keisha applying the white tips to my nails, when Dawna Hawkins bustled into the beauty parlor, a curvy brunette with a presence the size of Texas.

"Hi, Miss Dawna," Keisha said without looking up from my hand.

"Keisha," she replied in a husky, almost masculine voice. Dawna surveyed the parlor with smoky eyes, her gaze sliding from one booth to the next as all the girls busied themselves cleaning combs and rearranging gel products at their stations. "Miley, Jasmine, Lorraine ..."

They all glanced up in turn and muttered a 'Hello, Miss Dawna.'

A young blonde, barely twenty, froze as Dawna stopped in front of her. "G'morning, Miss Dawna," she said in a syrupy, Southern lilt.

"It's afternoon now, Tessa."

"Oh." Tessa glanced at the clock on the back wall. "I guess it is. Been here four hours already. Time sure flies when you're busy, don't it?"

Dawna cracked her gum several times. "Shampoo bottles are going to start flying, honey, if you don't go back into the store room, unpack them, and put them on the shelf like I told you to do yesterday."

Quivering like a mouse beneath the cat's shadow, Tessa scurried off. The atmosphere was tense, but as a couple of new regulars walked in for their appointments and the beauticians engaged with them, the atmosphere began to relax. While my nails dried, Keisha chatted about her five boys, aged two to eight. I'd long ago learned that the best way to keep your own life private was to ask other people a lot about theirs.

"Now lil' Dion, he looks like my momma's side of the family, but the rest, they all look just like their daddy." Keisha glanced at the clock, then motioned me back over to the barber's chair, where she unwrapped my hair, leaned me back, and began to rinse the hot oil from my hair. The water pressure from the sprayer was enough to flay the skin from my skull.

"I'll be." Dawna loomed above me sideways, blocking out the light from the overhead fluorescent lamp. She parted my wet roots with a sharp fingernail. "Is that your natural color?"

"Yes," I muttered, closing my eyes so she wouldn't see them roll. Having heard the question hundreds of times, I was used to it, but that still didn't make it any less annoying. Why was it if you had red hair, people assumed it was Reddish Gold 8B, Autumn Flame?

Just then, Keisha pulled all my hair into a ponytail, tugging at the roots so hard I felt my scalp lift from my skull. I fought tears as she twisted it tight, then wrung the water from it. As I viewed her from the side, I noticed her rounded belly and full breasts. I almost asked her how long until the baby was due, but she was a full-figured girl to begin with, so I decided to keep my mouth shut.

Dawna planted a fist on her rounded hip. "Do you know how many women come in here, asking for that color? And here you were born with it. Chicks must hate you, girlfriend."

Had anyone else said that, I might have been offended. But she had a way of saying it that made it come across as a compliment. I smiled back, not knowing what to say.

"You new in town?" she asked.

Before I could answer, Keisha chimed in. "She sure is. *And* she already has a date with Dr. Clint this weekend."

"Mmm, mmm, mmm!" Jasmine said from across the aisle.

I wilted with embarrassment as they bantered semi-vulgar comments around about Clint's physique. I was going to give Selma crap when I saw her tomorrow about spilling the beans. She must've texted Keisha right after we left the sub shop.

"How on earth did you catch him?" Lorraine laid a hand on my wrist briefly. "Half the female population of Wilton's been trying to get his attention since he moved back. We were all starting to think he was gay."

"What are you talking about, Lorraine?" Miley said, sweeping up a pile of silver hair. "You said you were *sure* he was. I was going to fix him up with my cousin Kenny."

Lorraine wedged herself between my chair and the mirror as Keisha tugged a comb through my tangled mess. "You come back here and let us know for sure, will you? Whole town's dying to know."

"Kenny will be so upset if he's not." Frowning, Miley propped her broom against the counter, then called another customer back to Dawna's booth. "Dr. Clint was so nice to him when he fixed up Kenny's Yorkie, Prince Henry, after the little guy ate an entire bag of M&M's."

I wasn't about to get in the middle of this debate, or return with information. But one thing I had figured out, if you wanted to learn a thing or two about people in this town, Dawna's Beauty Studio was the place to be. Blow dryer on low, Keisha separated the strands of my hair and then scrunched it so long ringlets started to form.

"Seeing as how he asked this fine lady out, Miley," Lorraine said above the whir of the blow dryer, "I'd say your cousin Kenny's chances are zero. Dr. Clint's one of them, what d'you call 'em? Metrosexuals. Fine to look at, but helpless with tools. No offense, honey." She winked at me. "Now me, I like a *real* man. The kind with dirt under his fingernails, who knows how to plumb a bathroom or fix a car. That's the kind of man who'll take care of you. A man like Archer Malone. Now him I'd marry."

All the women nodded and hummed, "Mmm-hmm."

Except Miley. Chin down, she tucked her broom next to her

station and hurried off to the backroom to join Tessa, her blonde braid swinging behind her.

"Now what'd you go and talk about marriage in front of her for, Lorraine?" Keisha snapped, her dark eyes flashing. "It ain't been six months since her and Jake broke off their engagement."

"Why are you blaming me?" Lorraine threw her hands up. "She's the one who cheated on him. I say her mourning period's long over. Archer Malone is fair game. So is Jake, for that matter — not that I'd ever date the likes of him." With a flip of her hand, she sashayed back to her booth.

Keisha clucked and leaned in close. "She's just jealous that Archer won't give her the time of day. Tell you what, though, if this town don't pass that levy, he'll be looking for a job somewhere else and ain't nobody around here gonna be talking about him anymore. Not much work in these parts. Only reason my William has a job is because Oren Rickman died when he drove his riding mower out onto the road into the path of an oncoming garbage truck. Came at a good time, though, if I can say so. Will finally got his job with the police department. We got insurance just in time. And little Billy was born."

"How many kids did you say you have?"

"Five."

This was my chance to figure out whether she did or did not have a bun in the oven. "That's a big family. Planning any more?"

"Lord, no. Got my tubes tied in May. The last three were an accident." She pressed a finger to her lips. "Don't tell them I said that, though. They don't know any different. I call them all 'my blessings'."

Glad I hadn't asked her due date. With one last fluff and twist, Keisha spun me around to look in the mirror. The conditioner had leant a sheen to my hair and tamed all the rebellious little wisps. She'd added just enough highlights to frame my face in strands of sun-touched gold. The nails were classy, yet subtle.

"Like what you see?" she asked.

"I do." I swung my head side to side. Honey-colored ringlets bounced freely. "Keisha, you have the magic touch."

As I counted out dollar bills at the register, something tugged at my memory. "You knew Oren Rickman?"

"Me? Not really. Will did, though. Why?"

"He had a dog, part Husky. Long story short, the dog's with me for now. I just wondered what would have made Rickman give the dog up?"

"I seem to recall he'd been sick off and on a couple years back. So maybe that had something to do with it? The dog was in some kind of training." One finger tapping her cheek, she looked up at the ceiling. "Bomb detection? No ... Attack dog? Naw, not that, either. Whatever it was, Oren wasn't able to follow through. Only reason I remember is 'cause Will kept complaining that they'd have money to hire another officer if they weren't financing the training for —" Her eyes widened. She slammed the register drawer shut. "A drug dog, that's what he was trying to make him into! You wouldn't believe the drug problem in Humboldt County. Bad as any big city."

Dawna, who'd been in the first booth dying the hair of an elderly lady, shot Keisha a warning glare.

"That's what they say, anyway." Keisha lowered her voice and mumbled, "You never know who's wrapped up in what around here."

There was more to that story, if I ever cared to delve into it. Maybe I hadn't uncovered any clues to direct suspicion away from Dad, but I did figure out that you could learn a lot in this town just by listening to the right people.

I tipped Keisha five bucks. Her face lit up like Christmas morning. She must have thanked me five times before I got out the door.

All the way home I kept trying to reconcile the fact that Oren Rickman had tried to make a misbehaving mutt into a drug-sniffing police dog.

As much as I liked that goofy dog, I couldn't imagine him doing anything remotely heroic.

chapter 23

CLINT AND I MET at Wilton's only fancy restaurant: Wild Bill's
Western Eatery. I'd driven myself there so I could drop Tara off at
Shannon's along the way for a sleepover. Plus, it helped avoid any in-
depth interrogation from Dad. I told him I was going to meet a friend
for pizza and possibly a movie, hoping that he assumed I meant
Selma. I'm not sure he bought it, but he didn't say much anyway.

When Clint walked up to me in the parking lot, he simply stared
for a while, a goofy grin on his face. He plucked a daisy from the
bouquet he held and tucked the stem behind my ear. "Your hair. It
looks … different."

I wasn't sure how to take that. So I waited.

He smiled, lifted a burnished curl and twisted it around his finger.
"I like it. I *really* like it."

"Thanks." I accepted the bouquet from him, its scent reminding
me of summers spent running barefoot through meadows as a little
girl. "I just had a trim." I didn't mention the honey-gold highlights
Keisha had artfully applied around my face or the twenty-dollar oil
treatment that helped tame my frizzy ends. He seemed to appreciate
the new outfit Selma helped me pick out, too, judging by the way he
kept sneaking glimpses at my behind. Amazingly, she had understood

that her style and mine were not the same and had me try on a lacey white baby doll top and a pair of faded slim-fitting jeans. They fit to a tee and transformed me from frumpy to *fab*-u-lous, as if she'd waved the magic wand of high fashion over me.

'You don't want to look too sexy or too formal,' she'd said. 'Just give him a hint of what you got underneath.'

The outfit turned out to be the perfect choice, as Wild Bill's wasn't actually all that fancy, but the place did have character. A carved oak bar from the nineteenth century, when Indiana was still on the western frontier, spanned the entrance of the waiting area. Behind it was a mirrored wall lined with shelves full of old liquor bottles. A pair of curving polished antelope horns was mounted above the doorway to the dining area — not that there'd even been any antelope in Indiana. There, in light almost too dim to read the menu in, we ate buffalo burgers and steak fries, washed down with birch beer. And we ate quickly, both of us more lost for words than usual.

This was a date. It was different. Awkward, exciting, but different.

When the bill was paid, we got in Clint's SUV and headed for the drive-in on the other side of Humboldt County.

The sunset that evening was a dozen shades ranging from purplish-red to pinkish-orange: violet and amethyst, vermillion and magenta, coral and blush. I marveled at the sky's brilliance, its vibrancy reflecting the joy I felt. I closed my eyes, capturing the image in my mind as the warm breeze rushing in from the open window caressed my face.

This was what it was to be alive again. To exist in the moment, grateful and honored. To breathe and savor every molecule of air. To feel the thump of my heart, strong and steady, inside my chest.

Clint slid his hand across the bench seat to tap my thigh. "What are you thinking?"

Wrapping my hand around his, I peeked at him through barely parted lids. God he was perfect. Not just his face or body, but *him*, inside and out. Everything about him, from the dimples in his cheeks to the way the ends of his hair curled in the humidity; from the toned lines of his lean, athletic legs, to the way he winked when he made a joke.

My cheeks bunched in a smile. "I'm thinking I've never dated a guy who drives an oversized SUV."

"Nice try, but I don't believe you."

"... That I never dated a guy who drives an SUV?"

"... That that's what was on your mind." He squeezed my hand and then let go, grabbing the steering wheel with both hands as he turned onto the highway. "Now, what were you *really* thinking?"

"I was thinking that even as crazy as life is right now, I couldn't be happier."

He slipped me a glance, then returned his eyes to the road ahead. "Really?"

"Yes, really. I'm here with you, Dad and I are ... well, we're getting along better, and Tara's more settled than she's been in years. Plus, she's making friends. Or *a* friend, at least. Funny thing is, if I could have lived my life out like I'd planned it, I wouldn't be here right now. I'd be gone already. All this, us, it wouldn't have hap-pened."

"And Florida? Do you still want to move there?"

"I don't know. Maybe someday. But actually, I haven't even thought about it in days." I pointed a finger at him. "That doesn't mean I won't complain when winter sets in. *If* I stay. I'm sure it's not as bad here as Chicago, but I still hate snow."

"So, you *are* staying?"

"You're here, aren't you?"

I expected him to look at me then. Or smile. Something. But he kept his gaze forward, the lines in his face serious. Dang it, I'd gone too far. *Think quick, Sam.* Ah! Change of subject.

"Your turn," I said. "What are you thinking?"

"Sam ..."

It was the pause that made my heart falter. I sensed a confession coming on — and not necessarily the good sort. A few years after Kyle died, I'd tried a dating service that one of my workmates recommended. Intellectually, I knew it was time to move on, but emotionally I couldn't commit. Of the twelve dates I'd gone on, four had extended to a few dates more. But with each guy they'd all ended the same. The speech had begun just like that: my name followed by a heavy pause.

Sam ... I don't see this going anywhere.

Sam ... I'd like to get to know you better, but I don't feel a connection.

Sam ... I don't think we're right for each other.

Sam ... I think we're better off just as friends.

The words didn't matter. They were all different ways of saying the same thing — that I wasn't *there*. In body, yes. In heart, no.

Yet all those times before, it had been more of a relief than a letdown. And now as I contemplated that this might be where Clint was going, it had an entirely different effect on me. It was as if someone had pulled the earth out from under me and I was hurtling into a bottomless hole.

"Can we talk about this later?" he said.

"Later when?"

"When we get there. It's just hard for me to concentrate on driving and be able to think of the right words. I'll tell you, I promise."

"Sure. Whenever you're ready."

The right words. Oh, shit. This was going to be worse than I thought. Was he in love with someone else? There was that mysterious text last Sunday when we met at the park — and he'd pretty much avoided me all week. Still, that was one isolated incident and I didn't have any proof that it was another woman who'd kept him away from me.

Was he moving out of town and hadn't been able to bring himself to tell me until now? Was it something personal? Cancer? Brain tumor? Bankruptcy? A secret past? Was he a recovering addict? Transsexual? Did he have a criminal record?

The next ten minutes were the longest of my life. I watched the verdant Indiana countryside roll by, washed in a glow of fading pink. The stalks of the corn were just beginning to tassel and the soybean fields were lush and green. In one field, they were gathering another cutting of hay. On the horizon, a cloud of dust, kicked up by the churn of the cutting blades, draped a veil of gold across the land.

We went up the exit ramp, then turned left and drove another mile, stopping at two interminably long stoplights before pulling into the pay line for the drive-in. The lady at the ticket booth was taking her sweet time collecting money and making change, chatting for several minutes with the people in the car just ahead of us.

Since Clint had made his announcement, I hadn't braved a look at him. I was afraid to. Afraid of what I might read in his face. Yet I was dying to look. To ask what had gone wrong. What I might have done differently.

"We can just go home, if you want," I finally said.

He whipped his head sideways. "Why would we do that?"

The car behind us honked. "Our turn," I urged.

Clint punched at the accelerator and the car lurched forward, then jerked to a halt as he stomped on the brake.

"Two of you tonight?" A woman with bright red lipstick leaned out from her glass booth. Matching red press-on nails tapped in a frenetic rhythm to the techno dance song playing from her iPod.

"Yes, two," Clint answered.

Cracking her gum, she stuck her claw out. "Twelve bucks, honeybunch."

I snatched my purse from the floor just as Clint leaned across me to open the glove compartment and take out his wallet. The pressure of his body sent sparks of electricity through mine.

"I got it," I said. "The drive-in was my idea."

I handed the woman a ten and two ones just as Clint raised his head, smashing it into my elbow.

"Ow!" we said in unison.

Clint rubbed his head. "You have pointy elbows."

"And you have a hard head." I clutched my elbow. He'd hit the nerve. I couldn't feel my fingers.

"I was going to pay," he said.

"But the movie was my idea."

"Yeah, but I asked you out."

The car behind us honked again.

"Sorry," I said. "I'm used to paying for everything. You can buy the popcorn, okay?"

Clint leaned halfway out the window. "Hold your horses! The movie doesn't start for fifteen minutes!" He sat down with a growl.

The SUV rolled forward. Clint drove cautiously, passing row after row. There were children everywhere. Toddlers in diapers. Tweens in tanks and cut-offs. A Frisbee whizzed past the windshield, smacking against the three-foot-high orange post on the outside of the exit/enter lane.

A lanky teenager raced in front of the car, throwing a palm up to stop us as he scooped the disc up. "Sorry, sorry." He trotted back across our path, then saluted in thanks.

A young mother in a bikini top and Daisy Dukes walked down the side of the lane, an infant on her hip. She couldn't have been more than eighteen, if that.

"I thought this movie was R-rated," I said. "I see more kids here than adults."

"You forget, Sam. This is Wilton. They don't have a mall to hang out at." He turned down the second-to-last lane, where the super-sized SUVs and passenger vans were parked. The last row had three RVs in it. "Besides, a lot of these families can't afford a babysitter. If parents want to go out, they just bring the whole family here. They get to spend some time together, and the kids stay out of trouble."

Around us, the shouts of children rang out, breaking above the laughter of adults as they gathered with friends. "I guess I can see that. It's just a very different world from Naperville, Illinois. I'd forgotten what it was like here. You get out into the world, big and fast-paced, and places like this seem so out of touch."

"Out of touch with what?" Clint backed into a space with a buffer of two empty spots to either side, then turned the engine off. Neither of us moved. We just gazed at each other in the dusky silver light, our seatbelts still fastened like we hadn't decided to stay. "I'm sure they don't feel like they're missing anything."

I looked away. There was more to this conversation than the social habits of upper middle-class suburbanites versus rural inhabitants. I cut to the chase. "What were you thinking earlier? I mean, you had me kind of worried — the way you said it. If this is it, if we're done, then let's just —"

"Oh, no. God, no." He unclipped his seatbelt and swiveled to face me. "I'm sorry. You were probably having heart failure. I'm not dumping you or anything. It's just ... I don't ..."

"Say it, Clint. Just say it. You don't want to commit. You don't feel a connection with me. We need some time apart. What is it?"

I undid my seatbelt, but kept my back pressed to the seat. I still wasn't sure how this night was going to end. Wasn't sure I was prepared for what he was trying to say.

He reached across the space between us, his fingertips alighting on my chin. He turned my face toward him. "I've just never felt the way I do now. Like I'm not in control. Like everything revolves around you — us."

"Does that scare you?"

"Yeah. In a good way, I suppose. Only because I've been there before. Happy, I mean. Deliriously happy. And when that gets taken from you, just the thought of letting yourself care about someone again is like … I don't know, like walking a tightrope across Niagara Falls." He paused, his eyes searching mine. "Before you showed up, things were, well, boring. Predictable, but a comfortable sort of existence, if that makes sense. Does it?"

"Perfect sense." I took his hand and squeezed it lightly, even as I shut my eyes to hold back joyful tears.

"I thought I was over the last heartache, but … Well, the funny thing is when I feel happy like this, that's when I remember it."

"Maybe the heartache is just a way of reminding us of all the good life has to offer?"

"Maybe."

The way he said it, though, made me think there was still some doubt in him, like he wasn't ready to completely let go. And yet, I understood.

My gaze drifted to the movie screen, the images nothing more than blurred patches of color to my unfocused eyes. Part of me wanted to dive in to this relationship head first. Another part of me wanted to back up, stick my big toe in to test the waters, wade into it gradually, make sure my biological urges weren't taking over my sensibilities. It was … confusing.

A long sigh made me look into Clint's face. He wore an apologetic smile. "I'm sorry, Sam. Here I am talking about my last relationship like losing her was the worst thing in the world and yet you lost your husband at a time when everything was going right for the two of you. I don't know how you managed." Placing both hands on my shoulders, he turned me around to face him and leaned closer, forcing me to look at him. "Tell me, how do you move on from something like that?"

"You don't. Not really. You just get through it. Moment by moment. Day by day."

A dam burst inside me then, releasing years of a pressure I hadn't known were there. Like someone had cranked open the fire hydrant.

He wrapped me in his arms as the tears escaped.

I wasn't crying for Kyle, though. I was falling apart because … because I remembered what it was like to love someone that much. And *that* was exactly how I was feeling about Clint now.

How do you tell someone that loving them frightens you? It was like the sensation you get when you're on a roller coaster and you crest the apex and the car starts to plunge. You're weightless, flying, and you have no control. You want to let go, lose yourself, scream like a fan-girl at a One Direction concert. But you also want to grip the lap bar with every ounce of your strength and return to solid ground before you hurl your last meal.

And then … Clint touched my cheek — and I forgot what I was scared of. His palm curved around my jawline, drawing downward. He traced the lines of my throat, the ridge of my collarbone, the slope of my shoulders. I leaned my forehead against his.

The previews on the screen flashed alternating light and shadow across his face. "When I'm with you," he breathed, "it's like I could jump to the moon, or grab a star out of the sky. Like I've got the world nestled in the palm of my —"

I pressed a finger to his lips, held it tightly there until the tension drained from his facial muscles. "Just shut up and kiss me."

For several moments, he did nothing but stare into my eyes, the connection between us crackling with energy. Then, in agonizing slowness, he tilted his head, brought his mouth to mine. I parted my lips, my breath a desperate invitation to his kiss. He slid his tongue between my teeth, flicked it against my tongue, darting, seeking, probing. The kiss lingered long, deepening and intensifying. Neither of us wanting to break it. Neither sure how far to let it go.

A group of young men walked within feet of my window, their raucous, beer-fueled laughter shattering the spell. I ripped myself away and laid the flat of my hand against my heaving chest. "Maybe we shouldn't —"

Clint dove toward me again, his mouth hard on mine, pinning the back of my head against the headrest. All I could think of for a second was that the gear shift digging into his hip couldn't have been comfortable. But somehow, the fact that we were in a public place where anyone could catch a glimpse of us made it exciting. Kind of like kissing under the bleachers at the school dance. You knew you weren't supposed to, but the fact that you could get caught heightened the thrill of it exponentially.

He lifted the hem of my shirt, his hand sliding beneath the top of my jeans and around the curve of my hip, his pinkie dipping below the lacy waistband of my underpants.

Oh. My. God.

I thought about hitting the lever to recline my seat back, but I wasn't sure with his height that he could actually climb over to my side. The backseat was free, though.

Wait. What happened to prudish, always-in-control Sam McNamee?

He laid soft, fluttering kisses across the bared skin above my bra. A tingle spread across my chest, filled my belly, and warmed the hidden places down below.

Oh, yeah. *That* Sam McNamee had never been groped by Clint Chastain. Groped? No, that wasn't quite the right word. Whatever it was, it felt spectacular. I didn't want it to stop. But here, now, it wasn't the right place or time. "Clint," I managed to push out, while suppressing a moan, "I don't think we should —"

"Maybe we *should* ..." — he tugged at the neckline of my shirt, stretching it down over my shoulder — "take this someplace more private?"

"Either that ..." — I kneaded at his thigh, massaging the lean muscles just below his hip — "or word will get around that the real show is back here. And then the management will kick us out."

"Or call the sheriff and charge us with lewd and lascivious

behavior. I hope that's a misdemeanor."

"Depends on the …" I stopped myself just in time. *Depends on the sex.* Here we were, going at it like a couple of horny teenagers. I sat up, drew back so my head rested against the window. "We're headed into new territory, aren't we?"

He removed his hand from my butt. I could still feel the imprint of it there. He grazed the keys with his fingers, where they were still stuck in the ignition. A pause opened up between us. Suddenly, I was aware of voices coming from around us, the bobbing beam of a flashlight, and the cloud of steam on the inside of the windows.

"Is my place okay?" he said, a devilish grin tugging at his mouth.

"Well, I'd say mine is out of the question. Tara's staying with a friend, but Dad's hearing seems to be just fine. Unless you want me to sneak you through the window? That could be kind of exciting, especially since my bedroom is on the second floor. We could be like Romeo and Juliet."

With a wink, he flipped the key in the ignition. "Into role playing, are you?" He clicked his seatbelt in.

"I'm open to it." I followed suit and buckled up. The movie had just started and here we were on our way out already. The yellow glow of the running lights marking the way, we rolled slowly past all the cars and trucks lining the rows. Many people were reclining in lawn chairs, coolers full of iced drinks beside them, speakers cranked high. On the screen, a giant starship floated across a star-strewn sky. "Clint, I … You know I can't stay the night, right?"

"I kind of assumed that." He stole a glance. "It's okay, Sam."

He lifted my hand to his lips and laid the softest of kisses upon my knuckles.

Tonight had already been a roller coaster of emotions. But I sure wasn't ready to get off the ride yet. As far as I was concerned, it could go on until I passed out from dizziness.

chapter 24

CLINT HELD THE DOOR open for me. Taking a step inside, I tried to let my eyes adjust to the darkness. The drapes were drawn, shutting out the silvery glow of nearby floodlights that might have made navigating to the couch — or better yet, the bedroom — a little easier.

The door clicked shut, throwing the room into total darkness. Clint twisted the deadbolt into place, but as I reached for the switch, which was just to the left of the front door, he caught my hand.

"We won't need that. Follow me." He guided me to the middle of the living room floor. "Here, sit down."

"Right here?" I squeaked. I couldn't see a thing. I half expected him to blindfold me, then tie me up. I wasn't sure we were ready for that. Maybe we needed to invent a safe word?

"I'll be right back."

I sensed him moving away. A few seconds later, a faint light emanated from the far end of the hallway. As commanded, I sat, sinking down onto a surprisingly deep-piled rug. I dug my fingers into the fibers. It felt like angora.

"It's alpaca." Clint put my daisies in a vase of water, then lit a pair of candles and placed them on the end tables next to the couch. A pale yellow glow lit the room. Soon, the scent of vanilla and sandalwood filled the air. "It's from Bolivia. Danielle brought it back when … I'm sorry. Forget I said that."

"You don't have to apologize, Clint. She was a part of your life. I don't expect you to never mention her."

"I know, but I just want tonight to be about us." And the way he looked at me made me feel like he really did.

"Shall we get started, then?" Stretching out on my side, I ran my hands over the plush fibers of the rug.

"Give me a minute." He rushed off before I could protest.

In the kitchen, glasses clinked. There was a soft pop of air as the refrigerator opened, and then another — louder — pop. A cork? My suspicions were confirmed when Clint came into the room bearing two tall-stemmed glasses of red wine and a still half-full bottle. After placing the bottle on the end table, he sank down beside me and handed me a glass.

I brought the rim to my nose, inhaling. "Cabernet Sauvignon?"

"I'm impressed. All I can tell is red, rosé, and white."

"Well, I spent a lot of time drinking by myself after …" I let my words trail away. I hadn't wanted to go there, but there it was.

"After Kyle died," he finished. "It's okay. You can talk about it."

"Yeah." I took a sip, looked once more into the depths of the glass, and took three big gulps. Warmth seeped into my veins, filling me with memories of a darker time. I'd avoided talking about it for too long. Until now, there hadn't been anyone I could share it with. Somehow, though, it felt safe to tell Clint these things. I gathered a breath, and let it out slowly. "I'm not proud of it. On weekends, I used to wait until Tara had fallen asleep. Then I would lock myself in the bathroom and tank up until I was numb. The night Tara woke up screaming with an earache and a fever and I was too sloshed to drive her to the emergency room was the night I realized it had to stop."

He put his hand over my glass. "Should I put it away?"

"It's okay. Really. I haven't been drunk since. Besides, you drove." After dinner, we'd ridden together in Clint's car to his place, so I wouldn't get lost. His house was in a growing subdivision and every other place looked the same, he'd told me.

"You know" — he tucked a strand of my hair behind my ear — "they say the opposite sex looks more attractive when you're drunk, but I don't think it's possible for you to look any more beautiful than you are now."

If there was even the tiniest crystal of ice in my grief-hardened heart, it melted right then.

Clint set his glass aside and bent toward me to brush his wine-moistened lips against mine.

I grew giddy with the taste of him.

He covered me in kisses. Shudders of delight zinged through my body. My fingers still pinching the stem of my wine glass, I tried to hold it steady, but a few drops spilled over the rim and onto the back of my hand. To the right of the couch sat an end table. I extended my arm, fixing to set the glass on its surface when Clint's hand curved around the inside of my thigh.

Oh Lord. Take me to heaven now, because I am ready to ascend.

I shut my eyes. His thumb stroked along the inseam of my jeans in small circles, inching gradually upward. Eddies of electricity shot from his fingertips. As his lips blazed a moist trail from my collarbone to the rise of my left breast, a shiver seized me. My body went limp in surrender.

The wine glass tumbled from my hand, spilling its crimson contents all over that gorgeous, tawny, soft-as-a-gosling's-down alpaca rug.

I shot up in horror. "Oh shit! I'm soooo sorry, Clint. Stay there. I'll clean it up."

"Sam, you don't —"

He reached for me as I brought my legs underneath me and turned my body toward the kitchen. But I forgot the end table was there and rammed my head square into it. It overturned, sending a stack of running magazines, the lit candles, the crystal vase filled with daisies and water, and the wine bottle onto the floor. The wine bottle was corked and landed softly on the rug.

That was where my luck ended. The lamp and the table came crashing down on it, shattering the bottle into a dozen shards. The tennis-ball-sized spot of wine was now a widening puddle. It might have been an even bigger puddle if the seat of my jeans weren't wicking half of it up.

Embarrassed, I froze. Suddenly, a roll of paper towels didn't seem like it would do the job.

My lip quivered. I fought back tears. Moments ago, everything was perfect. Now I'd ruined Clint's imported rug and made a complete fool of myself.

I stared at him as he bent low on hands and knees, puffing little bursts of air at the bottom corner of the couch. "Clint? What are you doing?"

He grabbed a pillow and started beating at the couch as wisps of smoke curled upward. "Just putting the flames out."

That was when I lost it.

I folded forward, forehead on knees. A blubbering heap of humiliation. I gulped in air between sobs, smoke overlain with vanilla and sandalwood stinging at my nostrils. At least it smelled good.

He rubbed my back. "Sam, don't worry about it. I was thinking about getting rid of the rug anyway. The only reason I kept it was, well, because it had cost her a stinking fortune."

"But it was so ... pretty and ... clean." The sobs rolled through me. I'd wanted so badly for this night to go well.

"Well, I could have let you put the glass down before I started seducing you."

With a sniff, I turned my head and peeked at him through a tangled mess of curls. "And you could have put the candles on the mantel."

"You're right. I could have." He cupped my ear, his thumb brushing the fleshiness of my lobe. He brought his face close to mine, the warmth of his breath curling inside my ear. "But I couldn't help myself. You're so …" — his lips nibbled at my jawline as I lifted my head — "incredibly…" — then moved to my throat — "perfect."

"So you're saying …" I felt my body falling gently backward, supported by his arm, until I lay beneath him. All the while, he never stopped kissing me, the tip of his tongue darting in and out teasingly. If this was foreplay, my mind was going to explode with euphoria when we got to the serious stuff. "You're saying you can't control yourself?"

"Around you? Not a chance." His mouth paused at the hollow of my collarbone. He hooked a thumb beneath the button of my jeans and popped it. "Do you want me to stop?"

I answered him with a dreamy smile as I slid my shirt upward and over my head.

chapter 25

I ROLLED THE WINDOWS all the way down and drove slowly, the speedometer barely topping thirty miles per hour on the straight-aways. For once, I was in no hurry. It was like I had all the time in the world, like there was nothing more perfect than this moment, this one single night, this simple life I had so unwittingly fallen into. I wanted to relive every second of the last few hours, over and over, wanted to savor the feelings that were welling up inside my chest, filling me with boundless energy and foolish hope.

And yet, I couldn't wait to find out what tomorrow would bring.

An orchestra of crickets strummed their ballad from surrounding fields. Above, stars glittered like diamond chips in a sky of coal dust. In the east, the moon hung big and bright above a sleeping earth. The corn stood seven feet tall, its thick stalks arranged in orderly rows, their emerald leaves whispering in the barest of breezes.

Hadn't I only just arrived in Wilton? The rain was so heavy that my car had hydroplaned more than once. I'd almost fallen asleep at the wheel, too. Hitting Bump had quite possibly saved both my life and Tara's.

What if, instead of lying in that ditch, Bump had run off into the woods, gone forever? I would never have met Clint. My dad would have been moved out of the house by the end of the month. And I'd be in Florida by then, still a dateless widow, no friends, no life.

The Harmony Road curve loomed ahead. I slowed down. I still couldn't go down this road without being hyper-vigilant. As if every time I traversed its length was a battle I would never stop waging.

The tree was still there, solid as ever. A smoothed irregular area, weathered gray over the past decade, marked the spot where Kyle's car had gouged the furrowed bark of the ancient oak. Its trunk was as big around as a pair of Sumo wrestlers. His compact car had buckled against its unyielding mass like an origami bird impacting with a cement block. In the nearby woods, the twelve-point buck that he'd swerved to avoid had collapsed, bleeding from internal injuries. He hadn't succeeded in sparing the animal. The great beast had slammed into his right front quarter panel. The collision had been just enough to send his car hurtling in the other direction, across the road, into the tree.

Kyle had died first. Instantly. The deer didn't expire until the second deputy arrived on the scene and euthanized him with his pistol.

Tara had survived relatively unscathed — physically, at least. She was too young to understand what had happened or remember the rescue workers plying back the door with the jaws of life to free her, but she was never quite the same after that.

My world collapsed that night. I hadn't wanted to go on living. But because of Tara, I found the courage every day to get up and go on. Maybe it wasn't courage so much at first as duty. I went on because I had to. Tara meant everything to me. Everything. My heart had hurt so bad some days it was unbearable. But instead of finding a shoulder to cry on, I had steeled myself to the world, closed myself off, buried myself in work I hated. As if clawing for success could somehow fill the emptiness inside me. But the loss was always there under the surface, tugging me downward.

How many times had I asked myself if he'd still be alive had I not been so adamant about winning the argument? If I'd only listened to his concerns, offered compromise, or gone after him …

I could turn it in my mind a thousand ways every day until the end of eternity. The truth was, I'd never know.

It wasn't grief I'd been running from all these years. It was guilt.

And it had taken a rangy mutt to teach me the power of forgiveness. To offer hope. A new beginning. Redemption.

My car rolled to a stop at the corner of Harmony Road and Hilltop. I sat with my knee locked and my foot firmly on the brake. In the distance, the twin beams of headlights were approaching the intersection at a rapid speed. The car was a ways off, but I opted to wait for it to pass while I mulled things over.

Since coming to Wilton, I felt … I wasn't sure. Lighter, maybe? Younger? Close, but that wasn't quite it.

The oncoming car neared. I kept my eyes on the headlights, cautious. The car sped by, a loud pulse of bass music rumbling its frame. Two teenagers hooted along to the music, if it could be called that, from the front seat. Its wake traveled through air and earth, vibrating the tires on my car. I hadn't recognized the two boys and hoped they weren't anyone Tara hung out with. Had I ever been that obnoxiously bold? No, Dad had impressed upon me at an early age that it was important to not infringe on others. That whatever choices I made or actions I took, they would stay with me forever. Still, I envied those boys their lack of inhibition. Then it occurred to me what it was that I was feeling.

Freedom.

The freedom to move forward. To live again.

The teenagers' car zipped down the road, its glowing taillights receding along the dark ribbon of road, before disappearing over the hill.

I was about to pull out when I noticed another car speeding south along Hilltop Road. It was coming so fast, I waited again. It pealed by, the muffler coughing. A truck, not a car.

The tang of smoke hung in the air. I inhaled deeply, held it in my lungs. Somewhere, someone was having a bonfire. Maybe roasting marshmallows or hot dogs. There was a mountainous burn pile in the back forty at Dad's from where I had cleared and collected the brush along the overgrown fence rows. Maybe this weekend I'd light it up and let Tara invite her new friend over.

After looking both ways, I rolled through the intersection. Air rushed in through the windows as the car gained speed, caressing my skin with the warmth and scents of summer. Soon, the smell of freshly mown grass, rich earth, and a third cutting of hay were overpowered by the odor of ash. I must have been close to the bonfire.

Yet as I scanned the length of the road, I realized there were no houses for half a mile on this section. The breeze was faint. Wherever the fire was, it had to be a big one.

A distant wail pierced my ears. It took me a moment to recognize what it was: a fire engine. That was never good.

As I slowed at the final curve before home, the sirens faded away. I paused at the last stop sign, a T-stop, and looked both ways. All was clear, but something made me pause and wait while my senses sorted things out. It wasn't until the rush of air through the open windows died down that I heard it. The sirens were coming closer again. Going in my direction. If they'd left from the firehouse on Templeton Pike, they could have gone around the 'country block' to head this way. Same distance either way, but that route had fewer stops.

A trace of dread wormed its way into my gut. What if —?

The sirens' plaintive wail shattered the stillness of the night. A clarion call of unfolding tragedy. I swung my head left to peer into the distance, toward my childhood home. Over the ridgeline there, a half mile down the road, a flicker of orange glowed eerily at horizon's edge. A billowing plume of smoke rose above the row of spruce bordering the front yard of my dad's house, twisting like a slow-moving tornado.

I gulped my heart back and slammed my foot down on the accelerator. The flashing lights of the fire trucks topped the hill far behind me, pulsing in my rearview mirror. They had taken the turn and were following me as I headed toward home.

chapter 26

Sᴘᴀʀᴋꜱ ʟᴇᴀᴘᴛ ɪɴᴛᴏ ᴛʜᴇ air, dying against a backdrop of stars as they turned to flakes of flickering ash.

I clenched the steering wheel and veered into the driveway, leaning into the dashboard as if pitching my weight forward the extra few inches would launch me into a wormhole that could propel me there quicker. The seatbelt cut a restrictive diagonal swath from my hip to my collarbone, digging into my ribs each time one of the wheels slammed into a pothole. The suspension rattled noisily as the car jounced over the driveway.

Damn it. I'd argued with Dad about fixing the lane before trying to sell the place. Its condition was going to cut into the house's value. First impressions were everything, I'd told him. Offers were going to be low, if there were any at all. Dad just couldn't admit it. Just like he'd had a hard time admitting that age was catching up with him, and he was no longer able to take care of a house and acreage. Yet he wouldn't move into the condo.

Now this. What the hell had he done? Put something in the oven?

Cresting the ridge, I let off the gas. The first fire engine was just now turning into the driveway a couple of hundred yards behind me. Beyond the line of forty-year-old evergreens that marked the perimeter of what we'd always called the front yard, I could see the flames wavering big and bright above the tin roof. House and trees stood silhouetted against a vibrant background of yellows and oranges. Through the glass of the big picture window of the living room, only a faint amber light showed. The other front windows were the same. The fire was somewhere in the back of the house, although by now it could have reached up into the attic.

I scanned the yard, the doorways, and windows, looking for Dad. There was no sign of him. The encroaching cry of sirens reminded me I had to give them the right of way, so I yanked the steering wheel to the left and drove over the grass. The breeze was pushing the ash in the other direction, but I kept the car at what I hoped was a safe distance from the house. I punched down on the brake pedal. Wheels sank into soft earth, leaving deep ruts in the carefully tended lawn. I had the seatbelt off before the car came to a complete stop. Without thought, I turned the key into the 'Off' position. The engine sputtered and croaked as I ripped the key out prematurely. I kicked the door open and hit the ground running.

A wave of panic crashed inside my chest. I raced toward the house, yelling for Dad. The closer I came, the more the brightness of the fire blinded me. In the minute since I'd first come into sight of it, the inferno had grown. Its flames curled beneath the soffits, licked at the siding up toward the attic.

A wall of heat slammed against my face. I reeled backward, coughing. The smoke was thickening.

Momentarily disoriented, I spun around. I pulled in air. Forced myself to think, to be rational. The heat was singeing my lungs, blistering my cheeks. My urge was to rush inside the house, search for Dad, rescue him. That might have made sense if I knew where in the house he was. If I did, though, I could wander from room to room, unable to see, the overhead beams splitting and crashing down around me, blocking my path. The smoke would overwhelm me long before the fire did.

Tires spun over the gravel at the top of the lane. The firefighters were almost here.

Every heartbeat pummeled at my hope. Every moment that passed was one moment closer to my dad dying. I couldn't let that happen.

The collar of my shirt pulled up over my mouth to help filter out the smoke, I darted around to the back of the house. The skin of my right arm, the arm closest to the house, burned from the heat alone. How could I endure it inside? What if Dad wasn't even in there? Would I be rushing to my own death for nothing?

"Dad! Dad, where are you?!"

Nothing. I called again. And again. Still, no answer. Called until my throat was raw and my lungs were scoured by smoke. Until a fit of coughing prevented me from uttering another word.

Flames crackled and popped. Tongues of fire reached outward and upward, engulfing the structure. I gazed into the windows, searching franticly, my eyes dry from the heat. I kept expecting a firefighter to appear at my side, ask me if anyone was inside, then rush into the mouth of hell, a hero defying death.

But no one came. They were still out front, shouting at one another as they unraveled their hoses, positioned themselves for battle.

Had they not seen me drive ahead of them? Surely, they'd noticed my taillights turning into the driveway?

Yet as I thought about it, it was possible they hadn't. There was a small rise and then a dip in the road between the stop sign and the driveway. The tree line along the drive could have obscured their view as I turned into the driveway. And when I got to the house, I'd left the car well off to the side. I had run around to the back before they came within full sight.

I started toward the front of the house. I had to tell them my dad was still in there. They had to know.

Only three steps into my mission, I pulled up. There. A figure, a shadow, cutting across the wavering light in the window of the back kitchen door. Low to the ground, as if crawling on the floor to stay out of the smoke. I was sure of it.

I raced to the door. Leapt over the steps of the back stoop. Stole the biggest gulp of air I could. Reached for the doorknob. Grasped it. And just as quickly snatched my hand back.

My palm burned with heat.

I tugged the sleeve of my jacket down to cover the inside of my hand, then wrapped my covered fingers around the knob. It wouldn't turn. The door was locked.

There had to be something nearby I could use to break the glass. I searched, but couldn't see anything I could use.

A boom exploded inside the house, like a small grenade detonating. The blast nearly knocked me off my feet. I stumbled backward, then righted myself.

That was when I saw it: a shovel leaning against the back of the garage, less than twenty feet away.

"Hang on, Dad!" I grabbed the shovel, turned back to the door and leveled the length of the handle like a battering ram. "Stay back! I have to break the glass!"

Eyes closed, face turned away, I clenched the shovel tight, brought it back and —

"Sam?"

I took a few steps back, breath held, listening. The fire snapped and popped above the low roar of heat. Had I imagined it? I wasn't sure. Had it come from inside? Or out?

"Dad? Dad, where are you?" Several moments passed in which there was no reply. Sweat poured down my face, drenched the front of my shirt. The only voices I could make out were the ones coming over the radio of the fire department. This was no time for indecision. I couldn't wait for them to come around back. Couldn't waste time going to fetch them.

Cocking my elbow out, I gripped the throat of the shovel handle, close to the metal scoop, and tucked my head down before ramming the blunt end behind me at the window. Glass shattered, most of it falling inward, but a handful of shards pelted off the back of my jacket and pants leg before clinking onto the cement. There was a jagged hole in the pane, barely big enough to slip my hand through. I tossed the shovel aside and yanked the end of my sleeve over my fist before reaching toward the long glass teeth.

Heat blasted my skin. I groped inside for the doorknob. It was like plunging my hand into an oven — and holding it there, when every brain cell was telling me to pull it out. I dipped my hand lower. There. My fingers brushed against hot metal. But to get my whole hand around it, I had to stretch, one more inch and —

A jagged tooth of glass tore through the underside of my sleeve. Instinctively, I jerked my arm back. Which was the wrong thing to do. The sharp edge sliced the skin beneath, burning as it tore at a vein. I pulled my arm up this time. Blood, wet and warm, began to quickly soak my sleeve.

I stumbled backward, the thumb of my other hand pressing hard just above where the cut was, trying to staunch the flow.

And then, a cough, faint, reached my ears. This time, I was sure it came from somewhere out in the yard.

"Dad?"

"Sam ... over here."

It *was* him. I staggered dizzily toward the garage. "Where are you?"

"By the ..." — Dad coughed several times before he could get the last word out — "wood."

"By the wood?" I spun around twice, my gaze sweeping over the stands of maples and clusters of forsythia at the edge of the yard. A couple hundred feet from the back of the house stood a fire ring, piled up with brush that Tara and I had trimmed two days ago. Surely he didn't mean there? His voice hadn't sounded that far away.

Ribbons of amber light rippled against surrounding branches and trunks. Ash drifted down from the sky like snowflakes of gray. Here and there, an ember glimmered in the drying grass. Fingers of heat scraped at my skin, reminding me of the danger I'd barely avoiding plunging into.

"Here, Sam."

Drawn by his voice, I dashed around the corner of the garage. A little too quickly. My foot dragged over a split log. I pitched forward, throwing my left arm out to break my fall. I hit the ground with my knees first, then my hands, jarring my bones all the way up to my shoulders. I pushed myself back to my feet and stood. A fresh spurt of blood trickled down the inside of my arm, but I pushed the pain aside as I caught sight of a pair of sooty jeans legs sticking out from the other side of the wood pile next to the garage.

Dad was lying there with his back pressed against the logs, his legs stretched out before him. He dragged in a mangled breath, wheezing as his lungs strained to expand. Soot smeared his face, reddened from the heat. Perspiration beaded on his forehead, collecting at his temple to run down his cheek in a tiny rivulet, leaving a streak of white against the black stain of ash.

"You missed curfew," Dad joked, but his words came out raspy.

"You didn't tell me I had one." I knelt down. The light of the fire didn't reach here. As far as I could tell in the dim glow, my dad was in one piece. "You okay?"

"I'm breathing, aren't I?" He was, but he sounded pretty ragged. He tried to push himself away from the stack of logs, but crawling out through a house filled with smoke had taken its toll. He collapsed back against the wood, closing his eyes tight as a cough racked his body.

"How did you get out here? The back door was locked."

"Front. I was … in the living room."

"Come on." I slid my arm around his back to scoot him forward and up. "Help me out a little. On three. One, two —"

"Bump!" Dad grasped my hand, pinching so hard it felt like a vice. His eyes were wide with desperation. "Where's Bump?"

"I don't know. Haven't seen him. We need to get you away from the house first. Get you some help. Fire department's here already. Now come on."

Even as I braced my weight into my thighs and heaved, Dad was dragging me back down.

A gritty sound came from his smoke-scoured throat. "No ... can't. The dog ... saved me... He —"

"Yeah, well, I'm saving you now. Trying to. So let me. 'Cause neither of us will ever see Bump again if you sit there like a sack of cement mix."

I dug my fingers into his shirt to hoist him up. His body hung from my grasp like dead weight, legs wobbly beneath his stooped frame. One labored stride at a time, I dragged him away from the house, my arm tightening around his bony ribs. When had he gotten this thin? Had he forgotten to eat?

Dad stumbled, his legs collapsing beneath him, but I held him up, heaved him forward a few more steps. We were free of the shadows now, nearing the front corner of the garage. All I had to do was get him another thirty yards, out in the open, where the heat and ashes would be less of a danger. Dad's feet dragged the ground, slowing us. But I carried him onward, aware of the blood gushing down my arm, yet somehow able to shut out the pain.

"Hey!"

I looked right. A burly firefighter dropped the section of hose he was holding and rushed toward us. My arms were burning with fatigue, locking up.

The man flipped his clear visor up to look Walt over, then pulled his oxygen mask down. It was Archer. "Is he okay?"

"Yeah, I think so," I said. Dad drooped to the ground. "But I'm going to drop him if you don't help me out."

Archer grabbed my dad's hand and slipped under his arm to relieve me of the weight. He inclined his head toward the far side of the fire truck. "Over there."

Just as we started on our way, Dad bucked backward. Fresh tears streaking down his cheeks, he looked into Archer's eyes, pleading. "You have to save him."

Archer glanced at me. "Is someone else inside?"

"No." I started forward. I'd haul him to safety myself if I had to. No sense risking all our lives. "Just the dog."

We went two steps, three, four. Still, the distance to the fire truck seemed vast. My own muscles had long since given up.

With a jerk, Dad wrenched his body sideways, tearing away before he threw himself to the ground. Unable to stand, he began to crawl back toward the fire. I lurched toward him, but my legs were heavy and I tumbled to the ground, falling a foot short. On hands and knees, I scrambled after him, barely latching on to an ankle.

"Let me go!" Dad shouted. "I have to get Bump out."

I couldn't let him go back inside. I'd felt the overpowering heat, sensed its power. He'd die if he went in there for that dog. That annoying, pain-in-the-ass dog.

And yet ... I would've plunged into that fiery hell for my dad. Even though he'd pissed me off more times than I could remember.

Dad yanked his foot free, but a cough gripped him and he folded, forehead to the ground. I threw an arm around his chest, hugging him tight. "Dad, he's just a —"

"He's not just a dog, damn it! He's my life." Firelight glimmered in Dad's gray eyes. He sat back on his heels and swiped a forearm across his face, smearing tears and soot. "I know he's not perfect, but I love that dumb dog."

I heard the love in his voice. Heard it emanate from the depths of his crusty soul and the furthest caverns of his stony heart. I didn't need to ask why. Bump, in his goofy naiveté, didn't judge. He loved unconditionally, with tolerance beyond human capability.

Archer placed a gloved hand on Dad's shoulder. "Walter, where would the dog have been?"

Dad pinched his eyes shut in thought and shook his head. "I don't know. I don't know. I lost track of him."

Settling on his haunches, Archer rested both elbows on his knees. "What room were you in together last?"

More sirens blared around us, their wails intermingling with the crackling and popping of the fire and shouts of the other firefighters. Dad pulled a hand down over his throat. "Before or after the robber came in?"

Archer and I exchanged a glance. I scooted closer to Dad and wrapped my hand around his. "What robber? What happened?"

"He can tell you about that later, Sam," Archer said. "I need to know where to look for the dog first."

"You're going in" — I jabbed a finger at the house, flames curling around open windows and licking the outer walls — "there?"

"It's my job. I'm trained for it." He pulled his mask back on, flipped his visor down, shimmering orange reflecting in it. "Which room, Walt?"

"We were in the living room when I fell asleep." He blinked back tears, his forehead scrunched in agony. "But I think ... I think I heard him back near the kitchen, or laundry room next to it maybe, barking at someone."

Nodding, I squeezed Dad's hand. "Yes, yes, I saw a silhouette in the kitchen. I thought it was you, Dad. It could've been Bump."

No sooner had I said it than Archer dashed toward the back kitchen door. I dropped Dad's hand and pushed to my feet, wanting to rush after him, stop him. I couldn't let Archer risk his life like this. Not for a dog. But my legs were leaden. And I couldn't leave my dad.

Not like he was.

Archer was on the back porch in seconds. He rammed his shoulder into the door and it popped open like a cardboard box top. Light exploded around him and he disappeared into a mushrooming plume of smoke.

I stood there for what seemed like hours, until Dad's hand brushed weakly against my calf.

"He'll find him?" Dad croaked, his voice the texture of sandpaper.

"Yeah, Dad. Don't worry." I sank back down beside him and pushed the wispy hair from his forehead. His face was hot to the touch. His cheeks were riddled with red blotches and small blisters. "Archer will find him."

I hoped.

chapter 27

PARAMEDICS SWARMED AROUND US. I shoved them away, trying to convince them that all I needed was water. They didn't relent until they'd looked me over from head to toe and asked a dozen questions.

Meanwhile, they tore open Dad's shirt, checked his heart and breathing, and affixed an oxygen mask to his face. When they decided it was safe to move him, they gently lifted him onto a stretcher. He fought them every step, flailing his arms, thrashing his head side to side.

"Leave me be! You have to help —" The effort sucked the air from his lungs. He gasped in several breaths before he could form more words. "Damn it, I said leave me ... alone. Help ... my dog."

"Did Chief Malone go inside looking for the family pet, ma'am?" one of the firefighters asked me.

I nodded toward the kitchen. He clicked the button on his walkie-talkie to alert the others, then he shook his head. "He should know protocol better than anyone. You don't go inside for a victim without backup."

A loud crash boomed from inside the house. Heads turned. Glass exploded, hundreds of tiny shards plinking against the concrete of the back porch. Tongues of flame speared outward from the kitchen window. The fire was growing like a monster devouring everything around it — and inside.

I flinched, thinking of Archer in there. Wondering if a beam had collapsed. If the fire had reached the propane tank. Worrying if he could get out. Cursing myself for not having stopped him.

They started to wheel my dad toward the ambulance. He flailed a hand outward, grabbing the tips of my fingers to jerk me with him. I stumbled alongside as the stretcher bumped over the lawn. At the back of the ambulance, one of the EMTs hit a lever and the legs began to fold underneath the stretcher. Someone else grabbed the end near Dad's head and lifted it up to guide it inside.

He grumbled something and they paused. Desperation shone in his red-rimmed eyes.

"Are you a relative, ma'am? You can come with him to the hospital."

Dad was shaking his head, trying to speak to me, but his words were rough with smoke and muffled by the mask. I leaned in close.

"You stay here," he pled. "Make sure my dog's okay, you hear?"

"Sure, Dad." I rubbed the back of his hand. Kissing him on the forehead would have been too awkward. He wasn't given to gestures of affection. "I'll call Clint. He'll take care of him." But even as I said it, I wasn't so sure there would be a living, breathing Bump to take care of.

I waved goodbye as they hoisted him into the back of the ambulance. The doors closed with a resounding thud.

As much as I wanted to go with him and keep him calm, I knew he'd be worse off if he thought that dog had perished because no one tried to save him.

I dropped to my knees in a rut in the tall grass where the ambulance tires had cut through the yard. Hands shaking, I dialed Clint's number. It was on the fifth ring and about to go to voicemail before Clint's voice came across the line.

"Sam, are you okay? I heard about the fire. I'm on my way." His words tumbled out in a panic. "My God, is everyone okay?"

The impact of it all hit me like a hurricane wind. I bit my lip, attempting to hold myself together so I could form a coherent answer. "You heard — how?"

"I passed a fire truck on my way home from dropping you off at your car, then saw an ambulance go by, headed in your direction. You didn't answer your phone. I called Archer's, but he didn't pick up. I managed to get your neighbor Ida's number. She said the fire trucks were swarming your place. Sam, are you okay?"

"Yeah, I'm fine." Although I knew I didn't sound very convincing. "They took Dad to the hospital. He's going to be all right. But ... but ... Bump, he ... didn't make it out."

"Oh, God. I'm sorry. Hang on, okay? I'm just around the corner. I'll be there in a minute."

I nodded, not even thinking that he couldn't see me, and hit the end call button. My eyes prickled with tears as I stared at my childhood home going up in flames. In there was the doorknob that I'd tied a string to, trying to lose my first baby tooth. Dad's vinyl records were in there, pictures of Mom ... Hugging my legs to me, I buried my face against my knees.

Memories flooded through me, tossing me in a somersault of emotions. Bad memories, good ones. Darkness, brightness. Yes, there had been both. Sometimes they were one and the same. The burnt toast my dad served me so many times ... he'd tried. He really had. Being a kid, I couldn't have understood what he was suffering. That depression wasn't a thing you simply slapped yourself out of. It sunk its claws in and held on hard, shredding your soul while you struggled to free yourself. It had taken me ten long years to learn that. It had taken Dad even longer.

I cried until my tears ran dry. Until I hyperventilated and keeled over onto the grass. I heard Ida's voice, soft and soothing, through the crackle and hiss of water hitting hot coals.

"There, there, honey." She sat me up, handed me a wad of tissues. "They said your dad's going to be fine. They'll have to keep him in the hospital for a bit, make sure his lungs are okay. Do you want me to drive you to the hospital?"

I blew my nose. "Not yet. I have to see if … if …" I couldn't say it. Frantic, I looked around for him, for Archer, but I was pretty sure none of the men still spraying down the fire were him. None had his wide shoulders. I shuddered as another sob gripped me.

Ida hugged me to her.

"Archer," I finally managed to get out. "He went inside for Bump."

She swept her fingertips over my cheek, then tipped my chin up as she smiled sweetly. "Archer's over there, honey. On the other side of the truck."

Relief swept through me, but was quickly dashed by fear. Why hadn't he come to me? I gripped Ida's thin forearm. "Is he hurt?"

"Far as I can tell, he's fine. He was walking around, giving orders." She waved a hand to her left.

My gaze drifted from the ruins of our house, toward all the shiny emergency vehicles, the deputy with his hand resting on the butt of the gun at his hip, the paramedics standing ready, the firefighters in their gear —

I stood, my knees wobbling like they were made of water, and started in the direction Ida had motioned.

"No, honey, no." Ida scurried after me, her hand alighting on my shoulder. "Sam, dear, you need to just sit down for a spell. They'll take care of everything. You've been through a lot. Really, you shouldn't —"

I broke into a run, weaving as I franticly searched among the faces. My eyesight was so bleary every firefighter looked the same with their masks on. A hand grabbed me from behind and I threw an elbow back, ready to push Ida away. But it wasn't her.

Archer gripped my arm. Unable to form words, I searched his eyes for the truth. The concern in the lines of his face gave way to compassion. In an instant, my heart shattered into a thousand tiny pieces.

"Thank God I found you," he said, gently pulling me to him. "I was starting to think you'd gone back inside."

It felt as though someone had ripped the bones from my body. I collapsed against him, fresh tears scorching my cheeks.

He stroked my back, his stiff gloves strangely comforting. "Shhh, shhh, shhh. It's all right, Sam. It's all right."

"How can it be all right?" I blubbered, sounding to myself like a five-year-old child. It was just a dog. How could I lose it over a dog? "He's … he's …" My words were smothered in sobs.

"Sam, stop." Archer tilted my head back and with his gloved finger, pushed my cheek to the right, so I was looking toward where I'd left my car. There, crouched in the grass, was Clint beside a grayish-brown lump of fur. "Bump's alive. I found him right away by the back kitchen door. He'd collapsed from smoke inhalation, but we got some oxygen into him and his heart's still beating strong."

I slipped my arms around his waist and hugged him as tight as I could despite his bulky gear. "Thank you. Thank you."

I felt like such a fool then. Not just for exploding into histrionics over the dog. But for suspecting Archer had anything to do with the arsons. And here he'd gone and done something heroic, damn him. How was I ever going to live this down?

"I'm sorry I treated you the way I did at the lodge. I shouldn't have said those things. It was —"

"Forget it," he said, his breath stirring the hair on top of my head. "Everybody in town was pointing a finger at your father. You were just defending him, that's all." He loosened his hold on me, pulling my arms down and away as Clint looked our way. He stepped back, arms stiff at his side, his tenderness replaced by boyish awkwardness, as if he'd said or done something out of place. But what friend wouldn't hold you and offer comforting words after an ordeal like tonight?

Clint motioned to us. I hooked a hand around Archer's forearm to pull him with me, but he kept his feet planted. He peeled my hand from his bulky sleeve. "You go ahead. I need to see what my boys are up to now, make sure everything's under control. Jake called in sick earlier, so we're a bit shorthanded tonight."

I left him and made my way slowly to Clint, careful of the potholes and ruts in the lane. The light from the fire was practically gone now, and the floodlight that normally lit this part of the drive wasn't working. I couldn't even remember if it had been on when I'd gotten there, I'd been so focused on getting to Dad. Either the electric had cut out from the fire or been turned off. Somehow I made it to Clint without falling on my face.

As I sank to my knees beside Bump, his eyes flicked open for a second, then shut. Little patches of bloodied fur shimmered in the moonlight. There were small gashes in his skin, leaving gaps in his coat. I ran a hand over his neck and his tail thumped ever so slightly. His breathing was rapid and shallow, and air rattled in his chest. The sight of him lying there brought me back to the night I hit him out on Harmony Road. I hadn't wanted to take him home then, but Tara had insisted we help him.

I didn't care if everything in that old house was reduced to ashes. I just wanted Bump to be all right. He'd made us a family again. Given my dad someone to talk to and be with. Calmed Tara by giving her something to focus on. And introduced me to Clint.

Nothing inside the house mattered. What mattered was who we loved. Even a stray dog with separation anxiety, bad manners, and an excess of energy. Or a cantankerous old septuagenarian with a poor memory and lousy housekeeping habits. Lord knew I wasn't perfect.

The scent of smoke had scrubbed my nose and throat dry. The

fire was almost under control now. The end of the house where the bedrooms were seemed largely untouched by the flames, but there would be smoke and water damage. The kitchen, however, was a total loss. Still, even if the rest of the house had survived structurally, it would be weeks, months maybe, before we could inhabit it again. If at all. The thought of all that lay ahead should have overwhelmed me, but I simply didn't have the energy to let my mind go there.

All I could do was focus on this moment — and the fact that a dog I'd known for so short a time had stolen my heart so completely that it ached with a tender fierceness right now.

"Will he be okay?" I twined my fingers in the fur of Bump's ruff as I bent to kiss his grizzled snout. The leather of his nose was bone dry. He smelled like an old campfire pit.

Clint hesitated before answering. "I wish I could say for sure, but there's no way of knowing, Sam. He's suffered a lot of lung damage. I'm going to transport him to the clinic and get him hooked up with some IVs and plenty of medication to help him sleep. He wasn't burned at all and while he does have some cuts from the glass exploding, they're mostly superficial, so things could have been much worse." Clint took some antiseptic and gauze out of his supply box. Carefully, he dabbed at Bump's wounds. "If he makes it through the next forty-eight hours with any degree of improvement, his chances are good. If he declines at all ..."

I squeezed his arm. "Just do what you can, okay?"

He nodded and together we lifted Bump onto the backseat of his SUV where Clint had laid a blanket down.

Clint pulled his keys from his pocket. "I've already called Melissa to get things set up at the clinic for him. I have the feeling it's going to be a long night."

"Clint, I ... I want to go with you, but I think I need to be with Dad now. Can you give me updates if anything changes with Bump. Good or bad?"

"Sure." He leaned in and kissed my forehead. "But I'll text so I don't wake anyone up. Call me in the morning?"

Nodding, I gave him a quick hug. He drove slowly down the lane. As much as I wanted to help Clint with Bump, I knew the dog was in good hands. But Dad … Dad needed me. I had to run intervention before he ticked any of the nurses off or walked out onto the street in his hospital gown.

If I had any doubts previously about which direction my life was going to go, tonight's fire had decided everything. I no longer had a choice.

But even if I had, I'm sure I would have come to the same conclusion.

My life, for now, was here. And I didn't want to be anyplace else.

chapter 28

BY THE TIME IDA and I arrived at the hospital, they'd taken my dad for x-rays. Soon, they'd be transferring him to intensive care for observation. Ida had driven me in my car and on the way I called Tara to fill her in on everything. The panic had been plain in her voice. Over and over again, I told her to breathe, kept reassuring her that Gramps was okay, and that Clint was taking care of Bump.

Ida tapped the top of my wrist as we sat in the waiting area of Fullbright Medical Center. I uncurled my fingers from the arm of my chair and turned my palm upward. She dropped my keys into my hand. The house key was lying on top of the collection. Small use for a house key now, what with the windows being blown out and big sections of the house charred. Just thinking about all the work to be done and the losses made me want to hurl right there in the waiting area.

And yet weirdly, it also made me grateful. To be alive. To know that Dad and Tara were safe and sound. To have a friend like Ida. Even one as unique as Selma.

Despite all the damage to the property, the truth was *I* had lost very little. A few clothes, some books. After a computer crash at work eight years ago, I'd learned to obsessively save my work online, so the manuscript was still intact. And still not finished. My ID and credit cards were in my purse, which I'd had with me in the car. Most of my belongings were still in a locked storage unit in Chicago. So why was I so upset about a bunch of stuff that wasn't even mine and a house that I'd walked out of almost two decades ago?

I closed my fingers around the keys, their little metal ridges digging into my palm. "Thanks for driving me here, Ida."

"Your car's a little newer than mine, and all the knobs and switches are in different places," she said with a wink, "but I managed to get us here, didn't I?"

"You did."

"Besides, you were in no state to be in control of a moving vehicle. You've been through a lot. Is Tara on her way?"

"Shannon's mom offered to bring her, but I told her Dad was okay and to just to stay there until morning." I checked the time again. It had been fifteen minutes since I called Tara, yet it seemed like five hours.

A male nurse shoved his way through a set of doors marked 'Radiology'. He beelined for me, as he took a pair of black-rimmed glasses from his pocket to put them on, and flipped through a set of charts on his clipboard.

"Ms. McNamee?" he said without looking up or introducing himself.

I stood, too tired to respond verbally.

"Follow me. The red line leads to ICU. He's stable. For now." Then he spun around, walking quickly toward the doors.

"I'll wait here," Ida said.

I wanted to tell her she didn't need to, that she should go home and rest, but the nurse was going to lose me if I didn't catch up. Anyway, if she left I didn't have a way home.

Home. Oh yeah. I didn't have a home.

The nurse punched a button on the wall and the doors swung

open. I made it through just in time.

After about fifteen turns, five more doors, and an elevator ride, we stood before another pair of doors marked 'Intensive Care Unit'. On the other side was a long desk with a high counter. Soft clacking came from a keyboard on the other side.

The nurse slid his clipboard across the counter. "Ms. McNamee here to see her father."

"Patient's name?" mumbled a weary female voice from beyond a monitor screen, the top of it barely visible above the counter.

The nurse spun the clipboard around to look again, as if he'd already forgotten my dad's name. "Walter David Schimmoller."

A hand appeared from behind the counter and pulled the clipboard down. More clacking. Then the scratch of a pen on paper. "Room 214," she said. A sigh of irritation followed. "But he's been sedated."

"Thank you."

"Fifteen minutes," she warned.

The nurse curled a finger at me to follow him. We passed half a dozen rooms, all empty but for one, where an old woman lay on her bed, tubes snaking out of every orifice, and a wall of machines pumping oxygen into her and monitoring her vitals. It didn't look good. Her body was a shriveled shell, unable to ingest nutrients or breathe on its own.

At the end of the hall, a pale glow spilled from Room 214 onto the tan linoleum in the corridor. Steeling myself, I turned the corner, careful to set my feet down softly with each step so my shoes wouldn't squeak on the waxed floor and wake him.

"'Bout damn time you got here," Dad barked, his voice raspy and groggy, but lucid. So much for being sedated. His bed was propped up as far as it could go. My relief at seeing him so bright-eyed and feisty was quickly followed by dread. A petulant, antisocial old man being held against his will is never a good thing. He aimed the remote at the

TV, punching a button on it with his thumb so repeatedly hard I was sure he'd bust it. A growl of annoyance rumbled in his throat. "Tell them to get me a different TV, will you, Sam? The volume doesn't work on this blasted thing. I can barely hear it."

"The volume will only go to a certain level, Mr. Schimmoller," the nurse told him, as he checked the chart at the end of his bed. "We don't want to wake the other patients."

I don't think that would have been a problem, considering they were either comatose or heavily drugged.

The nurse jotted a couple of notes on the chart, then turned to me. "He has some lung irritation, which will take time to heal. How long varies considerably. You may notice some wheezing, coughing, difficulty swallowing. Nothing to be alarmed about. But if he seems to be in any distress, just press the call button." He raised one eyebrow ever so slightly, as if to signal that volume issues with the TV did not constitute an emergency. "Someone will be along in a little while to check on him."

The moment he left, Dad mumbled, "Cheery son of a bitch, ain't he? Probably low man on the totem pole, so he pulled the night shift. That or he pissed his boss off." Putting a fist to his mouth, he coughed dryly, then cleared his throat and spit a glob of phlegm onto a tissue. He stared at the tissue. "Keep expecting to expel one of my lungs."

I looked down at the floor. "I'm sorry, Dad. I meant to change the batteries in your smoke alarms. I even bought a pack, but I just got so busy that —"

"Stop it, Sam. Didn't you smell the gasoline? Even if the alarms had been working, it wouldn't have mattered. The fire department wouldn't have gotten there in time to save the house."

"But you could've been —"

"I said *stop it*." After a moment, he added, "Did they catch the son of a bitch who did it?"

"Set the fire, you mean? No. Whoever did it was long gone by the time I got there. But you said something about a robber?"

"Yeah, but before you ask, I didn't see him. I was sound asleep in the recliner when I heard Bump barking somewhere in the back of the house and someone, a man, yelling at him, threatening him. There was a lot of smoke. I didn't see anyone, but I did see blood stains on the kitchen floor. Bump must've taken a chunk out of the bastard before he got away."

"I'll be sure to let Sheriff Driscoll know." I sat in the chair between his bed and the window. "How are you doing, Dad?"

"I feel like hell." He crumpled up the tissue and put it on the nightstand. "But I'll live, I suppose." His expression softened. I knew what he was going to ask.

"Clint is taking care of Bump," I said. "He's giving him fluids, monitoring him as closely as he can."

"Is *he* going to live? The dog, I mean."

"He's, uh …" I studied my hands. I'd broken all my nails going through things at Dad's house. I had blisters in places I'd never had blisters before. Why was this question so hard? I'd known for the last two hours that he was going to ask it. "He's a little worse off than you. He was in the house, breathing smoke, for a long time. Clint says the next couple of days are critical — and even if he makes it through that, nothing's a given."

I stole a glance. Dad was staring at the TV, a blank look on his face, his fingers curling around a wadded portion of his sheets.

"I'm sorry, Dad. I hope he makes it. We all do."

"If he doesn't," — he drew a breath, closed his eyes — "I'd rather God had just let me die, too." His eyes cracked open, his glance sliding toward me. "But I said a prayer on that ambulance ride. Told the Big Man Upstairs just to let me have this one thing and I'd live the rest of my life trying to make up for all the trouble I've caused." He squinted, pointing a finger at me. "Keep that to yourself, you hear?"

I nodded.

That was the first time in my life I'd ever heard Dad speak of God as an entity, not just a profanity.

It takes a lot to make a man like Walter Schimmoller believe in something bigger than himself.

In this case, it was a lot of dog.

"YOU TELL THEM THEY have to let me go," Dad said. He pushed his IV drip across the room, heading straight for the clean clothes I'd brought with me and laid on the chair the next morning. They were Clint's, and close to Dad's size, although probably not to his taste, but I hadn't been in the house yet to see if anything was worth retrieving. "They can't keep me here against my will, you know."

Barely 9 a.m., I'd only been here fifteen seconds, and already we were having a standoff. Great start to the day. Apparently, they'd backed off on the sedatives a little too soon.

I snatched the clothes away before he could tear his IV needle out trying to dress himself. "Dad, these are for tomorrow. You need to stay another day, so they can monitor you."

"They just want to keep me longer so they can charge me more, that's why. You'll see what I mean. Crying out loud, they probably charge ten grand a day rent for a bed around here. Couple of aspirin probably costs fifty bucks."

"You have insurance."

"Doesn't always cover everything. I'm still paying on my broken elbow for Pete's —" A cough stole his breath. I hurried to his side to help him to the bed. As soon as he was sitting, he elbowed me away.

"A lifetime of memories, of working every day, year after year, to build a life and own a home you can raise a family in and ..." — he raised his hands toward the ceiling — "it's gone in minutes. You think it's just stuff, Sam, but it's not. That movie stub from my first date with Ann. The picture you drew in first grade of your mamma, me, and you. The Christmas card you sent me of Tara the first time she saw Santa Claus … They *mean* something." His eyes misted up and his voice started to quaver. He turned his face toward the window. "Sometimes, when I'm sitting in that big empty house all by myself, they're all I have to remind me of all of you."

I hadn't realized he'd saved all those things. Let alone that they meant anything to him. If only he hadn't waited so long to say so, I might not have stayed away for so many years.

A nurse poked her head in, but pulled back after taking one look at Dad. She raised a hand apologetically and disappeared.

Dad swallowed several times before going on, trying hard to control the tears. Looking back, it occurred to me I'd never seen him cry. Not when Mom left. Not when his older brother Oliver died. Not when I left. Not once. Ever.

"That croquet set — that was her idea. The pup tent — her idea. She wanted to go to Yosemite. Sleep under the stars. After I bought it, she decided she didn't like the idea of bugs and wild animals and being without electricity. I kept both those because I hoped she'd change her mind. When she left, I thought she'd change her mind about that, too. Come running back because she missed us. Kept hoping she would until the day I learned she died. Shows you how dumb I am." He swiped a liver-spotted hand under his runny nose. "And the rest of that junk? I got it for a reason, damn it. All of it. Not just because I like to throw money around. I like to fish. Eases my nerves, sitting at the lake, waiting for the line to bob. Makes you forgot about things. Can't say I like cleaning fish or cooking, but there's satisfaction in getting to eat something you went out and caught yourself. All those poles? I kept every one I ever bought because they never really broke. I just needed a better one, a different one. So I got more. They're all in good shape, you know — or could be, with a little work."

He nodded, as if to reassure himself of his reasoning. But there was conflict behind his eyes, as if logic and emotion were at war. "Every time I wondered if I should throw something out, I just couldn't let go of the memories. Couldn't make a decision either, I suppose. I mean, what if I threw something out and then a week later needed it, or someone asked to borrow it? Guess the decision's been made for me now."

It all made so much more sense now. Maybe if I'd understood from the start, I could've helped him through it? He'd become a hoarder not out of laziness, but out of fear of making the wrong decision and then regretting it. He'd also held on to stuff in an attempt to remind him of the people in his life. I, on the other hand, made a habit of getting rid of things so I could forget. Neither worked very well for us.

With a grunt, he hoisted his legs up onto the bed and leaned back, the big puffy pillow swallowing his head. "When can I go back?"

"Archer said we can go have a look tomorrow. But I should warn you that what wasn't burned or smoke damaged probably got waterlogged."

A meal cart trundled down the hall, pushed by a volunteer with a cheerful smile. She waved as she passed us. Dad didn't see her, though. His gaze was fixed on the high, white ceiling.

"Wait here a few minutes." Trustingly, I laid the clothes in one of the drawers of his nightstand and shut it. "I have something in the car for you."

"Where exactly do you think I'm going to go dressed in a paper gown and toting an IV?"

"I wouldn't put anything past you."

TEN MINUTES LATER I stood at the foot of his bed holding the box of pictures.

His brow furrowing, he clicked the TV off. "Where did you find that?"

"In the attic."

"I put it up there? I could've sworn it was in the front hall closet."

"Nope."

"The picture box." He narrowed his eyes, then shrugged as if trying to downplay the significance of its contents. "Find anything else with it?"

"Like what?" I wasn't going to say it first. I'd let him be the one to open that Pandora's box.

He sat up, making his gown crinkle. "Oh, I don't know — marriage certificate? Old postcards, maybe?"

"No old postcards, but the marriage certificate was in an old filing cabinet you had up there. I put the important papers in another box and brought them downstairs. Unfortunately, I left that box in the dining room."

The dining room was next to the kitchen, meaning they had likely been reduced to ashes. That or a watery pulp.

"Oh." He rolled over, away from me.

I moved around the bed to stand in front of him. "These were hidden under the pictures." I held out the bundle of letters to him.

His eyes widened momentarily. "You read them?"

Laying the bundle beside him, I shook my head. "They were from Mom to you. So no, I didn't."

Lately, I'd developed this habit of speaking half-truths. The real reason I didn't open the letters was because I was afraid of what I'd find inside, and that it would re-ignite all the anger I'd learned to push away.

He picked up the bundle, looked them over, then held it out to me. "You *should* read them, Sam."

Arms stiff at my sides, I stared at his offering. In a way now, I could understand Dad being there while I grew up, but not really *being* there. Yet I could never accept that Mom had abandoned me. And I was tired of trying to reason through her side of things. I just wanted to forget about it and move on. Not reading those letters was my way of letting go.

"I can't," I said.

He tucked the letters beside him and turned onto his back. "When you're ready to hear what's in them, let me know. I'll tell you." He paused to give me time to consider it. "It's stuff you should probably know."

What did he mean by that?

At any rate, I had a lot to think through right now. The past twelve hours had been a whirlwind of emotions. I needed some sleep before I could make any decisions.

My pocket buzzed. I pulled out my phone. It was Clint. I stepped out into the corridor.

"Sam?" There was an urgency to his voice that squeezed the hope from my heart. "Can you come down to the clinic right away?"

"Sure, Clint." My mouth went dry with dread. I had to ask. "How's Bump?"

He expelled a breath, the pause heavy with unspoken meaning. He sounded so, I don't know, drained? "Just come, Sam. You'll see when you get here."

"Sure. It'll take me about half an hour, though."

He told me to be careful, then hung up. As I stood there gripping my phone, I considered calling him back and threatening not to come until he told me more. One glance at my dad squelched that thought. If Bump had died, what could I have done? Nothing. Except dissolve into a river of tears. Then Dad would have known. And here, now ... was neither the place nor the time.

"You know," Dad began as I returned to his room, "we had a dog when you were younger. What the hell was his name?"

"We called him Monty, short for the Count of Monte Cristo."

"Yep, that one." His lip folded into a snarl. "I hated that dog. Practically did cartwheels when he kicked the can. Wanted to get rid of him long before that. Even thought about taking him for a, you know, a 'ride in the country' and telling you he ran away. But he was your dog, so I didn't."

"Well, I wasn't too attached to him, either."

"Hah, you don't say?" He pushed himself up on his elbows, looked me square in the eye. "You don't feel that way about Bump, though, do you?"

I shook my head. Truth was, I loved that crazy dog. And the thought of him not being around, it made my heart sick.

"Life sure would be easier," he said, "without a dog to take care of, wouldn't it?"

It would. It would also be a lot emptier.

Yet I'd gladly clean up shredded softener sheets every day for the next fifteen years, just to have that dog back in our lives.

I squeezed his hand, felt the gnarled bones sharp beneath the papery skin. "I'll be back this afternoon, okay? Sheriff Driscoll wanted to stop by before they released you. I suppose he wants to get a statement."

He squeezed back. "Bring good news, Sam."

I forced a smile and hurried away.

chapter 29

IT WAS HARD TO see the road on the drive to South End Animal Hospital. Tears obscured my vision. My grip on the steering wheel was so tight, my fingers went numb.

The night I ran into Bump had changed everything. Today would, too.

I pulled into the gravel parking lot of the clinic and cut the engine. For a good long minute, I sat there, staring at the front door, trying to gather the courage to go inside and say my goodbyes. Only, I didn't know if I had gotten there in time. The way Clint talked, Bump was already gone. With Dad in the hospital and Tara still at Shannon's, it would be up to me to take him home and bury him.

How was I going to do this by myself? Would it be too much to ask Clint to help?

There's a lot of stuff in life you wish you never had to deal with. Stuff you can't avoid. But it happens. So you do what you're supposed to, all the while wishing you could be someplace else, doing anything but that. And as you do, people offer their platitudes, give hugs, then walk away.

They say they're sorry. In truth, though, they're just glad it's you going through it and not them.

Clint pushed the door open, motioning me inside. If he hadn't done that, I might never have gotten out of my car. I trudged across the parking lot, my heart so heavy I could've plummeted right through the asphalt and left a crater. Pebbles skittered before me as I dragged my feet along. I kept my eyes down. I couldn't look at Clint without falling apart.

The moment I stepped inside, he pulled me into his embrace, inhaling as he buried his face against my hair. Melissa wasn't at her station. The waiting area was empty.

I held on tight, not wanting to move, but somehow fortified by his touch. "Can I see him now?" My voice was husky with grief. So far, I was holding myself together. But I knew it wouldn't last.

His hand slid down my arm. He wrapped his fingers around mine. "Sure. He's back here."

We went through the examining room to the surgery area. Both were empty.

I turned to Clint. "Where?"

The whole place was deathly silent.

Until I heard the telltale thump of a tail thwacking against chain link.

Clint inclined his head to the left. A smile lifted his cheeks. "Last kennel."

I ran around the corner. Squeezed into the hallway were three narrow kennel runs. I knelt by the last one. Bump was curled up in the front corner, his head propped against the cement block wall, his back to the wire door, a haze of sedatives in his eyes. He lifted his head ever so slightly, like it took every ounce of energy in his body to do that one simple thing. I slid my fingers through the wires to scratch the top of his neck.

"He's pretty tired right now." Clint sank down next to me and slid an arm around my shoulder. "But by the looks of it, he's going to be just fine. His blood pressure is back to normal, and his breathing sounds good. I think it's safe to say he's in the clear."

My heart did little flips inside my chest.

"How? I mean, what did you —"

"Not much. I've seen a few animals afflicted with smoke inhalation over the years. He was one of the worst. I really didn't think he'd pull through. When I first brought him in here, I started the IV drip and watched him for a while before I realized there wasn't much I could do; so I broke out the cot and went to sleep behind the front desk. I woke up to howling about an hour ago. Figured that was a good sign. But just to be on the safe side, I did reschedule a couple of spays I had on the books for this morning." He opened the kennel door for me and I went inside.

I gave Bump a hug, mindful of all the cuts that Clint had painstakingly stitched and dabbed with iodine. "Dad will be so happy to see him. When can he go home?"

"Home?" Clint echoed sympathetically. "Sam, do you need a place to stay? I have a couple of extra —"

"Ida said we could stay with her." Actually, she hadn't offered yet, but I was sure she'd welcome us. I would have loved to stay with Clint, but given the recent turn our relationship had taken, the temptation for a midnight visit would have been there. It would have been awkward with Tara and my dad around. "Thanks, though. I appreciate it. So … Bump, when can he be released?"

"Tomorrow — as long as he continues to eat well and get better. Normally, I'd keep him here another day or two more, but he needs to be with someone who can keep an eye on him around the clock. Melissa had to leave for Michigan to visit her sister's new baby and frankly I'm a bit sleep deprived. I don't have any appointments until after lunch, so I plan on taking a good long nap before that. After four o'clock tomorrow, he's all yours."

"Good. That'll work out great. They were talking about letting Dad go this afternoon. That'll give me time to get him settled before bringing Bump home — I mean to Ida's." I rose to go. Life was so mixed up right now. I had no choice but to be in the here and now, taking things one minute at a time.

Clint closed the kennel door behind me, but before I could make my exit, he pulled me against his chest and planted a deep, long kiss on my mouth. It took me a moment to react, I was so numb from lack of sleep and my mind was in a million different places.

But as his kiss lingered, it carried me away from my troubles, swept me up in a wave of comfort, and filled me with the confidence that everything was going to be okay. As long as Clint was there to stand by me.

I rested my head against his chest, felt the swell of his ribs as they expanded with each deep breath, listened to the thump-thump of his heart, stronger and steadier than my own.

His lips brushed over the part in my hair and fluttered against my forehead as he murmured, "If you need anything, Sam, anything at all, call me, okay? I'm here for you."

Nodding, I splayed my fingertips across his chest. "What if I call you at three in the morning?"

"I'll come running."

"What if I'm freaking out because I can't deal with my dad a moment longer?"

"I'll be there for you."

This was all too perfect, I told myself. It couldn't possibly last. Something would happen. Just like I'd lost Kyle.

Yet just this once, I wanted to believe that it *would* work out. That there would be someone there for me. That I wouldn't have to soldier through my crazy life alone anymore.

"What if my dog —?"

His cell phone rang. He checked the display, hit mute, and stuffed it back in his pocket. "You were saying?"

"Maybe you should get that. What if it's a client?"

His jaw twitched. "Don't worry. It can wait." He tipped my chin up with a single finger, his mouth hovering inches from mine. "You were saying?"

"I …"

His lips brushed mine teasingly.

"I forget," I said, staring at his lips, wanting to taste them again. When I came here, I'd been so tired I could have collapsed on the tile floor and slept soundly. But after just a few minutes in his embrace my blood was racing in my veins, my pulse quickening at his touch. I could have endured anything, knowing he'd be there to pick me back up afterward.

I snuggled against his chest, clinging to him like I never wanted to let go. He swayed gently on his feet, holding me firmly. I felt safe in his arms. And that was, I realized, what I'd needed these past ten years.

The desk landline rang, startling me. Abruptly, Clint broke the embrace and stomped across the floor. I planted my feet wide to steady myself, suddenly aware of the fatigue weighing down my limbs.

He thrummed his fingers on the counter a few moments before he finally grabbed the receiver.

"Hello?" A furrow formed between his brows. He turned away from me. The voice on the other end sounded chatty and upbeat, but I couldn't make out the words. "Now? No, actually it's not a good time. I've been —" The voice broke in, insistent. He let out a short sigh of exasperation. "Okay, okay, but I don't have much time. I have appointments today, including a couple of surgeries."

Why had he just lied to this person? And who was it?

"You're *where?*" He swung his torso around to peer out the big front window. A look halfway between complete surprise and horror swept over his face. He slammed the phone back into its cradle.

In the parking lot, her curvaceous bum resting against the hood of a silver Audi Spyder, a gorgeous blonde waved to him. Her hair was swept up in a loose bun, but every strand was perfectly arranged and highlighted. She had on a pair of tight-fitting black capris. As she pushed away from the car and started toward the door, her four-inch heels accentuated the slender curve of her calves and her dainty size-six shoes, toes professionally manicured in a vivid shade of coral. If her tiny feet and tame hair weren't enough to spark my jealous side, I was consumed with envy when she stripped off her white half-sleeve cardigan to reveal the form-fitting pale blue blouse underneath that left no gaps in anyone's imagination as to what her cup size was. A person could have suffocated in her cleavage.

With every step closer she came, Clint wilted more and more. His backside was pressed to the counter. If he could have run without being seen, I'm sure he would have.

"Who's that?" I asked.

He pressed his eyes shut for a moment, then forced a smile as she reached for the door. "Oh, you'll find out soon enough."

The door whooshed open, letting a gust of warm air in. Her heels hit the floor like the clanging of a gong. She flashed an obligatory smile at me, then marched straight past me, pressed herself full length against Clint, and threw her arms around his neck.

"You have *no* idea how much I've missed you," she murmured. Right before she kissed him.

Clint grappled for her arms as he mumbled something against her lips and whipped his head back.

She moaned in disappointment. "You're right. That was rude of me. I just couldn't help myself after so long away from you."

Blood boiled in my veins. Who was this whore, anyway?

Her lips curved into a friendly smile. She stepped toward me, her hand extended. "I'm sorry. Pleased to meet you ...?" She tilted her head in question, one honey-blonde wave bouncing across her forehead.

I shook her hand, but snatched mine back as quickly as I could.

"Sam McNamee. And you are ...?"

"Oh, I figured it was obvious." She glanced at Clint, her blue eyes sparkling dreamily. "I'm his wife, Danielle Townsley."

Wife? My gaze darted to Clint, but his was locked on the floor. Just as well, the daggers I was sending him with my eyes would have speared him against the back wall.

Danielle glanced from me to Clint and back again, her fingers sliding the diamond pendant of her necklace back and forth along its gold chain. As if unable to bear the awkward silence, she finally spoke. "So, you must be a client of Clint's."

I waited for him to say something. To give me the signal that this was some crazy stalker and I shouldn't make any sudden moves. But he just stood there, plastered to the counter, as mute as a marble statue.

"Uh, sure," I said, my voice so small I could barely hear myself say the words. I wanted to dive into a hole at that moment, pretend this wasn't happening. But when I looked at Danielle again, she'd already stepped back to Clint and slid an arm around him in a half hug.

My eyes stinging, I spun around and raced out the door. I jumped into my car, but instead of putting my key in the ignition, I sat in the driver's seat staring down at my lap as I dug my fingernails into my palms to keep from crying. I pinched my eyes shut, but the tears came anyway.

This couldn't be happening. Not after last night. And just now ... I was sure that he ... that we ...

What the hell?

Knuckles tapped at my window. I gulped back my heart. Clint was standing there, a pleading look on his face. He motioned at me to lower the window.

I cracked it an inch. "What?"

"I can explain." He slid his fingers over the top of the glass so I couldn't close the window. Although I could have. It would have served him right. "This isn't what you think."

"That's what the cheaters always say on Maury Povich."

"Huh? Sam, please. Don't jump to any conclusions. We need to talk about this, okay?"

I glared at him. "So explain."

He glanced at the clinic door. Danielle waved at him. "I can't right now. Maybe we can meet later today?"

I shook my head. "I don't have time today." Which was the truth, but more than that I needed some time to let my emotions cool. To come to grips with this.

Twelve hours ago I'd thought my life was damn near perfect. Now, it couldn't have been more crap. All because he'd lied to me. Not lied, really. Just forgotten to mention that his wife wasn't really dead after all.

"Tomorrow when you pick up Bump, then? Please, Sam," — his voice cracked, but not half as much as my heart — "please?"

Jamming my key into the ignition, I gave it a murderous twist and punched my foot at the gas. The engine roared to life, humming greedily as I continued to feed it fuel. "I'll give you five minutes."

Then I slipped the car into reverse and laid rubber, watching him sulk in the rearview mirror as I rocketed out onto the road.

chapter 30

SUNLIGHT REFLECTED IN SILVER diamonds off the waters of the duck pond. A pair of mallards and four downy ducklings paddled across its expanse, the little ones swimming in valiant spurts of energy, resting, then hurrying to catch up. The mamma mallard hopped up on the bank to preen her feathers, while their father monitored the babies, who struggled to make their way up the steep, grassy slope to their hiding place beyond the cattails.

My arm curled under my head, I lay sideways on the park bench. Clouds rolled overhead, high and tall, a painter's vision. A teardrop rolled across my nose and I dashed it away. I thought I'd cried my tear ducts dry an hour ago. I sat up, blood draining from my head to leave me dizzy, my sight blurred.

Anger filled me and I squeezed my eyes shut. Anger at the arsonist for almost taking my dad's and Bump's lives. Anger that Clint hadn't told me the truth about his wife. Anger that I'd let myself believe that he and I had a future.

How could I have been so stupid? There must have been signs that I overlooked? Surely there was some lesson in this. What doesn't kill you makes you stronger, right?

I scoffed. Obviously people who said that had never had their souls crushed into a fine powder.

Well, I wasn't going to let Dr. Lambert Clinton Chastain hold the key to my happiness. I'd survived Kyle's death; I'd survive this.

I took out my phone and dialed Ida's number, hopeful. She answered on the second ring.

"Sam, dear," Ida said, "how are you doing?"

I drew in a breath and pushed out the only word that came to mind. "Fine."

In the canopy above, two squirrels leapt from limb to limb, bickering.

"You don't sound fine. Why don't you come on over to my place? I have two extra bedrooms. I don't know why I didn't say something last night, but there was just so much going on. You can all stay here while you get things sorted out. I insist. It's the least I can do."

I swallowed. I knew she meant it, but even this one small decision seemed like a burden right now.

"Thank you," I said. Two little words. And yet they sucked all the energy from my body.

"Do you want me to fetch Tara for you? Just let me know where she's at and I'll go get her."

"No … no. It's okay. I'll do it. I need to talk to her alone first anyway." After that, I planned on taking an extra-long nap. Maybe Ida had a bottle of wine in her house? Maybe I should pick up a box of pinot noir at the store before getting Tara? Heaven knew I could stand to have my senses dulled.

After hanging up, I shot Tara a quick text telling her I'd pick her up and that we'd be staying with Ida.

Where are you? she texted back.

At the park.

Doing what?

Just resting. And thinking.

293

I understand. See you soon. Can't wait to see Bump and Gramps. Glad they're okay.

Me, too.

Mom?

Yes?

I love you. Thiiiiiis big.

Hot tears pricked the back of my eyelids. That was what Tara used to say when she was really little. She'd hold her arms out wide as she lay in her bed at night. I'd hug her tight, breathe in the scent of her baby shampoo, and kiss her once over each eyelid.

I love you, too, pumpkin.

Although I knew I had to get going, I couldn't motivate myself to move. I didn't want to be around anyone, not even Ida or Tara. They'd try to comfort me, but they had no idea what I was feeling right now. Or not feeling. I didn't want to follow through with my responsibilities as the adult, pretending that everything was all right. It wasn't.

I set my phone beside me, wrestling with the urge to call Clint. But I didn't like where that would eventually lead: a fight. And I was too exhausted for that. I didn't want to think about his 'wife' or why he hadn't told me about her. As far as I was concerned, there was no way he could explain himself out of that one. Giving him five minutes tomorrow was simply a courtesy. If I didn't have to pick up Bump, I probably wouldn't even give him five seconds.

Yet he'd seemed so earnest, so desperate for me to understand. My fingers crept toward the phone.

No. Forget Clint for now. I needed to just worry about myself and my family.

The phone buzzed with an incoming text and I jumped where I sat. It was Tara again.

Forgot to ask. When are you coming?

A simple question, but I couldn't answer. My brain was on

overload, ready to shut down. I needed to rest.

I folded forward, my forehead upon my knees, my arms wrapped around my head to shut out the world. Branches snapped nearby. Stupid squirrels. Bump would have chased them away for me. I lowered an arm to peek at them so I could utter a warning.

But instead of furry rodents, I saw a pair of soot-stained ripped denims before me.

Jake's face split into an evil grin. The smell of gasoline on him was almost overpowering. He twisted his ball cap around so the bill was facing backward. "Fancy meeting you here again."

I shot to my feet, bolting to the left toward my car.

One step. That was as far as I got before his foot whipped forward, tripping me. I fell with a thud, my chin smacking the packed earth, my teeth cutting across my tongue.

The sweet iron tang of blood filled my mouth. A warm drop trickled from the corner of my lips.

He laughed. A gut-deep, diabolical cackle.

Footsteps circled me, dirty shoes kicking at twigs and fallen leaves. As he passed by, I noticed the big rip in one of his pants legs halfway between his calf and his ankle — and the puncture marks on his skin, the exact size and placement of a large dog's teeth.

A broken branch lay within my reach. *'Hit 'em in the nuts,'* Dad used to tell me in eighth grade, when boys teased me about my flat chest. *'That'll shut 'em up.'*

Two more times he circled me, his steps faster, nearer. I waited until his feet were pointing away from me. Forcefully, I flung my arm out. His laughter stopped abruptly. He pivoted. My fingers closed around the branch, pulled it toward me. In a blink, I tried to gauge where his crotch was, aim for it.

But just as I bent my elbow to swipe the branch up between his legs, his foot came down on my wrist. Hard. Bone-breaking hard. A scream tore from my throat.

The branch fell softly to the ground. He kicked it away.

I couldn't feel my fingers. Couldn't move them. There was an unnatural angle in the lower half of my forearm. I stared at it, perplexed. The edges of my vision blurred.

"You stupid, stupid, bitch," Jake said, his words slurred with drunkenness. He planted his feet to either side of me, straddling my legs, then sank to his haunches, his buttocks resting against my right thigh. "Shoulda minded y'own damn business."

I looked up at him, trying to make sense of it all, scrambling to pull my thoughts together, vaguely aware of the growing ache in my arm.

"Please ..." I squeaked out.

He ran a dirty hand up my back. "I like a woman who begs for it." When he reached my shoulder, he nudged me onto my back, so I was lying face up beneath him. He sat on my legs, pinning me there. An ugly smile twisted his mouth. "Please what, darlin'?"

This was like that night at the lodge with Dylan, but worse. There was no one here. And I was hurt. Badly.

A tear slid down my cheek. All I could think of was that I had to pick up Tara.

"Please ..." I whispered, "don't."

Casting his eyes upward, he huffed out a breath. "Wrong answer."

He raised himself up on his knees. Feeling the release of his weight, I wiggled backward, trying to get away, to free my limbs so I could fight him. Or run.

His right arm reached back. I pulled my legs up, flipped over, pushed up from the ground with my good arm. And then, out of the corner of my eye, I caught the dull flash of a wrench raised in the air, hurtling toward my head.

Metal collided with bone, ringing inside my brain.

Like someone had pulled the cord on the stage curtain, my world went suddenly black.

The last thing I heard was my phone vibrating with a text.

chapter 31

THE MOMENT I WOKE up, I gasped reflexively. But I couldn't suck in any air. Something was covering my mouth.

This must be what it's like to drown, I thought. *Slow. Terrifying.*

Instinct kicked in before panic could pull me under. I arched my neck back to inhale through my nose. Life-giving air flowed in, filling my lungs, diffusing through my body. As I moved my jaw around to figure out what was on my mouth, I felt a stiff, crinkly substance pulling at the skin around my lips. Duct tape. I tried to lift a hand to pull it away, but my arms were bound to my body with electrical cord.

For a minute — or maybe it was mere seconds, or hours — I could only make out a few things around me: a wadded fast food bag, an oily rag, an empty cigarette pack. I couldn't make sense of them. Or remember where I was or how I had gotten there.

Until the smell of gasoline permeated my nostrils, sending waves of nausea up from my gut.

Oh shit. He's going to bludgeon me to death, then burn my body.

I was lying on my left side in the backseat of Jake's truck — a red truck. Crumpled up like yesterday's gym shirt. My face smashed against a greasy burger wrapper with half-dried blobs of mustard and ketchup on it. A single burnt French fry teetered on the edge of the seat, sliding over the edge as we hit a bump in the road.

Wriggling my shoulders, I began to inch the cord downward in the hopes I could pull an arm free. A bolt of pain ripped up my right arm as the cord slid down past my elbow. I'd forgotten about the broken wrist. I bit the inside of my lip to keep from screaming and tried again. But the pain was worse this time. The shock was wearing off. If anything, I wished I could slip back into unconsciousness. At least then I wouldn't know what was happening to me.

I didn't want to know how the end would come. An instantaneous death would have been a million times better than this. I wondered if it was like that for Kyle — a moment so quick he didn't have time to contemplate it.

We whipped around a corner and my body slid until the top of my skull collided with the door. Sunlight stabbed through the opposite window, hitting me square in the face. I blinked at the brightness until my eyes adjusted. The back of Jake's head came into focus. Country music blared from the radio. I stared at the dirty bill of his ball cap, imagining the thousand ways I would kill him. If I could.

He turned his head to look back at me. I shut my eyes, pretending to still be out cold.

The truck trundled on down the bumpy road. A lighter clicked. I peeked between my lashes to see Jake lighting a cigarette. He cracked open the driver's side window. Hot air rushed in, stirring the smell of gasoline and tobacco.

Bile rushed up my esophagus, burning as it went. I swallowed, trying to hold it back, but a spasm squeezed my gut and vomit spewed into my mouth. I shoved my tongue to the back of my mouth to keep from choking on it. Unable to spit it out, I forced myself to gulp it back down in tiny, silent mouthfuls. My eyes watered. I kept swallowing, until my saliva had diluted the caustic taste.

I rocked back as he hit the brakes, then sideways again as we wheeled around a corner. My face was now at the edge of the seat. I couldn't see the back of his head anymore. Which meant he couldn't see most of me, either. I stared down onto the floor, searching among the wrappers and empty cups and crushed cans for — I have no idea what I was looking for.

Until I saw it. A wrench. With brown splotches on the business end: Bud Crawley's dried blood.

Tires skittered over loose stone as we left the asphalt of the road. We were on someone's private lane. My prospects were getting grimmer by the moment. Every time a wheel hit a pothole, the jarring sent a knife of pain through my crooked lower arm. That pain, oddly, was a blessing. Because instead of me becoming paralyzed with fear, it pissed me off that he had done that to me while laughing. As if he got his jollies from hurting others. I wanted to whack the bloody bastard senseless.

Through the screen of my eyelids, I sensed light and shadow alternating. Cautiously, I braved a look. A dense curtain of trees lined the lane. Sunlight peeked through tangled limbs. A quarter mile passed. A half mile. Three turns. Deeper and deeper and deeper into the woods.

Wherever we were, Jake didn't want anyone to find us.

Gradually, the truck slowed, then stopped. He rolled down the windows and killed the engine. For an excruciatingly long minute, Jake sat there, sucking on his cigarette, blowing smoke at the windshield. Finally, he flipped open a cooler beside him, took out a can of beer, and ripped the tab off. He guzzled it, belched, and guzzled some more.

Stagnant air intensified every smell inside the truck cab. If I hadn't known better, I would've thought I was inside an overflowing dumpster.

Jake got out. Slammed the door. And walked away.

This was my chance.

I listened to his receding footsteps. Heard a door creak open, then bang shut. A few seconds later, music blasted from a radio, voices and music jumbling as he flipped through several stations, finally settling on a country station. Which was like a screwdriver to my brain.

Now I was really irritated. I used to have a coworker at Top Floor Media who insisted on playing country music every afternoon when energies flagged. Instead of energizing me, it plied at my tolerance. More than once I contemplated sneaking into her cubicle and smashing her MP3 player when she went to the bathroom, but I was afraid security cameras would rat me out.

I pushed myself as close to the edge of the seat as I could and snaked my good arm over, reaching blindly. The cord around my middle tightened suddenly. Bolts of pain shot through me. I flailed my hand, knocking a half-full beer can over. Then, cold steel hit the pads of my fingers. I grabbed the wrench handle, brought it to me, and tried to pull my arm close.

Music blared as a door was flung open somewhere. I fumbled with the wrench, turned it in my grip, then slipped the handle end below the waistband of my pants before tugging my shirt down over it.

Jake jerked at the door handle nearest me. I froze, my heart thudding in my ears. He'd forgotten to unlock it. Keys jangled. The lock clicked.

"Heh, ssstupid bitch." He chuckled as he yanked the door open. "Trying to get away, were you?"

I mumbled a few choice words back at him.

He ripped the duct tape from my mouth, taking skin with it. I gulped for air.

In one frighteningly clumsy movement, he hauled me from the truck and set me on my feet. Eyes drifting shut, I slumped, feigning unconsciousness, but he shoved me against the wheel well and slapped me across the cheek. Hard. My eyes flew open as I stumbled sideways.

The wrench shifted downward. I clamped my arm against it.

"Bastard!" I spat, no longer able to contain my rage.

He stared at me for a moment, a foggy look in his eyes. Then he belched. A loud, gurgly, drawn-out belch. And laughed. Just before he forked his fingers through my hair and dragged me toward the shed where the music was blasting from. A fence, only half of it still standing, encircled a small paddock behind the shed. To the left, through the trees, was a dilapidated house, shutters hanging askew and every curtain drawn. Beyond that, nothing but trees and more trees.

My legs churned as I struggled to keep up with him. You'd think as drunk as he was he'd have a hard time getting from one place to another, but he dragged me along purposefully, mumbling as he went.

"Shoulda minded y'own God damn business … Stupid sheriff oughtta … nosy, blabbing … bitch and yer lousy stuck-up boyfriend think you're —"

Most of it was unintelligible, but somehow he'd figured out that I'd been looking into the arsons. The truth was that I hadn't known until he showed up at the park that he was the one responsible. But looking back, the clues were there. Why did he think Clint had anything to do with it, though? Besides, one date didn't make him my boyfriend. Although apparently in this backwater town it did.

Staggering back a step, he halted in front of a stall door. My knees buckled. My body dipped — and my head went with it. He yanked up on my hair, stretching my scalp. I yelped.

"Shut. Up!" he roared, spittle flying. He pawed at the latch until it popped up. The half-door swung outward. The sweet odor of moldy straw hit me, tickling my throat.

He shoved me into the dimly lit space. I landed in a pile of hardened manure. My eyes began to adjust to the faint light. A horse stable, judging by the size of the turds. I was allergic to horse hair.

Shit.

The door slammed shut. Jake stomped away and went back inside the house. There was no telling how long he'd be gone, but my guess was not very. I allowed myself a few moments to get my bearings and think things through. Sparkly motes of dust drifted across the shaft of light falling through the opening of the upper door. Or where it used to be. Broken planks lay scattered across the floor.

I rolled over and sat up to lean against the back wall. Bits of blackened straw and flakes of manure clung to my clothes. I tried not to think of the itch already burning at the bared part of my arms. Soon the hives would erupt all over my body to cover me in red splotches.

And to think, an hour ago I'd thought this day could not get any worse.

Squeezing my shoulders together, I managed to loosen the cord. But as much as I wriggled and rubbed against the wall I couldn't get it up and off.

A large eye hook was attached to the wall to my left. I went to it and slipped it under the cord at my back. The metal poked into my spine as I wedged the cord up further. Then I slid downward, pulling the cord up and over my head. My arms free, I untangled the cord from my hair, but not without losing several chunks.

I lunged for the door and shoved a hip at it, but it didn't budge. The wrench shifted beneath my waistband, slipping down my pants leg. I wedged the fingers of my good arm down my pants, groping for it.

"Gawd, woman."

I jerked my eyes up to stare straight at Jake as he propped an elbow over the top of the door.

"Will you ever give up?" he drawled.

The next thing I saw was the jagged edge of a broken plank coming straight at my head.

I CAME TO IN a pile of decaying straw inside the shed. It had taken me a long time to figure out where I was, because I was having a hard time remembering. When I finally did, I wished I hadn't. The light coming through the trees was now a paling silver. Hours had passed. Apparently, he'd beaten the daylights out of me.

Dried blood was caked to my cheek. My ribs ached. My head was pounding. I couldn't feel my fingers on my right arm anymore. One eye was almost swollen shut. And there was a chain around my middle. So tight I couldn't inhale fully without it compressing my internal organs.

But I was still alive.

Music blasted from the house. For a while, Jake warbled along with the lyrics. But as night encroached, his caterwauling faded away. Had he fallen asleep? And how long had I been here like this?

I rolled over, tucked my knees beneath me, and tried to raise myself up, but the world around me tipped. I forced myself upright to lean against the wall. The edges of my vision blackened. I couldn't keep my eyes open. Awareness drifted away. I fought to stay awake. Fought to remember. To think.

Then it came back to me: I needed to get away from here.

The problem was — I couldn't. I hurt. Everywhere.

The sickening aroma of gas fumes invaded my nostrils, bringing back the memory of an engine rumbling and tires crunching over gravel. Yes, I remembered now. Remembered Jake smashing my wrist. Shoving me inside his truck. Bringing me here. Hitting me, again and again and again. Although by then I was beyond feeling pain.

Then the sounds stopped. Even the music had stopped.

A door shut. Feet scuffed over gravel. Was that Jake coming for me?

A fist pounded on wood.

Why the hell would he knock?

I listened hard, but heard nothing more for several more minutes.

Pried my good eye open. A gas can lay tipped on its side before me, its contents soaking the dirt in a dark pool. Beyond, I saw nothing but a watery square of moonlight.

My eye stung. I shut it. Welcomed the darkness. Drifted away.

A BANG, LOUD AND sharp, rattled my skull. Adrenaline burst through every blood vessel in my body, startling me to alertness.

Somewhere between the shed and the house, there was a scuffle. Flesh pummeling flesh. Grunts and groans. Curses. Then —

"Where is she?!"

"Fuck you, Archer! Fuck you to hell and back."

Archer?

"What was I supposed to do without a paying job, huh?" Jake went on, his angry bellow fading to a pitiful whine. "Volunteers don't make no money, man. Miley and I were gonna get hitched next year. Because of all the trouble you caused, she won't even speak to me anymore. You ruined everything for me, Malone. Took everything — my job, my girl. I was next in line to go full time soon as Bobby retired. But no, you had to freeze hires and —"

"I didn't have anything to do with that, Jake. It was a county-wide hiring freeze. The money wasn't there."

"You're just a big, fat, ugly, lyin' son of a bitch, that's what you are! You wanted me out, that's why you threatened me."

"Threatened you? With counseling? I was trying to help. I didn't want you to lose your job. You're good at it. Jake … please, you have a problem. I only wanted to —"

"Problem? *I* have a problem? I'll tell you what my problem is: you. And I'm going to make you sorry you ever messed with me."

I heard the cock of a gun, followed by the rapid fall of footsteps.

Somehow, I stood. I staggered forward a step, the chain nearly jerking me back down. Locking my knees to steady myself, I looked out the opening just in time to see Jake running for the shed, a rifle in his grip.

I made for the far corner, but the chain wouldn't reach. So I stood there, as Jake raced toward me, barrel raised, his finger on the trigger. I backed up against the wall as he crashed through the door, slamming the butt end of the rifle into my stomach. It clanked against the wrench, hidden beneath my pants. He blinked once, then wheeled around as Archer dove after him.

They rolled around on the dirt in a tangle of legs and arms, both of them grappling for the rifle. Moldy dust rose up, choking my lungs. For a moment, I couldn't tell who was who, looking through my one bleary eye. Somehow, I pulled the wrench free, but it felt like a thousand pounds in my hand.

With a primal grunt, Jake flipped Archer over, pinning him to the dirt beneath his weight. He jammed the barrel against Archer's throat, right beneath his jaw.

I swung, aiming at the back of Jake's skull. It struck him behind his ear, sounding like a hammer hitting hollow wood.

The rifle went off. Archer lay staring at the ceiling, eyes wide.

For a moment, Jake swayed, his head lolling to one side. Then, he slumped ever so slightly forward — and fell on top of Archer.

"Archer?" I dropped the wrench, straining toward him, but couldn't quite reach.

He didn't answer, didn't move. But neither did Jake.

I looked for blood splatters everywhere and didn't see any. Had I just knocked Jake out, only to have Archer dying beneath him? *Oh, God. Oh God oh God oh God.* This was bad. Very, *very* bad. I couldn't escape with this chain around me. As soon as Jake regained consciousness, he was going to do something terrible to me.

Hopeless, I sank to the ground and buried my head against my knees.

Then, with one big heave, Archer shoved Jake off. My heart did cartwheels.

"You're okay! You're okay!" I blubbered. Tears flooded my eyes. I started weeping like a widow.

Archer rolled over to look at me. "Yeah, well, you sure don't look okay."

After he'd checked Jake's pupils to make sure he was still out cold, he scooted over to me and wrapped his arms around me. "I'm usually the one saving people, you know." He nuzzled his scruffy cheek against the top of my head, laying the lightest of kisses there. "But don't worry, my pride's still intact. Pretty lady like you can save my life any day."

Sirens sounded in the distance. This time, I was glad to hear them.

My day was looking up now. Life could only get better from here on, right?

chapter 32

SHERIFF DRISCOLL PULLED HIS notepad from his back pocket and tipped up the brim of his hat in a silent greeting as he entered my hospital room.

He scooted the vinyl upholstered chair closer to my bed and jotted the date at the top of the paper. His eyes were a calming earthy brown and he wore a sympathetic smile. "Tell me how it all went down, Ms. McNamee."

I told him everything, without embellishment. From the time I met Archer and Jake in the park and my tire got slashed, to my run-in with Dylan Hawkins at the lodge, to the moment they hauled Jake Taylor away, cussing and kicking, in the back of the patrol car.

In the week I spent in the hospital, Ida had visited every day and filled me in on everything she uncovered about Jake. Turned out he had had a lifelong fascination with fire and firefighters. So no one in Wilton was surprised when he went to firefighter school a few years after high school. By then, he'd fallen hard for sweet little Miley Harper. Several times during the three years that Jake was volunteering at the Wilton Township Fire Department, they broke up and got back together. When Miley started seeing another guy named Leroy Roberds, Jake made a pitch to win her back by proposing. She accepted, but Jake later caught her behind the bowling alley with Leroy. If it hadn't been for the crowd that gathered at Miley's screams, Jake might have beaten him senseless.

The reason Miley gave for breaking up with Jake was his alcohol and drug problem. In order to save Jake's career, Archer had suggested substance abuse counseling to him the day they went fishing at the park and I saw them. Turned out that the night Dad's house caught fire wasn't the first time Jake had begged off 'sick' when he was on call.

"So when Bobby Voorhees retired and Jake didn't get hired on full time," I said, "he started setting fires? That doesn't make sense."

"To a reasonably sane person, no, it doesn't." Sheriff Driscoll leaned back in his chair. "Jake figured if people were scared enough of their houses burning down, they'd pass the levy and he'd have himself a secure job."

"But why steal things? Wouldn't he have been more likely to be found out that way?"

Tara and Ida peeked in the doorway. I waved them in.

Sheriff Driscoll nodded at them, then turned his gaze back on me. "You'd think. But he started smoking marijuana when Miley Harper broke it off. He'd also been downsized from his part-time job at Armentrout's Hardware and soon after that another job at the farm supply store. He was hard up for money. Selling stolen goods was one way to get some fast cash to feed his habits."

"That all makes sense. Sort of. But why did he kill Bud Crawley with a wrench?"

"Indications are that Crawley knew something, whether about the fires or the stolen goods still isn't clear, but one way or another we *will* find out. It's possible Jake hadn't really meant to kill his brother, that he just acted out of anger. The wrench belonged to Crawley. It appeared he had just finished putting a tire back on his truck in the garage. According to ex-girlfriend Miley, Jake had a habit of slashing people's tires when he was mad about something. Crawley must've figured out Jake did it, then made him pay for the replacement."

Tara hugged me lightly, careful of my arm and stitches. My wrist was in a cast and I had several contusions to my head and ribs. Thankfully, I'd been unconscious when Jake laid into me and there hadn't been any permanent damage. In time, I'd heal, but I'd look at people and my surroundings differently now. Jake may have been locked up in jail, but that wasn't enough for me to walk from here thinking I'd be safe.

The mattress dipped to the side as Tara claimed a spot beside me, bumping my bum arm. "Sorry," she muttered.

"It's okay." I patted her hand in reassurance. "They've doped me up pretty good. Elephants could dance on my mattress and I'd barely notice."

She giggled, but then her face went suddenly serious. "I was so worried about you when you didn't call back, Mom. I told Ida. We went to the park looking for you. When we didn't find you, she called Archer. He had a hunch that Jake was after you and went to his place. I'm so glad he found you in time. I don't know what I would have done if ... if ..." Her lip drooped, then quivered as tears slid over her cheek and streamed down her neck. Her breathing rate began to escalate and grew shallower.

"Remember your breathing exercises, sweetie. Focus on me. Focus. I'm here. I'm fine. Just fine. I'm not going anywhere."

She forced in a huge gulp of air, held it, let it out slowly between pursed lips. After several more breaths, her breathing returned to normal, although it was clear from the pinched look on her face that she was struggling to maintain control. Ida rubbed her back, taking care of her like the grandmother she'd never had.

"What about Dylan Hawkins?" I asked the sheriff. "Have you found anything out about him?"

It was the drawn-out pause that made my middle tighten.

Shaking his head, he clicked his pen and placed it in his front shirt pocket. "Nothing yet. So far everything seems legit on his end. If he's been covering his tracks, he knows exactly how to do it."

"But the Ducati? What about that? Could he have altered the VIN somehow? It just seems like a strange coincidence."

"I agree, Ms. McNamee. But right now it's circumstantial evidence. Crawley's motorcycle appears to have changed hands several times before he acquired it, so we're having difficulty drawing any relation to his bike and Hawkins'. But I promise you, we'll look into it further. Jake Taylor definitely had links to a theft ring of some sort. Could be a more complicated system than we might imagine. Kind of like a spider web. For now, though, he's not talking. The dumb thing is that the judge would go easier on him if he did, but criminals can be unreasonably loyal to one another. The good thing about living in a place like Humboldt County is that folks look out for one another. Luckily there are more good people than bad ones around here." He stood slowly, almost like he was afraid to startle me. After tucking his notebook in his pocket, he came to my bedside and placed a hand gently on my thigh. His touch was sympathetic, his words like honey to the soul. If there was a Lone Ranger in this age, it was him.

He bent close, lowering his voice. "You sure you don't want me to press charges against Hawkins for —"

"No," I said quickly, before Tara or Ida could hear anything else. More than them knowing that Hawkins had tried to have his way with me, I didn't want them to know how stupid I'd been to try to trick him into giving me information. Ida might have thought it intriguing, me playing detective, but Tara would have had a full blown panic attack. She was barely holding herself together as it was.

"All right. We'll continue to investigate the stolen goods. We may never find out what happened to some of them, but at least we have a start. And if you ever need me, for anything, you call me direct, you hear?" He straightened, smiling at Tara and Ida in turn. "Good day, ladies. Take care."

The moment he was out of sight, Ida let out a breathy sigh. "Humboldt County's own Clark Gable. Or do you think he looks more like Sean Connery? If he wasn't married I'd —"

"Ida!" I chided.

"What? I was going to say invite him to dinner. And I wasn't talking about for me. He may be a decade older than you, Sam, but he's still a hottie."

Tara snorted a laugh and we all broke out in giggles.

"That reminds me," Ida said when she'd finally gotten her breath back. "How are things with that dreamy veterinarian of yours?"

My mood couldn't have turned any quicker if she'd shot me straight through the heart with a crossbow bolt. My lip twitched. "He's married."

She tilted her head in sympathy. "Ohhh, I'm sorry, honey. He seemed so —"

"Perfect. Yeah, I thought so, too. Well, he's not. No sense dwelling on it."

Just then the same male nurse who'd ushered me into my father's room after the fire bustled in carrying an armload of paperwork. "They're almost ready to discharge you, Ms. McNamee. The doctor gave you instructions and a follow-up schedule, correct?"

I nodded and scooted myself up to sit straighter as he laid a clipboard across my lap and flipped through it.

"Good. Just sign here, and here … and here."

As soon as all my things were gathered up, the nurse helped me into a wheelchair. I could've walked myself — although with the stilted, leaning stride of a peg-legged Hunchback of Notre Dame — but I already knew they wouldn't let me. Hospital policy, or some such B.S. meant to cover their legal hides in case I fainted on the way out and hit my head on a gurney.

When we got to the patient pick-up area, Tara had to go out with

Ida because she couldn't remember where she parked her car. I couldn't see how that was possible, given that we were at the Fullbright hospital, not the Cleveland Clinic. Most likely a van had pulled in beside her and she just couldn't see it a whole three rows away.

It was taking them longer than it should have. I started peeling back a hangnail on my broken wrist hand, looking up only when I heard footsteps stop before me.

Dr. Clint Chastain stood before me, looking as apologetic as if he'd just run over a kitten in my driveway. Beside him sat Bump, whining lowly. There was an uncharacteristic wrinkle puckering my dog's speckled forehead. Those odd eyes and mismatched ears melted my heart. Even the disappointment I felt toward Clint couldn't outweigh the love I had for that wayward mutt.

"I know you weren't going to ask," Clint began, the leash squeezed tight in his hands, "but I'm going to tell you anyway."

I opened my mouth to speak, but he held a hand up to stop me.

"Danielle and I have been separated for two years now. She's been all over Africa: Sudan, Ethiopia, the Congo. Treating kids who are malnourished, or suffering from malaria and a dozen other diseases you've never heard of. Refugees from war, mostly." He scoffed, looked away. "You wouldn't think it to look at her, but she really is a selfless person. It's what drove us apart. I wanted her with me. She was consumed with helping people who couldn't help themselves. So I let her go to do what she was meant to do. At first, I thought she'd eventually tire of it. But she never did. And the longer she was gone, the easier I found it was to live without her, rather than with her. So we agreed to part ways and finalize the divorce on her next trip back. She returned sooner than I expected. Surprised me. Stunned me, really. I was still trying to work out a way to explain it all to you."

"You just did."

313

"Yes, but I should have done it sooner. I'm sorry, Sam. I really am. But it was so much more complicated than you can imagine." He shoved his hands deep in his pockets, his face tight with regret. "I made the mistake of using the local attorney here in town, Natasha Plappert-Knapp. Papers were messed up, then not filed. Time went by. I just thought all divorces took that long to get cleared up. When I finally figured it out … God, I don't want to lose you over this, but it's my own damn fault if I do."

It all sounded plausible. And he did sound genuinely sorry. Still, it wasn't the fact that his divorce wasn't final that bothered me so much as him keeping details from me, even letting me believe his wife was dead. Then again, he'd never really said that.

A tear dripped from my chin. I curled my fingernails into my palm so the physical pain would detract from the piercing in my heart. Maybe, in time, we could try starting over. Part of me really needed him, but right now I needed to be with my family more.

"You know," I said, "if you'd just told me —"

"I know. Stupid of me, I wish I could go back in time. I just didn't expect things to go so fast between us. Or get so serious. I thought I had time to work it all out with Danielle first." He slid his hands from his pockets, clenched and unclenched his fists. "The reason she came into town, Sam, was to tell me the divorce papers were on their way. They came today, in fact. Plus, there were some other papers I had to sign, financial matters, like dissolving our joint bank account, separating out insurance policies. Boring stuff, really. But we took care of it all and there's nothing binding us together now."

"Do you still love her?" I blurted, surprised to hear myself say it. But I had to know.

"I care about her, yes. We parted amicably — which isn't to say there weren't harsh feelings, but we've moved on. She assured me that she has, too. And if you're asking if I want to wake up next to her tomorrow like I do you? Not even close. That chapter's closed. I want to be with you, not her."

I wanted to be with him, too. Desperately. With every ounce of my being. But … I had to be sure that things between Danielle and him were truly done.

"So … about us?" he asked. "What happens now?"

"Nothing. Nothing happens now." It took all my courage to say that to him, because what I really wanted to do was throw myself at him and feel his arms around me, holding me tight. And he would have done just that. But there was obviously a lot about each other we didn't know yet. If we were ever going to get together again, we needed to start fresh and go more slowly. "I think we both have plenty to sort out in our own lives first."

He nodded. "And later, down the road? Please tell me there's a chance, Sam. *Please*."

"I don't know, Clint. I really don't. Lately, it seems like all my plans just get bulldozed. I need to learn to deal with what life gives me, day by day. And I need to know that you'll wait until I'm ready."

Even if nothing more ever happened between Clint and me, what our relationship had taught me was that I *could* love again. All I needed to do was let it happen. A couple days ago, I had thought only Clint could fill that role. But now, I wasn't so sure. When I'd seen in that shed that Archer was alive, I'd felt *something*. I just wasn't sure what. After all, he'd saved my life. Maybe it was just relief, or gratitude?

Clint gazed up at the clouds, impossibly tall and framed in touches of red and purple as they caught the light of a setting sun. "Whenever you're ready, I'll be here."

I gave him my hand to let him know I was open to it. He bent down and kissed the backs of my fingers, the brush of his lips igniting sparks somewhere in the furthest chambers of my heart.

Ida's Camry rolled to a stop in front of us. From the backseat, Selma flapped a hand at me. She held up a bouquet of daisies and my chest flooded with warmth. Tara started to open the car door, but I held up a finger to let her know we needed another minute. She nodded once, then said something to Ida.

Unfortunately, neither Clint nor I could fill the awkward void that gaped between us.

Bump nudged my hand, sliding his big nose beneath my good arm. The hair was just beginning to grow back where Clint had shaved around his wound after the car accident. A three-inch jagged pucker marked the place his stitches had once been. I hugged Bump to me and kissed the top of his head as he licked my hand gently. "Thanks for taking care of him, Clint — and for bringing him here."

"So ... you're going to keep him?"

"Looks like it." I stole a glance at Clint.

The corners of his eyes crinkled with a smile. "The day you first brought him to my clinic, I thought you would. I was half tempted to take him in myself, but for some reason I didn't. I felt ... *knew* he'd already found a home."

Home. I didn't know where exactly that was anymore.

For now, I supposed it was at Ida's house. Because that's where Dad and Tara were. And Bump. The dog I hadn't wanted. The one that fate had seen fit to toss in front of my car on a rainy night.

As I leaned forward to stand, Clint grabbed my good elbow to help me up. I clung to his arm a few moments longer than I needed to. "You'll come by to take Bump for a walk now and then, won't you?"

He smiled, hopeful. "I wouldn't miss it."

Tara hopped out of the car and opened the back door. Bump dove inside first, his big tongue lolling to the side, saliva dripping onto Ida's meticulously clean seat. The door thumped shut and Bump leaned against my shoulder. Hot stinky dog breath blasted against my neck.

"Hey," Selma said, "sorry I didn't come inside. I'm scared to death of mercy."

"Mercy?" I buckled myself in as Ida pulled away.

"You know, those flab-eating germs."

Ah, MRSA. I snorted.

"What?" she said.

"Nothing. It's the painkillers. They make me a little goofy. Say, do you have an accent?"

"Me? I don't think so, but my momma *was* from Alabama."

"That explains a lot."

Selma sniffed the petals of the bouquet, sneezed, then extended it to me. "Newt said I could bring you these. He even gave them to me free." A tiny crease formed between her penciled brows. "Oh, hope you don't mind I didn't pay for them. I was going to, but he wouldn't let me."

"That's all right." I took the flowers from her as Bump followed them with his nose. I laid them in my lap. "I love daisies."

She put an arm around me in a half-hug, Bump sandwiched between us. When she let go, she looked me over more closely. "You look like —"

"Hell, I know."

"I was going to say like you could use a lot more hugs."

"Yeah, I could." I decided right then I was going to tell her about Dylan next time we were alone. She deserved better. And if she blamed me for anything, well, our friendship wasn't as strong as I thought. But I hoped it was.

Ida tilted her head to peer at me in the rearview mirror. "Your dad's waiting at my house. Hopefully asleep. They gave him enough sedatives to knock out a Clydesdale. Just to be safe, I popped in a DVD of *NCIS*: Season 1 for him. He won't budge. He still doesn't know the thing has a pause button."

Knowing Dad, he hadn't taken the drugs. Between the two of us, we probably had enough medication to start our own pharmacy.

"Oh, here." Tara handed my cell phone over the seat as we pulled away. "Someone named Rosa from Big Pine, Florida has left a bunch of messages. I answered the last time and she said to have you call her back right away. Something about a 'lanai'?"

After playing the messages, I dialed her back. It went straight to voicemail.

"Rosa, hi. Thanks for getting back to me." I paused, lost for words. In the end, I decided to keep it simple. "Say, I've had a slight change of plans. We won't be moving south any time soon. If I need any help in the future, I'll be sure to give you a call."

I put my phone away and stared out the window, watching the closely spaced houses of Fullbright give way to rolling fields.

Bump nuzzled his snout beneath my armpit. I draped my arm over him and pressed my chin against the top of his head. My vision grayed, the outline of Tara's head blurring before me. For a moment, I thought the painkillers had made me lightheaded, but then I realized it wasn't that at all. I was seeing a memory through Bump's eyes. My breath caught as I anticipated another gruesome scene flashing before me. But instead of fear or panic, a ripple of calm contentment pulsed through me. I saw Dad, standing above me with his arm cocked back, then lobbing a ball into a clear, blue sky. As quick as the picture had come to me, it vanished.

I hugged Bump tight. "Yeah, yeah, yeah. Don't worry. We're going home to see Dad, Bump. And I'm sure we can find that tattered old tennis ball in the backyard somewhere."

"Mom?" Tara rubbed Bump's ear and he leaned into her touch, soaking up the attention. "Where's Gramps going to live now? And what about us? Are we still going to Florida?"

"I think Gramps needs us here, don't you? We'll look around Wilton soon. Find a place for the three of us. With a nice big fenced-in yard for Bump."

Tara's cheeks bunched in a smile. "I'm glad we're staying. I like it here."

"Me, too, pumpkin. Me, too."

I gazed out the window as Ida drove us along the two-lane highway to Wilton. There wasn't a billboard or strip mall around for miles. I liked it that way. Maybe Wilton, Indiana wasn't where I'd planned to end up, but for now it was where I was meant to be.

"Oh, I almost forgot." Ida looked at me in the rearview mirror again. "I invited Archer Malone over for dinner tomorrow night. I hope you don't mind. Seemed like a good way to thank him for what he did."

The tiniest of tingles buzzed deep down in my stomach, growing until it filled me with giddy anticipation. Tomorrow seemed like a long way off.

about the author

N. Gemini Sasson holds a M.S. in Biology from Wright State University where she ran cross country on athletic scholarship. She has worked as an aquatic toxicologist, an environmental engineer, a teacher and a cross country coach. A longtime breeder of Australian Shepherds, her articles on bobtail genetics have been translated into seven languages. She lives in rural Ohio with her husband, two nearly grown children and an ever-changing number of animals.

Long after writing about Robert the Bruce and Queen Isabella, Sasson learned she is a descendant of both historical figures.

If you enjoyed this book, please spread the word by sharing it on Facebook or leaving a review at your favorite online retailer or book lovers' site.

For more details about N. Gemini Sasson and her books, go to:
www.ngeminisasson.com

Or become a 'fan' at:
www.facebook.com/NGeminiSasson

You can also sign up to learn about new releases via e-mail at:
http://eepurl.com/vSA6z

Made in the USA
Las Vegas, NV
12 December 2022

61975206R00194